THE FOURTH CENTURY

Édouard Glissant

The Fourth Century

Le Quatrième Siècle

TRANSLATED BY BETSY WING

UNIVERSITY OF NEBRASKA PRESS : LINCOLN & LONDON

Publication of this translation was assisted by a grant
from the French Ministry of Culture–National
Center for the Book and ♥ the National Endowment
for the Arts. © Éditions Gallimard, 1997, © 2001
by the University of Nebraska Press. All rights reserved.

Library of Congress Cataloging-in-Publication Data
Glissant, Edouard, 1928–
[Quatrième siècle. English]
The fourth century = Le quatrième siècle /
Edouard Glissant ; translated by Betsy Wing.
p. cm.
ISBN 0-8032-2174-6 (cloth: alkaline paper) –
ISBN 0-8032-7083-6 (paperback: alkaline paper)
1. West Indies, French – History – Fiction.
I. Wing, Betsy. II. Title.
PQ3949.2.G53 Q4813 2001 843'.914–dc21 00-61504 CIP

I dedicate this book to the memory of ALBERT BÉVILLE 1917–1962

We used to talk about the House of Slaves and
pictured to ourselves the wooden sculptures they
used to spot the runaways, the maroons; he
showed me the irons that were chained to their
ankles. But he also looked to the future: and now
the present is denied him forever. His name and
his example will always be inseparable in my
mind from the search we carry on in this present.

CONTENTS

THE FOURTH CENTURY

At La Pointe des Sables

Chapter 1

"ALL THIS WIND," said Papa Longoué, "all this wind about to come up, nothing you can do, you wait for it to come up to your hands, then your mouth, your eyes, your head. As if a man was only there to wait for the wind, to drown, yes, you understand, to drown himself for good in all this wind like the endless ocean . . ."

—And one can't say, he went on thinking (on his haunches in front of the child), one can't say there is no obligation in life, even though here I am a helpless old body just mulling over things already done-and-gone, the land with its stories for ages and ages, yes me here so I can have this child in front of me, and look, Longoué, you call him the kid, but look he has Béluse eyes a Béluse head. That's a race determined not to die. A tag end that just won't end. You figure that's just being a child—but that already is strength, that's tomorrow. This one won't do like the others, he's a Béluse, but he is like a Longoué, something will come of him, Longoué I'm telling you something will come of him, you don't know what, but still the Béluses have changed over time; and if not well then why would he come, why does he come here and not talk never talk Papa Longoué you understand, why all alone with you if there is no obligation, some malfini in the sky the eagle pulling strings, don't pull Longoué don't pull the strings, you just repeat yourself, you say: "Truth shot by like lightning," you are an old body Longoué, all that is left is memory, so OK, it would be better to puff on your pipe go no further, except why old devil why? . . .

Not a straw stirred on the roof of the hut. It was like a hunk of mud and grass stuck in the middle of the open ground—a site where the surface had been scored by water into bristling blades one had best avoid, where streams of runoff had stacked the earth along their edges and then the drought had dried it hard into sharp ridges—yes, it was all burnt to a cinder but through some miracle of heat it rustled in the morning like a dark tree. And all around (whenever one of the two people there turned toward the ferns and bamboo surrounding the place and tried to catch a breath of air, to catch the secret of this half-rotting, half-consumed wealth, that, even more than the passions of its sap, made the vegetation proliferate) bursts of a fragrance so burning and persistent that it really seemed to leap from this crackling hut, as if these bursts shot from a blaze whose rigid beating heart was the hut. And yet these two men, the old man and the child, merely let their gaze skim lightly over the curtain of trees surrounding the open space, far less to reassure themselves of the sight they were long in the habit of seeing (behind the first line of shadowy and silent bamboo, the ferns' thousand splinters, bright and deep, and still farther the tragic clarity of the plain showing through the space between the leaves) than to give themselves time to suspend the demands of this meditation, and take a rest from the silent dialogue that was their lot, and perhaps also to defer the moment when one of them would have to "think aloud" some word, some sentence, a word that would mark a new step along the way (for example Papa Longoué saying quietly and courteously, hiding the turmoil stirring inside, "No really, this time it was a Longoué who was not accursed"); to put off, in short, the need to broach another confidence: because words call for words.

And they immediately looked down at the ground in front of them with its sharp parallel striations evenly tilted by the wind toward the door built from a wooden crate; they contemplated only the red earth, fearing perhaps that all this vegetable upheaval around them would distract them from their conversation. More bound up in their silent search than they would have liked to admit, the one thing they feared above all was the irreversible power of words spoken out loud — as for everything else they went back to ruminating together over the dark, dense things of the past.

They looked at the fire in front of them, the three blackened stones, the charcoal burning beneath its ash, the live coals, the sudden puffs of smoke when the wind, ever so light and imperceptible, finally came through the trellis of bamboo. And only the stillness of everything—the clearing, the earth that was furrowed but dry and burning, the hut, the fire in front of the hut, the two statues crouched near the fire—gave the lazy smoke in the air some semblance of speed in contrast. And even the charcoal's crackling seemed only a weak echo, an intimate rustling reflection of the shouting and blazing sun already high in the sky at this time of day.

Mathieu Béluse had come, as he did rather often, very early in the morning—though when he came that way there was no guessing his intention or how he would make his approach. And as always, he would remain of course until nightfall, facing the old man, awaiting with a sort of savage indifference the rare moments when the latter would finally continue the calm and amazing story of the great-grandparents. A black cooking-pot already filled with green bananas, water, and coarse salt had been put on the fire. Implacable splendor of sky, of earth, of humble things.

—No one can say he wasn't born clever, acts like he doesn't know beans, but Papa Longoué is even cleverer, my son; you want to know a story you know already, yes, otherwise you wouldn't have come here with an old devil like me, and here you came without any money and not for a consultation: no illness, no enemy, no love no troubles—you just want to know if a Béluse and a Longoué amount to the same, but Lord how can this little boy know either end or beginning, yesterday has been dead so long, nobody remembers yesterday, it's been so long, Masterdanight, so long, and here comes a young sprout, sprung up just yesterday, he wants to map the course of night, so you have to talk, Longoué, you have to, soon you will be dead and gone and even the mangy dogs will have none of you. . . .

He poked the fire in front of him, blew on a bit of coal, which he skillfully tossed into his clay pipe, and then went back to smoking. In places his black skin was tinged with streaks of purple where it stretched tight over his bones. His ash-gray hair was still thick. In pants frayed at the bottom and a dirty jersey stuck to his body from years of continuous wear, he looked like a black mummy stripped of half his shroud. Yes. But his eyes were unbearable, from having located both the subterfuges of the present and the grave mysteries of bygone days at the same time. As for the future, his position as *quimboiseur* was sufficient evidence that Papa Longoué was its master. And as for words, he rarely used them: "Is there anything uttered anywhere in the world we see, any single crying word, that can make us know anything?"

—But what if by beginning everything came? Longoué, ho! At the end of your life there's a childhood. You see it, he is it; youth. He is thin perhaps, but he has the eyes. Yes, the power. He can do things. His eyes speak for him, I saw them. Because this one is a Béluse but he is like a Longoué, yes. He sits there two hours, stock still. He has patience. So, what if you do have to speak, you Longoué?

It seemed that the weight of the silence, the accumulating lightning, the mass of heat that the slow power of the two men crammed into the heat itself—by their motionless, patient confrontation—thus finally made Papa Longoué (more vulnerable this way than his young companion) in a hurry to get it over with as fast as possible; and it seemed that Mathieu thus achieved the task he had undertaken, to make the old man speak (in this language without price, all in how it was said and in repetitions, that nonetheless proceeded reliably toward some knowledge, beyond the words, that Papa Longoué alone could guess; because if he anticipated anything it was not obvious and, to tell the truth, he let himself be guided by the unpredictable consequences of the words; yes, this way of speaking was so right considering the thickness of the day, the weight of the heat, the slow memory). If he spoke it would make the past clear and perhaps explain precisely this passion that he, Mathieu, had for the past. Then gradually Longoué gave in, though he did not realize—did he?—that he was being subjected to the adolescent's law. On the contrary, he thought he was leading the latter (a talented boy, willing to listen to what old people had to say, a boy with a spark in his eye) bit by bit toward the moment when he could understand and possess the magical sequence of events by himself. But Papa Longoué guessed that his young friend had possibilities other than the gift of darkness; Mathieu, for his part, knew that the *quimboiseur* would be put off by logic and clarity. Consequently, they were both afraid of words and only proceeded very warily in getting to know each other. Both sensed however that no matter what they did they—a Béluse and a Longoué—would meet some time or other (thought Longoué). So the man gave in to the child and began to get his words ready, to follow what he said himself, to organize it, to extend it.

"The past. Tell me about the past, Papa Longoué! Just what is it?"

At that point the *quimboiseur* was not fooled. He understood perfectly well that he would get completely involved in the question, even in its childish form. And that this form was merely a final concession that Mathieu had wished to grant him, even though the boy could have simply asked: "What is left of the past?" or "Why do we have to go back over the past?" or some other straightforward, clear question without detours. No, he had given some thought as to how to put it. Longoué, for the first time, suspected that this person sitting opposite him was not as young as he seemed. He wanted to look Mathieu in the eye, sound him out more deeply, seeking in those eyes some evidence or denial. But he resisted, fearing perhaps to find there what he dreaded: a different passion—not the one eager for secrets but the beginnings of criticism and judgment; he had the good sense not to but lifted his face instead toward the blazing sky, as if looking for help. The red and black pipe was smoking in his hand. The heat everywhere was so vast and so sweet.

He put the clay pot on the fire, moving abruptly and almost recklessly, yet he was watching Mathieu, hoping that this sudden gesture would make him jump. The boy did not budge: quietly watching the green bananas, the gray scum on the surface of the water. . . . (This is not a child any more, thought the other somewhat bitterly, this is a man.) The food was already humming on the fire. The sound in the sun, the acrid fragrance of bananas, the dry smell of charcoal, the slow swaying of the trees (because the wind was coming up) was gradually numbing. Mathieu and Longoué remained silent a long while, forgetting the struggle. But it was another struggle to keep their truce, to stay absent. . . . In the end, the adult spoke softly.

"They are fools down there. They say, 'What's gone is gone.' But everything that goes into the woods is kept in the heart of the wood! It is just as well that I walk in the woods and never go down. Because when I look back toward my father my son is gone. When a man says 'The past' what he is saying is 'Hello my father.' Now, look at life, when a man's son is gone, he can never again say, 'Hello my son.' And my son is gone."

"Your son is gone," said Mathieu.

But it wasn't the death so much. His son was dead, ok. In the great war on the other side of the ocean. The Longoués would no longer be able to keep their vigil in the forest: the race was going to die out. For the ancestor begat Melchior and Liberté the son, and Melchior begat Apostrophe and Liberté the daughter, and Apostrophe begat Papa Longoué, and Papa Longoué begat Ti-René who begat sudden death. But it wasn't so much the death. The problem was he had to have a descendant, one he picked, his chosen one. A young sapling to sink your roots into the ground of the future. That was it. To be linked to tomorrow through the forces of youth. But Ti-René died too quickly. The only one left was this Mathieu — a Béluse.

Yes. The first Béluse begat Anne, and he killed Liberté the son. And Anne begat Saint-Yves and Stéfanise, and she was the one who lived with Apostrophe, the son of the brother of the man his father had killed. And Saint-Yves begat Zéphirin. And Zéphirin begat Mathieu, who went to war on the other shore at the same time as Ti-René; but Mathieu came back. He came back and he begat Mathieu the son, who at present was there with Papa Longoué (to ask him endless questions), just the way his own grandson might have been there too (ah! he too!) if Ti-René his son, unattached still and wandering, had not been killed in the great war on the other side of the ocean.

This much could be said: that the Béluse men had always fol-

8 *At La Pointe des Sables*

lowed the Longoués down through time as if to catch them. Anne Béluse was there to kill Liberté Longoué; the only thing that brought that trouble to an end was when Stéfanise Béluse, as a sort of reparation you might say, chose as her man the nephew of the one her father had killed. There had always been some Béluse on the heels of some Longoué; as if since the moment they had been delivered here after the long sea agony the Béluse men had wanted to extinguish the indomitable violence of the Longoué men by being its equal. So then Mathieu the father had followed Ti-René to the great war; although both had been officially drafted it would be wrong to think Mathieu did not, in fact, follow Ti-René — the government decrees simply corresponded to the requirements of fate, that's all there is to it. But Mathieu returned from that war. And this meant that, no matter what, the Béluse men were catching the Longoués. Not merely because Papa Longoué was half Béluse through his mother Stéfanise who was Apostrophe's woman, but also because the Longoué line would run dry in the person of Papa Longoué himself while Mathieu Béluse the son would live to become a father.

"Where is your strength, Masterdanight, where is your presence? Rip this earth open. Make words come out like *filaos!*"

Papa Longoué laughed softly because he was thinking of the Longoué men who, right from the beginning, had all left behind names that distinguished them from each other. For example, Liberté the ancestor's second son, who was given that name because his father had refused to crouch in slavery on the Acajou estates; and so on for all the others, there was always some explanation for the names. The names appeared out of the dark, it was just a matter of seeing them and grabbing them. Except, yes, except for the ancestor. What his name was no one knew because he had fled into the woods the very day, one could even say the very hour that he had been set on shore, and once there he named his sons but forgot himself (as he remembered himself). All, therefore, except that first stem who had been the archetypal Longoué and now — stupid, stupid — Papa Longoué himself the last of the succession, whose name even as a child had never been anything other than these two words: Papa Longoué. There was a sort of irony in linking the two words: Papa, which means tenderness and kindness, and Longoué, which is rage and violence. The last Longoué thus rejoined the first in the anonymity of the family name, but one of them had been a creator beyond reproach while the other was no longer anything more than a seer, and just barely a good *quimboiseur*. Thus the race was going to die out, just as it had begun, with the name of the root alone. Except that the first Longoué did not have time to be a person called "a Longoué" (even if he bore within him all the qualities of the family) and the last would only remain in the memory of mankind as a papa: Papa Longoué. With no other description, with no other dignified distinction; simply as the powerless branch that can be said to have been part of the tree, period. Now the branch lies there on the ground. As if all this forest that made the family, all this forest of men stirred to such excitement by the dry wind, all this wild, thick man-resin that had shuddered in the density of heat and night would now return into the earth, leaving the clear sky and the thundery sky, leaving on the surface of the soil behind them only this pathetic last sprout withered by marks of tenderness and kindness.

The wind began to spring up in the clearing. It felt soft on Mathieu's legs exactly like a savanna where the growth was not too tall, a field of short creeping plants. But this wind was growing; hurtled by its own power into the gully that passed in front of the trees, it gained ground: a weed about to get a purchase on the two men's breasts. Water in the vat of heat rising to where it means to drown the sun.

And the other thing that could be said is this: that the Béluse men and the Longoué men had somehow joined forces in the same sort of wind, with a fury and force that came at first from the Longoués, but then took root in the amazing Béluse patience. And (thought Papa Longoué, the *quimboiseur*, the man who was in charge of the future and who, in the person of Mathieu, expected to save the future) wasn't this final branch Béluse, with nothing in it that was Longoué? (Otherwise, why would everybody call me Papa Longoué? It's because I'm too mild, yes!) Maybe his mother, Stéfanise, had not really inherited the powers? He had always thought she had, but maybe she remained a Béluse to the end and maybe she passed on to her son this shortcoming of gentleness and weakness.

Longoué laughed nonetheless; he laughed to think that the sole act of official violence anyone knew of in the history of the two families had been committed by a Béluse, Anne Béluse who was the father of Stéfanise, and therefore unmistakably his own grandfather. What had Anne done? He killed Liberté Longoué. Out of love and jealousy. Ever since that time it had seemed that a deep, hidden violence lay sleeping in the blood. Maybe—who could say?—it was reappearing in Mathieu, despite all his education.

And then Stéfanise, who was born a Béluse, went away a Longoué: there was plenty of proof of that. She had plenty of time to change. Papa Longoué alone (—I, Longoué, whom they call papa—) had no time: he had almost not known his father, who died five years after he was born. And on top of that, he had entirely not known his son Ti-René because of the latter's tendency always to be wandering here and there, and especially because (since the *quimboiseur* had hoped that after a while his son would come back to the forest in the end), yes, especially because of the great war on the other side of the ocean. And thus Papa Longoué (—I, Longoué, who had no time—) had kept standing all alone, he had never been able to hook anything to anything, neither his father to his son, nor, as a result, the past to the future. He was the caressing surface of the wind but he was not the full-force wind clamoring deep inside itself starting at the base of the trees and rising up to the sun.

"You heard me," Mathieu exclaimed. "You are pretending!"

"Don't grow too fast, young man. I tell you, you are growing too fast."

"What do you mean growing? What did you say, I'm growing? What does that mean, Papa?"

Really the wind was rising. The coals on the fire rekindled in rhythmic bursts but soon went out, consumed by the violent air.

The cooking-pot seemed unsteady on the three black stones. The ground itself was moving: you would have said the sharp blades of clay were pitching toward the hut. The wind was not yet as high as a man is tall, but it rose steadily.

"This wind," said Longoué. "Yes! This wind! This is what you are asking for!" He went on proclaiming, which meant he was giving in: "Can anyone measure the strength of this great wind that rises up the hillsides?"

Because today they just hang around in that little spot of theirs, and they can't see! Where is this wind? What direction? Which one?

"They don't even see the boat!"

"The boat that brought them over?"

"The boat that brought them over," said Papa Longoué.

Hundreds and hundreds of boats came. "Do you understand? Why would they have seen that particular boat slip into the fog of their memory with its moldy gangplanks dangling along the hull like arms without hands. That particular one. That came into the harbor one July morning while the rain beat down like mad?"

Behind the swamps on the Point one could barely make out the gray walls of the Fort, distant cliffs crowned with bluish smoke that very rapidly disappeared into the screen of rain. Along the water-front there were only tumbling masses of some undetermined vegetation to be seen, and here and there the leprous wound of work or storage sites. On the boat, water was scouring the deck, streaming into the holds, drowning the foul cargo. The captain had ordered the hatches opened and the ports uncovered so the water would flow. It was half past nine in the morning, and the sun was shining through the rain.

(The Rose-Marie. She was impatiently awaited; there were not enough hands for the work of this country. It had required every-thing the ship's commander knew for two-thirds of the slaves taken aboard to arrive "safe and sound." Illness, vermin, suicide, re-bellions, and executions had punctuated the crossing with cadav-ers. But two-thirds was an excellent average. And the captain had escaped the English ships. Quite a remarkable sailor!)

The rain washed down the timbers, the sails, the rigging; it made the black spot marking where they had put the piece of sheet metal even more obvious. You could see the streaks of blackened wood swollen by water where the heated metal had been set up, next to the brazier. You could still see the thick remains of blood that were around it. Because rebels had been made to dance to the rhythm of the fire on the hot metal whenever they refused to walk during the half hour of exercise on deck. And the metal itself was there, twisted, humpbacked, blackened, bloody, and the rainwater striking it with a cheerful patter could not wash away the thickly aggregated soot of burned blood and rust.

At the bow lay the rope coiled like a snake overstuffed with prey. It served to drag a channel through the ocean, using mutineers chosen to serve as examples. They were dumped into the sea as if to dredge the bottom or to take soundings and assess the ship's position. And when they would burst into the blinding light, after the first moments of harsh sky, or brilliant night, none of the wretches from the hold could take their eyes off it, sometimes staring for a long time with a headstrong, demanding concentration. The rope more than the sheet metal had measured the size of the ocean, each time leaving behind in the depths of the abyss its burden of black flesh. . . .

"Hurry it up, Papa, hurry it up. Everybody knows all that. I've read the books!"

But all that apparatus had been left out in the rain: the weighted whips, the stiff straps, the gallows (actually more impressive than a big mast), and the hooked stick they used to thrust into the throat of anybody who tried to swallow his or her tongue, and the large tub of sea water for sailors to stick their heads in when they came back up suffocating from the depths of the holds, and the branding iron, a ruthless fork for anyone who refused to eat moldy bread or crackers drenched in brine, and the net used to lower the slaves every month for their sea bath: a net to keep them safe from sharks or the temptation to die.

The rain cleansed, readied for sale, absolved. The smell in the holds, however, grew thicker. The water carried rotten things along with it as well as excrement and dead rats. When the Rose-Marie finally was washed clean of vomit it was truly like a rose, but one drawing its sap from a living manure pile. That was when the captain decided to finish washing the boat from the bottom up. It was ten o'clock.

(Because the time is important in this delivery ceremony that inaugurates the new existence. Not existence, ho! but death, death with no hope. And yet hope came in the end. Because the order of events in this day must be meticulously and precisely noted. And because the slow naming of the hours was their only recourse until nightfall, before the escape into the forest shroud, escaping past the packs of dogs and men in relentless pursuit, all led by the master with his blue gaze who shouted to egg the animals on, while the other man, his most intimate enemy, the humpback with his sneering voice, obstinately keeping up with the man who led the chase, desperately panting but taunting by his mere presence. And because the time of day, after the long night of the holds, was still an ornament, an amazing luxury for those who had endlessly breathed in death, deep under the barely perceptible tide of the waves. Because the times of day, simply because they moved across the blazing sky, broke an opening perhaps toward something, some other thing, that would not be, would no longer be the low, rotten beams of a hold.)

"You are going to get lost in all your rain, if you keep on putting it off and putting it off. You are going to get lost. . . ."

Then the work crew lined up with big tubs and the slave count began. Each one chained to the one ahead, thus they climbed out of the bowels of the boat. As they staggered onto the decks a great bucket of water was dumped on them. A sailor scrubbed their bodies with a long-handled broom, scraping wounds and ripping shreds from filthy, already tattered fabric. A great blast of water struck through the rainwater like baptism for the new life. The crew laughed at these crazy black men who were stumbling idiotically out of the frying pan into the fire. Twice-soaked: sea water and sky water. The Rose-Marie deloused its manure pile.

Soon the deck was packed with this silent troop of men and women who did not even glance toward shore, although there was no doubt at all that this marked the end of their journey. Males, females, and offspring were squeezed against each other but kept their eyes lowered to the deck, yes, as if this deck had been a dry and yet kindly land, even though they were so well acquainted with the long wooden planking they had had to run on once every two weeks. As if the laths were strips of raised earth, sharpened by water and wind, in front of the cabin where the captain stood.

"A good crossing Monsieur Lapointe. A good crossing."

"Yes, Captain," replied the first mate. "Truly excellent!"

The good-natured master of the ship studied his cargo. By god, it hadn't fared badly at all on the voyage. They would be able to risk selling at the market straightaway, sparing themselves the traditional four days of fattening up the slaves. There was only one death rattle that he could just hear from time to time rising from the black mass.

"I don't understand," Duchêne murmured, "I don't understand their silence all of a sudden. During the ten years I've been doing this I have never caught them shouting or moaning, or even looking at the land, the shore, anything at all, when time comes to put them ashore. It's as if the end of the journey was the most terrifying part for them."

The first mate laughed awkwardly. Puzzles didn't interest him, only figures. Sometimes the captain got on his nerves, but he dared not admit it. All he saw there was cash, that's it. Soon he would be master of his own boat, then just wait and see.

That's how it went. And at eleven o'clock everything was ready. Done. The metal sheet stowed, the rope as innocent as tackle for the rigging, the gibbet once again insignificant: a small mast with no gallows and no hooks; the whips were in the weapons room along with the branding iron, and the net was still in the same spot, as if ready for a bit of pleasure fishing; the boat thus rid of its marks of hell was an honest merchant ship.

"Sign of a good sale, Monsieur Lapointe, when it rains delivery day! ... That's a good half of the washing and scouring! Beautiful day. The men are happy, the Rose is clean! Put the work crew from the holds ashore. ... Ah! Here we come, to pay our visit! ..."

The odor of vomit, blood, and death that even the rain could not get rid of all that fast was still there. But things had been cleaned and the odor would go away—until the next trip. Until the next cloying stench of death came to drop anchor in this harbor.

(Yet I can smell it just the same, thought Papa Longoué. Such a long time ago. From the very first boat—when this commerce was still no more than an adventure and no one knew if it would make a decent profit—right up to when the Rose-Marie came, and by then it had become a successful venture, yes, up to the morning that saw the two ancestors debark from the Rose-Marie to begin the history that for me is really history. I can smell it, that odor. Stéfanise my mother taught it to me, she got it from her man. Apostrophe who got it from Melchior who got it from Longoué himself, who was the first to stand on the deck of the slave ship ...)

(Not the absolute first but in any case first in relation to Béluse, which means that of those two men—the only ones on the boat who mattered—one of them, Longoué, was the pioneer, the vanguard, the discoverer of the new land. And at that moment. Because of all the foul smells that had smothered them in the holds, neither one of them had detected the cloying stink exuded by the boat; but they could see the effect this odor had when the small boat drew alongside bringing the port officials as well as the two white men, one of whom held a handkerchief over his mouth and his nose while the second, the man with blue eyes, scorning the refinements of his friend, gamely hailed the captain and, showing no fear or repulsion, leapt on the deck right next to the first row of darkies. And the result of this blue-eyed man's offensive gesture—because was it not an offense to the wretched men?—was to reveal almost as well as the humpback's handkerchief how strong the odor was. And long, long afterward, Longoué the ancestor knew that the imperceptible fumes from the boat were certainly just as dreadful as the horrible rankness in the holds; and in his memory, hovering over the journey's thick mass of rot and vermin he found that faint stink of death swept with rainwater that had so distressed the man with the hump. He found it again under trees and under roots. And he was able to make his sons from generation to generation, all the way down to Papa Longoué, smell this odor.)

"Oh good lord of patience save me! I swear, save me! . . ."

And so the man leapt on the deck. The captain shook hands with him affectionately and with respect. This colonial planter and his companion, who was greeted very stiffly, were implacable enemies: they could not leave each other's sides.

"Poor Senglis," laughed La Roche, and his blue eyes lit up. "He'll never get used to the stench of Negroes. But he can't bring himself to let me come out here and meet you alone."

The captain smiled kindly: he understood Senglis and his squeamish handkerchief.

"Well, friend, what handsome cargo! I hope you are saving me the best."

Duchêne nodded his head. Every time he arrived he put up with this ritual: the race between the two neighbors, each intent on getting the best bargain. La Roche always won. It was written. He had an eye for it and he was not afraid of the Negroes. He would go up close and feel them, there on deck, risking his life among these desperate slaves, one of whom would surely end up strangling him one of these days or knocking him flat before the crew could intervene. And Senglis wouldn't buy.

"See now, gentlemen! I can't do business before they're put on display at the market."

"That's for other people, Duchêne! I'll be responsible. Gentlemen, get to work, let's get the inspection over with."

The port officials consequently began their inspection. Really just a formality. The presence of La Roche made anything the "officials" said useless, and the sly captain knew this.

Then (it was noon), just as they all—the two gentlemen, the two officers, the agents from the Port—were heading toward the ship's bridge where the captain had invited them for a drink to celebrate the fortunate delivery, just at that precise moment turmoil erupted, incredible disorder inside the bunch of slaves. At first it seemed to be a mutiny (with the result that Senglis suddenly produced a pistol while the first mate made a dash for the weapons storeroom), but right away they saw that this did not mean a revolt, which would have been quite natural even if improbable at such a moment, but, bizarre as it might seem, it was a brawl among the Negroes, in other words, some settling of accounts.

And the captain who would not have been afraid of rebellion, especially in this harbor, right in front of the reassuring crenellations of Fort-Royal, stood there transfixed by what he saw: two slaves were fighting, they rolled and tumbled among their companions. Oddly the latter did not move away; occasionally they would fall because one of the two bumped into them, but they would just stand up again without a murmur, without a cry. It was as if they had not been run into by those two men but by some chance accident not worth considering, or rather by some power so dangerous, that it was preferable to submit without attempting to explain it or certainly not oppose it—and even, to be on the safe side, without seeming to pay the least attention.

The sailors could not understand: the captain was taking a long time to react. La Roche burst into great, loud laughter and shouted, "So you had a pistol, Senglis!"

And that freed the spectators immediately to rush forward.

They rushed forward, ashamed of the astonishment that had kept them frozen to the deck at first. Their fury hurled them toward Béluse and Longoué where they made their assault—two clusters of people who hung from their black bodies like two maggot swarms. But there was no Béluse or Longoué yet, or at least no one going by these brand-new names: there were only two fighters swept from one side of the boat to the other. One of the slaves had trapped his opponent against the rail, apparently intending to break him against the wet wood; but the eyes of both bulged equally and one panted as hard as another; in the midst of this unleashing of forces you could not tell who was stronger. The slave who had the upper hand was carried off by a first group of sailors to one side of the boat where he kept right on fighting. His adversary on the opposite side was subjected to the same fate and reacted against it in the same manner. It took almost five minutes to curb the bloody men and put them in chains. And another minute for the sailors to catch their breath, standing there in silence as if by contagion they too had lost the use of words. Awaiting orders, they all looked toward the captain, fearing perhaps that they would be asked to unchain the two Negroes, returning them to their places in the body of the herd.

"I don't understand," muttered Duchêne. "No. How can they be strong enough to fight? How? Or strong enough to want to? What motive could they have? What reason?"

"There isn't any reason," Senglis whispered. "You don't know what they're like!"

Unaware of this quick exchange, La Roche shouted to the prisoner who had seemed to be mauling the other. Yes, he addressed that Negro directly, though his words really concerned the captain.

"This is the one I want, my friend, I'll stick to my guns on that. Zounds, Senglis, when you want to get your Negresses knocked up you're going to have to pay a high stud fee."

"Then I'll take the other," cried Senglis. "It's settled, Captain!"

"Give them each thirty blows and then separate them from the bunch. They'll be all yours, gentlemen."

"Hey! You'll damage mine. I insist, Duchêne. I insist! Hold on, I'll have him punished myself."

"No. Not on board my ship, sir. I am sorry to go against your wishes. Give him the thirty blows. Don't worry, we have men who do an excellent job with discipline."

"Fine, fine, I trust you," said La Roche. And leaving the group deliberately he went to examine his acquisition close up.

With great difficulty, two impassive sailors restrained the frothing and foaming Negro with rope and chains. La Roche gazed at him for a long time; the slave withstood his gaze. The colon grabbed his head and pushed him to the ground in front of him.

You could see only the bloody nape of the slave's neck, his lacerated back held there under a heel.

The planter stared at the two sailors whose blank eyes seemed to glide over a spectacle with no density or reality at the far edge of the horizon.

"Unbind him," he ordered.

The two men were startled, not daring to turn overtly toward the captain and not daring to refuse to obey such a powerful gentleman. They rocked back and forth on their feet, then, making sure their weapons were ready, they unchained the arms and legs of the prisoner. The man stood up and faced the one who was already his master. He looked about him, took a deep breath, lifted his arm and almost smiled, as if coming to terms with his history and as if expressing his intention to put off until later any settlement of accounts. And then he drew a threatening sign in the air, a quick and half-ritual gesture directed at the colon. Then he stood straight and motionless and distant there beneath the July rain that seemed not to get him wet but rather to gush from his black and naked body like a secret dew. The crew expected orders to kill, or at least to slash away at the mass; besides, it was unthinkable that this Negro not be hanged. But Monsieur de La Roche turned slowly away and went back to rejoin the group of officers.

"One of these days you're going to kick the bucket," the humpbacked man laughed nervously.

"That's no shrinking violet, Captain Duchêne! But are you sure you won't damage him too much for me?"

"Have no fear, sir, the ship's cook is an admirable surgeon. And what's more he has all the salt and all the brine from the kitchens at his disposal since we are now in port. . . . Come along," the fellow added, "let's go in and have a drink! Though I'm afraid, alas, that I've exhausted my supply of rum."

"Never mind that, I thought of it. I've made sure you'll get some that's better. Let's go. Let's go."

"Ah sir," said the captain, stepping aside before the door to the bridge. "You are a savior for a wretched traveler deprived of pleasure or repose for so many long months!"

A deep peace then settled over the *Rose-Marie*: not the silence of adventurous high seas but the tranquil hum of honest occupations. And thus ended the first fight, which was the shortest. Dry and glowing like a valiant ember. The first silent fight. There is nothing more to say about it, except that according to the records by two o'clock the majority of slaves, including La Roche's and Senglis's acquisitions, had been unloaded. These two men returned to the small boat after having taken noisy leave of the captain. The rain had stopped, as if satisfied with having fulfilled its function on time. The green and yellow water of the harbor was churned by more and more violent eddies. The *Rose-Marie* pitched, swaying her masts — the very symbol of calm and serenity. The boat scorned the increasing violence of the waves; it had been given the lustral bath of the rain.

Senglis, in the small boat, had trouble with the busy, choppy sea. He grew paler still as he listened to his friend's sarcastic remarks.

"Senglis," La Roche murmured. "What did you mean to do with that pistol you were hiding? Don't you think I ought to tell our friends about it? Don't you think so? Don't you think I ought?"

And then he shouted above the lapping sound of the waves and the banging of the oars and the squeaking of the oarlocks: "Hey there, all of you, does anybody know what that Negro meant to be drawing in the air before me?"

Then the coxswain, who had come on the boat with them, turned toward the silhouette of the *Rose-Marie* outlined against the clear sky and roiled sea (which was odd, yes; because had he known anything he should have been looking toward the warehouses, in the direction the two slaves had been taken); then he spit calmly into the sea.

"A snake," he said.

Chapter 2

"You see, you can see for yourself," muttered Mathieu. "All they ever did was imitate, right from the beginning!"

Like a river the wind now carried minuscule branches of fern along with it, hooking them to the leaves of the bamboo where there were bays opened between them onto the distant plain; and the rustling of these transparent twigs against the feathery bamboo turned each bay into a splendidly sumptuous, real window draped in curtains that were delicate and luminous, a place where it would be nice to stand some night and wait for who knows what—something sweet and pointless. That, at least, is what Mathieu was thinking deep inside when the vertigo of memory lost its grip; not memory itself, but definitely the dizziness born of the words of Papa Longoué. Lost, Mathieu was trying to penetrate all the old man's onomatopoeia and reluctance and uncertainty to make the story advance and give some order to events. He had such a passion to know that, every now and then, he would sit up straight (not his physical body-self still crouched by the fire, but the force inside him), shake himself and really try to get close to one of those fragile bay windows opening into the mass of bamboo, and then he would feel himself escaping the drunken euphoria; he felt like he was waiting (the way one does in the books where it is always a beautiful evening) for something incomplete but tangible—and he did not see the winds, the one overriding wind around his physical body still there by the fire, he did not feel the first caresses of the rising wind move up his temples, he did not realize that the first straws were about to stir on the roof, soon ridding the cabin of its illusory fragrance by their movement, and, divided like this between the effort to put together a few revelations and the peaceful desire to lean out one of these bay windows, he scarcely yes scarcely heard Papa Longoué (but he was letting all the old man's mumblings settle, because in the other half of his mind he was conquering the drunken euphoria and, perhaps unwittingly, was really beginning to establish the chronology of this history) while the coals, neglected by the rising wind, gradually went out, and the *quimboiseur* finally asked clearly: "Why do you say imitate? I do not see it, I do not see any of that."

"So what about this," Mathieu protested, serious once again and attentive, suddenly abandoning his bay window, all the while trying to make the throbbing at his temples and the pulse of the wind against his body make sense together, "what about beating each other to a pulp all over the deck of the ship! Exactly at the moment that the two colons got off their little boat. And what were these two colons if not deadly enemies? Yes, they were enemies, and next thing you knew the two others followed them, like cattle to slaughter!"

And Mathieu went over to the opening through the bamboo to calm down, though he was still thinking about Béluse and Longoué, how they, rather than their two masters had fought each other—those masters who had never been able to settle their differences once and for all because one of them was forever pointing out that he was a humpback (as if it were not obvious), and besides, he didn't have to say this any more because the two Negroes had done their fighting for them! And the result was that they (the slaves) just inherited that as well, and even then, when the first blow was struck, the first day, just as they all would do afterward in this country, they got their misery and joy, hatred and love, for a person or against one, at the pleasure of their possessors, and constructed none of it on their own and they did this so well that it was no wonder that everybody in this country had forgotten the *Rose-Marie*, to say nothing of the sea she crossed and the country she came from where she had picked up her cargo of flesh. Yes. All that gone and forgotten into each day that went by, and every day the hand extended toward the manners of an other whose gestures nor voice they could never entirely imitate. But Mathieu came back from his bay window because he heard Papa Longoué pouring forth his long tale, descanting faster than the cascade of Morne Rouge, and:

"No," said Papa Longoué. "No, boy. What you don't know is bigger than you are. You don't know about the sea or about the land from before, you don't know what went before, you are like the last in line in the procession; it's all very well for him to lift his head in the air and turn every which way, he still won't know if the Cross is at the end of the road or if it is already inside the church greeting the altar candles in their paper windscreens, with the old women, each one proud as can be of her candle, all pushing and shoving behind the benches indicated, to the places belonging to the first one there. No matter what he does, the person at the tail end of the procession remains on the steps of the church. He can't get in. That is the way these people are. And you, youngster-that-you-are, you do not know what was inside the Rose-Marie. Because inside the Rose-Marie there was no hold. They were in a space above the hold, and not the hold itself, because the captain was a humane and organized man. What was the use of throwing eight hundred into the holds and arriving with two hundred, if one could just as easily line six hundred of them up between the decks and arrive with four hundred? And then Duchêne, the captain, had scraped his boat out ("A brig, yes: two masts with square sails and the third with no sails from which they had hanged someone just two days before their arrival"), he had created the space between the decks, with bars for the head and feet and iron chains. And who was it who said that the sailors came back up from the hold? I didn't say it. Actually, they would have preferred a hold to this place between the decks— there was no suffocating smell in the hold. And if I said that the slaves came up onto the deck, you mustn't believe, Mathieu my son, that they came up often. There were three steps between their floor and the deck; they had to at least bend over double to stand up in that space. Which means, sure as the sun is shining, that Captain Duchêne was organized, because he did not want to lose too large a portion of his load, and that meant that right from the beginning, back there as well, on the other side of the bottomless sea, over and above storm and illness and death, there had to be some planning ahead, a place to get supplies, and a Negro pen, you see. The Rose-Marie did not have a hold, at least no hold for the Negroes, it was planned in advance where they would go, into a special space, which means that even back there also there was order and method. It was deliberately planned. When the captain arrived his cargo was there already, no time to lose, the rum from France was unloaded—rum made without sugar cane—and whatever was there in the rottenness of the pen was put on board. That is, all the people expecting death who, however, were not yet dead, who were not lucky enough to be dead already. And rest assured, when the *Rose-Marie* arrived and stood off the coast there, the pen was already full. The entire country had been swept. Mothers sold their children, men their brothers, kings their subjects, the friend sold his friend for rum made without sugar cane. And thus they bought death with the money of death. Just so they could roll around, yes, in rum's death. Or simply so as not to embark upon the ship. So as not to have to be the six hundredth in the pen. And you see, that is something you don't know, you have no idea of what went on in the country beyond the sea. . . ."

The old man meditated upon this flood of words, trying to figure out if he had really been the one churning them out or if, rather, some other, some troublesome stranger had taken his place by the fire, knocking the clay pipe against the nearest rock the way he did? He was amazed to hear such a long speech, and to have heard it while he was speaking it, listening without impatience. Lord yes, a word from time to time was preferable; then each could find its place. Far better than in this stream of all-too-well reasoned words. Then the orator, fearful that Mathieu might be laughing inside, slipped a worried glance in the direction of the young man. Entirely fixated on the line of bamboo, he was almost not there. He was dreaming.

"You want to make me believe," he finally murmured, "that there was a history, before? Is that what you are saying?"

Ah! Youth . . . There is always a history, before.

They had not inherited the hatred, they had brought it with them. It came with them all the way across the sea. You put the food in, lay the fire, put on the water. You do it just right. You light it.

You wait for the wind to rise to the roof of the hut. The wind rises, rising past like a heat wave, and when it is up there, it is finished, your fire is dead, the banana is cooked, everything just right. That is how it was. They came across the ocean and when they saw the new land there was no longer any hope; going back was impossible. Then they understood that it was all over and they fought each other. Like a final display before sitting down at the table of the new land; to greet the new land and glorify the old one, the lost land. Maybe they wanted to bring their history to an end; not wanting to kill each other, maybe, who knows, they just wanted to cut each other a little, so that one of them could say: "You will walk into this new country but not intact! I, however, I am intact!" And then simply tearing off an arm, or maybe ripping an eye out, so he could proclaim to the other that the old hatred was victorious over the misery promised from now on. As if all the water of the sea, from the last shore they had left behind to the filthy vegetation of this harbor, had risen like a wall and driven them to this battle the same way this wind in one puff lights, burns, and extinguishes the charcoal under the pot of bananas. For hatred required both of them to live; it did not need one or the other to die; one of the two had to witness, powerless, the victory of the second. What victory? To have completed the voyage without a sigh, entering the unknown country with all his strength, and above all, above all, knowing that the other would be merely a cripple in this land, someone who could never possess it, never sing it, and that the victor made that happen! Captain Duchêne was certainly able to understand fury like that, but still he knew the voyage. He had no idea that hatreds could outlast the dreadful rough seas of the crossing; that these Negroes would still be able to find not just the strength but the desire to fight, after those weeks of slow dying. And the discovery filled him with terror; thinking as a result that he was truly trafficking in animals — wild beasts, not docile animals that could be domesticated.

Mathieu wanted to brush away the wind on his temples. The boy would not stoop to any such explanations; he had no intention of accepting such clear and tidy reasons. But the wind that is rising cannot be driven away.

"It's the way they were delivered," he said. "Too neat. Too simple. One sees the harbor, the boat, the Negroes, all bright and calm. I cannot!"

He would have preferred a description of the whipping session at one in the afternoon; seeing the boatswain carefully choose an instrument that was effective but not dangerous; hearing him consult the ship's cook about material or form (a strap or a roll of leather, supple or stiff); and the coxswain would intervene: "Better watch out, if you maim them you'll get it"; then laughter, the two slaves bound back to back to the mast, so that while he waited for his turn the second could feel the blows like an echo when they struck the other and he could feel the mast shaking, the shock of body against wood each time the whip fell; and the humming of the lashes, the panting of the man with the whip, the bruised bodies tensing and then suddenly collapsing, the spurts of blood, the indifference of the sailors who were used to such spectacles and bustled around the bunch of them, slightly dodging, perhaps, the whip's trajectory the way you dodge a hanging branch along a path, the two Negroes unbound, rubbed with salt, with brine and cannon powder, taken off the ship in barges, lying face down beside the others who would not even look their way, and the silence, the calm depth of silence that only whistling whips, footsteps on the deck, the muffled sound of skiffs and large rafts against the left side of the ship had punctuated; finally all the dirty, stagnant movements corresponding so well to the sadness of the rain as it ended, and here and there loud voices swelling outside the cabin, or perhaps the faint roar of waves against the mud of the coast, back there . . .

For he would have preferred, oh barge I the barge and he I on my belly the powder I the boat and beating on my back the current and the water each foot I the rope sliding for and dying the harbor country and so far faraway nothing I nothing nothing to end falling the water salty salty salty on the back and blood and fish and eating oh country the country ("the certainty that it was all over, irrevocably, because the barge and the skiffs were pulling away from the ship; that it was no longer even possible to cling to the closed but temporary floating boat-world; that now they would have to set foot on the land there and it would not move; and in the emptiness and nothingness it was like a memory of the first days of the voyage, a repetition of the first days when the maternal, familiar, and stable coast grew irrevocably distant; yes, nostalgic for the boat, despite the space between the decks, because it had certainly not seemed a fatal or hopeless place, right up to this moment when they had to leave it") and my his back so far faraway he whistles who gets up he gets up I the strength I master ("very quickly ho, the small boats sailing halfway to the land, there was a hand that threw a mess of dirty water through one of the portholes into the sea, as if saluting those who had left the *Rose-Marie* for good, for an inconceivable existence; yes, that familiar gesture, so familiar, of people in port washing down their vessel, and it truly seemed like the final flourish in the washed-out sky, at least for the two or three in the herd who had had the strength to look behind: the final punctuation, with that heavy slap of wash water falling into the sea and that scraping—that clattering—of the tub against the wood of the hull, then silence again, silence, silence") and I mud against the sky for shouting oho! ho! sun old sun in the crowd the death for two hundred a good batch granted you here all her teeth twenty-two years old a virgin the virgin her mother useless can do nothing too old without the mother here for the fields a good price over here on to the next look appraise handle handle in broad daylight no secrets and intact and health and docile ("and of course, the sailors had rubbed their bodies with the juice of a very green lemon so their bodies shone, exuding that acrid aroma of acid mixed with sweat that had so overpowered the starving men; but the wind from the east had swept away the smell, all that remained were beautiful and new complexions; with the result that the buyers—who made their old slaves lick the skin of those who had just arrived—were wasting their time and money, given that even the taste of lemon was gone now, diluted in the warm sweat and the scrapings of filth and the salt from the sea") I the end without hope and faces faces of animals cries holes hair but without eyes without gaze I the wind and taking off into the whip when raving raving raving and—he shouted: "Even so! Can you tell me how they got their chains off, so they could fight like that all over the boat?"

And he thought some more. "That's just lies. They couldn't unfasten their chains!" His voice as calm as the breeze over the grass.

"I know what is bothering you," said Papa Longoué. "You don't think they fought. You don't see the voyage. All lined up in that space, unable to lie down, or sit down, or stand up. Tortured nonstop by darkness and pain and suffocation. Men who want to kill each other but cannot. And those two separated with only ten bodies or so between them spent their time watching one another closely, counting each other's sufferings. And by the second week death had become rife among the people so they watched the distance that separated them grow smaller: the first, then the second, then another body had been thrown into the sea. Already, ten bodies had not been very many to keep hatred apart from hatred. But the number steadily diminished. So that by the end there were only two bodies between them, two women who moaned as if they were dying day and night. Only there was no day. The men heard none of that; they listened only for their own breath; hoping the other's would stop. You see, they were the strongest at the end of the voyage. And when they were made to go up on deck, the men were put on one side, the women on the other ("the males, the females"); therefore, because there were two women between them the men were unchained so they could be taken over to the bunch of men. That's how it happened. But I know what is bothering you. You saw that Béluse almost lost. You are wondering if he was the one? Eh?"

"That's not true," Mathieu said quietly.

Suppose Béluse was the one who scraped his back against the deck's handrail without wanting to? He was the only one it could have been, because the second Negro was then taken to La Roche's. The Negro maroon, the one they hunted one whole evening with dogs: Longoué. The slave, the procreator of slaves for the Senglis estate: the other. And this other was Béluse. He had been hurled against one of the cannons strapped to the deck but stood right up again, that is, before Longoué could crack his spine against the gun's mount, and he had grabbed a rope (the same rope used for dragging, the snake that had dragged their bodies down under the sea, unable to imagine right then or be aware that he touched it or how he was going to use it) and he had looped it so he could put it around Longoué's neck. But Longoué had slipped under the rope and with all his weight had held Béluse against the rail, simply replacing the cast iron of the cannon with the oak of the hull, as if in the meantime he had merely met with some trifling resistance; though it was clear that Béluse was almost as strong as he. Because Béluse, before falling onto the cannon's muzzle, had flung Longoué into the legs of the other slaves, not to catch his breath and not to get Longoué away from him, but in the hope of breaking his arm or his leg. And though they had then tried to grab each other by the neck and to break each other's backs, they did so less out of a desire for murder than to have an easy hold on the enemy: without resistance, like a toy. A taste for killing only came later.

All of that happened before the crew had been able to intervene. And certainly if Longoué had had—let's say—fifteen seconds more, he would have killed Béluse. Which meant that Mathieu did not want to believe in this fight. In that obscure region of himself dominated by the exhilaration and vertigo of knowing he did not want to admit, that Béluse had come so close to losing (not dying, losing), just as he was not yet willing to admit this: that Béluse had been able to live—stillborn—on the Senglis estates whereas Longoué had left the coast far behind to live in the forest on the hills.

"It's not true. It's not true!"

That Béluse, having forgotten his hatred, remained thus in the hut enclosure on the Senglis estate (watching days then years go by, and the huts became cabins: but really the cabin was a hut, the same piecing together of leaves and mud, season after season), and that he had begotten Anne, the one who murdered out of love—out of jealousy . . .

The wind the wind oh the wind. It had reached the roof of

the cabin, leaving the shallow scene; now it was making the straw bloom. The cabin was a torch stuck into the dryness with the wind both its soul and its invisible torchbearer. Or rather it was oh the wind a rider that knew no bounds digging into the flanks of the roof. And the torch shed no light—apart from the fact that the wind seemed to mock these two men run to earth by uncertainty, by forgetting, by memory itself when it no longer corresponded to hope;—apart from the fact that the wind seemed to want to blur everything, confusing everything while carrying it all off to the sky. But this torch kindled something like a passion, through the very flood and overflow of the mocking wind, through the endless crackling of the straw roof, through the heavy muggy heat at the foot of the cabin, where Papa Longoué, squatting before the young man—whom a moment ago he still thought was a child—sat in persistent, weighty contemplation, there far from the wind.

"Where is what is present, Masterdanight? Master, up and about as can be? A little-youngster who comes for knowledge. But good Lord, ho, who's complaining? Who can run after ghosts? And look. If one leans back he is scorched by the wind from the south! What is this boy looking for? I see all around. I see the green checkerboard plots below, the tarred road, nighttime on the road. How can you endlessly examine the past? Death comes. Death. It is the wave that rolls across yesterday's sand. Don't stir up the sand. Don't trample sudden death. And you, you men with no memory, you are happy! You are dead and don't know it. . . .

Do we not have a tornado on all sides like a hurricane laying waste that is to keep us from knowing where the earth is, or the sky?

During storms, remember, it's no longer a matter of business, it's life or death. You're not searching any more, you're fighting. Look. The whole crew has to handle the rigging except for those on duty between the decks, the ones in charge of the slaves under the direction of the coxswain. Tied to ropes they descend into the inferno. There the Negroes wait for the storm, wait for the utter frenzy, hoping to die once and for all or at least to take advantage of the moment to free themselves from the chains, never considering that tossed about by the waves like this all they would manage to do is break their wrists or legs in the iron pincers digging into their flesh. The men on duty there are in danger of smashing their heads open against the sides of the boat or of finding themselves caught in the stranglehold of black hands, while the storm covers up their cries and their comrades, tossed around by the fierce roll, cannot get to them quickly enough. And what if they do hang the one who strangled you the next day and ten of his neighbors along with him, that's some fine consolation. . . . The storm is the darkies' accomplice, it is not particular about its victims.

Then the coxswain, as he always did when emergency arose, first comes to check the ropes that were holding those two men; he has noticed that they never cry out, never try to kill each other or anyone else. One of them with difficulty lifts the arm tied to the hull to knee level, and makes a quick sign in the air in front of him. And, shrugging his shoulders, the coxswain contents himself with striking a good blow with his whip, giving the rebel's neighbors a share of it as well. He knows what the gesture means; before boarding the Rose-Marie, he was stationed at the holding pen for the Negroes on the coast back there. He took part in collecting the slaves, arguing over their number and quality with the men from the interior who sold them. He knows the customs of these savages.

Look. Today they don't know that gesture any more in their little lump of earth in the middle of the ocean! How did this young man get here! Was it written in all the swift passing days that one day a Béluse would come (a child) to account for the old treachery on the other side of the ocean so that the two coasts would finally rise above the storm and join? Rise above the shame of forgetting?

("Oh! Look. I'm telling you. It is not true!")

Why begin all over again, why spell out the first cry why out loud since all of history is resisting and here we are spinning while the day does not move forward? You can push and strain but the words roll around, they are in the wisps of thatch, they make a wall of whirlwinds. Who has ever been able to move a whirlwind wall? Soon it will be eleven, no, it is almost midday, we cannot do it.

"But to know what they were arguing about in the cabin!" Mathieu said suddenly. "If you are clever you can go back to where they were in the cabin while the other two were being beaten!"

The boy smiled, daring him.

"I can do that. Papa Longoué knows it all. What's the use of impatience, my son? You have read the books. And what is not in books you can't know. How Béluse fought on deck and almost lost."

"Ah. That's it! That's it!"

"Good. Let's slip in like water. . . . Here we are! They were bargaining in the cabin."

"Of course. It doesn't take a wizard to figure that out!"

"But here. You can see the place, hear the story tell itself. Because. Yes. Because Papa Longoué knows it all. . . ."

Mathieu laughed. Mathieu poked fun.

But suddenly and at precisely midday—while the wind was already abandoning the straw on the hut and rising toward the clouds—the last twig stopped moving; everything fell back into stony dismal heat, all you could hear were the cries from the plain, the distant shouts of men at work—and while these two conjurers sat there in silence, silent again in the swift motionless time where it had only just been eleven and now was already midday: a peaceful midday that outshone the other midday of the first day and the first fight—suddenly he saw the narrow cabin, with its strong odor. At first it had seemed to be a sort of office where work took precedence over convenience: guns and pistols padlocked to the wall, the chest holding the account books that on this boat took the place of a ship's log, the bottles of rum that had helped them get through the journey, all empty now, and the small box of red balls for registering how many of the cargo were dead. He saw new rum standing on the chest and the six men huddled tightly around some dubious-looking pewter mugs; he heard the words and did not even know whether Papa Longoué was speaking them again for his benefit or if, in all this outcry from the deeds of bygone days, it was the wind finally haggling over the price of flesh. Because in this struggle over names and secrets from the past for the first time Mathieu found himself the direct target of the *quimboiseur*'s power, with no time to figure out what was real. What if the old man had some knowledge of such a dialogue (but how?), or what if he had guessed at the words following some model he constructed for himself? And Mathieu heard the words above the echoes rising from the plains.

"Now gentlemen," said the captain. "We have to finish up."

He tried, between two hiccups, to get the best price and conclude the deal yet not antagonize the planters.

"The usual price!" said Senglis.

"The usual price! Look at all those red balls in my box. It is so full of dead ones that it is overflowing. No, gentlemen. I cannot give you these specimens for five hundred. The rum is excellent but one thing is really not equal to the other!"

"But the one you have taken off the boat was given thirty blows," said Senglis. "Give me a discount! Come on captain."

"I would never spoil a specimen, sir, if I could avoid it. If I tell you they are not in harm's way you can believe me."

"Obviously," said La Roche.

Instantly the captain was prepared to seize the opportunity; he was already high as a kite and suggested, "Six hundred and fifty?"

"Whoa there La Roche," said Senglis. "Work things out for yourself but I don't intend to spend my money on deals you've made."

The atmosphere in the cabin grew heavier, the air full of the smell of undiluted *tafia*. One of the men present was breathing hard. Sounds reverberating from the deck rustled like a thin curtain of straw.

"Gentlemen! Can we finally get down to business?" said the captain.

"Five hundred and fifty," said Senglis, slumped down beside the chest.

"I'm not asking for alms! I do my job conscientiously. I don't just go and buy whatever poor devils come out of the bush. I have people I've done business with for a long time. Guaranteed specimens. I have expenses to pay over there. I have to have finders, guards, accountants. I pick and choose. Finally, gentlemen, have you ever seen me throw my cargo overboard when the English frigates come? No, I take my chances. I maneuver. I lose days, weeks. And then, I don't pack them in. There are never epidemics on my boat. Well, almost never. This costs money gentlemen. Really."

"Yes, yes, captain," said La Roche. "We respect your good qualities. Luck has nothing to do with it. It's all Duchêne!"

"Six hundred and fifty."

"You know me, dear friend. I never haggle. I do however, have some authority over trade here. Isn't that true?"

"Oh, sir," said the captain pathetically, no longer so sure.

"Five hundred and fifty," said Senglis.

"Senglis, you are stupid. The captain has a lot to do. Six hundred, the deal is done, but we want a bunch of females, as many as we want, set aside for us at five hundred."

"You are killing me."

"But no, dear man. I invite you and these gentlemen to dinner tonight. It will be a pleasure to have you."

"Have me! That's the right word!" shouted the captain.

"My god. What a thing to say!"

"God . . . God . . . Do you know what time it is?"

And one of the assistants, intimidated by the argument but in a hurry to gulp down his rum, repeated stupidly: "The time, my captain?"

"You can say I am the last in the procession all you want," said Mathieu. "But I can tell that it was between midday and two o'clock, that is, between the time of the fight and when they unloaded the slaves!"

"It doesn't take a wizard," said the *quimboiseur*, laughing. "And you're not impatient any more are you?"

"What's the use," cried Mathieu. "Because it's all done! . . ."

The old man smiled. He stood up. "Already you want to run a

race with truth," he said. Then he crossed the clearing to the bamboo. Mathieu went over beside him.

The windows through the bamboo that these two men looked down through onto the plain had opened now into wide bays of sunlight. They saw the red earth down there through the branches framing it, checkered parcels of land outlined in stones and rolling in large plowed squares to lap against the first wooded depths where the hillside sloped upward. The sea of earth and the shore of dark trees seemed almost at war. In places there were thickets like beaches of ocher mud where the plowing met the forest. But these few areas, sprinkled with shrubs like rusty cobblestones, only marked a bit of pale lightning here and there at the far edge of the fields' brilliant red. The result was that the plain seemed intent on carrying the hillside off with a single wave, devastating the forest's rock, pulling the entire woody cliff to pieces. That is where it was.

Yes. That is where the fugitive had known that when he reached the hill he would be saved. He listened to the dogs but did not stop running. He was trying to tell by the sound how much distance separated him from his hunters. It seemed to him that the echoes were coming just as much from this brush in front of him as they were coming from the countryside behind. He could not be sure of his calculations; the only sure thing was that the dogs were gaining ground. The air was too free, the night too bright. Not enough water. Trails. High grass was better than the path. Cut across.

He saw the first row ahead of him. Thick trunks whose leaves merged. Oof! He grunted and leaped into it all. Into the night, the woods, deep and thick, the heavy branches, without being able to recognize any single element and the only thing spinning through his head was still the same crazy speed. The slope was so steep, the stumps so close together that he sometimes hung from the branch of a tree well before he reached the tree itself still ahead of him. He would jump from the top of a tree to the roots with just one big step. An acacia tore a gash in his skin. He lifted his arm without stopping and sucked the wound, panting, half-choking. The mixture of blood and sweat cooled his lips, and at the same time he felt the distant pain (as if this were a wound he had suffered in an earlier world) and, above it all, the prickling of sweat on the wound. But he already knew, just by looking at the lie of the trees and ground, that he had won. The dogs had lost. All he had to do now was climb all night into this forest.

He thought of the pen where they had been packed in and where he had been jubilant to see the other join him; he thought of the mud in which they both had slept, if you could call it sleeping, of the men in chains who had thought they were being taken away to be burned or devoured, of the ones who had hurled themselves onto the red-hot iron or into the sea, and of the other whom he had been unable to break like termite-infested wood, again and again he got a kick out of driving a stake through his shoulder (so he would not die), and he was on the lookout for the dogs running wild in the sky or still tenaciously lying in wait, he imagined the snake he would soon make and that he would stick in the ground next to the mud head, he thought of the man who had held him down by the neck with his foot, his back still burned where the boot had marked it, he thought, no, he was drunk with these flashes, with the fatigue, the blood and barking, even seeing the dogs run through the forest way ahead of him, as if the trees had become transparent, luminous, fragile, and seeing the sun fall with lions into the big ship's hold, a sun screaming and groaning in chains, burning the wooden hull that was instantly and endlessly reconstituted (to close the glaring prison forever), and seeing the lions or dogs leaping like flames while the storm reeled through the sky and the land.

(Eight o'clock. The pack had held to the trail since six that evening, it was in a frenzy of excitement. It found tracks again in the thicketed area in front of Morne aux Acacias.)

And he felt the wind: not around him or vaguely over his whole body, but running like a river through the furrows made by the whip on his back. As if this wind were going up a path across his back, going down all the gullies at once, taking every bloody crossover, every road opened into the skin. Fiercely he collapsed. He was now no more than a single cry of rage and weakness in the matted density of the hills, with the desperate howling of dogs in the distance. He lay down on his belly. He lay down so he would not have to feel the pain of the warm wind burning into his open flesh. So the wind developed into a kind of invisible flowering from this human trunk; and all through that first night it kept climbing that torn body and blazing out of it before falling abruptly back onto the plains to start its ascent again and its victory and once again splash down to the bottom of the slope.

(Nine o'clock. Men and dogs circling in front of the black wall. There was nothing to be done. It was as if this maroon had been trekking through the Morne aux Acacias since the beginning of time, as if he had been able to recognize the only place where the animals would never be able to track him down. Maroon from the first day. Maroon from the first hour.)

"He never even gave you time to find him a hut!" sneered Senglis. He had been able to follow the hunt by exerting prodigious energy. Now he was drinking his fill of the spectacle: seeing the black cliff as the end to his torment, the torments of this exhausting day as well as those of a lifetime of hatred and jealousy. He was someone who could be content with this for a consolation; and any such slim revenge, arising unexpectedly from time to time in the long parade of snubs, gave him the strength and courage to last for a long time.

"I'm going after him!" shouted La Roche.

Then he grabbed a small barrel that he had not let out of his sight for six hours. He had given orders concerning it the instant he learned that the slave had escaped. This barrel intrigued the other hunters, especially Captain Duchêne who, with his officers, had been invited to dinner and consequently had joined in the chase; he hoped there was a reserve of rum in it, and had even gone so far as to heft the thing but was badly disillusioned to find that its weight was nothing like what that much alcohol should weigh. La Roche merely shouted: "Duchêne, don't you dare touch that barrel, you'll rue the day!" The only thing the hunters could think of was that the master of Acajou had a bit of gunpowder in there, which he intended to send bang into that black ass. A notion reinforced by the restrained and savage fervor with which he had urged men and dogs on.

The men (the dogs were lying down, panting and muddy) went up to La Roche, pointing out that it would be crazy to try to keep going through the acacias; he probably would not have listened to them if his humpbacked neighbor had not said with a sneer: "Just leave him alone, he is right to want to get that Negro back," words that had the effect of somehow bringing the hunter back down to earth—which meant he stood there for a long moment looking at the cliff of tree trunks plunging into the abysses of shade that climbed the red shoulder of the sky above him. He was alone now facing the others who were growing impatient, and finally he turned around and with a wave of his hand simply ordered them to take the road back home.

Yes, that is where it was.

"So," Mathieu murmured. "The first thing he felt was the boot on the back of his neck." Long before he re-experienced the blows and the salt brine and the gunpowder, just at the moment when running had whipped up his blood and revived the pain.

"Because he was already a Longoué," the old man said proudly. He had not forgotten the country back there, no; but all that ocean to cross and the crop across his back, and even that other man—his prison mate on the sea, had already made him be a Longoué. "Yes, the other man too!"

"Then," Mathieu asked, "why did it not make the other one also a Longoué? He must have lost all that, therefore. Or else you have to explain to me what happened in that country back there across the ocean."

Papa Longoué stretched his hands out toward the plain.

He saw the former verdure, the original madness still innocent of man's touch, the chaos of acacias rolling down in a great swell to the high grasses; now there were woods that had been thinned softly lapping all the way down to the clear, checkered plain. All history becomes clear in this land before them if the changes in the land's appearance are followed over time. Papa Longoué knew that. He trembled slightly, thinking how Mathieu ought, at least, to learn by himself how to see the woods pouring down to a sieve of furrows, learn all alone how to feel the ancient madness quivering, there in that spot where the madness of men now imposed its rigid and patient greed. He had the power to feel this, and it filled him with oppressive heat and made him shiver in the sun. He stretched out his hands toward the plain: toward that other ocean looming between the land here and the mountain of the past. Not yet knowing that Mathieu had won because the young man was forcing him to follow the "most logical" path, and here he was arguing *that* and *therefore* and *after* and *before*, with *why* in knots inside his head, drowned in a storm of *because*:

"Because, ho Mathieu, we have to get to the beginning," he said.

"So he ran away the very first hour. . . . It was here, behind the hill's wall. And perhaps he knew that some day you would be here, papa, to show me the spot. He knew it; otherwise why would he have stayed there waiting so close to the pack of dogs, at the same spot where you would stand, between the bamboos?" He did not want to forget the boot on the back of his neck or the lash of the whip or the hunter's blue eyes; nor the name that he had heard in this language he did not know, so obviously a name: La Roche!

But the story had moved along simply and calmly: ardent, enthusiastic, part of today. The story of a man, Papa Longoué thought, who had nursed his hatred through the entire crossing, if this voyage could be called a crossing. And this man had not tried to think or create any order. Order and thought are for today.

"Let's sit down," said the old man, "and follow the path. . . ."

La Roche was racing ahead of the dogs, apparently just as much in a hurry to return home as he had been to make some headway on the trail of the maroon. Senglis made a great point of staying right there beside him. The captain and his two officers followed more slowly, marveling over the excitement of the two landlubbers. A few slaves brought up the rear; every now and then the old captain would glance thoughtfully at them, trying to see if their black masks hid either vexation or joy. But the slaves remained indifferent to the results of the chase. They said nothing because speaking was forbidden.

At ten o'clock they all crossed the river that ran along the border of the property; the dogs wanted to drink but their master kept them from it, shouting and pulling on the leashes. They all, men and animals, crossed the three planks thrown between the rocks of the riverbed under the hanging vines; then they plunged down the path at the end of which loomed the flat shadow of the house.

They had come the back way, a path scarcely marked between the erratic lines of trees. Soon they came alongside the group of huts where the field Negroes returning from their day's work were just arriving as well. The two groups briefly crossed paths without La Roche even seeing the men and women, shadows erased by shadow, who stood aside to let him by. They went into the big house through the kitchen where the oppressive smell of food cooking made their mouths water, and they wasted no time installing themselves in the main room where a young Negro woman, motionless and almost smiling, was waiting for them beside a table that was already laid.

Duchêne, Lapointe, and the coxswain pushed in close to the table, while the two lords of the domain had water poured over their hands. Despite the fact that they had dinner with La Roche here every time the *Rose-Marie* came to port, the seamen were unable to keep from ogling the unusual spectacle. The master of Acajou gave a great laugh; he made the young slave woman sit on his lap.

"Everywhere I go," said the captain, "all I hear is rumors of rebellion. What is actually going on, sir?"

"Oh, the person to ask is Senglis. He is captain of the militia or something like that."

"Laugh, laugh all you want. . . . Three thousand rebels in the south. Just as many in the hills."

"Bah, it's quiet here."

"And what do you think about the news from Saint-Domingue?"

"Come now. You're getting all stirred up over nothing, Senglis! Don't tell me you haven't shot enough of them to calm the others down. Besides, it's Duchêne told you that."

"Me!"

"Don't play the innocent. There are rebellions and then there are reprisals. That's the secret of your business. We wait here for you to come like the messiah with your three hundred head of slaves and we get had on a regular basis...."

"And to top it all off, now the Negroes he sells you are maroons."

"That's enough, my friend. You'll see—my maroon will bring me fewer worries than your new acquisition."

"Gentlemen, gentlemen," implored the captain.

"Fine, Duchêne, don't wring your hands over it. Here, I'll give you the girl for the night!"

And La Roche pushed the slave toward the captain.

"Oh, I'm too old!"

Everybody at the table laughed and shook merrily at that, except for Lapointe, who was testy and wondered angrily why nobody offered him any such a proposition. He was not a captain.

The girl was an extraordinary creature, scarcely veiled in an old scrap of yellow lace that she had found in one of the trunks in the house and over which she had knotted a piece of cloth that left her shoulders and chest bare and went down to her heels. She was certainly almost twenty but looked like she was fourteen. Her skin glowed in the lamplight. It was her proud custom to answer the only master with whom she was acquainted with a smile. As for the others, she did not have to take them into account: she could dare to turn her back on them despite her state unless Monsieur de La Roche gave her a look forbidding her to do so.

While the party enjoyed their meal (local chickens in a sauce, manioc cakes, cane syrup, yams, as well as a new vegetable growing on trees that they called breadfruit), conversation grew lively as they discussed the more and more frequent rebellions and then the Negro who had run away that very day: as if the men around the table were making some natural connection between these two orders of events or as if, without being aware of doing so, they were already electing the fugitive to lead present and future rebellions.

"You can feel it on the boat," the coxswain explained. "Every trip we make they are more restive. Now the crew is afraid of them; and not a single man feels sorry for them any more. And there is not a one among them who begs and implores. In the gathering pens back there they already know their fate and destination."

"Moreover, the minute they arrive they try to run away."

"Come on! How can that be?"

"I can tell," the coxswain went on. "I could see that that one would run away. You end up getting a sort of sixth sense for this sort of thing."

"Really, my boy, I'm going to hire you when I'm buying them. You can advise me as to which are the docile specimens."

"It's the way they both pretended to be calm. That one was an important man; the others were silent in his presence. He even settled an argument among them, there in the bottom of the steerage, bolted down. When we went down for inspection he drew his sign in the air in front of one of the men who was moaning."

"Ah! The snake."

"The snake. It was a strange crossing, sir. The crew seemed affected by the power of this Negro. Never before has the harbor of Fort-Royal been greeted with such cheers."

"But the escape? He was solidly chained."

"The power of that sign! Because I am sure that one of your slaves freed him. Think back. First we led away the batch belonging to Monsieur de Senglis. Maybe you remember that those two tried to fight again when the time came to lead the other one off to the slave quarters on the Senglis property."

"That was at three o'clock."

"We get here at four. We push them all into the first pen and go inside to wash up. One hour later he had disappeared. The others were where they belonged, and all of them chained, not even frightened."

"Bah! Many of my slaves were born here, how could they have

communicated with that African? Look boy, I was seventeen when my father died. My first decision was to mate the slaves who were fit to reproduce. That's how I got fifteen of them, with no other cost. Look at Louise, she doesn't know the mother and father who produced her. I brought her to the house immediately. But when I tell you that every day one of the women keeps watch nearby you will understand that I do know her mother. Bah! I have never smiled at a mother! Are we not in a new situation? No, no, they have forgotten their origins, this sign no longer has any power over them! I alone have power here, yes, I alone. Isn't that right, Louise?"

The young Negro woman nodded her head and smiled.

"I call her Louise, I don't know why. For the pleasure of it."

"Don't you believe it. They are still passing on some memory of their earlier state."

"Fine, we'll see about that tomorrow! A good whipping session will loosen their tongues. But tonight, my friends, let us drink to the health of the King!"

"And the death of the States General!"

"Senglis, no politics! Come on. I'm the only one who has lost anything, I'm the one to complain! Aside from that the night is ours!"

The half-lit smoky room gradually filled up with shouts, songs, and the dense reek of sauces; little by little the shining varnished benches were shifted around; the big sideboards shook; the already worm-eaten floor collapsed in spots; yellow cockroaches scattered away from where the lights were shining; the last bits of meat dried in the dishes while darkness encroached on the lamps. The young Negro woman, the only one paying any attention to the darkness, finally blew out the wicks, then without so much as a glance at the drunk men lay down on a sack near the half-open door. . . .

"Well, my friend, be my guest," said Papa Longoué.

Mathieu and the *quimboiseur* ceremoniously returned to the fireplace.

Nothing at all was moving there: the heat was motionless, the bamboo quelled, the bays blinded. The cabin no longer rustled, the embers were passive, asleep. But the young man lifted his head and looked up at the wind where it had veiled itself with clouds; it spun and made those transparent densities of sky waltz around a single crater. Gray clouds dizzily entwined around white clouds and in the center of the carousel the brilliance of the sun imparted something like a mirror of fire.

"Yes," Papa Longoué said simply as he bent down to pick up a cooked banana.

"Ah, it all seems like it's right here! Louise. The house. The little barrel next to the cistern. The door opening onto the two mahogany trees of the lane . . ."

"But you'll see, you'll see, you go down, you think you are going down, until the moment you suddenly come upon the road there today and then you greet yourself like a stranger."

"Even so! . . . Ah! I have gotten the better of you, Papa! I've made you do it! You are showing me the things all done-well-done!"

"But notice that before he went into the kitchen he had put his barrel down beside the door."

Mathieu waved it off as if he did not care. They ate slowly.

The last of the Longoués smiled, thinking of the men who believe they are the strongest. But they cannot keep any distance from a story. They do not think of it as something going on over here and the spectator over there. For them it is the same mix of wind at midday and at midnight. The spectator is down there beside the cabin, he never catches sight of the wind way up high. "I am the spectator, said the old man."

Mathieu did not know that in that same spot, long ago, yesterday, the fugitive had lain down, thinking of the woman who had freed him from his ropes; thinking I shall have her, I shall take her with me, while he looked at the midnight moon: hidden in the wind's madness it was tracing something like a pool of sweetness in the middle of ragged, spiraling clouds, a pale-yellow hole in the dark furrow of the sky.

Chapter 3

1

HE WOKE UP JUST AT THE MOMENT that this moon faded into the sky and the darkness of the woods became suddenly heavy with mist. He could tell that the shadows were depositing this mist onto the invisible leaves and ground, and it seemed to him that the damp air was the vanished moon spread all among the tree trunks. He watched the day gradually start to transpire from their roots as if it were the earth exhaling this light that rose to brighten the highest treetops. Then he understood that the spot where he had fallen asleep was the only flat surface in the upward thrust of the forest, the only bare ground that would be forevermore attached like a flat branch to the huge trunk of the hill. He was lying on his belly but by tilting his head back he could look up and make out the thick foliage above him. It was definitely daybreak, cool and comfortable, already heavy with the heat of the sun to come. He shifted gently then sat up all at once; he was numb to the painful tracks on his back, intent only on conquering the stiffness of his limbs.

After he had stretched he began feverishly to collect bits of liana and sticks that he piled in front of him. Then he noticed the two ropes around his wrists, still knotted as if interwoven with his flesh; the slave had only had time to cut the section connecting them to each other. He got rid of these bracelets, rubbed his forearms briskly and, squatting on his heels, began to assemble the bits of wood meticulously, using lianas to fit them together until they formed a sort of gnarled, reptilian body; one end of it he made thinner and then gave the other end a rudimentary head. He was so absorbed in his work that he did not see the sun, borne by the black trees whose highest branches vanished into its blaze, suddenly burst out over the hillside to his left. And by the time he had finished his strange task, the strip of sky between the ridge and the sun already resembled a great stretch of bluish water, sprinkled here and there with flimsy white boats. But he was looking at the two bits of rope on the ground; he was remembering that woman in her long dress, like a warrior in ceremonial robes. He stood up and walked along this earthen terrace. Because he already wanted with all his being to burn up the miles between the house and where he stood, ravaging the depths of the bottom-land savanna marked with dark greens and brilliant stripes of red, turning all this new vegetation that delimited his horizon to ashes, until he finally reached the warrior woman: her yellow veil laid out like braids on her breast, her red and black train hiding her ankles, her eyes glowing fiercely in the half-lit enclosure.

He returned furiously to his work, tearing hunks of earth saturated with dew from the ground and kneading them into the shape of a large, really bony head, all flat planes and wide gashes; then with his thumb he carved a mouth and two staring eyes, a sunken nose. Very carefully he chose a cranny between two roots where he put the head which he joined, mouth to mouth, with the creature he had made from wood and vines, wrapping its body around the mud head. They were so tightly joined that there was no way of knowing whether the red head wore a yoke produced by its own breath or if the hair was alive and seeking vengeance for its own existence against the one to whom it owed this existence.

He left it there and walked away; the day before him lay empty but already heavily charged with this land that he intended to know. With his left foot always wedged against a tree trunk he walked along the hillside all the way through the woods, avoiding the trail. He discovered where the land went down to the sea, and there the recumbent orb of a dune wrapped and surrounded by this one, selfsame body: seaward all waves and swells and closer in tufts and rolls of green made bitter by the offshore wind. One single body surrounding the spearlike sandy point which stuck out through its own excreta, piercing puddles of mud, putrid pustules, squatting ponds of water around which the sand acquired a glaze of filth. Immense silence sailing out to meet the sound of the sea; it seemed possible to touch the zone where these two orders of life met over the fringe of waves: the silent opening out of the coast and the mute rolling swell of sea life.

The fever he felt on awakening was calmer now, as if quelled beneath the great white sword tossed there close to the surge. He walked along the ridge following the coast and saw that, no matter what direction he took, the point was always there for him to see: and so he was the delimited point of focus while he himself, by walking, focused on and delimited the secret realm of the sand. He saw once again the other shore lying out beyond the sky as clearly as if this ocean were merely a channel; he reached out his hands toward where the roots that had plunged straight in now were stretched thin, toward the foaming bars he had crossed for the first and last time; he saw out there on the water's blue the endless blue-black line: there was not a curve to it, no end, no return. And the waiting—he felt again the same torments of waiting he had felt on the first days at sea, when the boat was still tacking along the shore, when he wondered every time he was taken on deck in chains for exercise whether or not the land was still there. Then one day what was there was the infinity of sea.

One day the sea was there, and arrival in this land of loops and detours, coves and gullies. Of course, the moment he came on deck, even before his second foot had landed on the splattered and streaked wood, he had grasped and weighed up this land; and having done so he kept his eyes down, fixed on the boat's planking, apparently uninterested in the panorama of the coast. But this was only a trick. He had not presented Captain Duchêne with the spectacle of a crazed animal looking all around and struggling at the entrance to the pen readied for it. Not one of the people there, not a single one in this group or in groups either before or after could have let the sentiment of defeat show—the mixture of acceptance and terror that filled them with turmoil. This was not defiance, because cargo like this no longer had the strength to defy anyone; it was instinct, modesty, an unreflective need for concealment. Perhaps it was weakness. Perhaps it was because the man had already assessed the difference between these two coasts (one of them stretched out infinitely and the other nestled in its curves), perhaps he had already sounded the mass of ocean brimming between their lands. Perhaps because this was no longer the moment to watch for a shoreline; it was time to get ready to live!

So he had followed the action at the slave market in a sort of dream. The rain continuing in fits and starts. Some women, pink and white. Some men, self-important. Shrewd ones, stubborn ones, greedy ones. Something gold bartered for a young boy. The rustle of dresses being dragged through the mud. Merchants shouting and gesticulating, hundreds of voices, thundering and high-pitched; the empty, silent faces of people still looking at him, waiting for him to make some decision. But he was bound together with two men and three women; the other man was close by and also seemed to have two women in tow. Of the entire shipment they were the only ones who were tied together and held aside: nine already marked animals past whom the unstoppable crowd rushed in their hurry to find a bargain, to haggle, to make their purchase. He saw the crowd go by.

Next they walked for a long time behind the cart through easy roads, down wide, muddy trails that were flat and even, except for the two lines of deep ruts through which the wheels moved smoothly without bumping. That was when he had been able to pay attention to the foliage lining both sides of the road, the trees and the deep shade, he felt that he was sure to find there the leaf of life and death. At a crossroads he understood that the other was being sent to a trail on the right; and you couldn't say it was true any more than you could say it wasn't: the other tried to get loose, not to run away but to fight again. Because they were both waiting for the moment to settle this business. But they were brutally man-handled; the sailors sent the other man head over heels in the red mud road, so that when he got up again his body was streaked with long layers of mud turning yellow on his black skin. Yes.

He had understood that they were being separated there for good, and when he arrived later at the low house sunk down behind the trunks of two huge mahogany trees, he knew that he was finally being taken to the last of the pens prepared for him and his companions. Before being shoved inside he was able to communicate by a single gesture with three or four onlookers (one of them perhaps a woman): dazed, paralyzed shadows along the walls of the big house. Although his two hands were tied together he raised them in the direction of the pen to show that he had no intention of staying there. Perhaps the woman had seen his gesture and then and there began preparing herself to come and set him free.

"But you don't know what happened back there in the country on the other side of the ocean! So long ago, so long ago, my son . . ."

—We don't know, thought Mathieu. We. We! And you don't even know, though you are the oldest man around, older than the houses and schools, older than the church and the Croix-Mission because you might say you were born the day the two of them went up on deck, when they saw the end the beginning, the prison the land, the desert the abundance awaiting them, and kept their eyes downcast looking at the deck the way we have our heads bent right now toward the red, sharp-edged mud; because there has not been one single empty time up to now that we have all forgotten together; not just the Longoués and the Béluses, that is to say the ones who refused and the ones who accepted, but even the others, chained to the Longoués and Béluses who followed the cart, without a clue as to why those two men fought like two brothers determined to stay together, also not counting those who took part in the hunt and were (this time old Mister Duchêne was not at all wrong about appearances) really indifferent as to whether or not they caught the fugitive, and also all the rest of them who never knew why a Longoué had to fight a Béluse, the people brought there who never wondered why they had crossed all that ocean and why they had survived at sea, for what work, for what existence, whether it was because the man, needing to muster his strength, had chosen this unthinkable way of going after some men, and they lived up to this very day in this state of absence and enveloped the Béluses and Longoués in their absence, gradually obliterating the wake of the boat through the ocean; until a young boy like me, after reading some books and growing up too quickly, yes, too quickly, finally looks at the foam on the surface of the sea and tries to find the place where the rope dragged blue, swollen bodies; until I, who have not forgotten because I never knew anything about this story, I come alone to ask questions of the oldest man around who is Papa Longoué, you, you who have forgotten without forgetting because you live in the hills, far from the road, and you claim that the events must not be followed logically but divined, foreseeing what has happened; no, not even you who, nonetheless today, despite the sun pressing down on your head, are now trying to establish dates and motives! It is because the two of us, you and I, want to climb back up the path of the sun, we are trying to pull the day from the past over us, we feel that beneath this weight we are too flimsy, and we are too empty in this absence, and forgetting to fill our presence; yes our presence in the world: a mighty grand word for you, for me, for our weakness and our ignorance, but a word we have to push before us like a cart without shafts because the world is there and because it is open and because, in any case, some day we will have to hurtle down our hillsides to it; because we want to understand for ourselves, you who understand and yet would understand nothing if I said these things to you out loud and I who understand nothing and yet already am able to understand you when you sit there like that not speaking in the great sound of the plain; because yes we want to discover, begin again from within, start from the moment when everything was not obscure, faded, start from the last moment in which we were able to look at the sun above Pointe des Sables, and sit down in the acacia forest to weigh this light and know that it was inside us! . . . *You grow more and more words distant*, but why not words why not long sentences when at sixteen, there are ghosts everywhere you have to stir up without knowing, and then I stop near the great plateau, day is drawing to a close, it is just about gone. I shout a great shout without knowing what it is I shout. Do you know your silence? And not in accusation, not to keep an eye on how things are divvied up between the man who lit the powder and the Negro who exploded into flurries of flesh and blood in front of the low house; not even to mark the line between the man who took the girl on his knees and the other one exclaiming, "By Jove! He is going way too far, making the black girl sit on his lap while we watch, even if we are neighbors and friends," because the humpback certainly would have liked to do the same thing (we know this), only he did not dare; no. But because, look Papa, I don't know, but it seems to me that the light all over the world would lack light if we did not have an account of the bargain, for us, for us, not the account of the seller content with his day (we have seen that already, the painting exists) but the account of the merchandise itself on display watching the crowd go by. There would be a voice missing in the sky and light, which is why I sit here beside you without speaking—for the voice—not for the accusation the suffering the death. And there is not one of us who knows what happened in the country over there beyond the ocean, the sea has rolled over us all, even you who see the story and the people in it. There. That is what we call the past. This bottomless sequence of forgetting with, every now and then, some hint flashing into our nothingness: my grandmother squatting in front of her doorway, she shouts at the young ones: "What! You can't figure out how old I am? What have they been teaching you at school, I tell you I was born the same year as the June-Fifteenth-Fire!" And that is what we call the past: that whirlwind of death from which we have to pull memory, so for you I am a child, one of the brats, you do not see that I have grown up since that first time when you told me to go home to my sister and put the tablecloth back on the table right side up so you could come into the house and treat the child or at least find out what was making him sick; and sitting there motionless before me you told me also to turn the statue of the Virgin around so the mother of god would not be offended; and then, without seeing him, you cured the child. The past yes because I have grown up since then and you do not see it, this need is the past, understanding a story what it means even before it begins and explaining it from underneath. Because if you had a clear idea of the life they lead down there, some day I will tell you about it, a life every day more sluggish, more dismal, more bitter, nothing bright, no mountain, no ravine, then you would see the past standing beside them but they do not see it. And I am not describing the details, there is no describing boredom, but that is the past: the fact of not finding the country back there across the ocean and why is that important since they both came; did they not bring the country with them? Did it not establish itself with them, and with them make the forgetting grow larger and larger in the past and magnify in the past the acacias and the huts on the Senglis property; because the country belongs to Béluse as much as to Longoué we never talk about Béluse, Béluse knew he knew what had happened on the other side of the ocean and so it was with him that the country was divided between him and Longoué until this day when you and I have looked at the foam on the surface of time, myself a young man whom you still consider a child and you an old dodderer a bit of bark whom I still consider to be knowledge and understanding yes despite the books whom I take to be the man who knows and disposes; but there it is, you are alone you have made your bargain you are the Béluse of the Longoués all the foam of the sea and of time have risen to your lips oh Papa. . . .

"But we have to follow Béluse," said the *quimboiseur*. "We left him too soon! After all he is your grandparent, ho Mathieu!"

2

First he noticed the old man weaving rush baskets off to the side away from the others: the only one to raise his head when the little group came into the yard. A calm, slow-moving man who stared attentively, the straw falling from his hands the way water gushes from a spring.

Next he saw how the huts were set up to make three sides of a rectangle with the fourth opening onto the slope on top of which the big house could be seen. It looked indeed like a fortified palace raised above the village of huts.

The sun was glaring down into the muddy yard and you could almost see the patches of water evaporate, the mud harden. What was amazing to him after being engulfed in the sounds of the market was this rustling, hissing, silky silence, shot through with indifference and resignation.

And so, this was where the boat was taking them.

He and the two women were thrown into a shed behind one of the huts. Water dripping from the straw roof glittered like a sun river spilling out of the sun through the sieve of dry leaves. Lying in this damp and this shade he could see part of the yard: the old man had not picked up his work again. He sat, patient and motionless in the light out there, still looking in the direction of the three newcomers. Disregarding the women beside him the man then lay on his side on the damp ground and contemplated the curious old man. Their gazes went straight down a narrow corridor between two huts, like thread strung in the bamboo. The question was which would relent the first. But the old man stood up without lowering his eyes; he crossed the yard and came into the passage, his head filling all the space and blocking what could be seen of the big house as it seemed to spring from the huts, his eyes more and more focused, widened, alert in their gummy sockets; he came into the shed and sat down peacefully.

"You detest me," he said, "but that's normal. You detest everybody right now."

The two women were transfixed, aghast. Ever since the boat had weighed anchor off the coast back there, not one of them had opened their mouths to say a word; suffering had been mute, as had hatred. Death: mute. Mute the drama hatched in the delirium of the steerage between the decks and settled by the *other* without speaking. Ever since the boat had anchored in this harbor not one of them had heard a word they could understand. All those voices and those shouts, the auctioneering enclosed them tightly in a ferocious deafness.

"Really, I'm not so old that I have forgotten the language. Don't look at me like a ghost!"

"But old Papa," he said, "it seemed unbelievable that such a thing was possible. So far, far away."

54   At La Pointe des Sables

"Well you see, it is possible. There are two roads. When all is well on a plantation they buy new slaves from the same region. Yes. It makes the work easier, meaning that you work faster and faster. When there is trouble they don't want to do that at all. They say the new ones bring an evil spirit with them, that they must not communicate with the old ones, that they forget to rebel while they are learning the local language; and then when they know the language it's too late, they have been brought to heel. So they are careful, they choose them from some different spot over there. It looks like as far as we are concerned everything is fine, because here you are. Right? Which means that tomorrow you will be put to work and very likely they will tell me to go with you to explain things. Once again I'll have to run up and down the fields like a youngster, at my age!"

This old man was like a hyena; all he thought about was his troubles. He talked so fast that it drove the three prisoners crazy because they could only understand a tiny bit of what he was saying, flashing here and there like the lightning in last night's storm. He would mix completely unknown expressions into his speech whenever his memory of his native language faded, or perhaps when there was no turn of phrase available in that language that would adapt to the new situation.

The man felt an uncontrollable repulsion at the spectacle of this puny, shameless person bemoaning his fate without even having thought to ask them if they wanted some help, something to eat. It made him shudder.

"What's the matter?" asked the old man. "Did the voyage disagree with you?"

"It's my back," he said quickly.

"Ah, they whipped you. You can't be a big-head with them, they're quick!"

The man in fact did feel the pain in his back again and all the stiffness in his body. He did not dare move, not that he was afraid of opening his wounds again, no, but he could see that any movement he started, even the least, would not be completed until he punched those filthy eyes. He held himself stiffly in the mud, focused on the torment in his back, also trying to figure out as precisely as he could in these circumstances just what being a big-head meant, and not even noticing that the old man had immediately gone back to what he was saying without giving another thought to the lashes or the wounds.

He started talking about a child, a little scatterbrained, she made your heart glad: everybody, masters and slaves, made a fuss over her because of her radiant, unexpected beauty. Orphaned in her infancy, she never seemed to have suffered from this misfortune because the people living there, the animals, the things, the earth, and the sun took the place of father and mother; and then there was her grandmother, whose existence was completely devoted to the child. Her name was Cydalise Marie Éléonor Nathalie, and she had decided they should call her Marie-Nathalie. At the beginning of his tale, therefore, she bloomed like a blue pool brimming with morning sunshine. Then she dulled but with no dimming of her beauty. From one word to the next, with no transition or almost none, she became opaque, untouchable. She had nothing in common with her surroundings. Soon she was no longer to be seen at the head of the little band of wide-eyed black children she used to watch over. Then she vanished for a long time; what they knew about her was reported by the house slaves: she was learning to read and write. The split grew even wider when she reappeared, a woman now and unapproachable in her youthful bearing: her finger always ready to point out some lack; her distant gaze as if the people and things before her did not exist; her voice reedy as if it were breaking, perhaps because of having read too many stories for her grandmother. And everybody kept a distance from her, ready to hate her; but she persisted in fulfilling her role in defiance of their hostility. They would drop their chatter about her but then go back to it again: the day of her first outing, her birth, her marriage, when she went into the church and sat like a proud young child on her bench. Riffle on the surface of the water, chalk mask, sea fire, cloistered dead woman: the tale rattled from one image to the next over the years. No one could see where or why this person was changing like this. And now she was springing—unfathomable, relentless, and numerous from the flood of words of this sly old fox, and she flew off, immaterial.

In fact (did he say this?) they could not understand why she had not married the lord of the low house. Stories. Stories of olden days. When she used to go all over the countryside, according to the old folks' tales, on foot but wearing a riding habit, crop in hand and thrashing away at the trees on either side of the road. And she would appear way up against the sky, up there where the trail joining the three plantations seemed to plunge down to the center of the earth, and at the crossroads she would hesitate, not knowing perhaps whether she should run to the low house with its two mahogany trees like guardians of death or if she should continue calmly toward the fortified house set above the huts like the peak of a hill. And when she appeared this way between the sky and the bottomless earth, she may have sensed already that she would never be granted knowledge of the kitchen where that Louise was now in charge, the traitor!

(And that her lot was to love all her life the very thing she ought to flee forevermore; and she would whip the trees, she would maul the hedges, and suddenly come to a halt before a slave convoy, clenching her fists, biting her lips, alone and fallible and erect, without a sound, in all the delirium of trees and birds.)

As if a force connected to the trees and sky suddenly loosed its fury on her. And she stood there motionless for a long time, a statue rent by the pounding of an indifferent sun. But her hatred as well as her love turned in only one direction: toward the same blue-eyed lord. Everyone knew she did not want to see him, that she could not; that every time chance or some obligation of existence set them face to face she almost vanished because she was so silent and stubborn—even when she had married the humpback with neither pomp nor pleasure and no one could help but notice "the arrival six months later of a dead child," whose hair (or at least a lock of it) had been burned by an old Negro woman on the threshold of the house.

All of this was what the slaves knew. Even *we* knew it. They pieced the story together bit by bit, almost without meaning to, like it was their job. Because not one of them would miss a chance to go against her, she was so changed, so distant, and so amazingly married to the humpback. As if a woman could not raise her child alone, the fruit of her flesh and the soul of her soul!

Rain no longer pattered on the shed's straw roof; the old man was breathing hard, lost in the sequence of his dream: he was reconstituting this strange, unreal story for himself even more than for the newcomers. The man was in pain (his back stiff and tight between the fiery fissures), hearing none of the long homily, or almost none, while the two terrified women suddenly threw themselves flat on the ground, their bodies lax.

(And she had made her rounds up in the peaks far above the bamboo and the wind swaying in the silvery ferns the day the humpback had said to her: "Marie-Nathalie, it is the will of fate, I love you!" She had laughed, it was the second time they had met each other; and she had caressed the oh so fragile flower of a hibiscus with the tip of her riding crop: content, flattered, distant.)

Then she had met La Roche. *We* knew this. It was no use her going by as if we were less real than the horse she was not riding, we knew perfectly well that she had met La Roche. A madman, half nigger in his head, despite his blue eyes. He made up insane stories. A hothead who used to burn himself with the excuse that he had an unhappy childhood. He found ways to amuse the girl. Maybe because their two madnesses melted together in the sun. *We* knew it. They looked at us all without seeing us, but we knew what was going on: how she would go to meet him first thing in the morning, leaving the house where her old grandmother did nothing but pray endlessly, hoping to tame her god so he would lay his hand on her granddaughter's head; and how she would run across the low part of the fields completely unconcerned about the slaves spying on her, without lifting their heads, their eyes at ground level following her as she ran; how, sometimes, she would have La Roche's coachman take her, she used to tap on the back of his neck and he would sit there very stiffly with a weak smile, without moving, so that we made fun of him when he drove like that, frozen in place with the girl behind him (but of course he was the only one who could tell we were making fun of him because we were just as stiff and motionless as he); and how the man and girl fell on the sand, no, in the sand: both of them drunk with the same salty taste; and how she would come back, pure, delicate, innocent with all the innocence of dusk; she was not yet sixteen; and how, ... and how, ... and how ... Because it did them no good not to see us, we knew every least breeze blowing over their heads, and the tiniest twitch of their hands and even yes even the circle around their eyes and the minute, imperceptible wrinkle of despair already throbbing against their lips that they did not feel; as if foretelling that one day she would actually no longer be able to bear meeting La Roche; and we were invisible as we watched every day to see the marks of mighty time on their faces, the progress of their pain: without these two who never saw us ever feeling the pain: without their ever suspecting that we, yes, we were watching that pain intensify on the face of the beloved. ...

But the old man had been silent for a long time. He watched, bemused, as one of the women moved closer to the man and curled up next to him; the man never stirred, apparently accepting that the woman gave herself to him. Motionless.

And they stayed there motionless until it was night, this woman snuggled up against the bulk of the man, she who had endured the voyage beside him without his even once having become aware of the moaning flesh next to him, without his even once having looked at the triangular head on the thin neck, the bony sway of her back, the straight hair stiff with dirt, vermin, and salt water; she had tried so long to get the man to look at her so she could lean on him, but whenever he would look her way all she saw were two empty eyes that would light up with hatred when the man looked over her body—passing over as if she were already dead—and caught sight of the *other*; and now she thought about the woman beside her in steerage, yes, she wondered vaguely where they might have taken her. She did not know that this neighbor had gone with the *other* into the pen on the Acajou plantation, that she had seen the *other* watching between the wooden slats and just holding his hands out to the young woman who came into the pen with her knife; and that the neighbor had heard the *other* run out while that young woman studied the five prisoners, hesitated, then turned away with a sigh (because: *setting them free wasn't really worth it because they would not have known what to do in any case, what road to take to get away;* or: *only one of the newcomers deserved the freedom he asked for so urgently;* or even: *he would be back soon to free the others*). She, the woman, destined from this moment on for the man next to whom she was seeking a bit of warmth, was now accepted by the man—not looking at her but already consenting to have this soft, warm presence beside him in the dampness of the shed.

Until night came. The two women were paralyzed. This one was trying to remember, whereas the other was not even a presence but a formless, incomplete throbbing that would never come alive again (unlike her neighbor on the boat the woman thought vaguely, unlike that companion whose moans had accompanied her own so well—in the same incantatory rhythm—as ritual as a chant and at the same time pointlessly female); and the old man silent now as the day declined, who had poured out all he knew—and his knowledge came down to the unreal story of a white woman, actually the mistress of the place, and the truth about her was something no words could ever discover: as if the entire existence of this country were so filled with this lady, pale as manioc before it goes in the oven, that this weedy old man had become entangled in the inextricable forest of words that he was unable to escape.

Motionless. As were all the other slaves whom the man would soon realize were mostly old men who worked on minor building projects or attended to repairing the outbuildings (pens, sheds, huts, stables), and especially women and children who worked in the fields, with the exception of a few women however, of whom all the others were jealous, who served in the big house and were self-important and squeamish when they came across their less-favored fellow slaves or when they had to speak to them. There were almost no adult men in the huts. The result was an air of frivolous freedom because the women were used to living among themselves with their only constraint the awful, mechanical work and their only annoyance (in this realm) the requirement that they take turns satisfying (one day one, the next day the other) the two supervisors and four overseers of the plantation. When the masters wanted to increase their stock they would rent male slaves from nearby plantations; this did not happen very often but when it did it frequently set off obscure conflicts that never saw the light of day, because the supervisors and overseers sometimes proved to be jealous of the Negresses they had under their thumbs to the point of making them pay in the fields (in harassment or lashings) for these forced infidelities that made them pregnant. The masters would rent males in this manner both for the hardest field work and as studs for their women, and it was known that the mistress herself decided who would couple with whom and perhaps took some extra perverse pleasure in disrupting the clandestine amorous arrangements of her managers and overseers. And right away the man sensed that his arrival on the plantation was something out of the ordinary and that it would be bound to disturb the usual order there; a white man (a supervisor) came to examine him and muttered as he assigned him a place along with the woman still clinging to him (coupling them and thus running a big risk by deciding on an arrangement that only the masters were in a position to decide). These two, he explained to the old man, would sleep in his hut for the night and the next day he would have to show them how to build their own. Then he took the second woman—so passive she seemed unconscious—away.

But the next day it was just barely dawn when they were shaken from the dust on the ground in which they had slept (where they had dropped senseless from exhaustion) by a woman who came into the old man's hut and shoved them outside where the mistress and the same supervisor were waiting for them. The man then saw the women who were all stirred up and surrounding the hut;

they formed a large obstreperous semicircle in the middle of which stood the impassive mistress, scornfully eyeing the uneasy supervisor. That was when the man remembered back to the story told by the old man; he looked at the mistress. Her wide headdress, a hat made of muslin that was turning yellow fascinated him; he thought he could see the sun (if the sun were there) through the headdress. He was transfixed by the sight of this human being imprisoned in such a mass of cloth: the beribboned neck, the breast pressing against the old satin ruching, the full skirt, laced boots, even the crop looped around her wrist. But he was all astonishment and detachment, of course, not knowing what satin was, or a headdress or muslin; and never having seen a boot be laced. He heard words ringing in his head—*marinatali, marinatali*—without really having any idea what they meant; he was alarmed by these words sounding inside him like clear thunder, and all the while he felt the burning lacerations in his back.

"Monsieur de Senglis should have had me informed," said the woman.

"You can make good use of him," said the manager with a nervous laugh. "He will give you good service."

She stared at him as if she were daydreaming. Then she turned toward the slave and said to the manager, "You will put him in the north crew."

"I was counting on taking him with me, on the woods road," said the manager.

"No, the north crew."

She left; but the minute she turned away she disappeared. Still walking, still visible on the path leading to the upper house, yet already absent; as if her presence depended above all on her eyes, her face, the potential weight of her words. This is how the man learned (said Papa Longoué) on the very first day that the master did not really exist except when he was looking at you. Despite the constant fear, despite the leaden hand that always seemed to hold you down in the muck, the master lost his powers when he had turned his back on you, as if he could only rule by establishing a flow that dried up as soon as he turned away. That was how it was with the woman. He saw her walking up to the upper house, and he forgot for a moment, in his head now empty of thunder, the pen they had been crammed into and the slave house, the putting to sea, the journey, the whip; he almost wondered what he was doing there, in that place. He forgot his fight with the other.

Motionless. Ever since the first morning hour when the sun was not yet showing behind the horizon, when the mistress had given them the once-over, until it was completely dark, the moment when, before beginning to build the hut, the man and the woman had packed down the earth at the agreed-upon site; and then the old man held a torch of resinous branches up so they could see, not out of solidarity but just to be with them where he could grumble and complain about someone as much as he wanted, because you would think that ever since he stopped working in the fields this old man never slept. They had almost finished the job when they heard a galloping horse and then saw the creature suddenly loom in the night; Senglis, spurring his mount on, made it rear up right there beside them. He looked at them for a moment then dashed off on the path to the upper house. Yes, all of them motionless in the stagnating hours, walled inside white, motionless death: the women who had risen long before it was time this first morning, who had certainly guessed that the mistress would come to look at the new man, who consequently had gathered around the hut, invisible and silent until the mistress appeared (she had caught sight of the group arriving the night before and at the crack of dawn had betaken herself to the managers' quarters to demand explanations and lose her temper and shout at the employee—doing all this without raising her voice, in that stubborn, haughty way she had), and somehow brought all the women together around her; they sprang from the half-light lingering beneath the branches, scraps of night that her mere presence as Mistress snatched from the darkness in the same way that this sun that was not yet lit was already making a whole world of light and brilliance bloom beneath the trees. The women were split between hostility on the one hand—because of the fact that the new arrival constituted a threat, the possibility that they would find themselves robbed of some measly privilege; because his potential power to disrupt the order of their shared existence, either by rebelling and setting off collective catastrophes, or on the contrary, by adapting too well and consequently usurping the place of the ones who were on top of the heap—and attraction on the other hand, the excitement aroused by the eruption of this male into their entirely female universe. They were stirred up and, without really being aware of it, already fearful that they might have to obey the man in some vague manner; these women had, however, under the tacit direction of their mistress, learned to bear their harsh existence and trailed along behind them not only the few men living permanently in the huts but also the white managers and overseers (despite the harassment these men subjected them to, which the women were resigned to accepting as some unconscious homage paid their power) and even the humpbacked master who everyone knew was subject to the cold grip of Madame de Senglis and therefore not exempt from the feminine law ruling the plantation. Decked out in their peculiar old clothes, bags, strips of cloth, indescribable fabrics, whose outrageous medley of colors made them seem one solid mass of nakedness, they were, therefore, the real ones in charge of the few men living in the huts, who were thus doubly diminished, enslaved and nonexistent, lacking the human qualities ordained by social custom but also stripped of the rudimentary power that distinguishes male from female among animals: no longer fulfilling their animal function of impregnating and freely reproducing, they had become accustomed to walking behind the domineering women; and the children too were disrespectful, paying no attention to the men but only to the group of women (not to one woman who might be their mother, but to them all as a unit, the all-powerful procreators); they were a band of ghosts frantic with hunger, pale beneath their black skins because of eating dirt and green fruit and spoiled fruit and all the leftover bits of animal and vegetable existence; children old beyond their years who already knew that they had to submit to the twofold power, one official and the other obscure, that would keep them under the yoke as long as they lived. Motionless. Ever since earliest morning, soaked in all the heat palpably rising from the night like thick perspiration, until it was night again trembling in its own fury: one single death between two gaping holes with this sun in the meantime beating its merciful burden of forgetting, of trepidation, of annihilation straight down on their heads.

Yes, until the moment when the man had been able to sit in turn in front of his hut: his body was buckled over in pain and the warm night rolled over it crying out that there was nothing to go back to, not the square of beaten earth where he had dared stand up against the other, not the forest where he had been tracked and had found refuge, not the stealthy approach, the haggling or the betrayal that was added to betrayal in an endless chain, not the stone cell in the slave house, not the cobbled slope, not the small boat beaten by the waves, the ship. The ship. Long after that endlessness, however, night was carrying him off beyond the storm to the country back there, but he was well aware that the woman was lying there in the hut, perhaps moaning, in that strange posture from which it was so hard to extricate one's body after the months spent between the decks; and it was as if they were still on a journey, as if this hut were only a strange extension of the same ship of death; it was as if they would never reach the destination (despite the new landscape, the close-cropped fields lapping into the hills, the astonishing dryness and the salt wind, the tortured red earth that seemed never to have known how to be wise or restful or moldy and sweet; despite the rhythm of chains and the frenetic tempo of harvests that he already could discern; despite the noise, the uproar, all the ravings of the masters carried by this old man's voice; despite a tiny river sometimes bursting through, just a trickle of water but resounding like a thousand seas and creating from a simple waterfall a tremendous torrent); as if the voyage had no intention of ever ending and he would have to hear the moans of this woman beside him for all eternity and see in the shadow of the *other*'s eyes something like the head of a snake protruding between two roots.

And, groping through the shadows, he drew a snake in the burning dust. A stiff and awkward snake that he trampled on over and over. Dawn of the second day was already swelling in the land.

3

The *quimboiseur* now wanted to make Mathieu happy. He wanted to reassure the young man and mend things between them. He stood up and went over to the cabin, stopping at almost every step to look out toward the plain. Mathieu had his arms around his knees; an upward-bound wisp of black smoke hovered around him. The sun scorched the earth.

Longoué went into the cabin and instantly reappeared as if he had vanished into thin air and then a second later materialized again in front of the shadow cavity that was the door. Mathieu, at least, giddy from the sun and the light flashing on the red earth (maybe he was also fascinated by the dark smoke rising from the fire to roll itself around him), hadn't realized how much time the old man spent inside out of sight. He only saw the little barrel: Longoué was carrying it at arm's length with his eyes shut against the terrific light.

"You carry it like it's the host!" exclaimed Mathieu.

Solemnly, the old man came back. Without looking at him he put the barrel down beside Mathieu. And Mathieu said, "That old dog! He watches those people come, weak as can be, possibly bleeding; in any case Béluse, at least, is sick, dragging himself around, almost dead. And what does he talk about according to you? It's just not possible, you made it up this very instant. That he talks about this girl with her riding crop!"

Papa Longoué was not looking either at Mathieu or at the little barrel. And Mathieu said, "As if there were something magic about the whole thing! Because you can tell me. They get off the boat, they meet up with these two planters and just guess where that pair is from—from a château in their France, they are two rich men out to get richer, or else they are heartless and unnatural like brigands, they are brigands, murderers, damned men, running away from their mother; and the other men, those other two who have some history back there that you don't want to tell me, packed off on the *Rose-Marie*, the two who end up making a beeline for the two others, going straight to these planters with their long-standing rivalry, with the result that the old man tells him (him, Béluse) right off the bat who knows what about the girl and the hills and the riding crop she uses all over the place. Because in the end, you can go on and on to me about why the girl, the woman really, comes like this to give them a once-over, and you say: why does she, white as manioc, come to check on the newcomer like some animal you expect something from? . . . And in fact, he is an animal. But so early in the morning, with the women all around and you would almost think she drew her force from the women there in a semicircle. All of them all wound up according to you."

"On the assumption you only wanted the logical sequence, events one after the other," said Papa Longoué.

"Yes, like those two landscapes, you say. One of them stretching to infinity, already lost in memory perhaps, so big, so flat, the plains of the past crossed over and over again endlessly, well, let's call it the lost land. And if the other one, the landscape here is drawn up into tight loops and bends and is so tiny, so quickly exhausted, it is because this is where the work and misery are. Not work, but the job one has to do from morning to night. Not work, the harness. Even today the ones who survive do their jobs, the ones who know and the ones who forget just do their jobs; not work. And consequently the land in their minds is small and finite, like the fields around Pointe des Sables. And motionless, you say? Even the wind you can't feel is not motionless!"

And without raising their heads they felt the wind way up above them plowing the field of the sky, and with its labor clearing something in them as well, the wilderness of memory where they were lost. But abruptly the wind died; the clouds seemed to freeze in the brilliant sunlight: liquid marble suddenly hard. Three o'clock. The plain crackled, you could hear its popping and snapping as its cloak of rising wind came off. A moon, the moon, emerged on the other side of the sun, just as round, just as white, separated from the sun by the clouds' flat plateau.

"They did not imitate," said Papa Longoué. "It was something they brought with them over the ocean."

He lifted the lid of the little barrel and spread out on the ground some leaves and yellow speckled flowers, the veins of leaves and some branches he began to peel between his fingers: he was leafing through pages. He did this carefully but also with an air of detachment (clearly rebuking the young man for the indifference he displayed toward the barrel and its contents; Mathieu of course looked at the leaves between the *quimboiseur's* fingers, maybe he even heard the crackling and maybe he even felt the dust on his own fingertips, but his eyes remained empty). Patiently, instinctively Papa Longoué went back to each leaf again to know it better or to crumble it better.

They did not imitate because in July 1788 this was the gesture the ancestor made, already, on the same spot—the outcropping between the acacias that, a good deal later, was to shelter the cabin made of crate wood. He had crushed between his fingers the leaves he had spent the day looking for, he looked off toward the low, flat house where the mahogany trees stood like guardians of death. And though this was the place where he stopped, it was not because he could foresee that some day I would put bananas to cook on a fire in the same spot and that you would come there (here) to ask me what and why, but because he already wanted to go back that same night to Acajou, and I'll tell you why, because he wanted to begin the story that is for me the story and kidnap the girl so she could know the taste of the earth and have her back marked by acacia branches, because he would lay her down there on the ground and she wouldn't even struggle. That would have been the first day, or the second if you like, and not—how could it have been?—already some morning in July 1788, because who knew about July? And who knew about 1788? For him and for me this was the first day the first shout from the sun and the first moon and this country's first century. Because all there was now was this tiny land surrounded by infinite sea and because this was where he had to stay. And strange thing, remembering the lashes on his back from the whip, if you can call it that because they still hurt and did not have to be remembered, he dreamed that the acacia tree and the thorns of the acacia would bring him revenge and satisfaction, he already saw the girl lying down in the darkness without even a struggle; he who was not yet Longoué but who had inspected (there is no other word for it) the country that day, going over the forest with a fine-tooth comb, into the deepest and fiercest corners, searching, searching and finding the *leaf of life and death* that he was now carefully exploring with his fingers and cleaning.

"Like this sun and moon over your head both at once," Longoué said. "It looks like just one fire, one brightness, you don't know which one lights the other. Whether it is magic that makes you understand the past or if it is memory and logical consequence that shine above the cloud before you."

"The first day for him, you say. And I can understand why we follow him first—yes, he is the Longoué of all Longoués; I can understand why we always have to go back to him," he mumbled into the woods. "Because he is your great-grandfather and he fled to this precise spot where you now are, I can understand that Béluse is not strong enough, we constantly leave him behind, he does not force us to stay with him, I even see that he gives us no words, words are clumsy when we try to touch on what he was doing; and for Longoué, you say, for Longoué there is the waiting, I do not know what he will be up to this second night, I hope—whereas for Béluse it is all decided: he is on the Senglis estate, he has been given a woman as his mate, he goes into the house, the mistress looks at him often, days go by, Béluse moves in, things go well, yes, I understand. But if the maroon is waiting for us, then why then and there on the first day, why—and don't try to distract me with your barrel full of leaves—why all that blather about that Cydalise woman, Marie-Nathalie—even if she loves La Roche but marries Senglis (so it seems), what difference does that make to us? They did not imitate, you say."

"Fine," said Papa Longoué. "Are you afraid of them? Of La Roche and Senglis and the girl, I mean? There they are; they are in charge. Do you really think an old wreck like me doesn't know how or why they talk? We can, we can. All this time they were talking over our heads we put out the nets we made to catch their voices and they never knew. They did not know we too were capable of saying *they are like this they are like that.* You are wrong not to want to look at my barrel; so then come back with me, youngster, you will see the sand pouring onto their heads. . . ."

They both forgot that enormous distance lying between them and the events, that ocean through which they dove to reach the bottom (not even thinking that things could have happened differently, that it would have been possible for there to have been other nuances in the words and deeds of yesteryear), they forgot the plain down below and today's burdensome job, as if these characters they brought back to life were more solid and more real. They were unaware of the path they had taken to get there or of racing furiously and heedlessly through what they were saying, no longer worried about offending each other; unaware that they were speaking "out loud" in the crackling heat; unaware that the *magic* and the *logical consequence* no longer were anything more than a pretext they used; that there were other truths to sweep them (two conjurers of the past) into their round. They did not suspect that this wind that fell so abruptly at three o'clock that it looked like the clouds up above had frozen in place was only imitating the past that suddenly descended upon them. That, without beating around the bush, this wind from the past would now sweep them away. (That Mathieu would emerge from it more threatened and shakier than ever; from that day to this devoted to conquering the present, the other face of this wind. That in it Papa Longoué would exhaust his last powers as a *quimboiseur!*) They forgot. Because they were already carried away by the gallop of a horse with Senglis astride.

Senglis: one hundred and fifty-seven years before, he rode his horse in the darkness between the house framed by mahogany trees and his own property set like a pinnacle above the huts and was no more able to imagine that all around him and

*far into the most distant future an unknown, underground world was develop-
ing, one that was still hesitant but that in the end, after the mute absence and clandestine blood, would suddenly emerge between the blades of earth and rise above
the night of shivering; a world sweat out of charred earth that would carry off into
the clouds the slow meanderings of an old seer and a young boy who listened
too well: where, in the clear sky and endless heat, it would become the sum of all
that had been suffered, the sprinkling of herbs onto the burned clay, the sketch of
the coast as it was gradually discovered, the taking root in the lump of black earth
and the dream made possible after the maroons' existence and after the struggle.*
And Senglis, stopping beside them and looking at the old man who
held high his torch made from a resinous branch, the woman busy
working (braiding vines into rope) who did not dare raise her eyes
from her task, the robust fellow who was sticking a post into the
tamped-down earth (arm raised high brandishing the stake, act
and object suspended in the bright light), did not really see these
animals who belonged to him, who were the undergrowth in his
forest; they only existed for him as things he would argue with his
supervisors or his wife about. Solitary, slashing through the night
on his horse, Senglis advanced through his own particular world,
free of all doubt or nuance, his only worry being what he would tell
Her-Ladyship-His-Wife—that was the title he gave her, probably
meant to convey that he had never stopped thinking of her as a
loose woman. He was in a hurry to impress her with all the details
of what had happened over the past two days, from the fight on the
Rose-Marie to the whipping, watching her for signs of excitement
or fear, or—far more likely—vexation. With this purpose in mind,
the allure of this pleasure, he had leapt onto his horse, as if drunk
with the sight of the girl crawling in the dust before the stunned La
Roche, then his intended pleasure hurled him onto the road like a
lunatic wind, where he drove the animal with every bit of passion
he could muster, finally flinging him there in the bedroom, suddenly rid of his usual fears.

"Louise," "the Negress," those were the only two words he could
think of. He may even have shouted them as he tore into the room
like a tornado without noticing how Madame de Senglis, strangely

calm and haughty, raised her eyebrows. He instantly began spewing a stream of incomprehensible words while she, supreme and in control of herself, sat there putting down the ladylike handiwork in which she was pretending to be involved (though really she had been waiting for him, peering into the seething darkness for hours on end, thinking up words to throw in his face). She nonchalantly leaned on her elbows with the patient demeanor of people who have learned to put up with a child's foolishness, and he went on: "You really should have seen, my dear. You should have seen it! A real fight if you can imagine it! And since La Roche chose one of them the least I could do was take the other, I know that's not how we usually do things, but anyhow. . . . Then when we got off that damned skiff, the priest who blessed them, you know our dear priest—probably on his way in a great hurry to some spicy rendezvous, this was absolutely the funniest thing, it really looked like he made the same gesture the Negro did. He moved his arm the same way, the only difference was the index finger, I could see perfectly well that he was just trying to get done with his chore. . . . But the others, the other two that is, the Negroes, it was amazing how for the first time, I was watching their stupid sign language, it seemed as if they saw the priest as some sort of colleague, they looked at the hand he held up to baptize them one after the other and La Roche's Negro, apparently seeing him as an adversary, begins making his own gesture, the snake you know, every time our dear Abbé Lestigne raises his right hand, so there they are both of them involved in this game—aping each other and the priest who meant to have the last word, Lordgod but he was funny with his sword all cranksided and the other one too constantly waving his arm . . ."

"But you should have informed me," said Madame de Senglis calmly.

"But let me explain. . . . You had to see it. It was that Louise, there's absolutely no doubt about it, the entire evening she was obviously smiling at him, it was Louise wasn't it, and she was sitting on his lap and he . . ."

But Madame de Senglis stood up and went to the window where

she listened to the night singing through great quivering sheets of heat.

"What Louise?" she said.

"You know perfectly well" (quivering himself because he knew she knew). "That Negress is in the habit of running things in his house, you know perfectly well . . ."

"Really," she said.

She turned toward him casually with a winning smile, then, suddenly leaning out the window, she began to sing along with the frogs (*tut tu tou tu*) in the vetiver pond.

"Marie-Nathalie, listen to me."

"But I am listening to you, my friend. Speak, speak."

Conscious of having already won this contest, she turned her innocent face to the light provided by the two candles. He became flustered, "Because I assure you that this fight took place on the deck of the *Rose-Marie*, La Roche made fun of my pistol. . . ." But he was instantly caught up again, carried away by a kind of intoxication and, feeling at ease, soon fell back into the bottomless pit of his own words. "Yes, now it's my turn to laugh. He claimed he had gotten the stronger man, which by the way is not at all certain considering that the second time they wanted to fight it was definitely started at the crossroads by ours jumping on the other. It's my opinion that they would put on a fine show if they were set against each other in an arena; in any case I saw ours just now building his hut and as for his, ah! it was not even six in the morning when suddenly there was a lot of noise behind the pen and a huge commotion as people came to tell us, no, it was maybe only five o'clock but we had to wait, you know how insane La Roche is, we had to wait while they went to get that little barrel that he would not leave behind as long as the hunt was on, and there we were beating the bush with the dogs and I saw right away that the trail would take us to the Morne aux Acacias and it was easy for La Roche to get us all stirred up, that fellow Duchêne was laughing up his sleeve I thought, possibly happy that something so terrible happened to our friend, and Lapointe with his scowling face, always after that boat he dreams of commanding some day, yes now it's my turn to laugh, we were there in front of the Morne aux Acacias, where were the superior smiles I'd like to know, and I, even though we had had to leave the horses, but I, nothing on earth could have made me because I wanted . . ." (And suddenly Madame de Senglis interrupted: "But we had agreed not to buy any adult Negroes; it is part of how we decided to save money.") Like a madman he went on, "Yes I wanted to and it was perfectly clear which one was the cripple and what crippled him was the barrel the barrel it doesn't matter we finally came back and I meant to know no I knew no I felt at first that this Louise please tell me . . ." ("What Louise," she said.) ". . . is that any name for, a Christian name in short, I saw instantly that she was, and I pretended to sleep on my bench that was some night some night all that snoring you know I wouldn't dare to swear it but I certainly think that our good La Roche this is funny was snoring like a sailor anyhow I was watching this creature . . ." (And she laughed because he was naïve enough to think that snoring can make a woman any less attached to a man.) ". . . it's been awhile now since she moved into his house, see it was around the time he began to steer clear of us ah! that creature probably made him drink some herbs in his rum and who knows what you know their filthy habits" ("Not at all," said his wife, "he is a free man.") "she made him eat one of those disgusting things that is one of their secrets it was probably a little before our marriage." ("No, after.") "You are wrong it was before our unfortunate marriage this is how it all had to end you don't take a slave and set her up in your house like a wife they get used to it and after that it's the herbs and potions those horrors they produce behind their cabins that woman was definitely cut out for that remember La Roche certainly harped on it enough my theory my producing stock my breeding calendar and when she was born he did not know whether or to what extent their taint their savagery had filtered into this creature's veins." ("Be that as it may we've done just exactly the same thing haven't we, so that we don't buy adult Negroes any more, it's simple arithmetic they only cost the stud fee or just getting our women pregnant and then watching them grow because as soon as they are four years old we can find work for them but here you've had to go and compete with Monsieur de La Roche and just like that allot who knows how much money for this African because Monsieur de La Roche is crazy about buying one every time there is a delivery.") "This creature and listen nobody knows who created her he dared call her Louise, Louise from the time she was a baby anybody could see the poison rising through her body at the moment when the children but these animals don't have children she was only interested in the herbs that have to be burned after weeding the crops of course our friend was her first alas and luckily her only victim how can I explain it way before his ridiculous obsession with moving this girl in." ("He is a free man I tell you no herb can force him.") "He is not free he was hesitant about killing her death is the only sentence for this crime however I admit he has found a pretty nice solution I have to tell you about the apparatus a sort of cross he invented with two squared-off tree trunks arranged on a diagonal leaning forward so that the head hangs down toward the ground and the effort required to keep it up so the blood won't run to the brain it's incredible pulls the legs tight in the straps yes of course we are familiar with other machines but I must admit that La Roche has found himself an extremely elegant manner of making the blood work whether it is in the feet where the ropes dig into the skin or in the head, he muttered so low that I was the only one who heard him: "I will not touch you" don't you see that he has had a magic spell on him and his house ever since the day when out of the blue he refused to recognize his neighbors and found his only pleasure in hanging out with lowly sailors who stay in the country no more than a month, it was seven years ago just before our unfortunate marriage." ("No, after, I tell you.") "Yes." ("No.") That creature was ten years old isn't it frightening to think that at ten she already was able she already knew and for seven or eight years it was a never-ending cliff he tried to climb up without hearing the appeals the warnings anything his friends said, like the Morne aux Acacias the other night if you'd seen him faced with the black wall he shouted "I'm going in there" the men had to hold him back and all this without his having let his barrel full of who knows what horror out of his sight even once, as if their diabolical practices had passed into his body or had put his mind in a whirl and again when the girl was strapped onto that crosslike thing he looked at her for a long moment maybe he saw her finally like a cliff that he had not been able to bring down lower she belonged to him never had he been able to tame her completely." ("But while you were merrymaking I had to go inquire of the supervisors simply to know why those three slaves were there.") Then, some sudden nobility increasing his stature, like an old tunic you notice one day and instinctively put on, he said: "You should not have lowered yourself to demanding explanations from our supervisors, Madame." But then instantly, rid of the tunic and back with the reality of his hump, racing off again blindly into the tunnel: "Really a terrific hunt and a supper fit for kings it was the girl who all the time the chase was on all the while the dogs were being driven into the ground to find the tracks again that had been lost right from the start the girl took care of everything, maybe she intended to celebrate in advance and then to make us celebrate later a failure that she herself had prepared you know our friend and his mind-boggling tendency to adapt to any circumstance he treated us like a prince, far too generous why squander just for the benefit of a few poor sailors really I, . . ." he laughed suddenly, ". . . his madness there's no other motive poison and madness that's it yes the next day, which was yesterday, he had them all lined up in front of the two mahogany trees except for the girl who stayed inside the house, you'd have thought it was a ceremony without any noise without any fuss just only the whip and he didn't want any of his supervisors to be the one to do it, madness I tell you, and repeating his futile question to those brutes, he went from one to the other: which one of you which one which one and at first the whip whirled without touching them but then lashed with great arm-loads into the crowd, the field slaves were maybe content in spite of being whipped because then they wouldn't have to work it's outrageous thinking about it, and the house slaves acting insulted that anyone could suspect them the women from the cabins everybody except the girl (then it was her turn to laugh, taking the crop from its hook near the bed, whipping and thrashing it through the air with long strokes then with a sudden gulp of laughter she stopped and exclaimed, "You can make good use of him, Madame! Really what a witty man that manager is. Make good use of him!"), but as he was punishing the entire troop of them like that here comes that Louise out of the house and right up to him where all calm she kneels down bows down still calm "It's me, It's me," and he who had I swear heard nothing if not the confession never even slowed his pace on the contrary he became raving mad shouting which of you which of you and whipping everywhere without looking while the girl went on it's me it's me the more she said it the more he sliced at the others . . ." And both of them, husband and wife, were now laughing and unable to stop, Marie-Nathalie running from one corner of the room to the other, lashing the damp, heavy air of this unhopeful night and you couldn't tell if the sort of rattle in her throat getting more and more raucous behind her laughter was going to explode into a magnificent burst of hysteria while on all fours in the middle of the floor, spinning like a crazy top toward his wife as she leapt from one patch of shadow to another and his hump almost all the way down his collar now convulsively silently rhythmically shaking like a sob of laughter (both of them husband and wife finally reunited in one single unreal fit of passion, above them the smoky brilliance of the candles), Gustave Anatole Bourbon de Senglis kept on repeating in a relentless and broken voice (his head between his arms, an occasional drool catching on the ill-fitting floorboards, and the flash of the crop descending to graze his crippled back): *cé moin, cé moin, cé moin,* it's me.

Chapter 4

1

THIS MAN WHO WAS NOW without his rootstock, having rolled in the one breaking wave that was the voyage (though retaining enough power and strength to pit himself against the other and in the rottenness of the steerage to impose his strength and power on the troop of skeletons ravaged by vermin and sickness and hunger— but having lost everything even his name beneath the uniform layer of filth with its stench of lousy water) and who was not yet Longoué but already knew every least leaf and every least resource of the new country, and who already knew that he would continue to assert around the forest, at this boundary to known existence, his incomprehensible and ineradicable presence—some unsuspected matter zeroing in on the earth and trees, tearing their forgotten secrets from them but making them tremble with a surplus as well or, better, a fullness of existence set aside in reserve for freer days—he now went back down to the tortured smallness of the Coast in search of the woman warrior in her brilliant clothing, for the last time he went back to the world of submissive animals and too-transparent masters, he took the path run by the dogs on his trail but in the opposite direction. And really, ever since he had flung himself into the curtain of acacias (later waking up with his back aching and that blue boat that sailed between the top of the trees and the sun, then making the mud head stuck onto the terrifying snake, then discovering Pointe des Sables gilded with filth like a pirogue endlessly rolled down to the sea, and sleeping again, waking up famished in the sweet damp of the underbrush, finding *the leaf of life and death* that he had pressed against his body, examining, assessing every nook and cranny of this country that filled him with infinite emptiness because he felt in it an absence of weight, of danger, a sign of an entirely new security but also the mark of some loss of existence, a floating, a truly futile and comfortable unreality—and sometimes he felt his wasted muscles with his hands as if he were astonished to find himself so light and in a world so bright), all he had been doing was waiting for this other moment when he would retrace his steps and plunge into the hole of sunlight where shrunken, inert fields stagnated and where the house with its mahogany trees seemed flattened as well behind its two guardians.

Perhaps amazed to breathe this salt smell that was slightly rotten but also airy and pungent (he had so long inhaled the heavy, stinking air of the steerage), and keeping the image of the Edge-of-this-land inside him as if he were watching it out of the corner of his eye, he followed along the foothills through the acacia woods. He knew exactly where he was going and headed straight to where the forest gave way to Acajou plantation, knowing that he would again encounter there—waiting for him perhaps—the girl with the black knife. To tell the truth however he was not thinking about the Edge-of-this-land or about this person waiting but acting as if instinctively, borne by the new transparency of things, his faculties reduced to just this one vague power he had inside him that forced him to act, to walk, to reach out toward some (he did not know what) animal abundance whose future and already compelling force he only lost sight of when the piercing torment he had to endure in his back made him seethe with rage.

He stopped at the edge of the tall grasses, scanning the layer of mist above the plowed fields and beyond them, ghostly in the thick heat, the house covered in mist, where every now and then a peaceful cry would flash like a splinter of glass. Boldly he skirted the field of grasses and went closer, seemingly protected by the motionless density of the sun and by this silence packed with silence: laminations of foliage weighing down on him and the plain. He saw the plain, scarcely emerged from the undergrowth they had managed to chop away and still bearing (like some beautiful animal bursting out of the water, already dry and gleaming in the sunlight while its belly still streams with droplets that it splashes about with every stride) the stubborn, blackened tatters of the former forest. A plainboat with half its sails off; but dangling from it on the wharf there are still piles of green canvas that will soon vanish, burned or hoed away. He inhaled the stubborn humus of the original verdure now ragged heaps mixed into the crumbly red clumps of earth. Beast cast up from where there was humus, he smelled the ancient odor that was stronger than the hoeing of clay, more real than the opacity of digging, certainly more actual than the drawn out shadows of the mahogany trees he now saw to his right. And it was at the edge of one of those shadows, there where an implacable day and an implacable night seemed fixed in endless confrontation, that he caught sight of the contraption tilting toward the ground as if to prostrate itself before the two great solemn trees or at least before the darkness they were able to cast thus into the sunlight and heat. But you could see that the closest shadow would never reach the apparatus, at most barely skimming it with its wingtip at the spot where the top of the mahogany tree spread no more than a sort of creamy, lacy gray. Then the shadow would quickly move on, no wider at this extremity than the distance between a rooster's comb and his plume: all day long the contraption would remain in full sunlight, its cruelty subtly improved by the shadow's slow movement toward the creature exposed there like that, moaning in vain for it to come until the moment she would see that the shadow had gone by without ever covering her and cast her back into the torrid universe of the afternoon for good.

He was not surprised to see that the woman with the knife was this creature: he was prepared for something of the sort. He merely laughed scornfully, seeing how she slowly tilted her head toward the ground then just as slowly raised it in a strangely rhythmic swinging motion, as if she were attempting thus to compensate for the frantic rush and terrifying blocks her blood went through in the circus of her body. He felt no impatience. Hidden where the grasses ended he watched closely.

So he saw the very thick shadow move around the mahogany tree; it touched the apparatus with the delicate tip of its farthest point (the girl long ago had stopped moving, not even shifting her head in the direction of that bulbous column of darkness that had wheeled to meet her) and finally seemed to go back into the tree while, at the same time, along its edges slowly turning brown, its black substance was eaten away as if it were a long needle that had heated up on the ground and became deformed as it did so. Suddenly, just at the moment it reintegrated with the base of the mahogany tree, the shadow, almost round now, lit up red and shattered—exactly as if it exploded (too ripe) in the persistent heat of the moment before dark.

Everything turned bright and radiant from this subtly streaming glow: the mahogany trees, the low house, the cross, the skirt draping dislocated limbs. Now the man held still, staring at the cross and its load; he felt an intense peace that sharpened his senses to the point where he noticed after the fact that the pitiful shadow thrown by the cross had followed the two massive columns cast by the mahogany trees the way a frail foal might have followed two strong mares around inside a paddock: it too had returned to its place of origin, drawing, at this time of day, a meaningless scribble of brown or reddish lines at the girl's feet in the dust of the center strip.

But the man had carefully prepared his present state of abeyance. All day long he had kept track of what went on in the plantation (the house servants who came to throw a bucket of water, the afternoon workers returning from their labor, the children who ventured to the edge of the mahogany trees; all of them silent, glancing hesitantly at the cross or going by in front of it without making the least sound in the dust with their feet, their heads bent low or their eyes staring, depending on whether or not they were brave enough to look at the apparatus—and once he had seen the man wearing boots standing in front of the veranda; he looked more violent stock-still than any wild gestures could have made him seem, as if he were insulting the machine, the plantation, the mahogany trees, the maroon hidden in the grasses all at the same time—then he went back into the house and did not come out again) and had run along the edge of the thickets to locate the dogs, going right up behind their wooden pen where he spoke to them in a caressing voice until they just sat there, slow-witted and stupid, watching him squat in the dust; then he had drawn signs that he alone knew on the trails they might take to pursue him: crisscrossing branches to block one path, making tracks to lead someone who took another path astray, and at a third intersection he put the invisible knot that draws danger to it. All this time he had heard the people working in the plowed checkerboard of earth on the other side of the grasses. He did not know that a vague sort of oblivion, and perhaps caution, good sense about fate, kept them riveted to their task; nor that an undertaking that was for him so natural and that was turning out to be so easy would have been inconceivable for them, incomprehensible, and worse yet, unattainable.

He was quiet now, keeping his eye always on the cross and what was on it but his head was full of a single idea, which was to find a knife to cut the ropes, because there was no doubt that they had dug into the woman's swollen skin. With this in mind he came up with the extravagant project of entering the big house, and when it was fully formed in his mind he set out to execute it.

He did so through the kitchen where he went right past the little barrel left up against the door; he very nearly tripped over it because it was of course night by now. He went in quietly: sniffing the smells of food for a long time; in front of him rocks blackened around fires stood out clearly in the half-darkness. He found the knife right away but could not keep from going farther into the house, a night visitor still under the protection of night. He moved noiselessly on loose floorboards between huge cupboards. He came upon the man who wore boots who, spurning his bed, had collapsed in the big living room with his clothes on where he now slept almost provocatively. Knife in hand, his mind empty and on fire, he never gave a thought to killing this man whom he had marked with the sign: maybe because, at this point, the only vague feeling he had about him was that such a man was certainly foolish to leave the doors to his house open like that when he ruled over so many slaves (that this foolhardiness, this madness had an element of the innocence that is the root of wisdom or bravery, and that one should not take advantage of it), or perhaps because he already knew that the man was not to die except at the place where the sign had marked him for the first and irreversible time.

He went back outdoors and headed for the cross but made no attempt to keep out of the diffusely lit areas that might have been able to betray him. He went straight to the woman: her pale face, her eyes rolled back, her skirt pulled tight by the two crossed beams, her feet swollen. First he cut the ropes binding her legs by pushing on her flesh with his thumb and sticking the knife between the ropes and the tormented skin without worrying about being careful. The woman moaned and opened her eyes. She recognized him immediately and at first she held still, watching as he finished unshackling her. Then she tried to struggle and scream. But her strength was all used up and her mouth was swollen. She uttered something like a growl of resignation; as if she had no hope of forcing her will upon the intruder and consequently despised her body because it was abandoning her. Then she moaned and tried to spit in the man's face. Her lips puckered to close over a thin, muddy foam that she was unable to control and that dribbled down over the dusty stripes of her chin and neck. The man understood what the woman meant to do, he laughed scornfully, put her roughly back on her feet, and when she tried to brace herself again just scooped her up onto his shoulder and carried her off that way.

It had been a long time since the evening work crew had returned from the fields; the dogs were subdued and did not bark; the path was clear in all directions. He, however, not at all concerned about the tracks he might leave behind, headed toward the Morne aux Acacias that had become his territory, his home. He could tell by the way she twitched almost imperceptibly that the woman had not given up all hope of resistance. Probably she never would. For the time being he made do with holding her in the crook of his arm, not entirely on his shoulder. From time to time he would laugh softly. He was filled with triumph as he gradually figured out how things were changing around him: the soft lumps of silent, plowed earth where he occasionally bumped into half-buried rocks and where a dry wind seemed to blow right through him, then suddenly the dense thickets that came up to his belt, so that the girl's head and her legs were gently whipped by harsh, maybe thorny, branches that he sometimes tried to push aside (but she was no longer moaning), and finally the cooing darkness of the forest at the foot of the acacias where there was no breath of air that threatened. He left this canopy however, and for the third time since his arrival turned off toward the sea. Pointe des Sables was a single brown stretch where a few puddles of stagnant water glistened. The sound of the sea filled it with a violent, sultry, becalmed life. He carried the woman to the first wave and dropped her into the water. Then he rolled her in the dirty foam and lightly rubbed the places where the rope had eaten into her flesh. She was motionless, as if she had fainted, maybe was about to die; but he saw that she was watching him pensively rub her belly through the cloth. She merely watched him, no longer trying to escape or lacking the strength to struggle. But he saw that he had not conquered her.

When they went back, arriving once again at Morne aux Acacias, she leaned against him; not letting herself go like someone being friendly and not with the relaxed manner that confidence and (in this case) gratefulness might justify, she did it somehow at a distance: merely pressing her hand against his hip, unable to keep from holding onto him when she stumbled over the roots. From this hand, the only thing from time to time connecting her to him (the darkness beneath the acacias being so complete), he could guess that she was only putting off a confrontation. She was growing stronger. She was waiting patiently, not admitting that he had freed her from her torture but now convinced that it would be useless to resist after this dreadful day on the machine. There was no way out. She would not go back to the plantation where the mere feat of her escape doomed her in advance. She would be unable to escape and live in the hills as a maroon with this man right behind her, tracking her and no doubt finding her again. She was not afraid of him; she did not know how to be afraid.

Alone among the frightened children of the slave quarters she was unafraid when, before sinking into their animal sleep, the people who worked the fields would find again the restless, angry strength, challenged but triumphant, to tell some of the stories they repeated every evening, as if, dazed with exhaustion, they found there a stimulant against this exhaustion or something to protect them from the day that soon would dawn (and she would go there alone and alone she would later return to the big house). The children who were her age and then the adults discovered her game (like a shadow she would enter the cabin where she heard the most unflagging voices and lie down next to the kids); they were frightened by her courage and her ability to listen to stories of that sort and then slip out of the cabin and go back through the mahogany trees to the house. They had even more trouble with the fact that she might be able to sleep alone on her straw mattress over there in the little junk room that she had been allotted. Slowly they shook their heads, thinking "such a little girl" or considering that it was just because she lived in the big house that she had so much courage. And when they would chase her away violently and forbid her to come again in the dark like that because the reprisals the master was sure to take when he found out about it frightened them even more, she still kept right on coming every night, sticking close to the boards or foliage around the cabin where she huddled all alone in the shadows and tried to figure out from the whispering that reached her there the thread of the story being told.

She certainly was not afraid of this man whom she had set free, this man who had insanely come back to find her. She would wait for tomorrow. Always the next day existed, thriving inside her with the unbeatable hope that she was right to have waited and that one day the next day would finally be what she was vaguely expecting. She was not afraid of the power of the man. So much sea had washed over him that she firmly believed she could escape this power. And besides, had she not been born in this new country?

Perhaps the man felt all of this merely through touching her hand. In any case he knew that she was not backing off, that she was getting ready to fight him. Which explained perhaps his quick, scornful laughs, that silent laughter, the times he would occasionally come to a sudden standstill. The topmost foliage was growing paler when they arrived at the spot where the maroon had slept the night before: the place where he had stopped not because he had chosen this place to be the future refuge of his descendants but because the way his skin had shivered when this very young woman had freed him from his bonds was still there inside him.

They collapsed among the roots; almost immediately the woman went into a fit of delirium. She caught on fire with no warning signs. It was a devastating attack, the sort one emerges from as quickly as one has been struck down or from which one dies. Right in front of him she went out of her mind, moaning and sometimes shouting. Motionless, without trying to help her, he watched over her until daybreak. Finally she lay flat on her face in sleep interrupted by convulsive movements.

But she woke up completely normal, almost warm in the filtered sunlight that spread a liquid profusion of light around her in a halo; he stared at her fixedly and spoke to her in a soft voice. She did not understand a single word he said. But still she listened to him, surprised at how interested she was in the impenetrable words. Perhaps he was telling her that she had grasped the power of the sign and therefore must know who he was or at least what he represented in the order of things and the place he held in the chain of life. Perhaps he was telling her why he had had the insane idea of going back to get her; whether he did it because he wanted a woman who would go with him into the woods (because perhaps he had learned at the market, while the sale was going on, that it was possible to escape and live as a maroon in the hills as long as you were not afraid of losing an arm or a leg) or if it was out of pure defiance toward the masters who had transplanted him to this spot. Did he want to force this fate in the mountains upon her, or did he dare? Did he think he was as powerful as that god the masters had, the one they feared so much but treated so casually? Did he not see, had he not had time to see that this god was the only ruler of the new land and that it was necessary perhaps not to submit but at least to adopt all the proper submissive behaviors? She was listening to him, solemnly, silently, but anger, grave and dark, slowly readied itself inside her; it was in a very calm voice that she began to reply, although of course he in turn did not understand a single word she said.

"Look at yourself! Just look at yourself! You are so thin that it seems like the wind from Pointe des Sables could turn you into a grain of sand in the sand. You are so dirty that the acacias pull their leaves back so they won't smell your smell. And you want me, Louise, the only relative of Monsieur de la Roche (because I know I am his only relative), to stay with you in the woods to smell your vermin all my livelong days! Listen, it's clear enough that you stole this knife from my kitchen. I have to admit you had the nerve to go into my kitchen. But I'll get it back, you hear, and I'll stick it right in your throat while you are asleep—like a pig, damned animal! You hear..."

Motionless beneath this branch falling in front of his face like a curtain or like a canopy, he started to speak again. It seemed he would never wear out. His voice bounced off the tree trunks and branches and returned to fill up the leafy cave surrounding the outcrop of land. That is what the woman noticed. Bit by bit she changed angers, literally. Her too many vague hopes finally spilled over. She gestured wildly toward the trees all around them. Unwittingly (and perhaps hours and hours had washed over them while he was talking) she became filled with a new emotion that set her free. In any case the sun's flickering red already lit the wooded cave when she passionately replied. The words they rattled off in this new land, musical or harsh, were obscure to him; he connected them with the heedless calm of this forest. Finally he became aware and amazed that she did not understand his language; he never imagined she might not know it. Had she not set him free in obedience to a single gesture? She, however, was carried away.

"Listen. Don't you see what they do when they catch you again! First they put you in the sun for days. I know what that's like, the sun took its time going across my head just once, that was enough.

Next thing is they cut off an arm or a leg. The best part is you don't die. You can't imagine the things they invent to keep you from dying! The sign, what sign? What are you going to do when I have to lean on you and the two of us will share two legs that can't walk at the same pace? Listen" — she stopped, the solemn shadow of night lengthened her, made her larger — "there is the sea! The sea is there!"

In vain she instructed him about her grand project. *Why always flee to the interior? When we stood tiptoe at the tip of Pointe des Sables we could sometimes see land on the horizon. People say it's the same land as this; the earth goes under the sea and comes back up over there, then it goes back under again and comes back up farther away, on and on like that.* The young woman swore to it. She had heard the names of the other lands; she was sure you could get there. Why forget the sea? They just had to steal a skiff and if they didn't dare do that (not wanting to alert people again or not wanting to be chased all over the place because of a stolen skiff) they could make one in the woods. If he didn't know how she would show him. The sea is beautiful, warm, so gentle. And then where it ends there was a land like this one, bigger and surrounded by sea; the maroons over there were getting together, they had chiefs, they were organized. The gentlemen often talked about Saint-Domingue. They had to get there! Have confidence in the sea!

Deep there in the woods, the woman who had forgotten the cross and who had eaten nothing all day peacefully began raving on again: she drifted, she laughed at the pitfalls, quelled gusts of wind, chased away the morning mosquitoes, poured sea water on their bodies to protect them from the sun, discovered too late that this made them burn even worse, sailed from one coast to the next, covering all the lands, went through lightning, rolled outward with the waves, opened each coast to the neighboring coast, each land to its sisterland, finally discovered the supreme exile where maroons were organized and made their own law!

The man never interrupted the woman's long delirious speech. When it was the dead of night he stood up and held some roots out for her to eat. In a daze she understood that all her talk was in vain, but she was too famished to turn down his offering, which she snatched from his hands and wolfed down without looking to see what he brought her. She was infuriated by her own anger and her comical hope. Rage made her weaker.

In the morning she made a sudden leap for the slope. But the man was not asleep and he raced down behind her and quickly cut her off. Still running she climbed the hill again. The man followed her. All morning long he pursued her into the hills. Finally she let him catch up with her and collapsed without a word. She tried to run away like this three times. Three times he caught her. Between times they did not say anything to each other. The man gave her things to eat; although she was more acquainted than he with what the woods had to offer, she made no effort to find food. She devoured what he offered her like an animal. On the fourth day when he had once again forced her back to the top of the ridge he walked toward her and, concentrating on the words, he said to her: "*Lan mè, la tè, zéclè.*" Astounded, she looked at him. He had understood those words. Lightning, the earth, the sea. Suddenly those words that she herself had said seemed foreign and clumsy in the man's mouth. That was how they began to communicate with each other. He covered her with his body, noticing for the first time how young she was. He had always thought of her as he would have thought of a woman, but she was so young. Strangely she told him, without his understanding: "I know my mother. He does not know it, but I know her."

And when their son was born three years later she had forgotten these ravings of the first night. She had forgotten the sea. They owned the forest. All the maroons, men and women, furtive and confident at the same time, used to come "to consult." The man was their center, their refuge. They would talk (though in the most roundabout way) of going back down to the plains. But he would shake his head impassively. He explained that the hills were the only place they would be able to hold out. He, however, was drawn by the Edge-of-this-land, and he used to go and wander along it. Alone he would follow the sea's contour out to the point, and seated by the dunes he would dream there: the stars said nothing to him. He had never seen the other land on the horizon. But he would drift, empty and powerless, along the edge of the foam. Sometimes he would go into the motionless water.

One year after the man arrived gusts of upheaval blew close by. The maroons all went down and burned several plantations to help the people down there who had rebelled. The man was occupied by the revolt, which was bloodily suppressed for several weeks. However, his incursions into the plain were brief. He would burn and pull back. This was how he conserved the forces at his disposal. When they finally knew that it was all over, that however many men and women had been massacred, he came to the conclusion that it would have to be "some other time." Possibly he thought the slaves were not worthy of his assistance. He had no intention of staying in contact with the lowlands. *Why don't they all become maroons?* He did not know what was useful about their struggle and their suffering. He did not understand that all of them would not have been able to crowd up into the hills. There would not have been enough forest to shelter them, let alone feed them. He did not know that their torments and even their accepting the situation served to protect him as a result. He was cut off from them. From the first day he had refused. Once when they were first together she had said, "You are stiff as an ashcake, stiff as *dongré.*" He took the word and said it his way: "Longoué, Longoué." She had laughed and pointed to them each in turn: "Louise, Louise, Longoué, Longoué."

When their son came she was determined: "I want to give him a name! This is the day I was waiting for. After today there's no other day! . . . This is it. Down below they tell a story about some lords who go to adore a god. Kings. If you could see how handsome they are in the story, all the wealth! I heard the gentlemen. Well, one of the kings is black as can be, they call him either Melchior or Balthazar, I don't know which. One or the other." And he (opposed at first to giving him a name from the plains) was conciliatory and decided it would be Melchior. It seemed the more likely name: Melchior.

When he was born the neighbors came running, timid and eager to please. Maroons, the ones who had not been caught again. They sang in the dark and drank stolen rum. Standing off to the side Longoué was watching the red fields literally chew into the forest. He was thinking that he had never conquered Louise. He had been reduced to demonstrating affection, weakness, as he would to a creature who was his equal. Even superior to him, perhaps. He had not taken her; she had accepted him. Every now and then he would feel the old rancor inside himself, and he saw it in her. Then they would stand there like stone, both of them, looking at each other. Luckily many of their times together he spent learning the words Louise spoke. He was obliged to apply himself to the task if he wanted to communicate with the other maroons. On the other hand, it was not necessary for her to learn his words; and he did not mind maintaining his prestige as an African, sharing as little as possible the knowledge he had of the country on the other side of the ocean. He therefore accepted her giving him something: the new language. During these lessons, improvised wherever they might be, affection would return. And so they lived in an equilibrium, each stifling their former anger. The threat from down below brought them even closer together.

One day he showed her the mud head and the snake, which, amazingly, were safe and sound in the shelter of a root. The earth had dried, cracking it all over, digging wrinkles into its cheeks and forehead and putting short, crinkly hair that looked like the mange on its skull. Louise shrunk away from it.

"It's a snake," she exclaimed. "It is eating him from the inside."

"No. It is stealing his spirit that leaves him living in vain."

"What is it for?"

"It is for him," he said.

He showed her the irons he had gone and gotten from the workshop on Acajou plantation. Two circles of metal linked by a short bar. They put them on your ankles. They came in every size, right down to tiny ones, like toys, that they put on children. He had chosen the largest size.

"You are cracked-in-the-head crazy! You've been back to Acajou again!"

"They are for him," he said. "For the other man."

"Don't show me anything else! I'd rather not know than get the shudders like this in the middle of the day!"

For the other man, who had stayed standing beside him while they had watched the buyers passing in the market, knowing that they themselves had already been sold. The man he had fought with on the deck of the boat and whom that time he had beaten, because at the crossroads where they were separated it only looked like a fight. The man he had crossed the endless sea with, watching the bodies between them disappear and each of them reading his enemy for the signs of slow death. The man with whom (this he told Louise) he had been thrown into the slave house back there on the other side. In the house, he said, you could see the long corridor paved in stones and at the end a peephole through which swept the sound of the waves. Narrow cells opened off either side of the corridor, and that is where they were shut up the second time. He told Louise that they put both of them in the same cell; they were inseparable for a long time. The same hole in the darkness, full of the growling sea, as if the cells were dug below it, as if they were soaking directly in the sea, prefiguring the steerage quarters in the boat, the resounding space between the decks and between the waves, echoing as loudly as any hold. When they were being loaded onto the boat, he said, they went down the paved slope at the end of the corridor and emerged, dazzled, to the vertigo of the sea where a boat, rolling in the foam, was waiting for them. The sound of the skiff bumping against the paved ramp was in his head. He spent a long time describing the house of slaves, even telling her about the sailors who checked the cells every night with their lanterns; he said how weird the yellow lights shut up inside lamps were. Laying out the reasons that this house of slaves just as much as the boat and even more than the market explained the snake and the irons.

(He was not Longoué. The neighbors called him quite simply Monsieur-la-Pointe because of his walks along the seashore. Louise called him Longoué, but they were the only ones who knew that.

She never said his name in the presence of others, as if she wanted to keep for herself the privilege she had taken. Consequently, his whole life he was the first of the Longoués without being so in name, and he was Monsieur-la-Pointe for everyone who had dealings with him.)

The other man, he said, was brave. Death is not the punishment for brave men. The punishment is the end of their bravery. The other one would have to be hard pressed until he became an impotent capon living without any reason to do so, accepting life.

"You are cracked-in-the-head crazy," she said.

But he held firm in his belief. "I know what I am," he said. *He brought the course of existence to a halt up above the Senglis plantation, where the other man vegetated.*

And in fact it seemed that there was an uneasiness slowing the rhythm of lives on that plantation, to the point of jeopardizing good yields from the harvests. Senglis and his wife left their affairs in the hands of their supervisors. They locked themselves up in the house, where every day he bent more crooked beneath his hump and she covered herself with makeup and powder, a funeral doll, a frozen image of decrepitude. She had the extraordinary whim of bringing the newly arrived slave into the house, whereas the most profitable logic should have demanded that she use him in the fields. But, even more extravagantly, she also granted him the privilege of keeping the woman he lived with. Their hut was still standing, but they often slept in the big house. Marie-Nathalie would call for the man at the drop of a hat, and when he was there she would just look at him calmly, sometimes even attentively, while she kept right on trying out various makeups. The man was uneasy and had to look around everywhere for some job to do, then made himself do it probably to forget that he was uneasy. The woman worked in the kitchen. She was seriously amazed at the strange goings-on in the place.

Madame de Senglis announced to her husband that they now had an excellent "stud" and therefore had absolutely no need to rent males from the neighbors. This revelation came to her at the end of the evening during which Gustave-Anatole (Bourbon) had recounted (and acted out) the events at Acajou plantation. But the first pregnancy, the one that normally should have preceded and authorized others, that of the woman mated to the man, did not happen. Gradually the whole thing turned into something of a crisis. It provided Senglis with the basic material for his jibes. "I don't see how he could increase your troop, that man who can't seem to get the cook pregnant." Day after day he would not let the subject drop. Perhaps his wife too was thoughtfully scrutinizing the man while she pretended to get all tricked out in front of the mirror; was she perhaps trying to figure out why such a piece of machinery would remain unproductive? The mistress began thus to verge on what could only be called insanity: having the man fed in her presence, forbidding that he do hard labor, attempting to find out about fertility herbs and potions that she ordered him to swallow. Not for a moment did she imagine that it might be the woman who was sterile. Not for a moment would she consent to sending them all back to the rhythm she had formerly imposed upon the plantation. She had to have that first offspring. The one born of the deeds of that pair, and she was dogged in her desire. It had become for her a law, a supreme goal, something tormenting her every instant. It seemed to her contrary to the order of things, contrary to universal harmony that this stallion had not—and especially since he had been given this woman—begun his work of reproduction. It was a mockery of fate for no good reason. In all this obsessive madness there was a minor incident: she herself gave birth to a son. She attached no importance to this. It was an accident resulting from a night of excitement (or perhaps indifference and apathy more intense than usual) that had brought the couple together, neither of them capable of responsibility for their actions, in a furtive and inexplicably inattentive moment. No contentment or disgust resulted from this night. The child was born—very strong and very beautiful. Madame de Senglis was not for one instant distracted from her major work. She turned her son over to the women of the house and immediately forgot him. As for the husband, from time to time he would visit his heir, rubbing the child's back and (though he hid this from the nurses) looking to see if there were not the beginnings of a hump, which to his extreme satisfaction he did not find. Marie-Nathalie would sometimes hear the baby crying; for a moment she would stop what she was doing, her arm in the air, fingers playing with makeup brushes, then she would slowly begin once more to adorn herself. You could not tell whether she was forty or a hundred years old, and she was twenty-seven. She shut herself up like that in this tomb, only coming out to return unflaggingly to her multiplication project that was always at the same point, zero.

"Béluse," she said very slowly. "Good-use. I named you Béluse for the good use I could make of you and I allocated a female to you. No, no, a wife. Let's say a wife. Here you are practically lord and master of your home. What are we going to do with the plantation if you do not breed?"

The astonished Béluse would sometimes run back to his hut where he had to put up with sarcastic remarks from the old man, who had nothing better to do in life (if that was life) than sit near the hut, weaving hats and waiting for the masters' favorite. It was easier for Béluse to stand the old man's hideous, smug smile than the mistress's dead voice. Though the slaves should have detested him, through some collective quirk he enjoyed widespread esteem. No one other than the old man ever mentioned the role assigned Béluse by Madame de Senglis's increasing folly, nor the futility of the attention lavished upon him. It must be admitted that it did not get in his way at all, even in his relations with his companion. The women perhaps showed a hint of condescension toward him. The supervisors, secretly flattered by their new power, felt kindly toward him. As the days went by the one who had shown him where to put his hut became bold enough to finally cohabit with the other woman, the one he had taken with him that first day. Who was still apathetic. He bullied and battered her fiercely and was no less fiercely attached to her.

One day when Béluse fled to his hut like this, he found the irons laid out in front of his door; he knew right away they were put there for him.

"I saw him," whispered the old man behind him.

Béluse started; the voice was coming from the hut.

"I saw him. He's a maroon! I can tell them right off the bat! He came without even hiding. I saw him. Virgin Lord, Béluse, I went inside. Then what does he do but come here, I'm shaking like a *filaos*. What does he do but stop, listen, look, then that's when he puts that thing in front of the door!"

"He thinks I'm afraid," said Béluse. "He thinks I'm afraid!"

"You are afraid," said the old man.

"I am alive," said Béluse.

He flung the irons far away while the old man laughed scornfully.

2

Here is what the Senglis property was like: a den of decay, impervious to the frenzied race against woods and brambles for wealth and profit playing out everywhere else. Here the bloody and savage pace had gradually given way to an even more animal existence, in which the domination of spirits culminated slowly in their wasting away. Senglis and his wife, by their mere presence deep inside a room perpetually smoky with candles, ran the property and did so more certainly than if they were bustling about with whip and shackles. But it was mold and lingering decline that they ruled over. The plantation was like a sluggish canker inside the virulent surroundings of other landholdings. Bit by bit the women slowed their chatter. Supervisors moved in and imitated their daring colleague; hypocrites, they sermonized; they let themselves be caught up in the slow-moving rhythm of things. Perhaps as a result, without being aware of it, they were developing a calmer, deeper attachment for the land they thus caressed when they should have been assaulting it. Indeed, the woods and brambles, the humus and proliferation regained no ground over the Senglis land, but you could see that the struggle at the limits of the property was no longer either fierce or victorious. The long, smoky, constantly progressing wound, like lines of algae and mud drifting with the currents on the sea, was not there the way it was around Acajou, for example, where it meant the arable land was advancing into the primeval mess.

Because after the maroon escaped, La Roche demonstrated a tenfold increase in activity. Into the fallow fields no one else had been tempted by (for all those hundred and fifty years that these men had been working fiercely to possess land, slaves, stores, and rum), he turned his gang loose; he went at the steepest slopes of the hills. For a hundred and fifty years the land slept there side by side with men intent on profit, when suddenly one of them seized it by the throat again. Soon he would call it: my property. As if another history were beginning. Planters held the plantation up as an example. The master was no more willing than before to invite them to his house but, at least (as they saw it), he was acting now like a normal man. His sole concern was to salvage cultivated fields from the land. Thus, contrary to the Senglis property, Acajou was a beehive and, consequently, a place of damnation for slaves. Physical and fearsome damnation, whereas on the Senglis land everything, even willpower, was rotting away in debasement and shamefulness.

This was the situation, therefore, on the two plantations when rebellion broke out everywhere. There is nothing to say about it, except maybe that slavery produced it: rebellion comes naturally anywhere that a slave can find a machete, a hoe, or a stick. Just as one cannot entirely describe the state of slavery (because of this one tiny, irreducible fact of reality that no description, no analysis will ever succeed in including: the frail spirit that awakes to pain day after day and sometimes becomes exasperated, only to lapse into the usual, the accepted, which is even more terrible than the spasm of damnation), likewise there is nothing to say about a rebellion of this sort except that it is hidden inside the wooden horse of suffering. A slave's rebellion is not one of hope. It is nourished by no hope, and sometimes it shrugs off revenge (which might be hope's supreme cry); it foreshadows, it ushers in the most painful and silent action (operation): taking root. None of the rebels cared that trends of thought, petitions, nightlong Assemblies or banquets had preceded their sudden upsurge for a long time and in other places. Nor that the mulattos, partially freed from the dreadful yoke of this society, were going to take part in the affair, but only from their own perspective: not hesitating whenever necessary to bay with the hounds. Their only concern was the strip of land burning there beneath their feet where something had to be found with which to cover themselves, something with which to strike when they burst out into the dazzling red glare. Cities, market towns, communes— the man who was slave to the land of the masters knew nothing of their ferment. His act was unclouded by the enthusiasm of words.

Béluse sneaked away right at the beginning of the unrest. For at least two weeks he joined one of the bands of men scouring the countryside. Bands created randomly in which men from different plantations joined together, seeing each other for the first time. But they spoke the same language. They had broken the barriers that had made each plantation an inescapable prison. They ranged over the free land, engaging in quick skirmishes with the soldiers and terrorizing the market towns. At first they kept to the hillsides and advanced from one district to the next. Then they became bolder and descended into the plains where they were massacred. But they held out so long that the ones who escaped alive, the ones who returned to their former shackles were able for a long time thereafter to greatly increase the store of tales told in the huts, evoking dead friends and the men who were still alive (waiting perhaps) on Such-and-such Plantation or in Such-and-such district. Because once the barriers were broken they could never again be made leakproof; and the most valuable outcome of all this was that from that point on the wind could blow right through from field to field. During these days of fighting, the moon turned pink at night and Béluse and all the others shouted.

"What she wants is my blood! And what I say is: No! No! And here's the question: Why doesn't she come herself? Well?"

They laughed, they shouted, carried away by the madness of the Senglis woman. They looked up toward the upper house, which, like Acajou, the wave had oddly respected. The slaves, who did not trust the maroons, were astonished that they had spared the two plantations. Usually the maroons did not pick and choose, they descended and they burned. For just this once it seemed that their actions skirted the lands held by La Roche and Senglis. The rebellion, made up of field workers in the majority, had no reason to hang around for long on the two estates. On the Senglis plantation there were few men; La Roche's was fiercely guarded. On pain of immediate dismissal, the master had forbidden his overseers and supervisors to participate in any way at all in pursuit or repression. As if this affair were of no interest to him. This said, any Negro who was not expected to be there and who entered his lands he killed. They all knew about it, except for a few strays or absentminded ones, the boldest of whom (who got there who knows how—expecting, perhaps, to find his victorious brothers dancing before bonfires of furniture) he exploded with cannon powder between the two mahogany trees—the two *acajous*. Senglis, who was a captain in the militia, *or something else I don't remember what*, was only lukewarm in his zeal toward fulfilling the duties of his office. Anyhow he was replaced for the lazy way he had disemboweled several Negroes. This lack of enthusiasm was judged very severely, but Senglis had withdrawn into himself; he no longer reacted. Except for the one time when, beside himself, he heaped abuse upon a Council of planters, reproaching them for "having only made mock of him at the time he was predicting these events." He then went back home to Her-Ladyship-His-Wife.

He arrived ahead of Béluse, who, well before the rebellion was definitively quelled, refused to descend into the plains—out of instinct or out of a sort of timidity not caused by fear. Perhaps he saw that doing so would be a fatal error. Perhaps he was just dizzy with the idea of leaving like that. So when he did go back Madame de Senglis welcomed him with real satisfaction, as if he were merely late. They agreed to say he had hidden as a precaution; the overseers themselves acquiesced. Because the fierceness of the battle had come to rest against the invisible walls of the estate.

Up in the hills Louise too was isolated and did not dare admit to having any interest in what she called "the war." When Longoué would return (he never spent more than two days away), she served him his food in gourds, remarking "that she wouldn't ask him anything, really nothing, since she already knew that all this turmoil was just for fun," until finally he had covered every last detail of the facts and the results. She did not dare admit that she was worried about the fate of Acajou. But one day Longoué told her that he, Longoué, was protecting Acajou and the Senglis house. *"Why the Senglis house?"* she asked without thinking, before she could stop, realizing too late that there was no special reason to spare Acajou. But Longoué laughed and said, "Because he is on the Senglis property and I want him to stay there." From then on she feared only for Longoué. She never participated in all the to-do of fighting and fire, and in the end you might say she grew used to it. But her relief was short-lived: she heard Longoué say, "That will be for some other time." The cares of existence were already wearing her out rather quickly. Although the man, her man, brought her all the necessities of life (from sackcloth, needles, thread—even a big thimble carved from walnut, bizarre there on the earthen floor of the hut, next to the pallet where Louise placed it solemnly—to clay pots of manioc, flour, and salt), she had to take care of everything else: breadfruit, yams, the tallow she molded into candles, the charcoal kilns she went to inspect. When people came to see Longoué, she made herself chat with the newcomers outside in front of the hut, while he had them come in one by one. She thus got into the habit of being friendly and it suited her very well. Sometimes there would be a burst of lightning; all the people of the countryside knew the power and daring that inhabited that body. After the birth of her second son she began to grow fat, becoming bit by bit the person her neighbors had called her from the very first day: Man-Louise.[1]

It was the hottest time of year in the forest on the hills. Truly, the

1. Man— is a title of respectful address in Creole, the equivalent of Madame. Ti— in the next paragraph is the contraction of *petit* (little) and is frequently attached to the same name borne by a younger member of the family.

sweetness of existence there was surprising, after the heavy mugginess down below. The dry, vibrant air wrapped itself around your body, but it was the way a cloud would, and there was no dark presence waiting to pounce. Suddenly you would see a clump of trees dancing in the distance—three feet away. You might discover an opening onto the green gravel bed of the infinitely receding hills—within shouting distance. The man now without his rootstock easily took root, however, in this lightness, bearing as if by default his name, Monsieur-la-Pointe (which meant his first son would long be called Ti-Lapointe before he took again on his own the name of the Longoué family and gave it some weight: Melchior Longoué), and looking all around the high ridges that were like waves on the sea, he forgot the sea. But, if there were no underground presences, hunger and sickness lay in wait. The sweetness of existence was only in the air, it yielded no fruit. Already Longoué, he, Longoué, was secretly scouring the hills, knowing every root and every branch the way a man, on the verge of sinking into madness, knows his spirit and feels it out.

And he was not yet used to the glimmer of the woods nor to its benevolence when he met up with La Roche. It was eight or nine years after Melchior had uttered his first cry in the cabin. Always feeling a bodily irritation, a physical frustration with safety, the facts of which escaped his mind. Longoué was restless, incapable of the stability that his own body refused. On the surface Louise seemed to have a grave understanding of his constant moving about, though, in reality, it left her perplexed.

It was one of those afternoons when every murmur falls silent; the branches of the endless treetops were projected in the blinding light through the thick, ferrous air, in shadows flattening themselves onto the grasses and thickets on the ground. Each bend in the woods was unique in the world. Longoué suddenly felt something like a premonition in the back of his neck, some ancient pain awakening, and then he saw La Roche less than ten paces away. They both stopped. Motionless, they stared at each other cautiously but unstirred by any fear that might disrupt their scrutiny.

La Roche sat down slowly on a stump after having placed before him a bundle he had been carrying on his back up to this point. No less slowly, Longoué squatted with his machete across his thighs. La Roche was armed with a pistol that he wore on his belt, but they both knew that the advantage it provided was very relative in the inextricable tangle of vegetation into which Longoué could disappear with one bound. They knew they had been walking one in front of the other, so this meeting did not feel like the result of chance. For nearly ten years, they guessed, they had been waiting for this moment that would bring a very old story to an end, the story dominating their existence all this time. Now everything would come together, a lesson would come out of it—through them, between them, against them. The result was that they were careful (also out of a perfectly legitimate sense of caution) to make no sudden moves. Slowly they looked each other over, La Roche perhaps more direct, erect and ready for attack, his blue eyes tightly glued to his opponent; Longoué impassive, sinking his expressionless gaze beneath the surface, massively vigilant but not without a certain amount of *potential* kindness. And La Roche suddenly spoke, using the words of his own language (when he knew that Longoué understood the country Creole, that they could communicate with each other that way); moreover, he spoke it unusually fast as if intending to force the maroon to make an extreme effort of attention in order to catch a few scattered ideas on the surface of what he said. But La Roche was more than astonished to see that not only did Longoué not force himself to exert any comprehension but he even replied in his African language, probably using it for the first time in ten years. After a few quick retorts they contented themselves with the dialogue that was not a dialogue: each one closed in upon his own injury, mutually inaccessible, as if instinctively they were veiling the immodesty of confidence or as if, forced as they were to confide in each other, they were trying nonetheless to preserve their free will or, in more human terms, their self-regard.

"And," La Roche said, "all these years she thought I reproached her for doing it: her sleeping-out-of-spite with that humpback.

The proof is that first she threatened to do it on the night we parted. She screamed her threat, no, she whispered it, her head stuck through the porch rails while I just stood there smiling then laughing out loud in her face. That is why she did it. But she didn't know that just the idea of it was what hit so hard inside, suddenly hardening me, even if she were just saying it over and over, before she ever did it. That is why I didn't hold her back that night. Because all the sand we rolled around in, she and I—I saw it as endlessly white and she saw it black. It was black inside her and I did not know it. It was at that moment, I declare, that I gauged the weight of my existence and found how pathetic it was! What was the use of all the racing, all the blood, all the greediness of my blood, and this desire, for what? For all these years she believed that it was the act I reproached her for, but it was the idea of it that came from her and uprooted me from where I stood. And her grandmother was, of course, content when she heard her admit what she had done wrong and decide so definitely what was required in reparation. Because that old woman was afraid of me, not for what I was nor for the pleasures into which I dragged her daughter's daughter, but probably for the wasteland, the desolation she had been able to guess lay inside me. But then, this is in us. No one puts his ear to detect this desert, but it is there. Why? So what reason, if one may call it that, was there for this divorce? It is incredible that I have forgotten it. Who will tell me the reason? Who then? And probably I can understand why she went back and forth between us, because she was influenced by the old woman who kept on showing her the advantages of the other side, the certainty, the stability, the chance to dominate a weak person who would consent. But I know her scornful stare when she thinks she has conquered someone. I know she dares not cry, but winning like that would make her cry. I am the only man to have conquered her. And I would have consented to her choosing him, that man. But she entertained the idea of this affair because I defeated her, that is where the dirty sand—the sort you would find at Pointe des Sables—developed. And how did I defeat her? I don't know any more! And for all these years she was, perhaps, imagining that I would happily come to get her and take her back to Acajou (carry her off like a gallant knight), even after what she had done. And myself, I see her still clutching that hump while he crushes her with his midget's weight and maybe she cries. The final joke will be on me when I weep and wail in turn, the day she dies. Because she will die, I'm sure of it! She is not eternal. She began to die the day she dared think that prostituting herself to Gustave-Bourbon was the best answer to all our stubborn arguments. Here she is, dying in her youth in the presence of the Negro with whom she is not and probably never will be bold enough to fornicate (as if their women did without it whenever the men, disillusioned, would let them do so), and covering herself with makeup to hide who knows what filth on her body, layer after layer, mummifying herself while she dies. She is waiting for me to come, she underestimates the power of the thing that devastated me, she doesn't understand that an awkward man who offends and hurts can also be hurt, no, be devastated beyond even the point of death, that there can be nothing left for him except this fondness for scorn, for dirty sand on his body. She has no idea that I am dead, on that night I too became dead. That from that day to this the only distance between us has been that she is dying when I have already rotted. Consequently, she thinks that all I reproach her for is that act and that, despite the act I will come and extract from her the consent she hopes to give. A double deception she should not have succumbed to, knowing me the way she does.

La Roche fell silent, and being a well-mannered man, waited for his interlocutor to speak. Tacitly, in the peaceful, scorching afternoon, they had agreed to speak one at a time; each one however it suited him and in his own language, foreign to the other. The birds began again to whistle in some far-off foliage where they had probably hidden; sometimes rustling sounds, heat detonating in splatters, furtive slithering, and long growls of wind stirred the woods. A sun dawned under every branch. Longoué ran his hand over the back of his neck, his movement slow and focused.

"It is not the boat. It is not the house. The boat—you have to get used to smelling that thing. In the house the trench-hole is full of disorder. In the sea, I don't know, the disorder is what holds you up. On the boat I saw him, him, and I get used to the smell. And a man it is true set his foot on my head, fine. But that man, he is going to die as it is decreed, not before. It is the pen. That pen. Where they made me lie down on the ground drenched in water; with shackles you can only sleep on your back. The rain it fell three nights and two days. But at night especially. You can't open your eyes when you lie on the ground and the water won't stop. It is that pen. Everything flays down from above. It makes your body heave, those white things falling. Even night turns pale, it repels your spirit. I shake like I was flayed white. There is no hope. That is the pen. Truly, I was ready to swallow my tongue, it was too much to bear. Two days and three nights in the rot. Death is the only choice. But death is not for me because the third day they bring him, they throw him down beside me and I come back to life. Then I forget about death; I don't believe in death anymore. Because he is there I have to stay. I am going to walk before him. Wherever I go he goes. The next night they take us to the paved house. But by then I am alive. The house, the boat. I bear it. The pen, that's it, that is where I scream, that is where I go pale. And then afterward, everything that begins again the moment they toss him next to me. It is that pen."

Then La Roche, delighted: "Fine. I carry the little girl off to the house. It seems to me that the horizon opens up in that direction. I become infatuated with her, Senglis definitely thinks I am allowing myself a bit of entertainment at home. That is the custom. But I am reckoning in different terms. You see, there is no man around there who doesn't think I am mad. I try to find out whether, over where you are, in the bottoms where you stagnate, there is someone to whom I can offer salvation. That is Louise, everything I have undertaken with regard to her is to know that. Since it was decreed that my own flesh would leave me I would nourish another flesh. In one fell swoop I would switch from a daybreak full of sands to a night with no torch. I even began to feel loathing when I met my people, my skin shrank at their touch. But you understand, when I touch Louise the shrinking vanishes, I am delighted with myself. And she, she, she! Would you believe that every time I would see her again I could hardly bear to breathe? I am damned, I accept the curse! Alone I am in charge here! But at what moment did the sin occur? Must it have ripened in some secret error, since the undertaking miscarried and Louise left?"

"The first thing I want to do is leave him there all alone in his pointless life! So I make the head and put the creature in its mouth. No matter what the woman says—he stays alone. And as for him he thinks that is what he wants. He shouts, 'No! I don't want to!' He believes he is the one refusing. He pretends to believe this because the whole time he is shouting 'No! And no!' he is shaking all over. And I think to myself: he's going to stay in the house, powerless. Why not his descendants too? A whole line to fall powerless. So then I go and I remove the creature, I scatter the head around. And one year later he has this son. He believes it is because he wanted to. He pretends to believe that, because any time he starts crying out for a good time he shakes all over. He gets the descendants he deserves. All of them in the house and unable to leave. Slave for every day to come. I take the creature away, too bad if it turns against me. But as for him, his son is the son of slavery. Listen well, it is the truth."

Silence grew between the two of them while, in contrast, the woods rustled with the subtle repercussions of heat. Down there evening was coming on; they saw it racing up to them along the horizon of the hills. La Roche dug in his bag and took out an object that he tossed gently at Longoué's feet. Long meditative silence. Longoué finally picked the object up.

"Ebony bark, stripped with a single stroke from the trunk! Let it soak for the time marked by two moons. Sea water is preferable. Lay it out in the sun for two whole days. Rub the inner surface and polish it. Make your drawing and carve. It is your profile, my friend. Quite true to type. Of course, the people who usually sculpt these things to guide us did not know you. You gave them absolutely no opportunity to study you. I had to draw the thing and, according to Senglis, the result is not half bad. Now, why did I not continue pursuing you? A whim of mine. I counted on arming an expedition against you, because in the end it would not have been impossible to get to you. But I suddenly got stubborn about all this land clearing. It seemed to me that, as a result, I was hunting you down more efficiently. And then, in time, you became irreplaceable for me. Perhaps you mark some distant boundary to my lands? No doubt. I am attached to you, especially because they call you La Pointe. The point, La Pointe, is that not absolutely the end?"

La Roche laughed softly while Longoué examined the grayish bark in which his carved profile stood out, dark red in the wood. La Roche was having fun.

"And what's more, I'm bringing you this! I spent a whole evening tracking you down just to give it to you. It seems fair that you have it, don't you think?"

He threw the little cask that he had pulled from his bag toward Longoué. Longoué caught the object and put it gently down beside the bark. There was something like amazement in the surroundings, life in acute arrest, at the sight of these two calm men seated face to face. La Roche who should have—it was his right—killed the maroon the instant he saw him. Longoué with no anxiety, without hatred it seemed, his machete slack across his thighs. Both parties to the present moment, these two separated by an abyss. Both equally mad.

"Yes, yes, a little barrel. It has been ages since it was dangerous. I would like for you to keep it wherever you go. It will worry your grandnephews, perhaps. What does that matter to us? Will our absurd progeny get wind of this story? They will have cleared so much of the countryside that they won't even know how to flush the creature that lurks deep inside them. Together we are going down the stairway to hell, you paler and paler in your sons, me drowned out in the stunned skull of an idiot. So, I am returning your evil sign this very day. Yes yes, this is a return. But, my friend, what living we have done we two!"

They smiled. Night was upon them. Far above the tree trunks it hesitated to cover up the extraordinary monologues. The two men lazed in the fire of evening, perhaps unsatisfied because they had poured out so little of what was bubbling inside them, but respectful of this peace and extremely respectful of this mutual incomprehension in which they found themselves once again interdependent. La Roche stood up and gradually (or was it in a single burst of motion?) disappeared into the shadows. Longoué picked up the cask and the bark, he was master of these heights that, all in all, the white man had conceded to him. Not conceded but acknowledged after loyal combat. The sea was there where the stars went silent. The shore was there, from which he could not see the other land. He shouted, in the language he spoke as an African: "I held your life in my hands. The whole time I protected you. It will be for some other time!" Something like a sweetness, a peace, a harmony with the stumps, the briars, the shifty bamboos and the sky came upon him. A birth in these woods, as if he were the newly arrived son of his son Melchior. Taking great strides he went back along the path to his hut.

Chapter 5

THE BIRTH OF BÉLUSE'S SON WAS the final downfall of the Senglis estates. Six crops had been harvested since Marie-Nathalie, livid beneath her makeup, last lit candles in the back of what she would have referred to as her boudoir, and she would certainly not have been able to say how much mold six years can accumulate in a box or how much of the cutting edge six years can remove from the blade of an ax. Impervious to time, dead in her inflexible and steadfast dream, she mourned daily for this birth that had become her obsession. Béluse, accustomed to the ways of Madame de Senglis, was no longer afraid of her dead gaze or the mournful mask where you could see her stiff wrinkles underneath the cream. In a soft, musical voice he spoke to this ghost, he walked it around the house and the mistress would cry out with delight when he took it to play with the Senglis child, and this ghost wasting away with an unbearable passion suddenly would come alive to ask him: "Béluse, when are we going to begin peopling our lands?" and he would soothe her with some story of fertility, filled with floods of black children, teeming with lush vegetation and cataracts of water, until finally one day even he felt sorry for her and he said: "We've got him, madame, he is on his way, a boy." And it did not astound him to see her light up like the sun, not exuberant but filled with fearsome happiness; he seemed content to bring the awkward future mother who laughed crudely and consented to obey the whims of the reclusive woman ("Turn around — Come here so I can feel him — Walk — Again!"), and content to watch the months that were the slow prelude to parturition slip by, during which he was finally rid of the mistress's attentions; it did surprise him, at a time when anybody could know about his paternity because it was visible in his companion's belly, that for the first time he had to be subjected to the taunts of the others ("Ah! If it was me she'd have given birth six years ago," or: "Now all the women are going to have to!"), as if the outcome of this waiting had isolated him in the end, and the outcasts were now aware of the privilege he had been granted. Because he scarcely gave a thought to the ravages suffered by those he called "the cargo." He had forced himself to work in the fields, but not too much; despite having become a good field hand, however, he had no inkling of (he was content not to see) the desolation of these hopeless jobs; he had become used to the daily sight of starving children (for whom every day he would steal some marvelous leftover from the meager dinners of Madame de Senglis), and the sickness accepted as final by resigned adults (for whom, when ordered to do so, he would go and get the veterinarian). He made no attempt to use the freedoms he enjoyed to bring attention to all this suffering; seeing it repeated day after day had finally persuaded him (as well as the others who were subjected to it but had no time to think about it) that this was the normal condition of life, once and for all. The vague hostility that was now all around him preoccupied him to such an extent that he began to try to make out the different worlds side by side or one on top of the other in the plantation; but, using a device basic to his way of thinking, he simply divided up this enclosed universe in which he himself spread out here and there like some neglected moss, according to its areas. He observed first and foremost the disturbing, authoritarian, "working" regency somehow exercised by the supervisors and overseers, with whom he had little to do, but he saw how they had people and things under their thumb and he felt their heavy-handed threat everywhere: men all of a piece for whom bloodying and maiming were just one moment (to be honest, the last) in the required constant policing operation that was what maintained order on the estate. Off to one side and beneath them was the sterile zone of the workers, but he did not think "workers," he thought of them as "the cargo, this is the boat's cargo they've brought together here": the people who dragged themselves from the huts to the fields and from field to hut, that's all. He did not go any further, not even to wonder why he had once joined with the rebels: whether it had not been for the rancor piled up inside him by so much degradation. Then there was the peaceful preserve of the house, the domestic servants, uppity because they were special, not thin or dirty or dressed in rags (and not fat or peaceful either) but surviving on leftovers swiped from the pantry: a marginal population that made do with the shadows where it *endured* in an animal way and ended up even becoming attached to its masters (privilege having such a power to exhaust the soul in the long run and turn it aside into the most gnawing dependencies), like the two women just bursting with motherliness who were fighting over the affections of the Senglis child. Then the bleak, dreary estate where Gustave-Anatole stagnated, distracting himself more and more with little perversions that he thought up: hating his slaves with the depraved hatred of a puny man: he persecuted the ones he most strongly disliked, forcing them, for example, to eat hairs he pulled out from under his arms (and the house slaves used to laugh, shouting to the poor man who had to do this: "Hell, you'll get something to eat now!") or making them smear their faces with the Senglis baby's stools. But everybody was able to see that those were games played by a feeble idiot, a lost man. Then finally, in the darkest recesses of the house, there was the tomb of Marie-Nathalie, the tragic mausoleum of her youth. And, perhaps so he would not think about it any more, so he would not dig deeper into the zones he had so vaguely outlined, he became gradually attached to the madness of the mistress. As a result he soon had a new position — that of protector. He knew that he was irrelevant to this madness, which had simply taken him for its object; and the blue-eyed overlord stuck in his memory since the day the old man had dizzied them (himself and the two women) with his words. Marie-Nathalie's innocent joy delighted him, however, as he watched her cuddle the bewildered mother, solemnly preside over the birth, pester everybody with recommendations, and then (once the baby was there) ponder long and hard over the best name. Senglis was amused by her incongruous behavior. When his wife announced, "We shall call him Anne!" and he had asked her: "Anne? Why Anne? That's a girl's name," and she had corrected him: "Think again, it's the name of the Constable of Montmorency, you certainly know how much I admire Anne de Montmorency, he was an ill-fated hero," and he had retorted: "Come on, you're not going to deck this slave out with the absurd name of a Constable of France, are you?"—and she declared calm as calm could be: "My friend, I see no harm in it, when your name, and who knows by what right, is Gustave-Anatole *Bourbon*." Bourbon shrugged his shoulders and was gone. So the child was named Anne.

But his birth was the cause, almost the signal of ruin. Because it was very quickly apparent that a success that had been so passionately desired, rather than whipping up the energies of Madame de Senglis, had instead overwhelmed her with a surfeit of pleasure, after which she let herself go. She was so wildly excited by the result, which had seemed so hopeless for so long, that the excess of her transports knocked the wind out of her sails, as it were. Béluse therefore did not have to "guarantee peopling" the land, did not have to continue the work thus begun. He was subjected to ridicule and teasing by the women who would turn to him as he went by and make coarse advances, but he would just smile sweetly and sometimes, when he felt like it, he would play the game and pretend to chase the brazen women who would pretend to run away, shrieking and calling out for help. Madame de Senglis forgot overnight her bizarre project. She paid no more attention to Anne than she had to her own son. She rapidly went into a decline, and Béluse vaguely understood that up until now the plantation had existed in the shadow of this madness. By its supernatural powers of contagion or hypnosis (failing the lure of profit that drove planters but that Senglis and his wife seemed so mysteriously immune to), it had been the only thing holding together all the worlds, the various sectors whose contours he had guessed more than determined. With the disappearance of this obsession the balance of the whole was compromised, and from that point on it was all downhill.

The triumphant land stormed the property. It being the natural propensity of proconsuls, the supervisors wallowed in short-lived pleasures in which their fondness for authority was still not enough to counterbalance growing shortfalls or incompetence. The property's already precarious economy was further subjected to repercussions that had begun to take place in the broader market. Senglis had to abandon the sugarcane mill that he ran, and soon he had had several discreet offers to buy the land as well as its machinery and equipment. It was a sure sign; but Senglis was already experiencing the death throes that would carry Marie-Nathalie off soon afterward.

The triumphant land lay fallow, available and insolent in the heat. Wild gangs of weeds, overgrowths of adaptable, insistent grasses circled the cocoa trees, thrust their tips up in the shade, hung around in the undergrowth carpeted with dry cocoa leaves, and then all of a sudden erupted between the tree trunks, smothering the plant—the domesticated tree. They waited to make their onslaught until the rainy season so they would be preceded by their tactical cavalry—gullies full of oozing water where the abandoned tree trunk would rot away. Then during the dry season they would crackle, wizened and dry, but they never surrendered their forces, merely lay patient in the drunken luminosity of the air; then once again they would pounce on their prey. Marie-Nathalie felt this assault all around her. Wild-eyed, she saw the unruly shore scratch the red or black leaf mold with its sands and the sand was fertile. When her powers of resistance were at their highest (it was a year after the birth of Anne Béluse), she clung to the heavy ticking on her bed for one entire evening, driving the enemy off and cursing: "Just dare come here! I'll spit in your eye! Hideous scoundrel, your body is bleaker than it is at La Pointe, I shall never get used to your limbs, yes the smell of your blood disgusts me, there you have it, I had to shout it out, you turn my stomach, . . ." and she would go rattling on in her death throes until Senglis murmured: "What did I ever do to you, Marie-Nathalie? Do I deserve this?" Then emerging from the chaos of her death she understood that he was terrified on his own behalf of the curses she had managed to utter, whose vague backwash still stirred within her, and she sweetly said: "But my friend, no, it is not about you," after which she cooled down without another word, fierce and reserved even in the clamor of her final solitude.

The triumphant land, benevolent and thoughtless. Béluse, disoriented by the death of his mistress, carved out a square for himself to raise crops where the forest was winning on the edges of the property. It was almost halfway to the hills and no one was there to keep him from setting himself up. Sweet potatoes, yam plants, manioc: all he could possibly glean to keep body and soul together. As for the rest, they used him during the harvest months or to tend the tobacco fields or pick coffee. He left the house thus and really began to get to know the country. He began then to ponder once again the old hatred. He saw that for the past seven years he had wanted to forget the other man. In the air around him he could once again smell the other's presence. As a slave who provided for his own needs but was still required to respond to every demand, no matter what, he satisfied simultaneously his desire to be somewhere else and the greediness of the supervisors, who no longer had to feed him or his companion or his son. He did not know that this was a situation made possible by the way things had evolved. He thought, perhaps, that he had snatched the right to withdraw into the hut of red clay reinforced with branches. Consequently, with no shame, he could once again imagine the other man trapped up there in the woods. He was discovering the new and triumphant land. But he stopped at the bottom of a ravine, between two banks with their crush of trees hanging over his head, and thought to himself: "You don't feel anything behind," probably meaning by this that he was not feeling this thrust, this gap that used to make you veer off back there in the land beyond the oceans and that used to make you know how puny you were in that land that stretched on forever. He guessed that here he would not be able to walk straight ahead without stopping until he met his death. He was not sucked toward the horizon and he was not unconsciously exhilarated by the broad reach of the land the way he used to be in the country back there. But he was also disturbed by so much diversity around him, such a great number of different landscapes concentrated in such a small space. By nature his love was for open terrain, and he returned with pleasure to the wide-open life of the farms. So in any case he did not object in the least to his son's roaming about.

Anne was always roving the high hills, especially since he had discovered someone to play with there; it was Longoué's second son, slightly older than he. Longoué had insisted on naming this boy himself, deciding that he would be called Liberté. Man-Louise found it natural. The country had changed; there had been the struggle and the advances made by the forest and Béluse had a special status, all of which had made it possible for the two children— both wanderers—to meet each other. It was immediately obvious that there was a mysterious bond between them. They would travel for miles and miles to find each other and as they went along had arranged for spots to meet, hiding places they alone knew about. Liberté Longoué often took his companion to where Man-Louise was making charcoal or tending her vegetables, and she thus became almost a party to their games. But Liberté was too canny to tell his father that he spent his days with Anne; likewise he never went to Béluse's cabin. Every day the two boys would fight fiercely, just barely disguising their instinctive need as a game: Anne would be the French and Liberté the English. They would emerge with cuts and bruises and gasping for breath from these battles that were not pretend in the least and Man-Louise would groan: "Those two! Always one of them has to kill the other!" They grew up outside their respective families and in the field of combat provided by the hills, where from the first instant they were in training for that death-night much much later, among the three ebony trees, that would send them hurtling toward each other. And so it happened that Anne, one evening while returning tools to the workshop on the Senglis plantation, managed to steal a machete and hide it in the woods without telling his friend about it. And when once again a rebellious outbreak caused unrest in the country, when they were maybe sixteen, maybe younger, Anne fought with the colons simply because Liberté had gone off with a band of maroons. They looked for each other, hoping for confrontation, but never found the occasion during the period of unrest. And, since everything calmed down in the end they went back to meet each other in the woods, exchanging recollections of the fighting and challenging each other once again. There was no one, except Man-Louise, who knew about this secret existence they had created for themselves, and it must be said that no one cared about it. They occupied the unclaimed neutral zone all the way to Pointe des Sables, where they fished and kept their realm intact; except on one occasion when they met a young slave girl (they could not say which of them knew her first) whom they invited in. They did not know that she would bring in the unavoidable night already prowling around their domain.

"*Night. Ah, night! Are you afraid at night?*"

Papa Longoué murmured these words, and the silence had been so thick that Mathieu jumped. Then he returned to the present, smiling and unaware that he did so, with a tentative, anxious smile. Yes he was afraid of the night, of going down the path between the steep shadows that were alive. He made an effort not to get up and leave right away but said, "It's not yet six o'clock." He did not want to be a coward in front of the old man. Then: "Who isn't afraid in the night?" He saw every wooden stake, every sharp blade of earth, the wretched cabin, the crazy ferns shrivel and fade and also grow thicker beneath the spreading mantle of gray. Papa Longoué moved the leaves around: "Night doesn't deal in hours, in the night you don't know what is going by. Stars. Look at the stars, does any word exist to tell how they live?" And maybe because he could not walk straight ahead without stopping at the ravine of his death the old man was trying to rise like the wind upon the darkness of the sky: "The fact is one can always keep on going up into the sky even if one is an ant on a wave."

"It's the barrel," said Mathieu. "That's what it is! But look. Your father's grandfather, a maroon in fact. That's the little barrel, if you touch it too hard it falls apart! But look. It has been there your whole life. And you, you held bark over my head in the cabin that first day when . . ."

"Yes," said the *quimboiseur*.

"But how?" said Mathieu. "Ah! I can assume that all this time you have been patching the cask so that by now there must not be a single piece of that wood still there, the wood from Acajou that La Roche had had fit together. But it's your little barrel isn't it, you hang onto it like a treasure without thinking...."

"No," said the *quimboiseur*.

"Of course, you think about it because you two are the only ones, right? Because we don't have enough as it is to brag about in this country where we would not even know how to live without going around in circles like donkeys, on top of it all we have to have a clan of seers in the woods who..."

"Now, now," said the old man.

"And what did he put inside? Because it's not possible, he didn't know about your "leaf of life and death" or those twigs you pour out in front of me. La Roche was no planters' *quimboiseur*, even if he was half mad. You put the leaves in. Fine, that's the hiding place. And what might he have stuffed in it for La-Pointe to open..."

"No," said the old man. "I put the leaves in when my son died, not before. The family used to fix the broken parts but never opened it. That's true."

"They never opened it but they repaired it. See that? Which means, well, that you don't even know what La Roche had shut up in there, because if we have to add them up it was a hundred and seventeen years between the time he threw it down in front of La-Pointe and when you opened it...."

"I don't know," said the old man.

"But I know. And then of course you could recite right off the bat what was in there, because I can tell by looking at your face, it's an absolute sure thing that you know all about it, but I'm a little-kid right? I have to learn to be patient and we have all, everybody, forgotten, everyone except this one family in the forest...."

"No," said the old man.

"Ah! Anyhow. There are a few. They were not all too young to lack respect for their elders nor too old to have any blood left in their bodies, and..."

"You are angry," said the old man. "Luckily you have the eyes. If you did not have the eyes nobody could put up with you. If you did not have the eyes I wouldn't get along with you."

Taken aback, Mathieu Béluse stopped his burst of anger cold, so to speak. He reached out and shyly touched the leaves scattered in front of him. "I'm sorry, Papa, I ask your pardon. I think I've got the shivers, that's why it happened."

"Well then, you've at least come for something—sickness; I'll give you some medicine!"

"But the thing I see is this: when people talk about rebellions. Rebellions! Rebellions are something in books, but for us it's us one red blood risen up in fields that are burning, that's how I see it, the earth bubbling up to fume down upon the plantations, rebellion is too calm a word, and well, I am the one who reads books, I am the one bringing the calm, but I see that today there is no running-wind over the farms, no, it's still prison still death and when one of them is sent away at Bois-Lézard he can always just go they don't capture him any more, not even at Joubaudière way down on the southern tip, and I see that we always say *some other time we'll do it some other time* and say it until *everything calmed down in this country in the end* yes that's our story—a long line of *some-other-times* bound together with dead people and nobody talks nobody speaks out loud of the dead to say nothing of how it is always dusk on the hills nobody, and to go back to the *animal wealth,* animal, you realize he made the first human gesture, which was to go up into the woods, you are certainly rather proud of that. Ah and luckily you said: the crowd of skeletons in the steerage, skeletons ravaged by sickness and vermin, otherwise one might almost have thought that it was a nice easy little voyage. . . ."

"Fine, but the thing you don't see is the calm you have to have to understand. You have to. I'm telling you, Mathieu my son, luckily you have books so you can forget the detail but so you can know what is being forgotten: the smell for example, the night crew, and the ups and downs on the Senglis plantation, everywhere the terrain changing, the trained dogs. All those things are what explain it to you! Because you will never know the price paid for every one of the books you spell out from *a* to *z*.

"You are right, Papa! Even if we went from here all the way to Grand-Rivière you'd still be right the whole way. But look at me, I see that he tells about the market and then behind that the boat and then still further back the house over there and still further back the pen where they were kept and still further back I can guess what was there but I see that he has forgotten the sea. No. Not forgotten. He did not understand the sea, what you can expect at sea, he never even heard Louise if all he did was get up and give her a leaf to eat, he never knew that the land on the horizon at Pointe des Sables is the same as here the suffering is just the same, he disappears deep into the woods and from that moment on we are all caught in a rat trap all of us."

"But why is it you call him La-Pointe? Because his name is Longoué, the same name I have."

Mathieu laughed. It seemed forced. He squatted there on his heels, shivering. He tried to sing, accompanying himself by beating softly and rhythmically on the little barrel (but his voice did not carry far because he was enunciating the words carefully, just for the *quimboiseur*):

A priest had a sword, *gadé sa!* Look at that!
The thimble was of walnut, *ki noyé?* What walnut?
Mr. Supervisor, Mr. Overseer, *couté sa.* What did it cost?
Crowns and louis d'or, *oué oué oué.* Yes yes yes.
Louis d'or and little barrels: *sa pa vré.* That's not true.

"Which means that you listen well and you remember it too!"

"Which means that I don't believe it! The priest with a sword is something that happens in pictures, not in this country! If he meant to baptize them all in a line upon delivery, almost in a ceremony, think about it, really, he would not have come with a sword. And then, because what we know about is supervisors and overseers not to mention accountants, why do you want them called supervisors and overseers in the old days? Managers, hirelings, how would I know? And at that time did they even know what a walnut thimble was, you see, it's impossible. Even your Marie-Nathalie in her cubbyhole with candles burning at noon, so what about poor Man-Louise? And before, in the cabin, you count six hundred, five hundred fifty but just take a look: is it crowns or louis d'or or is it really nothing but barrels of sugar? So?"

"Leave me alone!" the old man said majestically.

"Here's the best one: a coxswain. He can't be an officer. In the home of La Roche, an aristocrat. That was for officers."

"Godsalmighty! Just look at that! This little boy is crazy! I'm not the one who planted a forest of walnut trees, and as far as sugar is concerned I never asked more than half a pound per consultation. So? What's that all about—illustrations? Mr. Mathieu you're being cross, that's not nice!"

The quarrel was the result of an anxiety that intensified with the darkness: Mathieu made it happen on purpose to twist the words into something unpleasant; so it did not take long for the calculated vehemence of this argument to leave both of them disoriented, because the argument could not feed upon itself and got as bogged down as a *gommier* on the beach. Both of them became encrusted in the calm. A damp veil rose from the woods in the bottom lands so slowly that it seemed to be attached to the layer of green. The sorrow of night things penetrated the mind bubbling in excitement without extinguishing the clamor of yesteryear. "The sea," Longoué mumbled, "The sea is today. You are making me go down the river to today and I, I am showing you the river, there."

"Yes, straddling a barrel," said Mathieu. Then he was ashamed of himself and bowed his head. But Longoué was already far away reliving the celebration so often described to him by Stéfanise: the men all stirred up and threatening the plain, the big one-armed man who brandished in his only hand that supreme guarantor of bravery that a machete represented at that time ("the place I took it from—not many people would have gone in there!"), the child almost tossed from arm to arm, Longoué shouting: "Because they have proclaimed Liberty-Equality-Fraternity then I proclaim Liberty-Equality-Paternity! Everybody here listen: his name is Liberté," and all of them answering in a great volley rolling out into the darkness to the farthest branches: "Yes, Monsieur-la-Pointe," and the rising wind drawing the smoke from the torches, gourds of rum one after the other, squares of roasted breadfruit, Man-Louise seated motionless and serious in front of the cabin. "Why?" thought Mathieu. "All these questions not to find the answer, there will never be a *because*; the reality is that I know nothing and then more nothing. The rest is kept in the depths of the forest!" And just then he felt the wind, a trickle of water against his ankles, beginning to come up again: it was six o'clock. The sun tipped over behind the tops of the trees: the fiery red turned black all at once. The darkness had surprised Mathieu, he had to go down the hillside with his fear in his breast like a rock. There would not be a single bay of light to shine through the curtain of ferns. He would have to go down worse than a mule would until he reached the zone of the plains where some leftover day would stagnate until seven o'clock. Here he would take a breath and go back to his usual pace, without daring to cast a glance behind him toward the darkness of the heights. Questions, what questions? "It's this wind," said Papa Longoué, calm and invisible. "It's all this wind endless as the sea."

Roche Carrée

Chapter 6

BECAUSE IT WAS SOON APPARENT that he was not just like every other boy: he was quiet, he was not always waving his arms around everywhere. He would go off by himself or he would follow Man-Louise, but at a distance, not wanting to go along with her outright. She was cunning and pretended not to notice anything; she too was calm and thought: "I spent too much time with my eyes open in the dark while I was expecting him, he is tranquil as night and like night he cannot be understood." And when she thought he had lost track of her, she would stop, pretending to pick herbs or to take a rest alongside the path, groaning rather loudly: "Ah! Godsalmighty! How tired I am!" until she felt again his indefinable presence behind her. She would have been astonished to hear him admit that he was not fooled; that he knew she was waiting for him like that—he followed her because it was fun for him. And so, one leading the other, she initiated him to the first twisting paths into the depths of the woods, teaching him about the hidden trails beneath the roots of the mangrove trees, the patches of sky one could use to orient oneself among the cannas or the gum trees. Very soon he went down toward the sea and explored the Edge-of-this-land (secretly earning his name, Ti-Lapointe). There he turned naturally toward new realms, disregarding the sands both white and black, the dunes flattened so quickly by the wind, the slow freshwater channels glazed over in the heat; what drew him was the muddy mangrove swamp where he caught crabs and soaked in the nauseating smell. Life, the thing called life that everyone sees as the root's driving force, had left the Edge-of-this-land and penetrated the upland forest. Béluse himself, in obedience to this force, had advanced halfway to the outcropping in the stand of acacias, though he never went to look at the sea or stood peacefully by the waves. Every day the Edge-of-this-land faded more and more until it no longer even seemed to be a new land. The vegetation was cleared away, paths and mule trails popped up everywhere twisting along the edges of the sand; the ill manners of the coast took on the grubbiness of the people. Rows of sea-grapes appeared around the countryside as well as rough clumps of manchineels; or at least they became noticeable for the first time as if they had been planted in an orderly fashion to mark some limit. The child did not like the beaches lined with coconut trees or the paths of hot sand; he liked the purulent seething of the mangrove swamps. He went there all alone to look perhaps for the same mysterious proliferation of life that gave him strength in the forest. A hunter, he had no intention of sharing anything he ever caught, and he used to light fires in secret spots that only he knew about, where he would roast the birds he had bagged. If by chance he found it necessary to offer them what he had killed (surprised before he could hide it), he preferred just to give it all to them, and then he would stand there motionless watching Man-Louise and Liberté suck on little burned bones; Longoué said: "You don't get very many, but why do you go hunting if you don't like to eat them?"

He did not want to admit that he did not like sharing his bag any more than he liked to have company on his treks. But he was not selfish; and he took very good care of Liberté up until the day that the latter, aware perhaps that his brother was solitary by nature, also began to wander about and met up with Anne.

This life, this seething, this proliferation were powerful feed, fattening him up so that, in fact, he became stouter as he grew taller, broader and broader, solid, robust, impervious. Longoué, his father, was the only one able to approach him; but when this happened his child's face became empty of any sort of life as if he had to be cast outside himself and forget his own existence to listen to his father. He took things in, passively, neutrally, so that you could not say he was unhappy to be there, but then he also never made the slightest gesture or spoke the least word of acquiescence. Longoué seemed to think this sort of behavior was normal, and he enjoyed the resulting monologues (in which he talked a great deal and the boy was silent) that established, or so he thought, his paternal authority. Consequently, he never became aware that he could conceal nothing from the child who gradually became the depository of his knowledge, the confidant of his life and almost the judge of his actions. Right in the middle of one of his tirades the father would stop, for example, and without looking at the son, but peeking at him from the corner of his eye, he would ask: "So what do you think about that?" and though the child never answered or even stirred in the least, the adult concluded: "Right, right, you are right. That wasn't a good thing to do."

Because the earth had folded back upon itself and left the coast with no soul; leaving a degenerate space in which people struggled to endure between the coast and the uplands where it fertilized and multiplied its prodigious reach; and this is how the sector in which he—the boy—could play gradually took shape. The maroons were tranquil in their hiding place: they were only being hunted in principle now, so the planters would not lose their touch, to maintain a public law that, really, none of the planters cared about at all personally. That Anne and Liberté could become thick as thieves hinged upon that fact; because it was impossible to say whether it was because he was by nature kind and straightforward that Anne did not inform the supervisors of the movements of little Liberté, or if he did not do this because he knew or felt how futile it would have been to do so. In any case, the idea never came to him even during the bitterest of their quarrels. The maroons breathed easy during this period, they had almost ceased to be a dreadful exception, becoming a sort of tacitly agreed-to small population. Of course the fear they inspired not only among the masters but also among the slaves and freedmen, and especially among the mulattos—a fear that the masters cultivated—did not diminish. It was customary to threaten children that the maroons would be called to come and carry them off. Because for the people the maroon was the personification of the devil: the one who refuses. Perhaps when one of them was caught he was made to pay more than in the past for the insolent and incongruous fact of his existence; but this happened less and less frequently and the number of one-armed men dwindled.

It was also because there were more pressing concerns now for the planters, the main one being that the plantations now had to band together and combine their resources. Planters who were improvident or lazy let their properties be absorbed by other, more dynamic ventures. It is true that being obliged to do this was tempered by the fortunate system of marriages that made it possible to extend estates without reducing to famine or dishonor those who thus lost sovereignty over their lands; they became sons-in-law and proxies. A real caste system was established, weighed down by the authority of a patriarch. La Roche was the most powerful of these men heading dynasties.

After the death of Marie-Nathalie, whom he mourned in secret (Senglis and he met day after day for almost a month, trying to torment each other and bring themselves to the verge of despair by endlessly evoking the graces of the deceased), he was passionately set upon extending Acajou even further. He broke off relations with Senglis for good, referring to him only as "the humpbacked turnip," and systematically went to work on his project without a thought for anyone else. It was thus that five years later he married an heiress and had a child a year by her (something everybody marveled over given his age, contributing to the widespread legend that he was indestructible) but otherwise paid no attention to her. An absolute and maniacal Patriarch, the old bastard—that was what they got in the habit of calling him—went back and forth endlessly over his properties, his dreadful iron hand forcing wills to bend. Expressionless, impassive, he had no need to shout; high on his horse, whose trot and gallop could be told from every other trot and gallop everywhere, he would stare thoughtfully at those who had incurred his anger. A gaze that made them all, sons, employees, slaves and freedmen, shiver. He soon was able to calculate new profits because he had three sons and four daughters who were "of age," which allowed him to make productive contracts through the intelligent use of marriages. In the end the old bastard ruled as the despot of the largest concentration of lands in the country. But, fearful of having the unpredictable woman on horseback appear at every turn-off wreaking havoc on the branches with her whip, he never for an instant stopped his frenetic activity. Less and less did he accept that Nathalie was dead, announcing that she "was going to die." This mad notion exacerbated his energy.

The other thing that worried the planters was that the English, landing periodically in one spot or another, disputed the right of the French to exploit the lands. But in these clashes they displayed remarkable energy, determination, and heroism, thanks to which they saved their possessions; their conduct, which was dependent upon the troops of Negroes they had at their disposal, won them in addition a reputation for indomitable patriotism. La Roche volunteered his sons for the battle and saw them come back every time, safe and sound, haloed in newfound celebrity but more fearful than ever of his fixed stare.

The result was that the maroons were left to their forest and the child was able to grow up there in peace, extending his solitude, going deep into the woods and ensconcing himself there. This is how he prepared himself for his future position. At first he was not bothered by the relations between Anne and Liberté. He was delighted not to have the responsibility for his brother; now he could take off without a care to roam through the mangrove swamps or try to climb the huge kapok trees. In the beginning he would also follow the two friends, but having learned from experience with Man-Louise and probably now more skillful at camouflaging himself in the woods, he was careful not to be spotted. He took an interest in their terrifying battles, betting with himself as to which one had the best chance of winning and then being amused at how appalled Man-Louise looked. He was as aware as she was of the secret existence led by the pair of rascals but never showed it.

He was the first one to find the girl. Hidden in a mahogany tree that he preferred to the other forest giants because its branches stretched across the trail leading down to Acajou, and because he could see from there a large portion of the plain (the cornfields, the stretches of tobacco, the ripple of closely planted young cane between the red paths), he saw her come up from the far side of Acajou one day and disappear beneath the cocoa trees lining the property. He knew she was the daughter of a slave couple who had set themselves up on this slope the way Béluse had done on the other side. La Roche put up with this new situation although in general he kept his slaves in the immediate vicinity, close to his equipment and workshops; perhaps the man and his wife owed this indulgence to the fact that they had come on the same boat as La-Pointe: and we shall see that the old bastard retained a sort of affection for his maroon from the very beginning. It was strange how the son of a maroon who was risking his life in every instant (even though it was apparent that the hunt had slowed) and the daughter of slaves who worked at rolling tobacco—when they weren't having to bundle sheaves of cane—were able to rub elbows and speak and live together if they wanted to. From now on he posted himself on his branch to watch the girl, not because he was personally interested in her—because she was much younger than he or at least seemed to be—but because of the curiosity everything from down there aroused in him at the time. A curiosity mixed with defiance and an unconscious feeling of pride. Another day he discovered Anne and Liberté following the girl and pushing each other forward. She saw what they were up to and simply waited for them. He saw all three of them, solemn and self-contained, walk down the path and vanish. For a few weeks he amused himself by watching them: by turns reserved, laughing, or all wound up. Then he got tired of this community and from then on stopped following his brother. It was quite a while later that he became worried, when it was apparent that Anne and Liberté would fight for keeps with the girl as the stakes in the battle between them.

In this manner he grew up, acquiring a reputation for knowledge because of his size and his silence and even more a reputation for "power." Longoué could not acknowledge as he aged that his son might surpass him in the realms of mystery and the unknown. He insisted that the boy should take a wife and work a bit of land in the forest. But the other shook his head without saying a word and went right on with his ramblings. He had armed himself with a *boutou*, a solid stick that he had carved into a cudgel, and an old bag made of coarse canvas that he hooked into the stick. The bag and the *boutou* were already legendary. Nobody knew what he hid in the bag, but there were some who lived in the forest who whispered that it was the soul of a dead man who was obliged to serve him as long as the bag was hanging from the *boutou* and that the *boutou* was ready to drive off those who tried to open the bag. In other words, forever. Women did not seem to interest this young man, nor did *tafia*. Huge and peaceful as he was, one night in the utter darkness under the branches in front of the hut he suddenly said (this young man who never opened his mouth): "Man-Louise, from now on I am no longer Ti-Lapointe. My name is Longoué, Melchior Longoué." Then he went inside to lie down on the plank that served as his pallet.

"Did you see that?" Longoué asked.

And, after a long silence, Man-Louise replied: "It's because I looked into the night."

Because he was perhaps waiting for the old people's departure though he did not wish it. He loved Man-Louise wildly, but adoration more than decency kept him from ever demonstrating this emotion. He respected Longoué, but it was a respect qualified by condescension, because he saw Longoué as having much too much vigor, passion, thoughtlessness in short, for the "knowledge" that he had to take on. The heir to his father's secrets and already almost a grown man himself, he remained inside the hut. As Man-Louise and Longoué grew older Liberté took care of most of the shared labor. He understood Melchior's character and often said: "Leave him alone." Longoué laughed scornfully as if out of defiance. He figured that his first son was trying to surpass him and this made him furious: "I am his father!" But he was unable to keep from showing some pride in the fact. At every "consultation" he would hold in the cabin he whispered to the visitor: "Ah, if only Melchior was here, he would tell you that right away," and he whispered it with an air of saying that Melchior was very good at it but in the end he could not claim to be the equal of his father, and that if you really thought about it the slowness of old age was more valuable than the hasty aplomb of youth. Melchior however refused to see anyone at all, and the result was that all the people living around there yearned to consult him. Perhaps he was waiting for the day when he would be alone and would give what he was capable of giving; he would have killed himself, of course, to save Man-Louise or Longoué, but to exercise his power he had to be alone and the master. Consequently, the news that Béluse was dead seemed to him the first signal.

Longoué had kept Melchior informed about the whole story. Unaware of who Liberté was associating with, the old man sometimes would ask in passing: "Have you heard anything about that son of slavery?" Man-Louise hastened to reply: "Yes, yes. He is on the last bit of land on the Senglis property."

"Ah ah!" Longoué would say, satisfied. Liberté never talked to Anne about what had set Béluse against Longoué. By tacit agreement the two sons kept this quarrel and this hatred wrapped in obscurity, as if they were afraid of starting them all over again on their own account. They did not see that in tearing each other apart the way they did they were, in fact, heirs to that hatred. Each of them had been responsible for their respective families for a long time. But mature as they already were, they still continued looking for each other in the forest like children and meeting the girl. Neither ever went without the other to meet her, pressing her to choose between them, improvising wild speeches about their qualities, their worth, the work they were able to do, the treasures they had amassed. The girl would turn to one, "Monsieur Liberté," then to the other, "Monsieur Anne," giggling and swaying on her legs, until all three would burst out laughing and set off on an endless race through the woods. Anne, who acquired other machetes (and who possessed a hoe and a sickle) forgot the one he had hidden among the three ebony trees. Time went by and they did not abandon their habits or these childhood games.

And Melchior, who knew the whole story, interpreted the death of Béluse as a sign. First he knew that Longoué was obsessed with the desire to outlive his enemy; then it seemed to him that a whole epoch was vanishing with this Béluse whom he had never seen. It was Liberté who told them the news in that careless way he put on to say anything that meant a lot to him. Because this death made Liberté sad for Anne's sake; but he was also thinking that his rival would now have a cabin of his own. All Longoué said was, "He stayed alive until now, until now. I thought he would never die." Then he walked to the far end of the hill, the spot from which you could see down on the Senglis plantation in the distance and the Béluse cabin there below, which you could tell was there because of a patch of reddish earth between the leaves of the trees, almost within easy reach. And he blew into a conch shell, three times: the breeze carried the deep, clear, and raucous sound, making it echo across the hills, consecrating the death to the earth sparkling with heat; then he went back to his hut. And none of them knew (not Longoué himself or Man-Louise or his two sons) that he soon would be eighty years old. He sat down in front of the cabin and the others surrounded him in silence. "I did not want to kill him," he said. This hatred was almost peaceful and it spread its buds calmly in the daylight. Melchior thought: "Now it is really all over." A purple flower spun between his fingers.

And from that moment on there was no question of his doing anything other than what he was going to do. Lying tranquilly inscribed in his future death, Longoué no longer left the hut; but the idea of death was not an obstruction. Life went on in its monotonous way, each of them busy with their own work. They walked past the old master without seeing him, without seeing him the way he was, they would joke with him quickly; they had no time to think about death, they did not think about it. And yet the day came when Longoué made a gesture, a single gesture with his hand as if he were calling them; instantly they were all there around him as if they had been on the lookout behind the door, as if all they had done for ever so long was watch for this day, this moment, this gesture. Man-Louise stood a little to the side, Liberté at the foot of the pallet, only Melchior went up to Longoué. "Behind my head," the dying man said. "It's burning behind my head! Listen closely to what I am saying: La Roche, that's a man. Ah! Yes, that is a man." He clasped the sculpted piece of bark tightly against himself; his left hand groped along the ground toward the little barrel. He hiccuped softly. Melchior turned toward the two others to tell them that it was over. Then he squatted on his heels close to the old master of night now returned to the night. After a long time he stood up again; Liberté was standing in the same place; Man-Louise had gone out. He saw her seated in the clearing in front of the cabin at the spot where she always sat. He went to tell her to be brave. In her hand she clutched an old black knife so worn out that its blade was like an iron thread, more a spike than a blade. With her back against the big mango tree her staring eyes searched the land in front of her and the space over the land. He did not have to go any closer to know that she had followed Longoué without delay; she was going down the hill that no one ever climbs up again because she was unable to wait even a single day to rejoin him on the path; perhaps because she had feared becoming lost in these new woods, perhaps because Longoué bore within him a light that she treasured and that would light the road for her. It was clear that for the past few days she had been watching for this moment and that when the moment had come she did not deign to put up any defense. Melchior and Liberté did not weep, they did not moan. They simply sent the news around to their neighbors and dug a grave near the house for these two whom nothing had separated, neither the old anger nor the quiet, less turbulent days.

Melchior, calm and massive, took over for the stubborn old man who had therefore been his master more than his father. What else could he do? It was his nature and his destiny. People flocked to him, soon not just the hill people but people from the plantations. His power was so great that even in the cultivated lands it gained ground, as if all by himself he was a powerful forest laying siege to the fields. So the plantation people would climb up, fearfully or stealthily, bringing their problems, their illnesses, their miseries. Calm and impenetrable, he willingly saw them; he would hold the piece of bark over their heads and say, "I was waiting for you, you have come." He healed wounds and assuaged fevers. He was a good man with all the power of goodness that has been strengthened in solitude. When he grew alarmed about Anne and Liberté, he insisted that Liberté drop the role he was playing with Anne and the girl. He even offered, though reluctantly, to have his brother come along and help him. "Maybe so I'll carry your bag?" Liberté said with a childlike smile.

"You are just like him," Melchior told him. "Your foot is faster than your head." Liberté knew perfectly well that "him" meant Longoué. Both of them now were older, men in the prime of life, but they still talked to each other the way they did when they were children roaming through the woods. Liberté kept on living in the cabin. He raised vegetables, he hunted and he cooked for the two of them; but because the carefree, light-hearted way in which he did all this took the place of dignity for him, and no one could say that he was waiting on his brother. He agreed to be there and to take care of the everyday work. Melchior knew that this was because of the girl who had still, probably because she was somewhat simpleminded, not chosen between Anne and Liberté. The latter complied with his destiny, both accepting and tempting it. Just as Melchior accepted and tamed his.

Otherwise what would he have done? Because he had left the Edge-of-this-land, after having certainly learned from the mangrove swamps and the shore everything he expected to get there, because he had melted into the vast wave of the forest, because the sparse lands, the real and suffering existence, the half-dead Negroes came to him. Can we not say that he had taken root, that he was the first of his line? Better than the father to whom the peacefulness of the woods brought so much torment in the early days? Better than Man-Louise, who had spent her life guessing things but had never known anything with certainty? He had gotten rid of old Longoué's restlessness (not merely the hatred but also the passion for fighting, the liking to be on the move, the childish obsession with being the strongest); for a long time he had paid attention to the woods in all their depth, he had taken and strengthened the name of the Longoués. ("Because if you ask this question, Mister Mathieu, it is because you think he found himself with several paths to choose from. But that is not true. And I know that for you a quimboiseur is madness and stupidity. But that is not true. We don't know everything but we know something.") And he did know something, this man, patient and slow in the endless heat; so, fine, it was not knowledge, we were so ignorant, ignorant of ourselves which is the worst thing, but for him what was ignorant was the refusal not to know, which is already like a great knowledge; and therefore it is not about him that we should ask: *Why was he a quimboiseur in the woods?* Because while the father made the path the son did not just follow it; he stopped, he took enough time to stop and look in both directions, he had gone into the darkness and experienced there the song of the silent tree trunks: the song you hear when you stand motionless for a long time, until you have done it so long that you feel hairy roots growing down from your feet, planting you in the earth where you are altogether new and unpurposeful and tranquil, unknowing.

Chapter 7

BECAUSE HERE WAS A MAN who suffered, on the contrary, from something he did not possess; and bearing the name of a constable of France could not have given it to him. All his childhood he had endured the same old stories about "Manzel'Nathalie" (of course without knowing that Béluse picked up the expression from Senglis: "Mademoiselle Her-Ladyship-My-Wife"), so often that she had become for him a ghost, a white zombie wandering through tallow hallways and dragging behind her the corpse that was Béluse who went chattering on and on. The child was certainly more haunted by the never-ending evocation than afraid of the ghost. He was high-strung and violent, fighting with everything, a river rock, a dog, a child his age. So he was fascinated by the ease, the mockingly casual air, and the smile that never left Liberté's face even when he fought the hardest, finding there some complement or antidote to his own unaffected violence. And what were the things he noticed during his childhood? Béluse doing his job, never frowning, who apparently turned his physical and moral energies and his luck every day to getting through a superhuman labor (whether for himself or in the fields he worked for Senglis), as if trying to make up for those days he had spent in the upper house. The woman who seemed always curled up next to something, something not Béluse—often absent—but the notion of the presence of Béluse. Rising before dawn and going to bed after nightfall, but looking always as if she were curled up on some invisible support, like a liana grown too long. Targin, the supervisor who would turn up from time to time in front of the cabin and invariably shout from his horse's back: "So then, you think you are free because you live out here?" and then add: "Tomorrow morning you will come to the field where the big mombin tree stands." Or: "Make sure you're there at the manioc plantation!" And even more: the lightning flashing through him, the way his heart leapt into his throat every time he saw Béluse suddenly stop what he was doing and lift his head toward the hills! And as long as Béluse stayed there like that, looking up and lost in thought, his child's heart would beat like a drum; he was surprised that no one heard it. He was in torment: sometimes he had attacks that threw him foaming onto the ground, attacks prompted by his constant hunger and the weakening of his body that he abused, attacks that often ended in lengthy fainting spells. Throughout his childhood he suffered from illnesses that took all the longer to cure because no one knew any remedies for them. Until he was fifteen he lived, so to speak, in the company of worms that exited his body through every orifice. It took all that time for the decoctions he was made to drink to work; for a long time he could not get rid of the bitter taste of the thick grasses. But his edgy nerves served him well, allowing him to toughen up his body and resist consumption. With a poultice of leaves always covering some purulent wound on his leg, either on his ankles or his calves or his knees, he survived and he thrived. For him Liberté's ease (his ability to come out of the woods unscathed, never getting hurt, smiling about everything, and his agility even carrying a bag of charcoal) was a substitute for remedies or an additive to those remedies. He was always trying to make up for what he lacked in grace by making extra noise and being extra violent. Though his consciousness of the taboo weighing on the two groups (the Béluse and Longoué families, or rather the Béluse and La-Pointe families) meant he would not talk about Béluse with Liberté, he actually did not do so because he was not the least interested in Béluse, whose authority carried little weight with him. Anne's professed opinion about this (tinged with barely concealed scorn) only changed after Béluse learned of his participation in the group formed by the planters during the previous uprisings. The day that came out he got a dreadful thrashing, and then (although he was already lying there bleeding on the ground) a hiding with thorny branches, which left him half-dead for several days. It was no use his screaming that he only did it as a game—just to do the opposite of what his friend did (not daring to name this friend because he had an intuition that Béluse would be all the angrier and kill him outright); he only met with the somber eyes and fierce energy of this man whom he had considered up to now as a slave with no life or value. His opinion, therefore, changed in that moment, and in the end the almost lethal punishment did him some good. "Do you know," he later told Liberté, "the finest fighting I did at the time was to keep from dying beneath the feet of Béluse!" And he whistled out of pride in Béluse and in himself too. But the problem was still there: old men wanted to be fathers ("I'm his father") when the young were not feeling at all like sons. In Liberté, this sort of clash was tempered by his naturally gentle tendencies as well as by his ability always to be somewhere else, but in Anne it was the cause of crises that brewed for a long time. Liberté sincerely admired his fierceness, it was constantly on the alert, just looking for occasions. "It's a volcano," he said laughing. "You can't keep the volcano from smoking." He never held a grudge against his friend for the blow-ups he provoked, and consequently the hatred between them was limited to games and competition.

This explains both why the two of them were crazy about the same wild, unpredictable little girl who ran free in the countryside between Acajou and the Morne aux Acacias, and also the way they kept up this act for so long, apparently enjoying their joint courtship of this young girl who was too simpleminded or perhaps simply numbed, gradually worn down by jobs she had to do. And he made a timid attempt to get somewhere with her, but the girl very sweetly said to him, "Monsieur Anne!" and looked away, which kept him from going any farther. Suddenly he began to imitate Béluse, working relentlessly; lately he had by himself provided all three of them with their means of survival. And when Béluse died (very quickly, without any fuss, courageously as he had lived), Anne ended up in charge of the cabin along with the old woman (his mother) who overnight twined herself around her new support. Then he could no longer contain his impatience and violence—because Béluse had had a restraining effect on him, though Anne never guessed it—and he decided to run off with the girl. It took him some time to reach this decision, and meanwhile his relations with Liberté grew worse and worse; this was when Melchior became worried. Finally one day Anne went through the forest and waited for the girl and told her straight out where things stood. That he was happy with her, that he could work as well as anybody, that he had any number of perfectly new tools, that Man-Béluse cost nothing to feed, that he was sturdy and easily ran four hours at a stretch, that all she had to do was stop shifting back and forth from one foot to the other, that he got up at night because she was too much on his mind, that his work slowed down as a result (which was a complete and utter lie), that she would be happy as a fine lady (which was impossible), and that he would hunt the wild goats so they could have meat. Such a concrete plan appealed to the girl's imagination: at least one would have to conclude that this was so, because for once she did not just stand there like a bump on a log but hung her head demurely—instead of turning away. For her this was a sign of intense excitement. Anne was amazed. And when he took her by the hand and she followed him obediently he was upset. "Ah!" he thought furiously. "If it were Liberté she would have followed him the same way!"

Because he was suffering from something he did not possess; and perhaps he thought that running away with the girl was going to get this thing for him. From that day on, consequently, the fight was inevitable. When Liberté learned what had happened he began by smiling; then, light-hearted as ever, he left: Melchior watched him go, knowing already what was happening but making no attempt to thwart it. Because Melchior's strength and courage lay entirely in his calm. Liberté did not go to the Béluse cabin right away; for several days he lived in the woods silently reflecting. Perhaps unable to love or suffer, he made a pact with himself to go and ask for explanations, not concerning the fact (that Anne was living with that woman, the girl) but about the understanding they had had among the three of them that now was broken. And in reality he was not suffering, he was neither unhappy nor offended; he considered the way it had been done as a grave breach of faith, and it was this that he reproached. But he found the cabin abandoned, which disturbed him more than anything else! Obviously, Anne had gone off into the upland woods, a maroon. Moreover, he had no other choice. The girl belonged to La Roche; she was not free to dispose of herself. Anne belonged to Senglis. The special status given their two families (if one could call them families) that had allowed the girl to drift about as she grew up without having some man foisted off on her would not go so far as to authorize such a couple. As for getting La Roche and Senglis to agree, they had better not count on it, considering the complete absence of any relations between the two planters. Senglis would not give an answer and La Roche would have the guilty party locked up. And so, thought Liberté, the son of slavery had gone off into the woods as a maroon. "Longoué must not be happy," he went on to himself; it seemed to him that it was his fault. Because of this rather vague feeling he vowed to find Anne and settle the business; but he was in no hurry. Therefore he returned to Melchior. He waited.

Without knowing that Anne Béluse had essentially not benefited from his daring. Because Anne was suffering from an imbalance that the woman could not combat. He became a maroon in the woods but did not share in the maroon's vocation, which is to be permanently opposed to everything down below, the plain and the people enslaved to it, and thus to find the strength to survive. He did not have this strength, nor did he have patience. He was annoyed at how thick the trees were, and when he set off into the plain on one of the dangerous excursions he was forced to make— his new state having deprived him of any immediate resources— he regretted that the treeless spaces were so bright. Anne was a maroon by accident. He did not hold it against his companion, and besides she could never be aware of it. But one could predict that he would not live in the hills forever and that he would go back to the place his father had lived: which, in fact, is what he did when La Roche died. When that time came he set himself up permanently on the thin strip of land that later would be called Roche Carrée, Square Rock (perhaps because of the shape of the nearby hill, perhaps because La Roche had pushed the checkerboard squares of his fields all the way to the edge of that hill) and then was taken back to work on the Senglis plantation by the humpback's son. His attempts at the life of a maroon never were and never became the result of any obligation, any irresistible urge or passion involving his entire body; rather it remained the result of a fit of temper and, you might say, a desire for a woman. And he returned to work on the Senglis property (what else could he do?) as a farm worker, a day laborer; not a slave. But it amounted to the same thing; the only difference being that after slavery had been abolished he would raise his head in the direction in which he thought Melchior was living and no longer was there a flash of lightning bursting in his breast, nor did dread weigh down his heart.

Though there was cleared land in front of the cabin at Roche Carrée and one could tend—more than cultivate—a few vegetables around it and feed a rooster and two hens (and though it was impossible to grasp it, to see it as an object, something whole and complete in this aura of impoverished existence where each separate object was blotted out in the dull, daily mud), it was also, one had to admit, very much part of the woods, lying shrouded in the fringe of the forest that thrust its way up the Morne aux Acacias from that point on. Thus, like Anne, who was divided between two torments, Roche Carrée was simultaneously the servant of the plain and the sister of the forest; it balanced there on the unclear boundary between two worlds. So Anne would come to love the peaceful contradiction that the cabin kept alive, but he had not yet reached this point. He was exiled in the woods, and for the time being all he was cultivating was his tantrums. Not only was a fight inevitable, but it was also inevitable that violence would kill grace. The one who laughed at everything, who had stored up inside himself enough steam, enough water caught in mid-air, enough rising wind to keep himself far away from old Longoué's stubbornness, was not prepared to make the decisive act; he would know how to fight but he would not know how to kill. He would know how to take the blow but, in spite of being the more agile, he would not find within himself the fire that was required to strike the same deadly blow. And thus, once one granted that fighting was inevitable, one had to accept that violence would kill grace. That is why Anne, hurled by his entire childhood toward the three ebony trees, killed Liberté with a single blow.

They began by watching each other closely in the morning (almost a year after what could only be called the abduction of the girl), both of them thinking as they awoke that day: "OK. It has gone on too long," and moving through the woods closer and closer to each other. All night long it had rained and the rain kept on, damming up and provoking their common resolve. An endless warm cascade that wove a second forest into the forest. Raindrops coiled like real lianas around the lianas. There was nothing to do in such a deluge; this chance occurrence decided the day and hour for them. As existence came to a halt because of the rain, Anne found he was impatient and jealous because he thought that Liberté would also have been able to carry off the object of their common desire. They did not spy on each other out of meanness or secretiveness, and certainly not to put off the fight, rather they did it to play their childhood game all over again, following trajectories that on that day the hurricane made newly tempting. Beneath the thickest of roots, gnarled and knotted above ground into tunnels and caves, the damp humus was steaming, a blue steam that slipped through the interlacings and rose through the tumble of water; like charcoal kilns when they burn out. The violet glow of young tree trunks, the red of fleshy flowers standing up to the rain, wild and erect in the gale, and sometimes, miraculously spared beneath the branches, a tremulous puddle like a small island in the raving din of all that water. Around midday the two men moved closer and closer, each intent on jumping out to surprise the other; Liberté won the gamble because all of a sudden he stood there right in front of Anne. Anne, preparing to maneuver to turn his adversary around, had thought him far behind. Even then they did not spend much time insulting each other because they were tired of having waited so long; what grave insults suitable for such a solemn occasion could they have found, considering how well they knew each other and the great delight with which they had been exchanging insults for the past twenty years? Contrary to established custom, they fought each other without a word. Liberté never took his exasperating smile off his face, and moreover the rain was on his side: soaking into the large tree trunks, the whipping branches, the sturdy vines, it gave them a sort of viscosity that was to his benefit. Agility goes well with rain. His superiority, therefore, was established, but the blows given or taken, the gasps for breath, the twisted arms and cracked ribs hardly counted in a fight where there had to be a survivor. Anne, far more enraged over how long the fight was taking than over the superiority demonstrated by Liberté, suddenly broke away and without a thought rushed toward the three ebony trees arranged in a triangle as if put there by some meticulous hand that also cleared a space among them from which other species were banned; he took refuge beneath their cover. Or at least Liberté thought that Anne was taking refuge at that spot because the insane rain was turned into a mere tornado there and you could keep your eyes open in it. Anne spun like a madman, he was a caged mongoose, inside the space surrounded by three ebony trees; he churned up the thick moss on the ground, the carpet of delicate grasses, the nettled, brambled shoals that kept the clearing a spotless pool in the midst of the surrounding disorder. But he found the machete right away, he gripped its green, moldy handle, he swung the rusty, nicked blade that had lost its edge years ago. Liberté ran at him; he had no time to stop. He gave a mighty shout, a colossal sound, a boundless *"oué"* yes resounding echoes through all the rain and out beyond: to show his approval of such a simple trick, his astonishment that he had not predicted it, his satisfaction with such a beautiful stroke of the machete. The filthy blade ripped into his left shoulder, tore through the flesh almost to his heart. The smile never left his face, the wild and joyful song was still resounding beneath the trees. Shuddering, Anne listened to it go on and on into the distance into the burst of rain giving birth to darkness, while he watched the red stain spilling over at his feet. "Serves you right," he said. "Serves you right." It seemed to him that the friendly dead man there wanted to congratulate him but that the rain put up a fog splattered into drops of water and gusts of wind between them.

He had not reached the dark heart of his anger but, torn between sorrow and pride, he had been able to focus—at least for a few years—on a single act (one that was, moreover, irreparable, that no one could erase or mend) and so could give his torment a precise image: a smile, a shout, a trickle of red water snaking through the rainwater. Because inside him he had something far more than regret over having fought alongside the planters, far more than obsession with the ghost of an old woman—Manzel'Nathalie was an old woman for him—descending suddenly in broad daylight upon him. ("Yes, Mister Mathieu, Veritable-Constable that you are! Because you think people in this country have been waiting for you to sound their suffering and their anger. I can hear you saying to yourself: 'They didn't know, they didn't know!' And what are you and what am I? Even if the hatred went away with Béluse and Longoué, how can you guess the violence that Anne bore in his own breast? And when you say: 'The past,' how can you know if there even is a past when you cannot see the irrational violence, violence without a cause, planted in his heart like a damned-fig? Because the past is not in things you know with certainty, it is also in everything passing like the wind and impossible for anyone to stop in his closed hands. Because they didn't wait for you to come before trying to uproot the damned-fig; and if they wanted to point the spot out to you, how would they have marked where it grew? Who would have given them whitewash to mark it? So then you say: 'They have forgotten!' But it was not something they knew before you came, they knew it long before Béluse and long before Longoué. The boat they were shipped in was not the first boat. Because when, right at the start, Longoué ran off to become a maroon, one might say this happened because he made no effort to know the low country, he just suddenly entered the past that stood there beside him; that is why I call him the first. In one evening he recaptured the years that had piled up ever since the day people were unloaded off Pointe des Sables; and he became the first. That is why the boat is the boat they were delivered in. But the others were there; before him they had borne it. Huge numbers of them were unloaded as replacements for the exterminated people; but also there were those who had been exterminated themselves who could not have imagined anyone would be brought to replace them. How could he have made Béluse into a Longoué if Béluse did not hear the past calling over the hills right from the beginning? This was because Béluse was destined for other work and there's no use protesting, Mathieu Béluse! my ignorant great-grandfather guessed perhaps what the work was. Because if blood came only in the second generation it is because Longoué wanted it that way. He is the one who united the maroons; he burned the cabin at Roche Carrée after having pinned Béluse down on the cabin floor. Who prevented him? Why do anger and violence take roundabout routes to reach this first generation? Did they not think that it was first necessary to get to know the country, down there as well as up in the hills? Longoué said: 'His son is the son of slavery.' But that son was the one who would plant the machete, driving it home in an attempt to uproot something without knowing that its root was within himself. Because the reason that he lacked this thing, the reason he did not possess it was that he had not felt it; but it was inside him. And you can see that knowledge doesn't give this thing to you because there you are shivering feverishly without even having thought to bring a machete. Because the past is not like a palm kernel, all straight and smooth with a tuft on the end, no, it begins with the first root and keeps on going, budding and budding endlessly into the clouds.") And the past was there flowing through the plain just as much as it was exploding on the hills. A natural division because the plain was here and the hills were there, but not a division that had enough time to harden and set! Like a burning land emerging suddenly from the water and rapidly cooling once and for all! It was to reduce this division to ashes and sprinkle it everywhere right away. To do this there was Anne, the murderer, who did not know what ran beating through his blood. To do this there was Melchior, sturdy and robust. Rising above repulsion and scorn to do this work down below that was yet to be learned. Melchior who had rid himself of childishness, tantrums, and noise. A stout man who walked slowly. He understood that the noise was to stifle irrational violence. He was looking for the reason. Or perhaps he had already been chosen and called and it was really and truly the reason that was looking for him.

He did not follow the maroons when they would go down to wreak havoc in the plain from time to time. They did not misunderstand him: they knew that it was not a matter of cowardice, they said: "Fine. He has different work to do." Melchior watched them go off (Liberté among them, trying to find Anne during this whole period of unrest), thinking that perhaps they were going off to fight because the people in the plain were rebelling; that is, thinking each time that the people who were scorned—the slaves, the men in chains—were prepared to die to allow the proud, the unconquered maroons to make the spectacular gesture of burning and doing battle. Then Melchior pushed farther into the shadows; he was quietly amazed that such a little country could have woods and lands that went so deep! Likewise he did not want to avenge Liberté in single combat or even by striking Anne with some calamity like grief or illness or impotence. Vengeance moreover was pointless. For a long time Anne expected Melchior to act: strike him a blow in broad daylight that would knock him to the ground or pronounce a slow curse that would cripple his existence. But nothing happened to disturb the monotony of the days; this waiting was for Anne, of course, far more of an ordeal than any vengeful punishment. Longoué (La-Pointe) had turned hatred into an everyday throb of pain, he had tamed it; Melchior, unconcerned with those weightless obsessions, extinguished hatred by refusing to take revenge. But this action that had no consequences was still irksome and calling for some event that would revive the whole affair or would bury it forever. Tall-Stéfanise, the big woman, achieved the latter when she went to live with Apostrophe.

And rather than pondering over "an eye for an eye," which would have crisscrossed the ground with an endless boardwalk of murdered and wounded men, Melchior applied himself to founding a line. For a long time he had known a woman, the daughter of a maroon (he would not have dreamed of choosing a companion from among the people down there, despite the respect he was beginning to have for the weight of their existence and its value), but bemoaned the fact that she was so afraid of him. She was paralyzed in his presence, and though he went out of his way to run into her more frequently, his state of affairs had not advanced by so much as one smile. He had a depth that made him seem (on such occasions) futile or shy. He also had an obviousness, a clarity that terrified people in a different way; not to mention that his situation kept him isolated. He resolved therefore to ask her father for the girl; it was just one way among others to get a good result. But when he went into their hut he was discouraged by the effect of his arrival. The three occupants displayed neither turmoil nor panic but were stunned and paralyzed. The fear and respect shown by the old man was particularly disturbing to Melchior, who could have been his son. The youngest, the girl, had withdrawn to a corner next to her mother deep inside the hut. The intruder forced himself to smile.

"So what I've come for," he said, "is to ask for her."

The old woman gave a cry but stifled it immediately. The youngest, who was unable to hide her interest, craned her neck.

"Yes, yes," stammered the old man . . . then: "Come here!" he called out emphatically as if to exorcise his terror.

The girl came. Her fear was already gone, but the two parents still trembled. The father launched into a mumbling speech extolling the countless qualities of his offspring, but Melchior, unable to bear the atmosphere of fear—even terror you might say—quietly interrupted saying: "Good. Then she must be there tomorrow morning at sunrise."

"Yes, yes," said the old man. "She will come." And the next morning she was there.

He never knew whether they gave him their daughter because

they did not dare face his anger or if they were flattered by his request. He never knew whether the young woman accepted of her own free will or if she gave in to this threat. With the slow passage of days and nights these problems vanished. He had left the hut immediately, making no attempt to imagine the scene after his departure: the exclamations, the fear, or perhaps the exuberance. The next day, long before the sun burst over the top of the trees, the new arrival was seated in the spot where Man-Louise always used to sit. He caught sight of her when he left the cabin, and the thought flashed through his mind: "Man-Louise has come back." Then he smiled from a distance calling her to him, and he had the deep, slow pleasure of seeing her walk toward him with no problem, no fuss.

He was the first in the line to stop camping out on the land; he decided in favor of patience. A Longoué with no curse upon him. The only one, yes the only one who had been able to choose his destiny and lead it unswervingly by the hand without a single hitch: from the first shout of a sugar worker heard in the forest dawn to the last firefly seen in the night at the end of his long life. Slow and perceptive as long as he was still standing. The only one really. Because did the ancestor not experience the curse of being captured, deported, sold into slavery, that man who used to reflect upon the infinite horizon in the country back there across the ocean? And Apostrophe, who died five years after his son was born and therefore never was able to pass the word on to him. Papa Longoué himself, who could not hook anything to anything, neither his father to his son nor, consequently, the past to the future. Ti-René, the carefree vagabond, who went off to the great war and brought forth sudden death. All of them. Cursed in their own way; all but one: chosen to nurture strength and patience. This Longoué, Melchior Longoué, who had reclaimed the name of the line; the only one who wore peace on his brow until the end. And though he was there for the death of his son, Apostrophe, he had three years after that to talk to his grandson about the flickering insights he had collected during the long years he had spent in the woods. He had to be the only one, he was compelled to be; for the entire family (as well as for the maroons who were the family's echo in the surrounding forest) he was the thick, heavy root taking hold in the land. That is why Liberté, who quivered, light as a leaf, died. Liberté, the one most cursed, was he not? Because he did not at all deserve or foresee (smiling and unconcerned) his fate: struck down in his prime and laughing at his death. Liberté, the smiling corpse carried by Melchior on his back from the stand of ebony trees to the cabin and buried beside the grave of Man-Louise and Longoué; to the extent that he was even able to locate the grave under the jumble of nettles, stinkweed, and sweet lianas proliferating there. And Anne Béluse, who in that inevitable fight planted the machete into his body, driving it home with a single blow, had not looked ahead either: with this act he uprooted or tried to uproot the wood embedded in his breast and unintentionally caused Melchior Longoué to take root in the fertile Longoué loam!

Chapter 8

While some people withdrew deeper into the shadow of their forest and others gathered strength from the clay they endured, an unasked question grew larger and larger, spreading over the space, the ceaseless crackling, the peaceful emptiness everywhere. Unconcerned with crises or torments, it bore on its immaterial body of the unuttered question the struggle and misery of everyone. Because the little barrel was there in the cabin where every person who came to consult could see it—assessing it with a glance but not daring to contemplate it for long.

"They say that Melchior no longer carries the bag around, he has switched to the barrel."

"Don't speak the word! You'll go up in smoke."

"If you go inside you walk down unlit paths forever."

"They say La-Pointe was burned with Man-Louise. They are in there."

"Did you see a grave when you went up?"

"They say there is no grave. They are inside that thing, nothing but ashes."

"It used to belong to the old bastard. He has really lost his money this time."

"The old bastard wasn't looking for La-Pointe. The two of them had an agreement."

"It's his horse. He comes on horseback. When the creature gallops La-Pointe is there."

"A snake."

All of them, anxious about the barrel, that is about the ferment hidden inside its depths that, perhaps, would create out of all the sorrowful echoes and all the silences a single voice swelling louder in bright light. Anxious too about the tension they watched building everywhere (because they were no longer content to merely follow with their eyes a horse-woman without a horse racing to an assignation) and they thought that this tension was taking shape up in the hills.

"People say they are going to come down and there will be fire everywhere!"

"There's going to be fighting, there's going to be fighting. Close the cabin up."

"Saint Anthony of Padua, there's going to be fighting again!"

Already good at expressing action, either what was going on or what they foresaw, they only did so jerkily and bit by bit in roundabout sentences, never suspecting that this action was inside them. And, unaware of this fact, they were trying to put together some logic from the mysteries surrounding them (because power that is too obvious is a mystery even when it takes on the dread shape of an old tyrant or the density of a Negro without malice); some connection between the dark nights and lightning flashes, between a humpback and a horse—they were looking for some semblance of continuity, at least, that might (even if they were unable to sustain it for long in the realm of spoken truth) reassure their minds or strengthen their desire to live.

"When you take the path up the hill it feels like it's that thing! Nothing but woods and more woods, night with more night. Cool on your breast, hot on your back."

"I'd rather die, really I'd rather die."

"Listen up, there's going to be fighting again."

"Jesus-Mary, there's going to be fighting again."

"They say the humpback is going downhill."

"The old bastard will take the plantation."

"No, he will marry his daughter to young Senglis."

"You're touched in the head. The son of that humpback turnip!"

"He's always asking. Five distilleries and still he proposes."

"And they say that thing is as full of machetes as a toolshed."

"They say there's powder in there too to burn things."

"Melchior is the strongest. He controls all three: the bag and the boutou and that thing too."

"Just look, there's going to be fighting again!"

They were all—all—infatuated with the words that surface and warn but nonetheless do not define existence; from one sentence to the next, from a secret to an assertion, weaving the voice swollen with mystery that would bring forth their light. They were worn out by the cane, ground down in the cocoa, rolled flat with the tobacco, but capable of lasting beyond the transient hoeing of weeds. And capable, if not yet of understanding, if not of taking action, at least of singing about a magnificently adorned future (like a paralytic's illusory dream); touched also from time to time by a reticent memory, the former land surfacing like some deceptive itch left by an illness that has gotten well on its own. Without their daring to believe that, perhaps, they were feeling the future act thus attributed to powerful proxies stream from one thing they said to the next. The act: the drive already pronouncing these words among them, or rather, the articulation (unheard-of syntax) of their incoherent chatter.

"Who is going to get us out of here?"

"Nothing here but flamboyant trees, ebony trees, acacia trees."

"It's Guinea, it's the Congo, ditto ditto."

"Rain and more rain, sun and more sun."

"The snake, the snake."

"They say that everything is going to be free, not just the freed slaves."

"So your whole body can get some sleep then all night long."

"A house for you with two thousand bathrooms."

"Not just the mulattos."

"A house for you with seventy-two mattresses, twenty-eight dining tables."

"You don't know how to eat from a table."

"They say that she still goes looking for him and the old bastard he's not happy."

"The son of the humpbacked turnip."

"Don't mess with that stuff. If someone's waving a steel bar around in the air you'll wipe your back with it for sure."

"Damn it all there's going to be fighting."

"They say in the forest, look, the *acomat* tree and you get lost in the coolness no wind everything plants you don't see the green sky the forest is right down on your heads."

"Okra is slippery, ash-cake choke you! Not all you eat is food."

"They say—what a joke, this is for forever. Nothing changes!"

Because the little barrel was there; it was there through storms, hurricanes, dry-season dust, dawns, unbridled nights. Not one of them could say what was in it, if there was anything in it at all, or even if La Roche had ever hidden anything in it. And so the question no one asked but that was on everyone's mind was really very simple, very direct: *What is inside that thing?*—then, as time went by and forgetting came, the question died in its simple form but now immaterial kept on through the air, spreading out over the space of heat, waiting to be picked up again in a new form; or, failing that, waiting for someone to have it inside himself at least, transparent and unsuspected: like a veil of mist rising from a road—from a distance it makes you blind, but if you walk right in the middle of the road you can't see it there at your feet at all; or waiting for someone finally to answer it without knowing it is a question, a veil that hangs over the passing days and does its haunting in the obvious renunciation of outcasts:

Because to begin with Melchior saw his first child be born, a daughter that he named Liberté in memory of the brother struck down with a single blow among the three ebony trees. Melchior felt he could not do otherwise. He recovered, perhaps, a bit of the energy dissipated by his dead brother and set it flowing again in a single stream inside this newborn body. And Liberté the daughter made no appearance, so to speak, among the works of her father; she was so reserved that she vanished from everyone's memory; but she founded the family of Celats that would stubbornly persist far away from everyone or rather would merge with the mass. Because the daughter who had been named Liberté like her father's brother had perhaps suffered from her name: from the confusion into which she had dissolved, where she seemed to have been done away with; whereas all alone with her energy she was vaguely preparing for her separate and simple, mutual and headstrong existence within the destiny of outcasts. From the first she had refused to be either one thing or another; people would never be able to say: "This is what she did—went with this man and they lived way out back behind Roche Carrée, they had nine children and four died before the age of five." People would never exclaim over her because of how her eyes sparkled and her voice propelled you forward—no, already at birth she was just one branch among others. She stuck out just barely because her name was Liberté; in fact, this name that was not hers by rights was precisely what made her incapable of directing her energy outside the ordinary or making herself be noticed by exceptional words or deeds. Consequently, people glanced at her once and then left her to her hidden work. She vanished. Like the family that would follow; nobody heard anything about them from that day long ago to this: until the moment the young girl with flashing eyes would stop and say: "Here I am, I'm Marie Celat." And so this family that had evaporated like that into space and merged with the masses, would suddenly emerge now in a new form—that of this young girl. Nobody who saw her could keep from saying: "Here is Celat."

Because the question was present when you were near the little barrel ("that thing"), but without the wretches' knowledge of its materiality, its question-body had merged with the exertion of poverty; and now it was emerging (today) in its new form, "How, how can all that time be put into a little barrel?" Yet the one entrusted with the form was unable to formulate, never even thought he had a question inside the turmoil of his mind. And the question inside his mind lit fires. He cried out. Believing that he was discovering, as a clever man, the flaw in the whole or, as an ambitious man, the palpable, underlying bonds sustaining blood and sap; whereas what he sensed was the question throbbing (unformulated in his thought just as in earlier days no one would speak of the little barrel by name) and pressing against his skull the rising tide of answers.

"So they can keep on forever putting hundreds of candles out for the dead on All Saints' Day, and they can set the cemetery on fire if they want, but they will never succeed in recapturing the lineage! Because he, La-Pointe, was the first to make a mockery of the chain of the dead!"

"But damn it's beautiful on All Saints at night in the cemetery, like a crop of fire in the distance! Unhunh, it's beautiful!"

"Yes, a beautiful memory for people who pass on! But no matter what they do, any of us, we'll never get the lineage back again. You can't use candles to make them cross land and sea to reach out their hands to you, your dead!"

"But still, people ought to mourn their parents, or be there with them and put three flowers beside the grave . . ."

"Yes yes. Each one in his little path, raking the sand and laying out seashells to make it pretty. But none of us (and not you and not he) none of us even know whether the dead have reached out their hands and zombies are not talkative enough to tell us because they are just there temporarily to take the place of the dead. It was he La-Pointe who first turned his back."

"He turned his back."

"Yes. And as usual I disagree with you about La-Pointe! His was the act of a man (not an animal, even if there is something splendid about how animals act), a proud and thinking man: he goes up into the woods. But he scatters the head, and then his next idea is to go and leave the irons in a cabin though he is not even sure Béluse lives there. He lets him keep on living with this story on his tail. Your opinion is that he is right: because he has to get to know the new land. Because he thinks that Béluse has started down "legitimate" paths by way of submission. But at the same time he, La-Pointe, made a mockery of the lineage that he should be guarding. Because I see that ever since they left the country back there he has been the guardian."

"So now what are you able to see concerning the zombies?"

"Don't make me laugh. When they saw (when we all saw) that the dead were not dancing with them in their magic dances they invented zombies. Not so much to frighten as to reassure themselves. This way they think the dead come back among them. Come back among us."

"So then you are stronger than a zombie are you? It's obvious that you aren't afraid of the dark!"

"And the barrel. They don't dare say its name. Mind you it's more like a little cask. They don't dare say its name, La-Pointe doesn't dare open it; as if La Roche had the power to force anything on him at all. And you after all, you put something you call *the leaf of life and death* inside it. Don't make me laugh, the dead are gone for good, you can crumble your leaf all you want but that is not what will make us move a single step in space. Because we are on the branch without roots; from time to time we shiver for no reason at all in every wind."

"Well then, look hard, Zombi-Mathieu. I have never dived into the sea, and if you are not satisfied go and plow your field in the sea, you'll have a big field at least! The truth is that you would like to see a serious battle between the two men in order to know if Longoué could really master Béluse. But they are both gone, and if you want to see this battle you will have to go and dig up the two graves on the Morne so you can call them.

"Papa Longoué, you're being cross, that's not nice!"

Because of the infinite amazement of space inside his head; because of the barricade before his eyes, the depths of the forest, its smothering germination, the dazzlement; because of the piling up of deaths, of births, of battles, into which one stumbled unknowingly. The eternal question scarcely left a minute's rest or any corner not on fire so the birth of Stéfanise could be observed and praised and sung. And yet this birth was part of the question, it was cut into the question the way a *malfini* slices across the sky. Tall-Stéfanise, born in the woods, who would follow her father Anne when he went back down to Roche Carrée (after abolition), but who kept always a bit of moss in her heart, a bit of the maroon in her soul. And she used to go back up into the stand of acacias whenever she pleased, no longer to protect herself against the plain but because it was what she liked and what her man liked, or rather it was her destiny and the destiny of her new lineage. She who had come, long as a day with no manioc she was, stretched out long the minute she came from her mother's belly, and she grew faster than a *filaos*. You could hardly tell she was a girl (girl or boy, what difference did it make: with the same job to get through she would get through it like two men; and a girl was just as well endowed as a boy for the only inheritance to be had: being born and dying), yet in her girl's heart smoldered all the love and all the insight the world can have.

Scarcely time enough to notice she was there before she was jostling her mother around, making her talk and shout and live at last; screaming at her father: "Don't touch me! I'm not Liberté Longoué!" which never failed to leave him dumbfounded, grouchy, and defeated. She watched over the last days of Man-Béluse, the old woman (who had never completely gotten off that boat, and was happy for the unexpected support from the child). She hoed the land. Scarcely time enough to see her grow before they were calling her down from the hills. Tall-Stéfanise, full of real noise. Through her the long passing of lives, torments, and battles suddenly began to run faster; blood sped up. Eyes searched more sharply; passion exploded. The river current led to her! Stéfanise was almost a delta. Because after Louise and Longoué, after Anne and the girl, after Melchior and Adélie she took over for herself the inevitable and you might say mechanical attempt to catch up to the past; this instinct that was entirely womanly, sometimes assaulted, sometimes urged on and sometimes rejected by the man, but always victorious. And she brought with her such sunshine that, despite the monotony of doing the same things over and over, it seemed that she had created herself, born in abrupt birth from her own light.

Then how could they have come so close to erasing, skipping over the morning that she appeared in the hut between the chatter of the old woman, Man-Béluse, and the silence of Anne who was ignoring it all? Memory must have run riot to have risked missing something like that, chancing such a dreadful loss. (*"And how, how can all this time be put into a barrel?"*) Because Stéfanise had around her all the forest's own invention, the sprouts and shoots that raced with her toward the sky, the sieve combining life and somnolence, the mute bloom of sap, the abrupt explosion of the germ far from the seed—and the result was that in the end the woods and the girl together gave off a sort of brightness where more than one clumsy man would try to plant himself.

Chapter 9

BECAUSE APOSTROPHE, Melchior's second child, was born immediately after Stéfanise, Anne Béluse's daughter. Immediately, but *after*; a year after. During this year Stéfanise accumulated the light dew of living that made her someone who was always *a little more* than Apostrophe. It made her the one who would go to him and take his hand, and then lead him through existence without dominating or outdistancing him (on the contrary, she would stay modestly behind, gently pushing him forward); but though she was *a little more* than him she never was aware of this *more* (in which the delicate dew had bathed her). She even felt the torment that comes with an obsessive need to be useful, to be necessary to the other; though this is so much a part of being an affectionate woman, it was very unusual for the daughter of a maroon, especially in a country where it seemed there was not only nothing to do but nothing to be attempted. Every day she would say to Apostrophe: "*Ou pa ni bisoin moin, ou pa ni bisoin moin.*" Every day repeat it: you don't need me. "But for what?" he thought, not daring to ask, at a loss. She thus believed, or guessed, that there was something to do, some role he should play. And in fact, with her gentle prodding, he did play this role; but he suffered from a sort of constant bewilderment, which, because of life's mischievous ways, created a good *quimboiseur* out of his tranquil person.

Melchior very early on took an interest in the little girl: she gave off a sparkling radiance all around that drew him to her. How he heard about her and from whom were mysteries. But the fact is that she was not yet nine years old when she came into the cabin and called out to her father, Anne: "I saw Papa Melchior, we talked to each other!" Anne sighed and thought: "I'm not done with those people. He's up to something or other."

But he did not forbid the little girl to meet with "Papa Melchior." She was too naturally attracted to him. It would have looked like seduction except it concerned a man who was almost old and a child who was drawn to the slow walks and all the strange things he endlessly taught her. Anne could sense the powerful affinity between them.

Thus, what it took for a Longoué, a fearless woman, who was out of place among the Béluses, to go up of her own free will into the hills (with no need to change her nature because it was her nature that drove her to do it) was this monotonous piling on of one thing after another: Senglis decrepit but stubborn had to be determined to hang onto his plantation (and his plantation had to not be devastated by the maroons); Béluse had to have moved up to the cabin at Roche Carrée; he had to go halfway to the woods; La Roche intent on clearing land had to leave Longoué alone up in his forest (and Longoué had to protect Acajou Plantation or at least take care not to attack Acajou), and "the woman beside him on the boat" had to give birth to Stéfanise's mother. All in order for Melchior to become infatuated with a little girl sprouting with such dazzling abandon in the thick dark surroundings, and in order for Melchior's son, a year younger than the little girl, soon to come along everywhere they went, understanding nothing, or almost nothing from the silences and sudden outpouring of words that so delighted the man and the little girl. But by following them around like this without speaking a word, Apostrophe acquired a density, a presence, that Melchior and Stéfanise took to in the end. Thus it was through Stéfanise that Melchior acknowledged his son, a Longoué whose self-assertion was so effortless, whereas Stéfanise still needed the (real) noise and (real) excitement that she created around herself. And it was through Melchior that Stéfanise approached Apostrophe, reaching this serious, bewildered nonchalance that lay beneath the stillness of his nature and gave her so much pleasure and so charmed her.

Because Louise, then, jaunty and agile in her strange garb, had to have taken the kitchen knife (the same black knife that he would later steal before cutting the ropes tying her to the device); she had to have gone into the pen to set this man free—so he would go up into the hills and so La Roche would go after him and not catch him, and so La Roche ten years later, arriving alone in the woods with his madness and his unconcern, would take him the barrel and throw it at his feet. And Louise, whose heart also was full of uncontrolled violence, full of heedless, unaccountable noise, and who was only contained with great difficulty by the strength and stubbornness of Longoué (until the day they both died when all of a sudden she longed to follow him), had to have cut the rope without taking time to unbind his wrists: not knowing whether she was obeying the sign from the land back there or if she was succumbing to a necessity nurtured by the future of the new country. And Louise, who was not yet Man-Louise (good-natured, slow-moving) but felt this stir from somewhere else, this liking to breathe, in short this expectancy, had to have presumed in her perfect body and her pride Stéfanise's unbridled body and her (real) noise—that Melchior would rediscover. Because for Melchior the little girl was first of all not like a daughter but, instead, like the image of Louise the way he would have liked to have known her before she took on the genial good nature of Man-Louise. All this monotonous and un-dreamt-of flamboyance above the dense sap of miseries and battles just so Melchior, solid and robust, would recognize in Stéfanise— sprouting up into the sky like a *filaos*—the image of his original mother, fierce and warlike. Just so that—all the while overlooking his own neutral and uninteresting daughter Liberté, who was absolutely not jealous of her father's preferences if she even noticed what they were—he would recognize Louise in Stéfanise, the child of disorder, Stéfanise. And so that he would adopt her truly as his daughter from then on and would give her to his son so she could be his daughter a second time (so that the daughter and the son would grow more closely attached to each other than double plums). So that in his life all the reasons, past and present, for his being alive would be thus summed up—not leaving out anything: even that he almost died because of Stéfanise, or that thanks to La Roche he was saved because of Louise and Longoué.

He once went into the market town during the day in search of some little treat for Stéfanise. He wanted to because of the little girl, but he was also driven by a curiosity that he had never lost. He connected the child who had recently turned up in his life with the life down there. He felt it daily coming closer to his own, and this is why he wanted to give Stéfanise a trinket, or some kind of food, anything permeated with the smell of the town.

There was little danger. The people living there knew him; sometimes he would go near the town and no trouble ever came of it. Maybe whispers: "There goes Melchior Longoué," trailing here and there behind him. Neither the planters nor the constables would have been stupid enough to follow him. But these conventions were turned upside down by a pair of swaggering military men too pleased with themselves to bother with local customs. Fascinated by the faint murmur accompanying Melchior, they stopped him for questioning and he was proud enough to give them his name. He never would have pretended not to have his wits about him. The soldiers immediately led him off, followed by a denser and denser crowd of people. News spread everywhere: "They've caught Melchior Longoué!" or "We've captured a dangerous maroon!" Melchior was prepared to take the risk, the huge risk (in relation to his childish pretext for being there) because he vaguely wanted to confront, with no weapons, no fighting, the bright and orderly world of the plain. Couriers scattered in all directions to tell the planters.

"Stupid scoundrels!" old La Roche shouted when they came to tell him, and he jumped on his horse.

When he got to the market town Melchior had already been led off to the bailiff, who was extremely uneasy about the whole business. La Roche went straight to the prisoner.

"So, you are the son of La-Pointe."

"My name is Melchior Longoué."

"What next! You don't have a name, my boy! Besides, you are the son of La-Pointe."

"Melchior Longoué."

Melchior looked calmly at La Roche just the way Longoué used to. The old bastard gave a mischievous look in return; it felt like he was back in his youth!

"Longoué eh? What are you doing with a name? Does it get you anything to eat? First, have you been freed? Are you free? Damned La-Pointe. Ah! What a fellow! . . . So you walk around like that without your bag or your cudgel either? Not surprising they caught you. Too bad! I would have liked to open it—your bag. Just to look at the spirit you have working for you. Eh?"

He could not bring himself to leave Melchior. Old times coming back like this had him full of life again. He was almost begging for an insult, some gesture, some sign that would have reminded him of his man marooned in the first hour.

"All right then. Since you are here, give me a consultation. So these rascals will at least have been useful for that! Come on, I know you are a *quimboiseur*, no sense dodging."

The courtyard was lined with beds of pink, yellow, and red poppies. Hints at the harmony of a French garden could be seen in the low hedges here and there and in the token lawn. But there were plants impervious to pruning, paths rustling with grasses, brilliant bursts of flowers far taller than the foliage to show just how fanciful such a parody was. The prisoner let his gaze wander; he was thinking.

"Well? Is there something? Just make sure you don't tell me I have a lover. Right?"

Finally Melchior looked at La Roche, then he said softly: "Perform the marriage. The boy is more able than his father and you love your daughter. She will be happy."

"Damn La-Pointe! Damn La-Pointe!" La Roche burst into loud laughter, satisfied perhaps with these unexpected words.

"Fine," he said. "I'll do as you say. But if you've tricked me, watch out!"

He was still laughing when he went into the room where the planters, who had not gone to see the maroon, were meeting. The gathering was in turmoil, opinions shooting back and forth.

"Let's make an example!"

"Since he's there we can't back off!"

"My friends, let's turn him over to the authorities."

"Eh! The authorities will give him back to us!"

"Easiest thing is to toss him in a grave."

"Let's hang him high up on a short rope!"

"You know the fear he inspires. A *quimboiseur*."

"That's nothing. Let's let him go."

"And pretty soon they'll be saying: 'Let them all go!'"

"Soon? They've already said it."

"Silence!" thundered La Roche, putting an instant stop to all the racket.

"Sir," a young planter began. But La Roche looked him up and down without a word and the foolish man fell silent. Every single one of them were, one way or another, dependent on Acajou and its master.

"So," the old bastard said quietly, "all year long you never think of going after them in the woods you can see from here through this window and where all you would have to do is reach out and gather them. Even with thirty dogs and a gang of people you wouldn't dare go up there. But because two troublemakers disguised as soldiers have a little fun policing the roads you can let loose as much as you like."

"But sir . . ."

"And you probably think that it's time to provide our population with a first-rate incitement. Hanging a maroon, a *quimboiseur* to boot! What more efficient way to spark the unrest in all their heads? Right? Not that we aren't already plenty bothered by all those abolitionist coons. Let's give them a good, spectacular pretext for protesting—why not! Right?"

"Sir, we're determined to resist!"

"Well then, resist this!"

The old man pulled out a pistol and pointed it toward the men there.

"I can see I have to defend your interests against you. . . . Besides," he chuckled, "I got the idea from Senglis."

They looked on in consternation, certain that he would not for an instant hesitate to make use of his weapon. This was not a man who would brandish a pistol without using it if necessary.

"Fine," he said. "I'll go down and give the orders. I'll have him branded with the iron and then we'll turn him loose again. Which will satisfy everybody, right? You'll stay quietly right here and an hour from now we'll be able to go back home. Right?"

Outside a small group of people was discussing the event. "Melchior Longoué—he is strong. You'll see—he'll get away. He has the bag and the *boutou* and that thing." "It's not possible, they'll brand him and then whop! his right arm." "Even so! He can replace as many arms as you don't have teeth in your big mouth." "So he's really got a bunch of arms!" "Just watch, it's the old bastard who's going to fix things for him!" There were fifty of them there, pressed up against the hedge where they could watch how things progressed from a distance.

(Melchior thought about all those people on both sides of the hedge, who were ignorant enough to believe that he had come there by chance, that he had gotten himself caught out of carelessness, that he would escape out of fear.)

"All right," said La Roche. "They are going to lead you away—a mere formality. Afterward you will be free. You see, I'm not one to bear a grudge. But I know what I'd do if I were you! All right then. Marriage, eh? OK, agreed. If you know what the sickness is you know its remedy."

He winked his eye at the maroon. He was overjoyed.

He gave his orders in a deluge of jocularity. His jubilation made him friendly and offhand, and the astonished colons watched him come back into the room swinging his weapon from the tip of his fingers like a toy. He crudely joked with most of them. "Come now, George-Lucien, you'll never see the end of clearing, I'm going to have to give you a hand." "Do you know what people insinuate in Paris? They claim we're illiterate barbarians. To think that a quarter of my fortune goes to improve the ordinary fare of these gentlemen, really!" "Eh, my dear Depaume, do you, at least, know how to read?" Encouraging good humor in everyone there until gradually this turned into a warm sense of confidence, certainty in the future; thinking up serious projects (a few measures of repression, a plan to cut back the allotments of manioc to the cabins)—real pleasure in life—until suddenly a police officer burst into the room shouting: "Sir, sir, he has escaped!" *Incompetent man.*

"Before or after branding?"

"We were taking him to the workshop as you ordered; suddenly he shoved one of his guards and disappeared down an alley!"

"Get your horses!" several of them cried. "This time he's fair game."

"I've gone after one of the same sort," said La Roche. "It's hopeless. Stay calm! Don't give the others the pleasure of seeing you come back empty-handed and exhausted. I know what I'm talking about!"

And since the hubbub did not stop: "Gentlemen," he announced, "Let's move on to more cheerful matters. Since we are all gathered together here I am pleased to inform you of the upcoming marriage of my third daughter, Marie-France-Claire, to young Senglis!"

Then in all the confusion of compliments and congratulations he chuckled alone to himself: "Damn La-Pointe! Damn La-Pointe!"

"Because their names were something they set store by. They were perfectly willing for you to have a name provided they gave it to you. If they had decided on La-Pointe, just try and make them acknowledge that you want Longoué, because Longoué is like a good, solid ash-cake in crab soup, and unbending as a campeche tree. Get them to stand for it! That your name is for you and chosen by you? They'll never agree!" Unless they take some particular pleasure in it. For instance, it was Marie-Nathalie who did not want them ever to call the man anything but Béluse (not Pierre, not Paul, but Béluse) and who took so much pleasure in rolling the word around in her mouth: Béluse. Because she knew that the name had arisen from her own good humor, from the laughter rising inside her and that had been so hard to contain when that supervisor declared: "C'est pour le bel usage, madame!" *You can make good use of him,* he said, and her first use of the servicing, the *bel usage,* that was to make such a marvelous madness swell inside her until she reached a point where all she had to hang onto was the one, the hypothetical impregnation that she had ordered up, was to join it to the man who would fulfill the role; so that the man meant to mate would, in fact, be named for his projected good use: Béluse. In such cases, yes, they would kill you rather than take the name from you, even if in other cases—when you dared choose one and decided on your own that it was yours—they would have killed you just to take it irrevocably away. Then they would proclaim: "He has no right at all to have a name." Except, again, if the name was flattering to them or flattered some part of them that could smile condescendingly about your daring as if to say: "Come now! We have to let them have that, we consent to it." For example, there was the woman who lived with Targin, the supervisor, not with but beside him, to take care of the bit of amusement he needed at home (—eh *no! no one knew why but he became attached to that creature he had taken from the slave pen the night that all three of them were brought there— the man and the two women*), to say nothing of the housework and cooking. And when he was one of the first to die during a period of unrest and was distributed in pieces in one of the fields he had ruled over (such a horrific murder that at that point Senglis came very close to losing his estate to it, because the other planters loudly demanded that he change the rules regarding security on his land and even that he act in their interest and quit working it), the woman who was already very old but still strong went to live with one of the plantation slaves on some sandy land that was no good for planting. She took the child she had by Targin with her; he had grown up behind Targin's house and she had tended him as one would care for a little animal, always turned loose in the yard behind the house, away from Targin. Just as the child became the child of the new couple, the eldest in short, who was not—except perhaps for his lighter skin—distinguished from his brothers, in the same way people got in the habit of calling the cabin the Targin cabin and the family the

Targin family. Thus the supervisor had without knowing it a line of descendants in name the same way he had had a son without giving any thought to the matter. And this family, whose surname of Targin no one contested, improved the place, gained ground on the sand as they went downhill, and then across on the facing hillside they carved out for themselves a small area that was not well-defined; that is, it was a space where people never knew exactly what was being grown, a property of sorts, indistinct and unobtrusive, a jumble of vegetation that logically came to be known as the Thick Thicket—*La Touffaille*. Until the day when the little patch of land would be considered worth something, but that is another story.

I am talking about someone from down there, you understand, where they would give you the name that suited them; because as far as a man from the hills was concerned, the best they could do was to cut a piece of bark and carve it (making something like the grandparent of identification cards) and hope that if luck went their way they could put their hands on you. The people in the hills chose their names: they weren't called This or That, people were not in the habit of naming them; they chose and then went around telling everybody: "This is it, Such and such is my name." You see how that's different. They named themselves before anyone named them. They baptized themselves, so to speak. Although in some cases in fact they acted more and more as if it were a baptism, choosing names from down there; like the mother of Anne Béluse's children, who insisted that the boy born a year after Stéfanise (that is, the same year Apostrophe was born) be named Saint-Yves. She felt nostalgic for ceremony, and likely if she had had a dozen children after that one (as she should have) there would have been a certain number of saints parading through the cabin. She would not go back and forth for long before scooping up the brat from the cabin floor and declaring each time: "He is six months old now, we are going to call him Saint So-and-so." After all. It was necessary to get into the ways from down there because in Anne's mind it was already decided that he would return to Roche Carrée. At least

Melchior, when he adopted something from the plain, would always go for the roughest and most durable; like that time when, walking in the market town one night through the narrow passages separating the houses, he had heard a split second of protest from someone: "So now he is starting to apostrophize me!" From this the certainty that an apostrophe was tougher than tough gradually grew in his mind and it became the name of his second child, the son he was hoping for. But best of all—everyone ended up resembling his own name. Just think of Saint-Yves Béluse, in a country where it was hard enough just to hang on, I say hang on, not live! and where all the land around as far as you can see did not belong to you, when you think that even as a child Saint-Yves Béluse began to dig in the earth, bringing back plants, gathering seed to bury them somewhere (without even knowing at first what those seeds were going to produce—whether okra or wild pigs), with the idea of getting some money for the crop he produced. Not so much because of the money, which was something unknown in his house at the time; but for the pleasure of owning something and strutting about displaying his ownership. This man—raised in the woods and without any contact with the people from down there until the age of thirteen—hadn't the name he inherited rubbed off on him? Because I ask you, what's the use of owning something when no one else in the country has property unless it is to turn your nose up at your brothers? If you are trying to hang on, fine; but if the vainglory of owning things gets into you in this country, where all you ever get for working a piece of land is misery and grief? Even when he was very young he was already thinking about how to organize what he cultivated; he tended the biggest timber, ebony or mahogany, because he foresaw that one day they would bring in a profit. Can you imagine how much time an ebony tree takes to make you a profit? But Saint-Yves planned way ahead: he anticipated caring for his dark woods and his vegetables one of these days at Roche Carrée; and one day, therefore, he would cease being a slave on the official papers though he would keep on being a slave on the land. *And did he perhaps go up in the hills to uproot the three ebony trees and saw them up?*

Stéfanise, at least, her arms whirling through the air, jets of mud between her toes, her voice carrying like a trumpet across the ravines, did not thoughtlessly accept the tide rising from the village either. During the period that she lived in the cabin at Roche Carrée, after abolition and before she went up to Apostrophe, all the neighboring young men used to come and hang around her: "Mademoiselle, I love you, I want to live for you," "Why don't we do like the colt and filly?" "I went that way to see if you were gathering grass for your rabbit"—the shy, the brazen, and the practical ones. She would laugh and ask Sylvius, Félicité, or Ti-Léon: "What is your name?"—and when they were too ardent she would run away shouting: "*Ou té dan goumin-an?*" Were you in the fighting? Because she so loved hearing that story told over and over again, that it was, in fact, the only way to make her stay there with you. Suddenly she would be attentive, the big toe of her left foot digging a hole in the red dirt when the boy who caught on quickest, a beguiling big-mouth, skillful at "picturefying" recounted the great *goumin* of abolition.

Yo té di nou, they told us: gangs of bastards if you think anything is going to change here you can just sit there and wait, you'll be covered by the dust of the centuries but you will still be standing around in the same place, come on, get a move on, cane doesn't stand around waiting—and what do I see at the very end of the road all of a sudden women women women it looked like heaven's cat-house Man-Amélie out in front holy smoke the three police-men all they did was jump on their horses it's all ours forward they shout forward you would have seen hoes machetes and in the midst of them a mulatto who comes to shout my friends my friends this is no way to do it *aargh*! they vanish him faster than you can say hell and damnation everything is ours we hurry women women noth-ing but women in front and suddenly—Stop! Rifles completely blocking the road troops bayonets, stop who hollered stop, ahead carnival run wild, I see twenty thirty fall beside me, there's smoke not long before you go deaf and suddenly I'm on the other side we get through where are the soldiers and I see the women women

women each one with a rifle we go down and another comes waving a handkerchief go home and *aargh!* he runs faster than a marmoset we go down and not just all the houses furniture wrecked the gate gone not just the road but all over everywhere fields roads, it spills out where are the soldiers the women who bind cane the men who cut it all together enough to be hit over and over without feeling it *Yo té di nou*, they said to us: bands of lazybones and sluts on your feet up with you it won't wait nothing is different—we're there with our toys and where are the supervisors Man-Amélie her gun like a *boutou* she shouts who needs bullets you don't know how but out in front of you like a *boutou*, her dress is hooked up like pants she screams my son *pa moli!* Forward my son and then really soldiers soldiers gunfire gunfire but just look it's a river out of its banks how many more downed fifty a hundred us we get through nothing stops us and suddenly there's one man who shouts *Chelchè rivé l'esclavage fini* Schœlcher is here and slavery gone victory *Chelchè rivé* Schœlcher is here and another one comes: the French Republic is bringing you your freedom and its delegate is the honorable minister Schœlcher *Yo té di nou*, they said to us: good for nothing savages on your feet get to work Beelzebub even Beelzebub wants none of you this will be for centuries of eternity—that's it: victory, slavery over, I look at Man-Amélie lying there with her dress up over her head and her head pulled from its roots at right angles her hand on the gun like a *boutou* she's not shouting any more not hearing the din any more the noise everybody in the street victory she hears hell and damnation victory for all those dead with her in the road victory!

"Ouél!" shouts Stéfanise, "smoke in the sails—*la fimin dan vouèl!*"

But the one telling the story had better not take too much advantage of this smoke this *fimin* or rather this wind in the sails, adding things that were not true, saying five thousand instead of five hundred, getting drunk on the sound and action he described, because there was nothing Stéfanise did not know about the great battle, and she would get indignant whenever someone embroidered on truth and shout at the foolish braggart: "Go away, go away! You added that you damned liar!"

Because it was still throbbing through the air not yet forgotten not yet lost, the women women women streaming down and not just maroons like proud lords of misery and mud but everybody the exhausted the silent the submissive in a single surge. It was in the air where anybody could sniff it, from Melchior who had come closer to the land and people down there, risking his life among them out of curiosity, to Stéfanise focused on the account. It was in the air, where people sensitive to signs of its life, that is those who like Melchior bore this daily death without giving in to it or those who like Senglis were no longer intent on profit: all those, in short, who were unencumbered and who had a place on the edge of the bitter confrontation between destitution and rapacity, could feel it and herald it; or, like Stéfanise, feel it and remember it.

Senglis especially suffered from these changes around him because he was able (just as Marie-Nathalie had been formerly) to pick up any breath of air that stirred his stifling atmosphere. Less imaginative, however, than his deceased wife who was beset in her final hours by all the vegetation she had spent her life laying waste to, he heard another wave breaking with a heavier, more ordinary load, closer enemies, and in his agony (well before the great battle that Stéfanise would be so carried away by) tried to hold off the mob of slaves that he watched swelling around him and besieging him. Those were the days when his son was beginning to pay court to young Marie-France-Claire; Senglis, delighted by such a match, cherished the hope that there would be a definitive union that would incorporate his plantation into the Acajou estate but under the authority of his son. A fanciful hope, just like everything he had undertaken. This dream aside, he had become more human and was rid of his obsessions. Forgotten in the darkest parts of the upper house, he no longer made an appearance in the affairs of the plantation, which the young Senglis vigorously took over, to the great displeasure of the supervisors. But this moment of respite, of blissful calm, only heralded the violence and desolation that would spoil his end.

Tortured by the seething mass of populace around him, he

shouted from deep inside his room: he could be heard everywhere and the children holed up inside the huts. Then he muttered endless advice and recipes: for farming, repression, accounts. This was an agony that went on forever. He felt the fondling touch in the air, the endless rustle of things to come that he would, however, never see. Finally one day he called for La Roche and his son, quaking at the mere idea of any such a move, had to screw up his courage to go after the father of Marie-France-Claire. But then La Roche came running top speed escorted by the young Senglis, frantic after a headlong dash boot to boot with the old bastard.

"Ah!" said Senglis. "You came! They never leave me alone for an instant, I always have to be defending myself, do you hear them? There, there. I wondered if you would be able to get through, ah!" Then, changing the subject and suddenly almost smiling: "We certainly did hate each other because of her, don't you think?"

"My dear friend, my dear friend," La Roche repeated.

"I knew it, though we didn't dare say so: you loved her as much as I! Because I did too, La Roche, I did too. Listen, listen, I was never able to tell her that Anne de Montmorency was not the Constable of France, at least as far as I know. That's stupid isn't it? It's stupid. But you. How did you disguise it? Ah! Don't deny. See: Marie France-Adelaide, Marie-France-Eloise, Marie-France-Claire, and for the last daughter you weren't able to resist, Marie-France-Nathalie. See what I mean! I bet she is your favorite."

"Ah!" wept La Roche, "so it's true that she is dead. She is really dead!"

The candles guttered gloomily. These two old men who had never entirely renounced their duo were seeing each other for perhaps this one last time in the half-light of the room. But Senglis, as if speaking these words had rid him of some problem troubling him, sank back again even more furiously into his delirium and cried out as he died: "Be careful my friend, ah, they will carry you off also, you don't know them, it is the mangrove mud, I am sinking into it, hold onto me, hold onto me!" —while La Roche, a practical old man with neither dreams nor visions, held out his hand to him, and wept over the horseback-riding woman who had lived at this place, and every now and then he would estimate what the property would be worth when it passed on to the son.

Because life, the desire to die, the thirst to possess, blinding you on your path, prevent your feeling the root or understanding the raging stream flowing over space: unless, like Senglis, you are no longer any more than a transparent rag blown away by the least breath of air and drifting along with the surge; or then again like Longoué Melchior, you are an unshakable cask quaking only at the hidden thrust of the root. Then, yes in those cases you understand what is going to happen. Otherwise, you sit there thinking: "But where then, where did it all go?" All the heap of seemingly obsolete things — until the day when the heat drives straight through you like a stake; but heat can also dig you out. There is all the monotonous cry you do not hear: so that La Roche would leap on his horse and ride straight to the village and say to Melchior: "I know what I'd do if I were you." So that he would then give orders *that the prisoner be taken to the workshop, that it was no use tying him up* (and neither of them had mentioned the barrel that was still, however, sitting there between them like a monument, nor Louise who was alive there in their gazes). So that the people who had watched the goings-on from a distance would come back, some to a house built of metal sheets and packing boxes and some to straw-covered shacks, all of them exclaiming: "I knew he would get away! What man could ever hang onto Melchior Longoué?" And so that Stéfanise, already driven by her nature toward the cabin among the acacias, would however linger at Roche Carrée and would yell every day at the top of her lungs the story of the great uprising, understanding as well as Melchior the truth that was so obscure (at that moment and even today): that the lords, the plantation lords or the maroon lords of the forest, would be forced to renounce their brilliant pact; the latter would return to a feudal land without luminosity while the former would not lose a minute in weaving together a new sort of fabric across the land; that for once the people from the uprising, slaves or people from the market towns had lit their fire themselves; that they would open their road into this country—so vast and so small; that life would leave the thick crossroads and the damp carpet of the forest to settle around Roche Carrée, in the region where the soil was finely sifted, and all the places where men would suffer and die without any echo to their cries. And perhaps Stéfanise like Melchior foresaw the absence, the nothingness, the forgetting of death that would be the result of all this, and this was why she went up into the woods, so that at least there would be two or three who in the clearing in front of the cabin would stir the rubble and the ashes of the fire.

Because where did it go, where then did all these things that come up in your mind go, the things that burn your brain without your experiencing the fire, though still suffering its burn? You ask: "But really, papa, we don't even know what we have to dig for?" It isn't misery, you don't need to look for misery I tell you, misery will look for you, and don't try to enter misery with words. No! Your head starts spinning. Like a frigate bird that has only one wing to beat against the sea . . . They thought that if they just cut off the right arm, and then just the right leg—they ended up amputating one whole side of the body: a lung, a testicle, an eye, an ear. And maybe this is what we have to look for in the heap: this piece of you where the burn streaks through like lightning, a piece that has stayed far from you, however, in the forest or on the sea or in the country over there: the right half of the brain.

Chapter 10

BECAUSE, DESPITE THEIR ASTONISHMENT and indignation, these two agents were obliged to finish their task (because they were appointed for that purpose and because any signs that they had botched the job would make for very serious trouble with their new employers); so that law would thus be victorious everywhere. Law: the premise, that is, that slavery was abolished, that all persons would be accounted for by the registration bureau, at least as far as recording their identity was concerned, or certifying any papers that pertained to them. The two agents, therefore, had set up a table on the main square, behind which they barricaded themselves for protection against the pounding tide of humanity. Incarcerated in their dungeon of registries and forms and buttoned up tight in frock coats, their ears fiery red and rivers running down their bodies, they stared into the blurry wave of black faces in front of them. They were thoroughly official and let nothing of what they felt show, at least not in the tone of voice they used to call out "Next" or "Boisseau family"; but from time to time they would lean together and egg each other on in some practical joke, or crouched there behind their papers they would vent their anger.

"This is impossible, impossible," the first agent said briefly. But then he immediately recovered because he was in charge of questioning the applicants and called out "Next!"

"Lapalun plantation."

"How many?"

"A man, a woman, three children."

"Family Ofthree: Détroi," said the first agent. "One man, one woman, three children. Next!"

"Family Ofthree, two plus three: Détroi," repeated the second agent who was in charge of writing it down. Before him every face was the same blur, each with a hand held up in front of it to take the piece of paper of which he kept a copy.

"Plaisance area."

"How many?"

"Myself, Euphrasia, the children . . ."

"How many children?"

"Five."

"Euphrasia family, one man, one woman, five children. Next!"

"Euphrasia family, two plus five," repeated the second agent.

"Just me, by myself," said the next man.

"No mother, no father?"

"No."

"No wife?"

The "next" man snickered.

"Bymyself family: Tousseul. One. Next!"

"Bymyself family: Tousseul. One," repeated the second agent. He held out the paper certifying existence if not identity.

This was the great battle's epilogue: the distributing of papers that would sanction entrance into the universe of free men. Near the table a certain reserve, almost solemnity was required. But the farther one got from it the greater the excitement among the crowd. On the fringes there was outright exuberance. Throughout the village, behind closed windows and locked shutters and blinds: jubilation and noise. The former plantation slaves, women included, were there. But so were the maroons: majestic in their rags; wherever they went they wore their mud and nakedness like dignified finery, and they were, in fact, the only ones armed with machetes. The entire environment being one of rags and tatters, they managed to be simultaneously the most deprived and the most magnificent. They approached in small groups like firm and steady islands in a boiling sea. They did not speak or gesture and you could smell in their wake the stench of fear they aroused but that was quickly swept away by the excitement of the day. The maroons were torn between the satisfaction of people who see their existence given legitimacy or their past confirmed, who can now, oddly and without a care, go up and down the maze of little streets they used to have to travel furtively, and the vague regret for days gone by when the dangerous life they led set them at the highest order of existence. These mixed emotions made them restrained in their bearing and even silent. The result was an exaggerated appearance of modesty that distinguished them even further. They were special because (in addition to having machetes) when they reached the table they themselves would pronounce their name and the names of their relations, unlike the mass of people who, generally speaking, had a great deal of difficulty stating names or referring to any existence as a family. The two agents could tell the difference; this sign of independence seemed to them an insult and made them even more indignant.

"What an idea. Can you imagine?" sighed the second agent.

His colleague was beginning to exhaust the list of customary first names that he was now giving to a whole line of these savages as surnames.

"Clairette family . . ."

"Anaïs family . . ."

Their ears growing redder and redder they huddled together the whole time, alarm in their eyes, complaining to each other behind their papers.

"Old La Roche was well-advised to ask that the registration bureau send people to every plantation so we could be spared such a crowded scene! This is awful!"

"Ah, my good friend, the Republic does what it wants! . . . Next!"

The man barking out names then started on famous names from ancient history.

"Cicero family . . ."

"Cato family . . ."

"Lethe family . . ."

All of antiquity paraded by, or at any rate what they knew of it by hearsay: from Romulus to Horace and Scipio . . .

"Scipio, that's hilarious! Listen to that!"

Unfortunately they reached the bottom of their knowledge all too soon. And it was at that moment that they heard a voice that gave them a start: "Longoué family," it said. They abruptly pulled themselves together.

"What? What did you say?" barked the first agent.

"Longoué family," said Melchior. "One man: Melchior Longoué, one woman: Adélie Longoué, one girl: Liberté Longoué, one boy: Apostrophe Longoué."

"In the first place Liberté is not a name," shouted the first agent.

"It's OK, it's OK," the second said quickly. "Longoué family, two plus two."

Melchior took the paper.

"You shouldn't have given in," reproached the first agent under his breath.

"Oh," said the second, "Longoué or Aristides!"

They assumed they would have their revenge on those who followed.

They had to acknowledge a Béluse family and a Targin family among others, however. They watched the people who had registered as they walked away: most of them waved the sheet of paper at arm's length; a few solemnly studied it as if they were trying to take its secret by surprise. These agents did not feel like demiurges; they were not at all proud of feeling their power; they believed they were buffoons, rather, in a cruel parody of decorum. When they had used up all the first names, all of antiquity, all the natural phenomena (like the breezes, Zephyr and Alizé), and even names borne by people from their own region of France, some corner of Bigorre or Poitou: Clarac or Lemesle (playing a good joke on their neighbors back home), they resorted to asking their clients and would even go along with their taking local names: the names of plantations or neighborhoods. Thus there were families named Plaisance or Capote or Lazaret. When impudence became too obvious they amused themselves by turning the names around so that at least they would be farther from their origins. Senglis, for example, resulted in Glissant, and someone from Courbaril would be named Barricou. La Roche's name became Roché, Rachu, Réchon, Ruchot.

And it was their further misfortune that neither of these two agents was a chemist or seaman or an astrologist or botanist. Then they would have had inexhaustible mines to exploit, an endless repertory; instead they had to make do with rather slim pickings (Mars or Shark, Firtree or Wrecked); they regretted that this was the case and every now and then considered going to get some scholarly tomes that would have opened new horizons for them.

The afternoon, prostrate in the heat fermenting in the crowd and bubbling up against the fronts of the buildings around the square, dragged on. The agents had been served elegant refreshments, but they quickly found themselves preferring large carafes of water with *tafia* added. Stripping off the austere bearing of civil servants that had held them above the general confusion, they unleashed their pleasure in mockery. They did not notice that, as a result, they were contributing to the general excitement; that the former slaves preferred this unbuttoned aggression to the chilly moderation originally presiding over the registration procedure. Suddenly, in all this chaos it was night; lamps and torches were brought. Shadows exaggerated the already excessive scene. Everyone was shouting: the people waiting to register, the clerks, those already registered.

"I'm going to remember 1848," shouted the second agent.

Dogs were barking everywhere, the gendarmes' horses bucked and reared, smoke from the torches circled around and round them, filling heads with even greater intoxication.

"You mentioned music!"

"Hold on, that's it!" the first agent gave his approval: "Doremi family! . . ."

Names became grotesque in the most literal sense (or at least that is what they thought). Finally, however, they did not even react any more; the first agent looked at the black face in front of him without seeing it; he stopped feeling or thinking, and after a moment demanded: "Choose a name." Soon he reached the point of groaning: "Choose a name, *please*." The imperturbable tide, fiercely indifferent to their taunts, had won out over them. They were aware of it and their rage grew bitter. That is why every now and then they would sit up straight and seriously insult those people jammed together in front of them like a curtain between them and sweet existence.

"I've had enough, I've had enough," muttered the second agent.

"Hadenough family!" the first agent immediately announced. "One man, one woman, six children."

"Hadenuf family," repeated the second agent. "Two plus six."

At night the formerly freed slaves came out of their cabins and the mulattos left their houses. Both groups were rather straitlaced, and they walked round and around in the crowd of people until in the end it swallowed them up. The freed slaves timidly tried to take part in the gaiety, but they were unable to savor the collective pleasure because their freedom had been due to some individual merit, perhaps to the affection or gratitude of a master; it had been given for some clear, narrowly specific reason. It was as if they were excluded from the wild enthusiasm of the moment. They put on a show of being knowledgeable, of being people who have already been there. Their laughter was indulgent and their smile patronizing. The mulattos, or at least the ones who had deigned (or dared) come out into the streets, made it known that if it had not been for them, their conviction, their battles . . . Now that they had what they were after it was a good idea to take advantage of the occasion to up their prestige. People gathered in groups to hear them. They spoke French well, ah! There was no denying: "Monsieur Dachin, he can spin out that French!" But these miniature forums were soon borne off by the swell. The mulattos retreated in annoyance over the Negroes' ungratefulness.

Because that was the danger: that this great wave would come tumbling in through the half-open door. That the names tossed out at random, ironically or with a sneer, would become covered by the dust of the earth, the honorable patina of time until they caused those named to have undreamed-of pretensions. A person who has a name is like a person who learns to read: if he does not forget the name, the real history of the name, and if he does not forget how to read he is raised up. He begins to know about his mother, his father, his children: he learns to want to protect them. He leaves behind the gaping hole of days and nights, he enters into the time that reflects a past for him and compels him toward a future. Now he conjugates his verbs whereas up to now a single indeterminate form covered all the possible modes of action or futility for him. The most intuitive of the men in charge of the country sought (and were already finding in the pretentious foolishness of their mulattos) some way of getting around this danger. But there were others like La Roche, not very many it is true, who pushed reasoning to extremes. They wanted to go backward by any means at all; they would create the past, *their past*, swept into public view by the great wave, and they would not let go of it again. It became sort of a sacred calling to be perpetuated. They refused to take one step farther into the dissolution.

Because La Roche, who was almost a hundred years old, was in no mood to approve of so many new things. The necessity for reforms, simply for the sake of his own interest, did not escape him; his mind was alert and he saw that in the future (because he was not at all willing to quit this existence) there would be a captive mass that he would not even be obliged to feed any more. From this perspective, perhaps, it was not such a bad business: according to Senglis, what was the difference between ordering slaves around and forcing free men? The old bastard chewed these arguments over, but soon he found others every bit as convincing: the unpleasantness, in fact, of having to devise proper appearances and qualify one's schemes and buy consciences (offered, it is true); having to abandon an absolute world to enter into the ambiguousness of the marketplace. The shamelessness of no longer being out in the open but pulling strings in the shadows. The old planter was disgusted by all the many predictable ways his existence would shrink. The young men might get used to it but no one could require such a brute effort of him. And then his world had one great merit that was henceforth threatened: docile obedience, the stern, impeccable docility that he was made for. He would lack subjects—not just people who obeyed when he pointed his finger or looked their way, but people who were *waiting for* the moment to obey. And now what did he see everywhere? A definite predilection for dispute, for arguments; not recognized, of course, but suspended in the naïve bubbling turmoil of this abolition. A propensity for disorderly conduct, or for squawking. And why not admit that he was also afraid that the maroons down from their woods might deposit in this fermenting must the leaven of struggle and relentlessness. But above all he deplored the everyday, nagging character that this relentlessness was soon likely to take on. Ah! Was he perhaps prey to the nostalgia of the great silent challenge he had breathed in from the direction of the hills? And now all that was becoming horribly banal down in the fields, quibbling over a few pennies. Couldn't these people just be born and die without any fuss? Or at least foment some magnificent rebellion that might enliven his old age? No. He would have to be subjected to the humiliation of fighting and overcoming a miserable mess of ignoramuses and incomplete people. Should the maroons not have stayed there in their forest? And not come to scatter here in the plain where they would soon run through their magnificent resentment? Adding nothing of their strength to the stubborn meanness that was brewing? It was clear that his work, or even more—his mission was to *create new maroons and furthermore imprison and isolate the people who would now be called field-workers.* Ah! In the future (that he would still be master of for a long time to come) he saw the only positive inheritance he could leave his great-grandnephews: he would undertake systematically to surround and hence smother the plain. So those who escaped it would never have the leisure to come back and spread the word about how they accomplished this bit of petty daring! As for the maroons, he would make some new ones just for his own pleasure. Yes, his grandchildren would know nothing about this. In his omnipotence it was *his past* (his, his alone, his as he stood erect beside his woman on horseback) that he would prolong! The cantankerous old man planned his defiance. He alone was powerful. So just who would interfere with him like that, claiming to impose upon him some bankrupt existence when he himself had never committed any offense against its laws or regulations? What offense? What wrong? . . .

The question, consequently—*"Why did La Roche die on a slave boat?"* —remained incomplete. It was too direct to take into account the crazy, mad dimension or in any case the unreason into which the old bastard was now advancing. As if he were borne toward some culmination that would have provided his life with the permanent luster of a magnificent demise. The question needed something more; just as La Roche had to be seen in the proud and logical continuity of his life, but also in the drunkenness and dissipation of these latter days. Take the question of darkness farther with a word from darkness. Trace the steps of the haughty planter from the moment when, at the bedside of the dying Senglis, he had, perhaps for the first time in his life as a grown man, not held back his tears but wept, until that evening when he dressed himself meticulously (as if for a ceremony) and had himself carried down to the foot of the cliff. Between these two moments flashed the steady gleam of one and the same *absence*: La Roche as if carried off somewhere else, in search of the *cause no one would reveal to him*. Follow him from this point, starting from that cliff, through the few events that might answer the question, at the same time that they would change it, or rather make it complete.

So that night the old bastard, unsteady on his feet, was playing conspirator. Not three days after the slipshod formalities of abolition, he set out to provoke the new order. *The old man expected a secret shipment of Africans!* Stamping his feet in pleasure, he swung a light from the top of the cliff, to which came an answering signal from out at sea. A small boat approached; "lights out" almost completely, it seemed. La Roche leapt spryly aboard and, playing to the hilt his role as smuggler, kept silent to the best of his ability. The little boat took a long detour out to sea to elude any possible surveillance and they reached the ship, which was not far out but hidden in a small cove. The men helped La Roche up the ladder that he would not otherwise have been able to climb all alone; at the top however, he *leapt onto the deck.*

"Ohé, Petty Officer Lapointe!" he shouted.

The ship's commander gave a start; he could not get used to the way the planter had never consented to address him by his title, Captain, on the pretext that he had known him as Petty Officer Lapointe, and what's more the name reminded him of some black maroon, who knows which.

Because, in fact, it was the *Rose* that had anchored in the secluded cove like this, to smuggle its cargo ashore! Captain Lapointe had replaced Captain Duchêne, who had died happy of a stroke just as he raised his arm to swig down a tankard of *tafia*. The ship-owners put their trust in Lapointe, and in actual fact he had proven himself the man for the job since recently the slave trade had become so dangerously complicated. Austere, fierce, and stubborn, Lapointe was fixed on immediate objects, on the precise maneuver for the moment, and would never trouble himself with any assumptions about the future. He had become familiar with the structures and organization of this business, gradually finding out the extent of Captain Duchêne's boastfulness (he had never admitted to the tight rein his employers kept him on) and the requirements of large slave ships: the return these ships demanded, Lapointe thought, kept the captains cornered between the hazards of the voyage and the strict expectations of La Rochelle or Bordeaux. The system was now so cumbersome that it was necessary to give the colons a stake in it in order to get them to help at the other end of the line. The unflagging La Roche thus had added this string to his bow—until this trip, probably the last for the patched-up, old, and wheezing *Rose-Marie*. The old man had, with the reticent backing of colons who couldn't afford to treat him with disrespect, improvised a special reception for the ship. He had persuaded them that this reception was mandatory, that the expenses committed eight months before for this voyage had to be covered, that there was a way to conceal the delivered stock in the area around the distilleries, and that once they were settled in, the Negroes' arrival could easily be back-dated or at least not declared, and that, moreover, this shipment was being delivered at ridiculously low prices. There was so much panic and confusion that he managed to convince a certain number of them that, provided he work out the practical matters, this mad project was solid.

Accompanied by his first mate, the former coxswain—who was so clever concerning the psychology of Africans—the captain stepped up to the old planter and his escort (two terrified black servants). The *Rose-Marie* did things the traditional way.

"Well, Petty Officer Lapointe, you have here a fine cargo! I hope you'll save the best for me!"

The old man paced up and down the deck, exuberant and short-winded at the same time, spluttering sounds that he instantly swallowed; then he raised his finger to his lips and whistled several sharp, sustained *shs*! The two or three absolutely necessary lanterns were turned down low and added to the conspiratorial atmosphere. It was a moonless night and the coastal bluffs threw a uniformly deep shadow where they were. Toads and night creatures could be heard spinning out their steady song at the top of the cliffs.

La Roche left Lapointe and his men abruptly and headed toward the mass of people one could barely make out on the deck. He had grabbed one of the lanterns on his way by. The sailors could see the yellow spot swing back and forth as La Roche lifted the lantern up to chests or faces. It was like the silent fluttering of a lightning bug against a field of black flesh. The speck of light elegantly moved farther and farther away accompanied by the satisfied purr of the one carrying it. Then suddenly, without a single sound, it disappeared. Or rather, after its silent extinction, swallowed up in the thick shadows, a clear cry could be heard from beneath this dark mass, like someone laughing for joy; then this shout that later none of the survivors could remember, that is, understand. Worried, the former coxswain had already headed off in that direction; Captain Lapointe called after him, "Above all, no firearms!"

The *Rose-Marie*'s first mate was immediately on the scene: in the total darkness no one saw him disappear into the magma. The sailors rushed forward with axes and sabers, rapidly clearing their path. The fighting spread; no one thought of leaving the old *Rose*, that is, not until they heard two huge splashes and the infinitely proliferating drops falling back into the sea. That was how La Roche's servants chose to escape the furious melee and get back to shore. Then, in one great surge, the cargo headed for the rail. Despite the chains and ropes, they all leapt overboard in the hope of reaching the land that was so close by. The sailors tried to prevent them but Captain Lapointe shouted again. "Let them, let them go!" The shouting died away as they all did everything possible to climb over the rail and churn the water frantically for the fifteen or twenty feet separating the boat from the foot of the cliffs. So the rain of black bodies fell.

"Let them all go to the devil!" shouted Lapointe.

What he did not say was that really he would have had no idea what to do with his merchandise now that La Roche was dead. He was stuck with this corpse, and considering all the noisy racket they had created in the night the best thing to do was clear out as fast as possible. The Republic did not joke around when laws were broken. Consequently, Lapointe gave orders to help them overboard: sailors grabbed hold of the Negroes who huddled on deck and did not respond to being hit. They threw them into the water without bothering to take off their irons. A lot of them were already reaching shore, spreading themselves over the steep ocher rocks like a layer of cane syrup on a buckled and rusty sheet of metal; others were helping each other in the water and some sank straight to the bottom.

Lapointe shouted to raise anchor and leave this disastrous spot. La Roche's clothes were a mess so Lapointe had someone straighten them, and a skiff was sent off to leave the body on some rocks at a little distance from the cove. The corpse in its white suit was glowing faintly as they pulled the skiff back aboard and the ship stood out to sea. As for the first mate, wrapped in a sheet and weighted down with a ball and chain, he was thrown with no ceremony at all into the sea along with two other sailors who were victims of the skirmish.

This is how the final battle ended: clumsily, bogged down in shadowy confusion. La Roche alone on his entablature, his eyes rolled back to stare at the harsh stars overhead, and this flood of exiles close by already searching for stones they could use to break their chains, while the Rose-Marie vanished out to sea. That was the last ship of the slave trade. It moved away from the coast, old, battered and hesitant, having abandoned the old bastard on his stele of rocks, having provided him with a troop of exemplary maroons, people who would never be on display in the market, who would never follow a bumpy cart rolling slowly down a mud road. The old colon thus was well taken care of for his final display: he could sleep there in the night warmth, surrounded by the felt of cliffs, accompanied by the shouts of battle; he could sleep, having known right to the end the world of contrasts that he had wanted for himself, with no gray zones or compromises. He who was already erecting in his catafalque of rocks the impenetrable ramparts behind which his descendants, debilitated by so much stubbornness and bitter solitude, would be permanently immured. Because he came to die on the edge of the land he had ruled over, not on its humus or on its sticky clay, or even on its hot sand, but in the hollow of a rock that his dead hand seemed still to grip. Rejected by the land and thrown up onto this sterile rocky spur where the wave spray would never once touch him. Waiting for some local inhabitant to come upon him by chance and run in panic to tell the police. After that he would be laid to rest, a half skeleton crawling with black flesh, in the huge mausoleum that would be built on the high ground at Acajou.

And on this last boat of the slave trade moving away from shore the way a crippled old man after a final outburst leaves behind even the memories of the successive girls he had, Lapointe, gloomier than ever, was considering his fate. He had dreamed, to the extent that he dreamed at all, of flawless operations, majestic entrances, the required account in detail, substantial benefits (not merely in the profit they guaranteed but also as a sign of what he was worth); finally he dreamed of retiring on some ancient, solitary moor—he looked out at the thick, flat darkness and laughed bitterly at his own bad luck, which had ensured that the rank of captain he had worked so hard for and that, right to the end, the old ape had denied him with his mean pretense, had actually gotten him nothing but disappointments. Because now, after years of notable service, he would have to account for a cargo *already arrived in a good port*, that neither English frigates nor the Republic's ships had forced him to throw overboard but that he had nonetheless lost, where?—not in the sea but on the land itself where he had been responsible for delivering them. The owners of the *Rose-Marie* would be inclined to skepticism, they would smell treachery, they would go over the secret report in which he related the affair—which he would have such a hard time writing—with a fine-tooth comb. If he even got that far. Because he was also in charge of a crew that two days hence would demand its pay and no doubt would mutiny. Where in damnation was he going to get the money? That didn't even take into account the *Rose* herself. Soon there would be reports about her everywhere: the last ship of the slave trade reduced to a ghost vessel, with no food or water, off the English and French shores, from both of which her privateering was banned.

Thus *"Why did La Roche die on a slave ship?"* was not the whole question. It did not include the old overlord's obsessions, his refusal to endorse in any way the actions of his descendants or their potential profits, his intent to remain at the dead center of the moment in which the horse-woman left him after she herself had set him this milestone. Completed, the question became: *"Why did La Roche die on a clandestine slave-ship?"* Without this additional word it made no sense, and there would have been no sense in even asking it. When those two agents collapsed onto their chairs, incapable of shutting their registry books, defeated by the smothering work and even more so by the terrifying indifference of this great wave they had faced, the old overlord of earlier days lay dead in the blaze of the day—his long voyage continuing now only on those solitary rocks through a night with no bearings. Yes, from that moment on, the *Rose-Marie* fleeing across the monotonous sea was foreshadowed in his life. Already there was nothing left of them (the man and the ship united through the same gesture) other than this indistinct movement at night just off the coast, at the edge of the land where the people who had escaped the fifteen-foot-deep water dragged themselves toward the steady song spun out along the ridge of the cliff . . .

"Because, Mister Mathieu, you see this sun over your head. But how many days have you just stood there without seeing it? Tell me, how many?"

Yet Mathieu's thinking was too wide awake and raced ahead of him in all di-

rections; he ran into all the lives and deaths crowded together with no time to put them in order. He turned this way and that in the crater of heat. Then, stopped dead in his tracks, he explored his mind from every angle and made no headway in its spinning machinery. The dry season swept him away far above the cabin.

Blazing fire exploded onto the highlands and the plain. Bamboo frayed in the heat, scorched ferns made hazy holes on his arm. When the wind rose up to the sky and melted into the motionless, cloudless blue desert, the roof of the hut had hardly quivered. The straw, stuck to itself by the blaze more tightly than when the rain massaged it, no longer exposed to the wind anything but its skeletons in dense compression. The red, the greens of the plain, the sumptuous ochers of clays, were all wrapped in a yellowish layer subtly shading their splendor. The real height of the dry season assailed the earth.

"But you don't know anything about today, papa! What's past is past, so tell me what still remains of it down there? Yes, tell me! It's been ages since you even went down as far as the tar road, do you see that speck down there? Listen, I'm going to go down soon. I do my looking in full daylight. What is night? I am not waiting for night. I am not a coward (yes I am afraid, fine, I'm afraid), I can see in full daylight, using the eyes I have today! We have to go down, papa, we have to."

"Yes, yes," said the old man. "Go on down, the time has come."

"But why don't you? You are the oldest person around. Are you never going to be done with your eternal counting of leaves? Look, I tell you, there are some traces, you see, and there are the registers. Knowledge."

"But all I can read," said the old man, "are the great sky and night asleep inside it. You, go down, go on down, the time has come!"

So, in a fever, Mathieu stood up and took off with long strides along the downhill trail. He never even said goodbye to Papa Longoué but hurried in the direction of the tar road, he chose to forget the procession of faces, gestures, words, an entire plantation of men and women each with its own distinct foliage, each arching against the sky in its own particular manner. Because wasn't what remained

for him, Mathieu, the thing pounding inside his head, the thing
throbbing in that half of his brain that he had been chasing after
for so long (enduring the pounding obsession all the while), was
it not this bend in the path just before it opened out onto the
canefields, there where the two lemon trees framed by a few yellow-
red peppers made the round edges of a green, shady peacefulness?
Was it not this mud-hole filled with harsh, cutting dust, in front of
the lemon trees where with each step he felt like he was falling from
the top of a cliff? Was it not, after this bend where he never failed
to stop as if tied there by his ankles, the silent light of fields that
looked abandoned but where you might also think that the irons
Béluse threw down there had taken root and multiplied to take
a firmer hold upon you? Delicate and lifeless, the hissing silence,
the brilliance of leaves stretched out blazing, was this not the real
face, the only gesture, the word? Who could reveal what even one
of these fields had been able to cover with the emptiness gradually
buried beneath its mud, how many voices, hoarsened by *tafia* and
the tom-toms to celebrate the final cutting, had it extinguished, so
that finally one man might fall before the field and recognize it and
say: "You are the Real One?" And instead, Mathieu, who could not
do this, wanted to distance himself from Papa Longoué, erase him
from the surroundings, cut the string and let this inflexible old
man go on ahead, while the others who were tied through the darkness to the *quimboiseur* would all fall helter-skelter into the water
hole. Because, the land Mathieu saw fuming there before him, is
not the land *always the thing still there?* "Because someday will they not
have to turn it over on itself so it will become profitable to make up
for all the years when it let itself be duped. Saint-Yves had it right!
When he hid seeds in the little bag hung around his neck he was
already trying to cajole it; because really some day the land will have
to stop its lies and the people who work it, far from any kind
of loudspeaker proclaiming their eternal damnation, will have to
find the clearing in the forest finally, the path downhill and the two
lemon trees. Because it is both Role and Actor, because moreover,
everything that is suffered and fulfilled comes about only because

of the land, because it exists, because it lets one stand up just enough to keep from dying?" Mathieu borne along like this toward the heated idea, the abstract but blazing idea set, perhaps (waiting for him), down there on the last leaf of the last stalk of the last cane-field, a mile and a half, no, let's say two miles away where he would reach it in half an hour, forced back into the darkness the proces-sion of faces, of specific desires, of profitable corpses that turned up in the wake of the old *quimboiseur*. He struck Papa Longoué from his mind. He meant to remain alone with the liberation blossoming inside him, "I tell you that in the end they will cultivate it, really cultivate it, not just slave away up and down its body for no rea-son." He meant to whirl around in this day fraught with a single grand idea and spin, drunk with the hot earth until he was giddy. He even called to a man (the only person on the road, trailing a wake, it seemed, through the blur of heat), a man completely gray: skin, rags, legs, pointed straw hat, all gray, merging with the grain of the earth. "Whose is this, hey, whose is all this?" And the country man smiled and answered: "A fine day to you. This belongs to Mr. Larroche. All of it, it's all Mr. Larroche's."

"Oh, yes, of course, Mr. Larroche's. Obviously."

Mathieu, stripped of his fine idea, came back down to earth, back from his dream of a flaming land; he went up to the leaf he had been focusing on from a distance, eager to pick it (while the man went on his way, occasionally turning around to look at the city youth who had strayed there), and, of course, there was obvi-ously neither a thought nor an answer on the leaf. It was a cane leaf with two yellow stripes along its edges; it was sharp and it crackled and Mathieu turned it over and over between his fingers. The leaf spoke no word of the great shared secret.

He heard Papa Longoué laughing. He thought: "Anyhow, I don't care who won the fight"; but he found himself once again inside a huge barrel rolling nonstop down the road and through the bung-hole dazzling as a plume of fire before his eyes Papa Longoué ap-peared grinning sardonically, "You cannot do it, I tell you, you can do nothing if you do not climb back through the source."

"But at least," thought Mathieu, "I'll stop at Stéfanise!" He laughed quietly to himself.

Tall-Stéfanise: inside the cabin she picked up the barrel and for no particular reason moved the piece of carved bark, and she went out onto the clearing, her great long body like a male papaya tree. She was thinking "OK, I have to go tend the yams." *(Because, hey! it was not just the supervisors who knew how to get their cooking and everything else done for them. You always had a woman to serve you, didn't you? Standing there beside you while you, before your gourd bowl of codfish and breadfruit, acted important, explaining how the point of work is that it is never done. Right?)* And as she went by she spoke briefly with Melchior in the hut he built for himself close by so he wouldn't bother them. Melchior said: "It is too bad what happened. Your father was in such good health." And for the thousandth time she replied: "Yes, it's simply too bad." They each knew this was not just talk and that the words were just to make contact.

Mathieu, alone on the road, laughed. He was looking through the bunghole, and in its dazzle Stéfanise was making off with Apostrophe's hoe or his machete, or the packing box he sat on to receive those come to consult. And when Apostrophe asked for the thing in his poky, vague way she pretended to look around, muttering, "Well now, well now," until she finally came in full of triumph: "It had fallen behind the big pot!" And every now and then, her trumpeting voice would rise singsong and wheedling as she exclaimed: "Postrophe, my-man, are you going to tell me thank you very much?"

Dry Season at La Touffaille

Chapter 11

1

I tell you,
when he returned to La Touffaille where they were all waiting for
him, the mother self-absorbed, the sons shouting for no good
reason, the daughters expectant in their scatterbrained way except
for the eldest, thin as a rail, who stood there obstinately beside
her mother, and when they all saw him get down from the mule,
take the animal to the pen, finally come into the room they had not
moved from, knowing, just by the way he went by to go to the
animal pen, without glancing through the door to the room, yes
knowing that things were not going any better—at that moment
he was already without hope, he was giving up for the first time;
and the way he held himself stiffly when he came in was so he
would not show it. Because if he let them see that he no longer had
any hope, then it would confirm everything, and he would have
to expend ten times the energy just to put a stop to the wailing or
withstand the gloom.

The three sons, all so exhausted by the same worry that they
seemed a single man in triplicate (despite one of them being stocky
and withdrawn, the second all thin and gangly, and the third an-
gelic—almost pink beneath his black skin), all went with no transition from their shouts of excitement to a somewhat timid silence
and looked at him on the sly while the girls (except for the eldest),
on the other hand, rushed at him with a whole list of questions.
But he sat down without saying a thing and they all sat vacantly
around him.

Occasionally they would hear a mango falling on the tin roof
and the mule snorting noisily in its pen. Night noises, in short.
Things one only heard at night but that they were sensitive to now
as if it were already night keeping them silent at this time of day.
They heard the thumps on the roof and the scraping sounds in the
pen that they, nevertheless, were not in the habit of hearing—

except in the torpor of night before fatigue overcame them completely—and the fact was that for the moment there they were, open and defenseless before the gaping void of the afternoon. And he, the father, was taking a long time to speak. From where he sat he saw the bit of thistle-covered ground that went up behind the house to the mango tree, the few square yards of trampled clay like some rummage-sale crest dug up to decorate the rise of the little canefield out front. He could just see the green edge of the cane at the top of the slope and he imagined the slope itself, smooth and peaceful. To the left the path went on as if overwhelmed by the woods, strewn with rocks and slimy puddles; to the right it descended precipitously to a crossroads where plums grew and then all the way to an inlet where the river smoothed out and the children swam while they brushed the mules. And so he, the father, sat there like that, as if it were as much as he could do to sit and hold himself rigidly in the silence. But tumult assailed him: La Touffaille rushed in through the door at him—the land carefully planned and well-laid-out geographically, but also the place where they picked herbs, the whorls of branches, the thick clumps of fruit, the background of cacao trees, the yam plants' trembling tendrils, the buckets and buckets of sweet potatoes, all of it tumbling around inside his head. He was nothing but a voice now, an attempt at voice, a pain of voice trying to clear a path for itself through the engulfment of La Touffaille; and in the same way all he could hear echoing was a single, uniform voice when he knew perfectly well that there were eight of them answering him, seven if you took into account that the mother never opened her mouth, or rather six because Edmée, the elder, barely spoke as well.

"Senglis said there is no guano."

"But the ship was there the other day, not ten days ago!"

"He said that that boat was not the guano boat."

"But then, it's still going to come!"

"He said the boat will not be coming any time soon."

"But then we won't have a single bag, not one!"

"He said we have to make do this year without guano."

Then silence: *the girl thin as a wisp of smoke always stubborn there beside the sea and waiting my dear I don't know what she is waiting for,* her eyes looked blind her mouth seemed locked shut ah that was Edmée; the only living, dark, incomprehensible one of the Targin family. Their history, the life they endured was now no more than the dried-out throbbing of the earth, and she alone, Edmée, stood in the midst of the others, all of them Targins, but reduced to merely "father" or "mother," "sons" and "daughters"; indistinguishable. The faintest of silhouettes merged with the earth.

"He said he will only take twelve cartloads; business isn't doing well and he will only buy twelve and won't pay in advance."

Then silence, and the mother beyond despair, going back over the days, grasping at the simple moments at the automatic gestures of existence (so as not to see the death hanging over her head): the three boys and three girls, led pitilessly by the eldest, who splashed themselves (or pretended to) with the green foamy water where herbs had been soaking—the pot with red glaze inside, with pink or blue veins worked into the clay, the one reserved for the parents—the leaves stuck to the children's skin, while they shivered (or pretended to) and the eldest cleaned them off with a bunch of herbs that lathered up to her elbow—every morning and every night bursts of sound around the big rusty, iron jugs the water spilled from, tepid and more pleasant when it had spent the afternoon warming in the big reservoir set up under the bamboo gutters—breadfruit cut into cubes in the black pot, peelings in the very top of the cauldron to wedge the whole thing shut, plus moreover a rock for additional weight when the water boiled hard—the kitchen below the room they lived in, its floor of burnished earth leading out to the foot of the cacao trees, whereas the big room was adorned with a white wood floor that sagged everywhere—the wood, charcoal, and ashes trampled down in a corner—the rock worn thin set between the big room and the kitchen like a rickety step in a staircase—eating around the table, all lined up on the two benches on either side except for the father, who had the only real chair—every now and then codfish steaming in sauce made with red butter and the smell of peppers in the house—manioc dust all around the table at the end of every meal—siesta time that was so pleasant during which the girls had to be deloused at length while the boys shaved each other's heads (dried coconut-head) with the razor they took out of its greasy rag—the slow, never-ending battle against flies—unremittingly round and around, the deafness creeping over them from the fidgety din—flies, flies.

Then silence, dry season outside; and this was well after the day Stéfanise went up into the acacia trees for the last time, but you see dry season never changes, sit yourself down on your heels in the dust and when you are ready to get up you are quivering dust, yes it was in heat like that that Stéfanise said to her father, Anne Béluse, when both of them were shrunk flat in the floury dust in front of the cabin at Roche Carrée: "It's been ten years since they gave us our papers. If I stay here one single cursed day longer now I will be yellower than that piece of paper!" And Anne, out of sorts (because haven't you noticed how people who are violent are always stunned when something unexpected descends upon them), answered: "You can just stand there and try to tell me that it's on my account that you are still here eating my manioc?" But Stéfanise was too strong for him, rather than listing all the work she got through, she laughed softly. And Anne, sweet as a lamb (because haven't you noticed how those same people are sweet at heart), made the list; not one of the work she got through but a list of the times she went up into the forest to hang out with Apostrophe: the day, for example, when Sylvius had brought her a piece of cloth, who knows how he got it, and since she was not there he hadn't wanted to leave the present but went away with it; and the evening the Acajou lands caught on fire, and he, Anne, had gotten all the gear out to say nothing of the woman or Saint-Yves, and they had spent the night in front of the cabin in the light of the fire, while that Stéfanise, hey, she was off in the woods nice and cool...and Stéfanise laughed. But though she had always trumpeted abroad anything that upset her, this time she did not admit to her father how Apostrophe was eluding her: he made no effort, whereas so many men would have been willing to, yes, and how she had to go back up every time to rekindle his memory—while Melchior and Adélie smiled quietly.

But then this was long after that time, Anne had had a chance to take back his last violence, having made up with Stéfanise; then he died falling from a tree: he had screamed bloody murder as he came crashing through the branches—and Saint-Yves had taken the cabin. But when Anne died, twelve years after Stéfanise went up into the forest for the last time, there was still no child to shout under the acacia trees. Melchior, settled down with Adélie in the shack near the cabin, just couldn't understand how it could be. In a country where children sprang up everywhere like wild sage, Stéfanise moaned all day long just to have one and it never came. So it was the Longoué's fate that they would always suffer to perpetuate the family. Perhaps such a rare species does not reproduce just like that, eh? And the Béluse family also began to cut back on the number of kids in the cabin; but who could count the offspring they had outside, whether it was Saint-Yves or Zéphirin or Mathieu the father, all of whom were apparently sterile or almost so in their own homes, but who cast their seed everywhere outside with the greatest of freedom? Because only the Longoués stuck to having a single heir, sometimes accompanied by a brother or a sister created for the sole purpose of supporting the work of this heir, the one chosen to perpetuate the line. This is because there was, in fact, something to inherit, something that the person called to be heir had to be judged capable of fulfilling. And it is certain that a Béluse (despite their desire to imitate, that is, the pretence they made of limiting their family) was free to waste his seed anywhere outside, it was of no importance. Whereas a Longoué, eh, he had to conserve himself. And in compensation the Longoués lived long lives; but you needn't think many people in the country could outdo La Roche or Senglis in the race to live longest; or reach almost eighty like Longoué-La-Pointe, much less Melchior's ninety-one! They were rapidly wiped out by wear and tear. Moreover they were in a great hurry to multiply everywhere at once to make up for that death galloping to meet them. As if death would get tired, faced with such a dense field, or waver in the end? But look, this time Stéfanise and Apostrophe were going too far. She just filled herself full of laments, and he was preoccupied with exercising his practice. Even if a Longoué is a rare creature, ought they have been so insistent—putting it off for fourteen years just to raise the price? And Stéfanise's energy during these long sterile years thrust her upon Apostrophe: she overwhelmed him with thoughtful attentions and wanted to know everything about him; which meant that she gradually was initiated into the *quimboiseur's* secrets. Apostrophe felt it was improper for a woman to step so close to the realm of darkness, but like his father, Melchior, he was withdrawn from whatever was going on; he was always dully present but could not come up with anything to say. Apostrophe dodged the issue and just went along. Ah! that Stéfanise! Next she was picking up the little barrel and putting the piece of carved bark on her head all by herself. She became bolder, until soon she was giving care on the sly to sick people who were accommodating because they were happy to "consult" without having to pay; and Apostrophe shook his head. . . . *Fine, she was my mother, but what a phenomenon; for more than twenty years she made his head spin with her talk and reached the point where she knew as much as he did; except she actually suffered before she succeeded whereas he, completely absent in the forest and almost without willing it, laid his hand on you and soothed you, even if everywhere else it was the dry season and the sun was a sledgehammer on your head.*

Or, after that period, the sizzling at La Touffaille that would swell into a ball there outside the better to roll inside the house: they thought the roof would lift right off because of the pressure, and the next minute they saw it would flatten a manioc cake with boiling oil on the floor. La Touffaille cooked; it made you wonder why Senglis wanted so badly to chase them away and put his cattle there. Not even cattle would have been able to stand it on the side of that hill.

But he, the father, did not budge. Who would have had enough willpower to lift a hand to any job at all there when the truth was blatant: no money no guano no harvest (except for the dozen wagonloads of cane, which added up to just about zero), and the pig (the only part of which still showed was its head), and the hen's eggs spoiling in the heat? And all of them, at least the three sons and the three daughters who were so quick to take action, just stood there, absolutely vacant, around the father. The mother self-absorbed, Edmée, the eldest, thinner and thinner as she sweat. Until evening came (there was nothing to cook in the pot) and they heard the rumbling tom-tom like a sign of an unlikely storm in the dry land. Moths in search of light stuck to their skin. All the day's sizzling and crackle accumulated in the flash of lightning bugs. The beating sounds grew louder over there, probably to help in the descent of darkness. In the room those nine statues finally came to life, the father sighed: "Saturday today, they are beating the drum at Monsieur Pamphile's place . . ." But I tell you:

She—and this for me is the only gauge in time as it draws to a close—she was not yet born, one can imagine that neither the father nor the mother saw in their minds that one day together they would have a girl who would open the path for eight others (two of whom would die as infants), and then myself, in my mother Stéfanise I was only like a lament in search of its own body, when for the umpteenth time fighting broke out everywhere! We have to assume that La Roche's nephews had adapted to the new situation or that quibbling in the fields for a few pennies was not really profitable, or that the piece of paper turning yellow inside a closed gourd did not provide much extra, or maybe even that the mulatto gentlemen were weakening in their conviction and fight, don't we? Whatever it was, once again they all surged forth because poverty makes you as inexhaustible as a butterfly, and many of them shouted: "Long live Guillaume!" because there was some Guillaume with a number after his name making war on the other side of the ocean.[1]

"And why not 'Long may we live'?" said Mathieu.

Whatever, it's the same old story: they are in the hills, they are in charge; and then they go down into the flatlands where people are waiting to massacre them. That is what happened in the far south in a place always burgeoning with trouble. Now look there, it is abandoned beneath the sand. All that time fallen. And why not say long may we live, it is because you are surrounded by the sea: consequently, if the sea casts Guillaume up on the sands you take Guillaume number and all, and you wear him on your head to make your advance. And notice that this time really

1. Here, Guillaume is the Gallic form of Wilhelm I, King of Prussia. Prussia defeated France in the Franco-Prussian War, taking Alsace and Lorraine as the spoils of war. Wilhelm was crowned emperor of the Deutsches Reich at Versailles in 1871.

no division exists in the masses; everybody's mind was on the same thing. The same can't be said for the mulattos who for the moment have a grip on the crank-starter: the proof is that a certain number of them were shot and the others thrown into jail for life. Everybody into the same one, taken off with the people whose papers called field-workers: former maroons, slaves, freedmen. If it were not for Melchior or Apostrophe up there in the forest you really would have thought that nothing had ever happened back there in the infinite land.

"Nothing did happen," said Mathieu.

All of them joined together in this, the same plundering all over again. As if I could not see it, and you too despite holding your hand in front of your eyes, yes, fighting and division in the country back there over the ocean? This is how it was:

You are there, you open your eyes, the light says it is morning. Woods all around rising up to the sky. You close your eyes, you rock there in the sweetness. If you hear a sound it is the twitter of a hummingbird. You see your luxuriant body on the finely braided mat. But the wood is an ascending shaft inside the house and the sky is the roof. You stand up, you go outdoors, you see the houses. The dogs as big as zebus, sweet as papaya. You walk, no one answers. You too are sleepy-eyed. But you walk. Then there's the river, the horizon turns yellow. But yellow, yellower than a leaf in dry season. It falls in the distance, so far away that you are reeling inside its body, and for you the streaming water is like a lost thread in flesh that has neither rest nor hunger. You can walk until you reach death, you see no end to it. Where is the sea, you know nothing of the sea. You go on down the river. You put the water on your back and carry it out to the middle. The water is on you, you become more flowing than the river. You alone, you are the forest and the river and the houses. You think, someone has to say who will be in the work to come, who will plow. You think, there are not enough machetes for defense. You think, the line of slaves will go by in three days, a two days' walk toward the setting sun. You think, hide everybody in the woods starting tomorrow. Because the forest that bears its own sky beneath its branches is also inside your head. You alone in the light. You stand up, the water comes with you. This is the infinite country. You walk toward the houses all in a straight row. You stop. Too much silence. The relentless horizon shrinks on your skin. You are caught. You see that you are caught, all of them there with guns, the disemboweled dogs, not a sound, not a false note; you see him, he is sneering, full of vengeful venom he stands among the people and points to them; and just then you hear the first scream and the first woman forced out of a cabin, struck with the flat of a sword. There is nothing to say, the forest leaves you, the river leaves you, ten of them are already upon you, then in spite of the terror all around, you hear the chains they are preparing: this is how it was. Ho.

But now look, look at today, at the moment, that is, that they all tear down the hillsides shouting "long live Guillaume the First or Second," and you would think nothing had happened in the country back there. They act like moths flying everywhere, bumping into everything, and this makes them at the same time as densely united as the hairs on a head; they end up with the same song, they speak as one when they shout. They all want to rush ahead, and there is no longer any maroon climbing up into the forest trailing chains like a snake behind him. They are all running, they are part of the same river; I agree that the country back there has been forgotten, but then why does the old story repeat itself over and over, eh? The moth-of-misery that flies up, and the hand that slaps it down? Why the gunfire again before they once more fall back down into their oblivion, their happy-go-lucky lives?

"They don't fall back down!" said Mathieu.

And now you have gone through the forest and reached the pen you will be crammed into. You are deader than a fallen cachibou full of black ants. In your head you cry, "I'm dead before tomorrow. Wherever they take me I'm not going!" But this is the thing: the other man has not taken advantage of the treachery, anyhow what would he have done being in charge of a village of old men and sick people with no food, he's lucky that his masters take him not even hearing him squeal like a pig and that they throw him into the mud of the pen next to you.

"Into the mud of the pen," said Mathieu.

And today, I mean at this moment when they all without exception for the first time went tearing down the hillsides, you can tell that it is all over, forgotten. Wherever you have been taken the sons of your sons have risen up and the sons of the sons of the other man too, they bathe together in a different river; but soon soldiers come in and the dust settles on their heads again. That's the way it is. As if the ones who are dead had been created to be a sun that rises and then sets, changing nothing in the day that goes by. As if they covered your head as they passed with a dust that would make you stand there petrified. And the sea that had brought Guillaume bore him off immediately who knows where. Now, this was long before she was born at La Touffaille; because time goes by for the people shouting in the south, but it is also going by three years later at the moment she was born (that is a year after I found inside the body of Stéfanise the lament I was chasing after), and twenty years on down it is still going by (because the past is not simple, ah! There are so many pasts coming down to you, you have to do a real juggling act if you want to catch them, not just stand there with your arms over your head like a slow-poke waiting for them to set themselves down in some cool spot nearby) when she had already left La Touffaille to find me (Ti-René was on the way, the lump he was making in the world was apparent) and when the three Targin sons, you could call them René's uncles, began to despair.

They were still a single, unvarying voice, just try to figure out which one was talking and which one listening, they were all three the voice of the Targin son, just as there had been the father's voice and the ever so infrequent voice of the mother and the voice of the daughter (it too divided into three branches), without counting the sound of the even more sparing voice of Edmée the eldest, which had pulled away from the rest of them when Edmée had met Papa Longoué: the three sons, busy in the animal pen, while their single voice discussed the work, the land around them, the despondency abroad in the land. The youngest who was barely fourteen contributed the barest bright note to the monotonous dribble.

"Manzel-Edmée, thin as she is has chosen the right moment to get her feet out of here!"

"What do you mean, thin? She's getting rounder and rounder in front."

"What do you mean, rounder? She's a stick with a nice little bundle hooked on her front."

"Do you think we're going to leave too?"

"Sure thing I'm going, I'll be heading to town."

"You'll leave the girls here?"

"I don't know myself, if Monsieur Senglis offers us the land up above Pays-Mêlés, it's because there's not much to do in it!"

"You don't understand anything. He says La Touffaille is a good place to put cattle, now with the Central Plant they are bringing bulls in from Brazil and La Touffaille is good for grass and feeding cattle."

"The land up there is good. It's just that you can't take cattle up there."

"I don't know myself. Whether it's here or there, I'm going to town."

"What are you going to do?"

"Who cares! I'll find a job that's for sure!"

"So then he has a khaki shirt and alpaca trousers!"

"You are going to leave your mother?"

"Manzel-Edmée has left. Why not me?"

And in the mule pen the three sons worked together like always. They avoided any work that would separate them, they arranged things so they would be together. The eldest cut along two sides of the heavy, rough fertilizer bags before turning them inside out and sewing them back up with big stitches; the second was cleaning straw and putting what wasn't any good onto an old manure pile; the youngest was braiding rope from thick lianas that he hooked to a beam. Minor tasks, almost invented in order to wait for better days. The straw roof of the mule shed hissed in the dry season. Was it only the youngest of the three brothers (his feet together at the base of a post, his body tilted back, swung from the rope he was braiding) who perhaps guessed that the occasional moments of dizziness came over them there in the sun because they were giving up?

So all of those people, and the ones before and the ones after, created to be the light and the sun of the day going by! But fallen nameless, like a sun with no horizon in a day with no light. But they are the light that is lit underneath, they are the cemetery with no sand or candle or seashells that makes fire beneath your feet: you forget about Guillaume or whatever other pretext, you look at the mark beneath your feet and the torches. All those men, lit even before your father's father was born, making little lights for you Mathieu. The nameless fighters whose deeds you don't even know. Raised up for you Mathieu. So that you leave the infinite country back there and then are here taking into your body the red land with its limits. All those suns blazing day after day, but you never find the grave in the forest, just an occasional yellowed bone under some rotten root. So that one day Stéfanise, who for months has run everywhere along the hills so she can better bear the flesh of her flesh and not die of fear faced with Apostrophe, will choose the moment when Apostrophe is away and, aided by a neighbor, will push this little pile of meat through her body all the way to the floor of the cabin. Without a cry, fearing that if Apostrophe were to hear he would come running full tilt. This woman who spent her life making noise. And so that she would look at the little pile, all stiff and black on the cabin floor and say to her neighbor with a laugh: "This one is going to know who's the master" — thus relieving herself of the terror that had been growing larger and larger inside her at the same time as the child. And no one, you realize, had thought at first to name this thing that was full of blood, a bit of meat with his eyes shut whose name was already Papa Longoué. From the first day. And even if later they decided to give him some name like Melchior, let's say, or Ocongo, or both at once, it doesn't matter, he is already Papa Longoué. As if he were born an old man to be the papa whose only son would be struck dead far far away.

But Stéfanise, apparently vindictive, comically furious that this child had taken fourteen years to present himself, kept to her promise and definitely showed him who's the master. She was crazy about the boy and took him in hand, even stepping ahead of his grandfather Melchior, and making all the decisions. Melchior smiled, thinking that, perhaps, Stéfanise was putting him (Melchior) on the same level as Apostrophe. She gave no sign of wanting to monopolize things or use violence to impose her way; the child simply followed her everywhere. At first in her arms like a boutou and then spiraling alongside her and apparently of no concern to her. But for him she had rediscovered the monologue that the Longoués so treasured, and without looking at him she would talk out loud about every thing she was doing and describe every place. It was up to him, as he drifted here and there around her to remember what he could. So the outbursts that she had flooded the hills with in earlier times were transformed into a constant stream of words, neither soft nor shouted, just normal. Clear, plain, and simple. And this is how the grievous story began for Papa Longoué, he was still a child and scarcely standing; it was to be his forever. Because all his life he suffered from toiling after a knowledge he had been called for, that he certainly was worthy of possessing, but that relentlessly eluded him or rather left him constantly unsatisfied: perhaps because the knowledge was no longer enough, perhaps because he was out of breath from running after Stéfanise, and perhaps precisely because Stéfanise, despite her light, was not the person (a woman) required for transmitting the knowledge. She seemed to know it and fear it, because from the beginning she said over and over that she wanted to make the child into a Longoué, as if he were not one. It is true that Apostrophe was away too much and did not concern himself enough with his descendant. It seemed there was a hole opening up again between Melchior and Papa Longoué that Stéfanise was desperately trying to fill while Apostrophe swayed on the edge of it, unconcerned. Nonetheless, of all of them, he was the one best adapted to his situation. As if, absentminded and perpetually wandering, he had remained the only one to dream of the great country back there, of the infinite coastline curving neither out nor in—and that at his death he would take his solitary dream with him. Or perhaps, alone among them, he never felt that curiosity that had driven Melchior toward the market town and kept Stéfanise at Roche Carrée for so long. He did not suffer in the least from being essentially cut off from real life, from the abject poverty that he was part of nonetheless. He felt neither a lurking scorn nor tender anxiety for the people from the valleys and ravines: he simply saw them, occasionally he spoke to them, he tended them. He never suspected that such indifference distanced him almost entirely; that in a different way and on his level the gap that Melchior had so patiently crossed was being dug again more deeply. Also, it would not have been possible to achieve all at once nor once and for all harmony between these different worlds. And because of this new detour, because of this backing away Papa Longoué was subjected to the discomfort bestowed upon him thus by Apostrophe, to the precise extent that he had been endowed with an ability to sense discomfort. Which made him, all in all, a Longoué while at the same time he was not. What would have been called great sensitivity somewhere else—latent in him and not in the least sustained by reason, and perhaps nothing but fatigue after having chased around after Stéfanise so much—marked him with an anxiety and weakness that he never got over. It was this weakness that made him valuable. And he probably would have succumbed to it all, smothered beneath the frenzied instruction of Stéfanise, if Melchior, without being obvious, had not filled him with quivering and with an infinite capacity to smile and be patient that would help him get through the irksome, nocturnal regions so full of seductions and things he could not grasp, the regions destined to be his particular life, without going under.

So he was five years old, beginning to stare in amazement at the frenzied turmoil of Stéfanise, when one day Apostrophe stayed in the cabin and did not get up. The child did not understand all the excitement. He watched Melchior bending over Apostrophe, the gourd full of boiled herbs, the steaming cloth wrapped around the sick man's chest, Adélie sitting in a corner staring straight ahead, the precise and orderly stirrings of Stéfanise who was suddenly silent, who helped Melchior with no thought of being in charge of anything. And later it seemed to Papa Longoué that this was a moment in which he had grown older all at once, that is, he had merged with his own nature all at once and had joined the nameless old man who was inside him, because in the end all he remembered about this day, apart from the preparations and all the turmoil of illness and death, was the animal cry Stéfanise uttered from five in the afternoon until noon the next day. One single terrible scream, the scream of a mare in the throes of death, the scream of a wounded mother, the scream of earth disemboweled: for one whole evening, one whole night and one whole morning it rolled across the hills. As if Stéfanise for the first time was screaming for all those who had not screamed; she filled the country with voices, for all the people who from the first day, astounded and feverish, had not had time to climb the peaks of suffering with their scream; for all those who had turned their story into a long, tearless processional. As if taking onto herself all the suffering accumulated everywhere among the locust trees, in the flatness of the fields, the yellow bay water of the Cohées, in the stagnant sweetness of old backwaters. She screamed without stopping, as if separated from the occasion and never once looking at Apostrophe lying there. The people he had cared for, whose miseries he had relieved, for whom he had been the only doctor they could approach, the only possible confidant, the only dreaded authority (in that way he had played his role well—in spite of the dream that carried him elsewhere—in the slow maturing of the new land) came and went beside this scream, walking alongside the scream, and they in turn never once looked at Stéfanise, the motionless source of the scream. And Papa Longoué the child was drowned in this scream the whole day long, and it went on inside him long after his ears no longer heard it. He emerged from it not suffocated but soaked to the marrow: a knowing old man who, from the age of five, in his nameless child's body, was brewing all that was necessary to know and bear such lamentation.

And thus, for the three more years during which Stéfanise went back and forth stupefied and automatic as a pendulum, he was ready to take in Melchior's words. The latter did not clutter his mind with recipes or specific knowledge but through these murmurings, like an invisible whistling bird up in the branches and just as constant and insistent as the bird, gave him a taste for water seeking itself out, for stalks that grow, for rocks that crumble, for earth that works; for everything that quietly and patiently comes to life beneath the sun.

"Look," said Melchior. "Stéfanise is always racing around everywhere. She will tell you the words, as for me I haven't time for that; I'm already standing on the other side of the hill. I am going to go back to the country over there with my feet covered with mud. You must not leave Stéfanise, she makes noise and you may think she doesn't know, but I tell you, she will put you where the earth is good."

"Look," he said. "Don't try to run when your time comes. The ones already gone call you from their side; their strength is greater than your strength."

"Look," he said. "You have this forest of acacias, but you must be sure to go down onto the flatlands and eat the *icaques* that grow in the savanna and suck on the lemons from down there. . . ."

Then he would go with the child into the flickering darkness where no one could follow them, places that Stéfanise herself never reached. There he showed the boy Apostrophe, more real and alive than the shadow inhabited by dream who had lived in the cabin, a smiling Liberté who asked to carry the bag, Longoué running after Man-Louise, who was carrying a large golden loaf of bread in her hand, Cydalise Nathalie surrounded by voracious, soil-depleting plants, the old bastard who buried himself beneath the rocks, then the others, penned up on the boat and on all the boats that had come before that one. But above all he made the child touch the indescribable darkness, the side of it, that is, where these transparent woods merged with the heavy forest of the country back there, at the point where the fantastic germinations, the stunning shoots of these two forests created beneath their domes a single sky for the lands that were so distant from each other; then the tangled knot of herbs connected by the *leaf of life and death*; and the memory, that was no more than a greater willingness, able to transform a bag into a tomb, a little barrel into an abyss furrowed by black paths, a piece of bark carved into a screen against the powers; and the future, which was stagnant.

From all this night quivering and because of his own clairvoyance Papa Longoué got his frailty, and this darkness thus prepared him to confront the clarity of Stéfanise. The way that one swiftly plants cuttings that will take well in a friable, airy field for the next harvest, the child whose tilth Melchior had seen to was able to bury in his breast the precise words that Stéfanise tossed there, learning the livid stench of the boat, the healing herbs sorted from the rest, and the dead who come back when called.

Well, so she was my mother, but what a phenomenon! You cannot imagine how far inside my head she went; luckily I was equipped to resist. As Melchior said: "She is going to take you in her hand, she is going to put you on her shoulder. If you are not strong enough to stay there without wiggling you'll tumble off. But if you hold sturdy as a palm tree then you will see from way up there on top of her tall body everything around that needs to be seen." And I can tell you that I never tumbled down. I can tell you that I saw. Now, ah Godsalmighty! Those degenerate men who pretend they can see and who mislead those poor people. There is one who has set himself up down there who pretends to see with his eyes shut; he sells them spring water pretending it will cure them, just the same way as when they take holy water at church believing it will make the sick swelling in their big feet go down; he's a crafty one but he's going to end up head down with his eyes in his hair. He does things like this:

You see, one day a fellow shows up, someone I know, an old man who claimed he would never come up here, and he said to the so-called seer: "My mule, I just don't understand at all, the more I give him in his bucket the worse off he is, tongue hanging out and not eating." The fake says: "Ah! So you have a mule?" Then the old man gets mad, why shouldn't he have a mule, he's a respectable man and the longer this goes on the more he thinks the animal is going to blow away in a breeze being so despondent. Soon its ribs are going to go right up into its head and goodbye from the other direction. And the fake says: "It's nothing, nothing at all. You just have to make the mule swallow Perlimpinpin powder in a bucket of water. There you go, that's two francs." The old man stands there absolutely motionless, he says: "And what is Perlimpinpin powder?" The fake exclaims: "What? At your age and respectable as you are you don't know what Perlimpinpin powder is? Ah! My ears are going to turn into water! You take some America powder, you mix it with Perlimpinpin powder, you add essence of min-nin vini, because you see, if you don't put in the essence the animal will never come and drink the dose, and then finally you put in some extract of Spanish bull-feather, that's for strength. There you go, that's two francs." The old man repeats: "America powder, Perlimpinpin powder, essence of min-nin vini, Spanish bull-feather." Then he stands stock-still, stiffer than ever, and says: "Fine. But just where am I going to find all those powders?" "Go on!" says the fake. "And where do you find redfish if not in the sea, and blackfish if not in the river? The pharmacy has powders. You just have to go down to the pharmacy and Monsieur Toron, a fine mulatto, is going to show you the powders all lined up on shelves. For four francs you'll have them. It's one franc per powder." And there's this old man adding up four plus two, his head bursting with sweat; then he pulls out a rag and manages to count the big pennies and the little ones, copper pennies and pennies with holes, until he has two francs worth lined up in the fake seer's hand. That's the way that man is. A fake. He's not a person who could have stood up to it if he had been confronted with the voice of Stéfanise, not even for a minute I tell you. The first minute she said his name he would have been reduced to dust. But it's true, ever since the day that Melchior kept standing there against the big mango tree with his boutou beside him, there are no more of them. No. No, none left.

Ever since the day that Melchior, in the same spot as Man-Louise (but he was standing, standing up against the mango tree, his thick, straight body leaning on the trunk), had waited for the sight of Stéfanise and the child coming for the last time down the curving path through the trees; then he shut his eyes and he was brought down like a sturdy man, one never weak or tired, whom the dry seasons skip over. And when Stéfanise had buried him in turn in a grave (after Adélie and the others who had departed there), when she had packed the soil down well at the spot—there was perhaps not a single one of them any more in all the country. Not a one, except for the oldman-child who was all frailty as his name said, who could create darkness at high noon. Not a single one left to kindle the zombie population risen up to attack, or to sink a Senglis into the death throes of delirium at midnight. Their zombies were of no use except to terrify the children, and their power was limited to tormenting a neighbor.

It was no surprise that from that moment on the people down there learned so readily to despise each other, to climb on top of each other; that is, someone who thought he was farthest from the highlands looked down on someone still close to the hills, and so forth. Not surprising that they so readily confused fake seers with the real ones; that they despised the color of the forest on their skin and felt in their flesh the temptation to get out of their flesh. Because the country back there was dead for good; fine, agreed there was the new land, but they never did take it into their guts, they did not see that there was only one sky over their heads, they looked off into the distance for other stars, not to mention their river that had dried up and their rootless forest. As if this country was a new boat at anchor, where they crouched in the holds and between the decks without ever climbing into the masts on the hills. And on the contrary they sank deeper and deeper, every day crammed even more tightly into their ignorance of full daylight, having left at the top of the masts the oldman-child whose vertigo (the frailty) was his greatest merit. It was no surprise that these Negroes complained about each other. They were no longer towed along by something that took its strength in the infinite country back there; they thought they could go where La Roche or Senglis were, or maybe even Lapointe in his moors or his office in Bordeaux. This is how those two agents, like bitter prophets, had sent them all off to Poitou and the earldom of Bigorre where they would wander with neither hearth nor home. But poverty gets to you, in spite of yourself you cross back over the ocean; soon you are landing in the narrows of yourself. After all, it was just one more precipice to get over, one more ravine, a water hole like the one that during his lifetime Melchior had gone beyond. You cannot leap over the abyss or climb up the cliff in a single stride. And already, the time once again, undivided, they had all risen up in the south, at that moment, yes, Anne Béluse, who bore within him the crunchy earth from the bottom of the hill, had been sent to the town cemetery, wrapped up in a white cloth hanging from a bamboo pole like a hammock. The first of his line to depart thus, preceded by a man riding a mule and swung from the shoulders of four neighbors jogging along and taking turns in teams of two (the sagging cloth under the dead man's weight almost dragging in the grasses along the trails) and singing and chanting to keep the pitch of excitement high. And from now on the Béluses would take this trail for their last journey; it seemed as if this was the day they had waited for to enter the community down there; this was how Saint-Yves went, who died the same year as Melchior, and so did Anne's wife long ago, and this is how Saint-Yves's wife would go tomorrow. But meanwhile Zéphirin, the son of Saint-Yves, had become a grown man; and a year after the birth of Ti-René Longoué he had a son, who was Mathieu Béluse.

2

"But you are going too fast!" said Mathieu. "Can't you announce the dates one after the other and quit spinning around back and forth? Swirling like the dust at Fonds-Brulé, ho?"

So! You hope there's a ledger, one of those big notebooks they open up at the town hall right under your nose to impress you, that can tell you why a Béluse followed a Longoué that way, or why Louise had obeyed the gesture he made when she already considered herself related to La Roche, or even how it happens that all those African languages flew out of their heads like a flock of finches? Open your ledgers, fine, you spell out dates; but as for myself the only thing I am able to read is the sun blowing down on my head like a big wind. And the first days, they are up there, a single cloud, almost blue, marking time, you try to climb into the throbbing but those are days heavier and deeper than the underside of the earth, they are hardly moving in the midst of the sky's brilliance, you can hardly see them start off in your direction, then bit by bit it turns into rain, it all gushes down, the day before yesterday is a sigh, yesterday is a flash of lightning, today is so bright in your eyes that you do not see it. Because the past is up there all tightly clustered about itself and so far away; but provoke it and it takes off like a herd of bulls, soon it is falling on your head faster than a cayali hit by a slingshot.

Not even letting you stop in a bend in the road to look around and take in the close-cropped savanna, its rough green surface splattered with red. Here and there little herds of *icaques* grazing on the savanna, their rough leaves hiding the yellow fruit. Swift expanses quickly exhausted where a thicketed area suddenly toppled into the rustling of a clump of bamboos. The smooth flight of a red furrow soon knotted by undulations or colliding with three surging *filaos*. Everything resoundingly bright and dry, pale green and light brown and around it the great hills or dark highlands. But the original humus was spread evenly everywhere by the same labor; in the very middle of canefields a gaping tangle of vegetation would suddenly reveal cascading water deep in the crevices. Now the past poured down on your head does not allow you to dawdle alongside the patient toil that had raked the forest like this, raised the savanna, distributed the humus, brought men together. One would have to have known the moment when the sea of earth launched in assault against the cliff had subsided in the acacia woods (thinned out from now on). Discern the side, that is, where the savanna and fields had met with the forest (still shimmering in its crazed germination, higher up than the acacias) that had itself rejoined the heavy forest of the infinite country. But the roaring din of the past on your head did not let you verify this moment or take the measure of this side. Consequently, it was better to teach people, whether they were creatures of the humus or creatures of the cane-fields, how their feet had taken them from the savanna to the forest and from the forest to the savanna. Imagine a closer understanding of the hows and whys, for example how the earth had been abandoned here and worn-out there. Why worn-out? Worn-out for whom?

Because, I tell you, what division was there between her and me, ho, when we met? And don't droop your head like a lady-leaf! — at my age I can certainly talk about how and why my son was born. Maybe if you see me going too fast it is because I want to get to the moment when my son was born, so that I can race right off to the moment he died! No? And meanwhile I will certainly have to close my eyes to see her again, you here being the first person I have spoken to about her, ever since that day of the hurricane. For me she is the measure of time passing. There is one day before her and one day after. It's no use hanging your head and pretending to count the herbs in the barrel — I could be the brother of your father's father, and then she would be your great-aunt. Look. Did she climb up here to meet me? No, no! This time it was youth calling out in all directions: a young, beardless seer shut up in Stéfanise's cabin and a girl grown-up-too-soon who spent her time washing her brothers, tending the animals, binding cane (her thin body like a zoclette-piment, her mouth drawn back in her face) and driven to despair from one harvest to the next, without even knowing she was desperate or shy. And when one of us, I do not know which, saw the other, just try to prove whether it was in the hills or in the ravines. As for me I heard her name, Edmée. It was the first time I heard a name like that; I had not spent much time around the savanna. Edmée, it sounded like the breeze saying aidez-moi, help me, and I was there, not knowing any words to say but there I was. With her almost triangular head and her eyes glistening deep inside there was no need for words. There was a flame tree standing for our sake (I am not one to brag) and it took no less than the fury of a hurricane to uproot it. Now, it was in '90 (since you are demanding dates I'll give you this one) that my son Ti-René came. She was already living in the cabin where Stéfanise tried with all her might to make the best of it; we hadn't told Stéfanise anything, and then one day she sees the other one arrive, without a word, no explanation. Two armed statues in the cabin, myself speechless in the middle. And I never went to La Touffaille either, I would have died rather than ask, ask for what? She stayed a week, *then she went back down to get a few things. The father did not see her, the children cried, the mother vacantly watched her leave. That was life....*

And it did not occur to any of the girls to fling insults at him. And five years later, in the days when their carefree airs had faded in the dry breeze, they still stood up for their sister. The father who was taciturn at first, seemingly detached from it all, gradually grew bitter. He reproached his first daughter for what he considered her desertion. But the reason he was so aggravated that she was gone was that he had long ago given up on La Touffaille; he only made a point of it because of the other girls, none of whom ever spoke of leaving. And the boys as well, who no longer had any hope, condemned Edmée. As far as the three girls were concerned, they were calm if not optimistic and saw no reason to blame their older sister for their misfortune. One of them in particular, such a beautiful girl with glowing skin, hair all black and smooth down to her waist, plump arms and legs, looking like a coolie woman—just as pretty, with her soft singsong voice on a single reedy note, calmly and timidly defended her sister and never let even one cutting remark get by. Since her name was Aurélie, the sons, encouraged by their father's silence, shouted: "Aurélie and Edmée: it's all the same cooking-pot!" But the passing years left a venomous deposit in the father's heart. One day, exactly five years after Edmée's departure, he announced there would be a wake the following Saturday. A private wake just for the family. And he said it was for his daughter who had died five years ago. When the day came he had a white cloth ironed and placed it over a crate near the bed; on it he put a bowl of holy water with a branch. As soon as it was dark he lit two candles beside the bowl. The daughters cried that curses would rain down on them all. The mother did not open her mouth. He demanded that they all take their places, and the wick on the tin lamp was turned down. The sons surrounded him beside the bed; the mother went off alone in the big room; the daughters crouched just outside the door to show they were against the whole thing. But he wanted the rites of a real wake observed. He had food and then drink passed around: blood sausage that he had gotten somewhere else, rum, and syrups. Monsieur Pamphile's tom-tom spread out into the darkness. Its heavy beating and occasional rattling patter carried across every hillside, over the motionless woods, down barely marked trails. Morosely it emerged onto La Touffaille, where all the things that brought wakes to life (hoarse-voiced storytellers, lewd dancers, shivering children, victuals, and familiarity with the dead person) were absent tonight, just as absent as the woman presumed to be dead. The blood sausage was cold, and they all mechanically chewed their bit of it. The tom-tom had too far to travel and died away in the black hole that was the big room, where the lamp gave far less light than a candle. The stubborn father talked nonstop, as if to replace the storytellers. The words he said were La Touffaille itself: its dismal struggle, its disintegrating history, from the time when beating the tom-tom in the countryside was forbidden until the day that Senglis proposed an exchange with them after demonstrating how La Touffaille could no longer yield anything other than debts and destitution. And was it not true that the police had come around several times, once last November—furious over being stuck in the mud where the road curves by the plum trees, and then the other time completely beat, covered with sweat under the dry season sun? They were no longer very insistent, those policemen, they would just come around to be admired and talk in loud voices about how debtors' prison did, after all, exist. If you had the law against you then there was nothing left that might save you . . . and thus, beside this empty bed where in his mind, no doubt, he had laid the cadaver of La Touffaille, the father gradually forgot Edmée and her running away with her *quimboiseur*. The sons gave the ritual responses, clarified a point, or carried the laments one step further. The girls at first talked to each other in hushed tones ("Lord God," whispered Aurélie, "I don't see how she can do it; if I spent just one night up there I'd be dead, even before waking up in a dog skin with a ghost lying on top of me so he can kiss me!" Then they imagined the various transformations awaiting their sister if she displeased Stéfanise or her son), and as the night progressed they huddled silently inside the bedroom. The long hymn of abandonment encircled them with its calm detail. And toward morning despair entered them in turn. This mortuary parody touched them more deeply than the woes of existence and destroyed what was left of the ardor that up to now had kept them steadfast. More numb than petrified they joined their father, not to curse Edmée but to lay out the misfortune of La Touffaille item by item. That is they brought the weight of their silence to this quiet litany. And when the father, obsessed with his ceremony (even after he forgot its pretext), made them all come up to bless the bed, the girls wordlessly obeyed. The tom-tom had died away and clusters of white tinged with pink were forming on the distant ridges. Heat already radiated from the earth. It was clear to the participants that this wake had killed La Touffaille for good. They lay down in the room around the empty bed and listened to mangos falling on the roof, their eyes wide open to the day, not knowing what it would bring; and, in spite of themselves, they turned their heads toward the mother in the twilight, feeling that she remained the sole force, the one cord binding them to this place. But the mother, clenched tight inside herself, had not said a word. . . .

Ah, I'm always amazed at the frivolity of minds! There you are squirming around, you aren't listening; for you La Touffaille is nothing and the Targin family just wind. You wonder what becomes of the mule. You too leave the land behind in order to run around everywhere chasing wisps of smoke. You too are after Perlimpinpin powder. Well fine, an unfinished story is like a tom-tom that rumbles in the kindling wood! Look, you can get hold of the master if not the mule at the moment the man arrives at the pharmacy. He has been climbing down the hills since morning and his body is covered with sweat, but he looks quite spruce in the clothes he put on before coming to town. The ragged ones are stuffed into his Carib basket. Look, he is standing there in the middle of the store turning his head right to left, surveying it all and staring at the green, white, and black jars. He stops in front of one that is huge and red, thinking: "No mistaking, this has to be the one where they put the Spanish bull-feather." And Monsieur Toron, a good mulatto, who has already seen what is up (all he had to do was watch this yokel spinning like a merry-go-round right in the middle of the pharmacy), steps up to him. "So, what can I do for you?" And the other man, thoroughly suspicious, introduces himself: "Here's the thing. I have a mule that won't open its mouth even to say amen. And so they told me you could make up something for me that would force him to drink. Perlimpinpin powder." "Ah, fine, fine," says Toron. "Perlimpinpin powder. I see." "Yes," the old man says. "First America powder, then the Perlimpinpin, which is the most important, then some essence of min-nin-vini, because that, you see, is what makes the mule come and drink it, and then Spanish bull-feather to build up its strength." "Fine. Fine. I see," says Toron. Then he calls his assistant: "Anatole! Make up four powders for our friend's mule." Then he explains to the assistant, a young man who is extremely proud of his new eyeglasses, which powders to use and where to find them on the shelves behind the office. ("You know, we don't want to expose rare products like these to accident willy-nilly.") The old man, meanwhile, seeing the assistant on his way out, even if this assistant was wearing new eyeglasses that made him look like a black octopus washed up on the beach, goes on anxiously making explanations and comments. ("No, no," Toron exclaims. "He is an excellent assistant. Between us," he says under his breath, "he knows as much as I do.") Then your old fellow sits down stiff as a ramrod to wait for the excellent assistant to wrap up a bit of flour or white sugar or bicarbonate of soda, who knows what, in four pieces of paper on which he writes the powder's name.

OK now! There he is, lighter now by the four francs (transformed in a flash into crumpled papers), standing there in front of his mule. The animal huffs and puffs like a volcano, but his master is huffing and puffing almost as hard. He has run all the way from the pharmacy to his cabin without stopping or looking left or right, not even changing out of his Sunday clothes or stowing the four papers away. He grips them tightly in his hand, and sweat has almost soaked through into the flour or the white sugar. "There you go, there you go," he says. "If you don't eat now and if you don't drink now, it's because Lucifer made the eyeglass-man's hand shake." Then he gets the bucket, pours some water in it and stirs the powder in, then straddling the mule he opens its inflamed mouth and pours the whole thing down its gullet; the creature's red eyes are wide open beneath the torrent, but it is not even strong enough to dislodge him and finally the old man gets off satisfied. The Perlimpinpin is doing its work in the skeleton's stomach. It won't take long. And of course, two days later the mule was dead. There's the old man, you can see him confronted with the swollen carcass. He feels the mule's legs—stiffer than bamboo—finally he cuts off a piece of tail and stands there with the clump of hair in his hand, thinking: "Now, you and I, we're going to go give Monsieur Toron a piece of our mind."

And all this time the registers were functioning! They registered the coming, the cane, the dying. Consult the old papers and that's what you see: coming, cane, dying. Down in the valleys and up in the hills. So it is not necessary for a young man to climb up into the forest and lead an old unattached wreck to the brink of speaking. You did not make me do anything, it is the malfini eagle in the sky that makes me: the one that pulled the strings right from the first, and he is the only one grasping the past in his beak! I tell you Mister Mathieu, if you too go after Perlimpinpin powder instead of digging in the grave on the hills, your head will become just as empty as Pointe des Sables. You will stay there under the moon like a rock that is nether cold nor hot. That's the way they do it in this land. And so in the end they are even afraid of a fake rocking in his rocking chair. They are afraid of Abbé Samuel, thinking that the priest will likely as not shake his robes on them to make them cripples. Ever since the days when sermons predicted that fires of hell would get them if they didn't stay submissive — that constituting virtue and duty — they have been afraid of passing close to robes, either white or black ones. Because they think the priest's robe is going to come after them and change them entirely. They are afraid of midnight, they moan that midnight is lying there on a branch waiting for them to go by. Their minds are all withered up like that. Well, you don't see any of the past things planted there in the earth to speak to you. Not the registers, not Papa Longoué, no! Just take a young cane plant, watch it grow in the ground until its point bursts into the sky, then follow in its tracks to the Central Factory and watch how it turns into molasses and cane-syrup, into sugar or into tafia, into gros-sirop or coco merlo; then you understand the pain and underneath the registers you hear the real words of earlier days, that over such a long time have never changed. You hear them.

"Damn it all, that's the real truth!" said Mathieu.

3

All this time other men were building the roads. Colonial roads leading to the Factory without a thought for the things stagnating on either side. The ones leading to the police station, their black tracks cutting through the savanna. The ones winding to towns and ports, where they come down to rickety wharves where boats are taking goods aboard. These roads have no time to penetrate the land's exuberance; as anyone can see they race along as fast as they can from the edge of the fields to the edge of the sea.

All this time people were building up cities or what they called cities because there was no other word for that unspeakable thing. Tin roofs and crate wood jostled together into a canker crammed between mud alleys; at one end stood the church and at the other end the Croix-Mission. The long central road was pretty open, to be used by tilburies and light carts, crinoline dresses and high-class funerals: the vivacious façade for pomp and ceremony. And not twenty, not ten but five yards behind it would be this teeming plague crawling openly down toward the cemetery enclosure. So had the former maroons come down from their hills and the slaves held on in the valleys just to end up in this swarming misery? All equally undefinable: not Longoués or Béluses or Targins? And had the long story become bogged down in the mud of slums?

But one of those cities! Chosen from among those piles of shacks to be the example and the leprous energy! Frenzied pandemonium day and night simply in order to muffle any other voice in the hills. Quivering in the yellow dazzle of lamps, announcing at every crossroads that it was alive, fabulous with torches and displays, with haggling and blood; gripped by an eternal carnival that played in its theaters and its streets. And to stifle the cry of death heard everywhere else, it put on black robes and powdered its face to mimic death. It hurtled people together into the arena of its ferment: its mulattos and its whites, its men of color and its masters colliding. A city where the music started up at dawn just as gallant men who felt it their duty to follow the noble custom would appear for their appointed duels. But where, in the same wan glow, razors also flashed around gaming tables. An extravagance, moored to the prow of the earth where it could throw up its screen of deaf frenzies against the confused babble of destitution. But the voice rolled down from the heights! And in one morning it swept the turbulence and dissoluteness away in ash and flames; the people who had stunned this land were stunned by it as it became completely covered with lava instead of flour and its robe darkened the sky. This city in heat felt all across it a heat that petrified the walls, the roads, the mud, the year, the day, the surrounding air and even any idea one could have of a city. And when it withdrew the only thing it left men to show it had been there (unless you count the ruins) was a layer of rock hanging over those ruins and an old Negro, the sole survivor, terrified of being scalded alive in an underground jail where he had been thrown. But so was there anyone who wondered why these things happened? Why was there this Negro that no one would have considered calling a "man of color," why was there this rock balancing on the top of gaping walls that had to be held by iron chains? Who wondered if this was not the end of the growth of swarming cities once and for all? The city—the unspeakable thing swelling its voice to stifle the call from the upper reaches? The city—the receptacle where the history of the land and the knowledge of the past become bogged down and lost in its confinement?

Let us leave the city, its suffering without echo, its stunned desert. All this time the land continued to spread out over itself, leveling everything. It carried the wilderness humus and the compost of cultivation toward each other, silently into its folds. Bards soon appeared in the bright spaces that thus opened up, emerging from nowhere to praise the beauty. In a country where singing is like becoming, free bards were bound to come. They were born of their own bliss as soon as the original thick vegetation allowed their slender voices a bit of space. "How lovely and how fine it was to cut cane in orderly lines to the tom-tom's beat, joyful and confident in one's work while in the distance the sea breeze caressed the sweetness of the flowers, the fruits, the leaves and the branches!" The bard, just barely separated from the hills, just barely risen from the canefields where men like him were exhausted, went mumbling on about the fragile beauty, never seeing the death robe that cloaked this beauty. He made great efforts to keep the ooze of the trampled cane at a distance, until soon a cane leaf for him was no thicker than whatever fit into the words of a song. The bard rocked back and forth pretending sensual delight in this bright spot. He had forgotten not just the hills and their steep demands, but also the exhaustion, the red ants, the bleeding, the desert of cane stretched out beneath the sun, because the bard was dancing along a road not made for his feet. He drove even the memory of the primordial mud far from him. He was chasing after other pleasures, still not yet aware that he would see them endlessly slip out of reach (and unaware that, even when passed out from satiation some obscure lack would still endlessly cast him off to the side of the road)—so that one day he would have to come back along this trail, to the crossroads before it opened out onto the colonial road, and his two feet riveted in the hole before the lemon trees, he would attempt to intercept the force churning his soul. So that he might understand, at least, the man stirring in the forgotten depths of his soul. The man: no longer Melchior or one of the Targins, and not Mathieu or Papa Longoué, but that undefined person (Sylvius, Félicité, or Ti-Léon) who experienced the real weight and measure of a cane leaf in his flesh, and who on Saturday, perhaps, would beat the tom-tom for his own pleasure at Monsieur Pamphile's place and who every evening, wearing his pants fringed at the knees and full of holes, would lie down on his tilted plank (when not on the dirt floor of the hut)—so some bucolic bard could send out into the perfumed air a procession of hummingbirds and so that later one Mathieu Béluse, no less a bard, would stop and try to close his fist around the gurgling of a song caught in his throat.

But even this man was moving ahead. One son or another had amazingly escaped the fields and become a truck driver or stevedore on the wharves, a tax collector or pharmacy assistant, an employee at city hall or a teacher, or simply chronically unemployed and always out looking for odd jobs, and to this son he turned over the task of taking in the field with a single glance, measuring its depth. He himself had merged with the field and his only horizon was two handsbreadth above the ground (at the level where the stalks were cut) or ten feet up where the tall leaves reached. But still he moved ahead: because all this time during which the plantation overseers and accountants were increasingly recruited from among "people of color," and during which the "people of color" fought first to have this right and then to carry off the rights that followed naturally from this one (the right to act as a citizen and elect a mayor or representative, the right to be not his own equal but the illusory equal of another, the right to open a store and to parade, the right to embellish the night with a frothing garland of words), and often with all the fury and nobility of heroism, and all the self-sacrifice of someone who believes in the virtue of his fight, and for results which, in short, had not all been useless (because occasionally a stifled cry would land like a coal on all those erring ways, occasionally it would turn out that someone would be lifted up, suddenly turning and seeing behind him the past, unearthed and speaking to him), and which had even contributed toward bringing a bit of earth into the earth—he, the man, the sugarcane cutter or the driver at the central factory, stuck between the two extremities of the cane plant, never had so much as a moment to raise his voice, never located even one silence in which to temper his real voice so he could brandish it before him, and consequently, all this bustle about ballot boxes, official sashes, horsewhips, revenue, bravos went right over his head; he never shared in any of it and thus all the fuss sometimes taking him as its pretext, the enthusiasm for change and for profits that from time to time would refer to him by name, in the final analysis left him there in his mud, unchanged. He was a spectator on the side of the road who cheered the changes and even went down into the nearby market town, first riding in carts then later in trucks, to put a piece of paper that would change everything for other people into a sealed box—but a spectator safe from the trap (loving the sounds of celebration and always ready to cheer whatever changes were passing through but, after these drunken spells, always back the next day the way he had to be in the closed universe where there were no more big-mouths or officials to come to his aid). In his eye, after the splendor of grand occasions, there always flickered the light, shrewd rain of dismal knowledge.

All this time, therefore, the tiny land that was turned in upon itself in loops and curves, in hills and ravines, drew the new plantations tighter and tighter in a circle around this man. (Stéfanise might have asked him: "What is your name?" and in all innocence he would have replied "Sylvius. That's my name.") There would no longer be anything to distinguish the highlands from the valleys, the man who refuses from the one who accepts, a frantic maroon from a dying slave. And so, kept apart from this evolution of men, this man who ate today the same thing he ate yesterday, did however move ahead as the land evolved where the savanna and the fields met the woods. He cries over himself; he still has a precipice to get over. The past continues as long as he has not gone over it; and the moment he goes over it the future begins. There is no present. The present is a yellowed leaf joined to the stalk of the past on the side where neither his hand nor even his gaze can reach it. The present drops from the other side; it is endlessly dying. He is dying.

And at the foot of the precipice, the last one, the castrated bards, men of refinement and good will, left to themselves and enchanted by their frame of mind, packed down underfoot the roots where sometimes a bleached bone would peep out and danced their graceful dance on land where anonymous heroes whom no one could bring back to life cried out, where candles were burning, the entire underground cemetery lit by nameless fighters whom no one could get to rise up from their earth, because it was an established fact: their struggle was in vain (the way they came down like a wild river, the way they rose up like a wild wind: they had not even scorched the skin). It was better—for the people who lived there it was the only possible opening and also a constant temptation—to try to dry up the ocean, not to go back to the infinite land on the other side, but to run across the muddy bottom of the sea, among the creatures of the deep who would be completely amazed to find themselves out there in the open, dying. This way they would reach Lapointe's office and help him finish his final report. And because this report told stories that were hardly defensible, it would be best to deck them out in flighty, butterfly-like words, honeyed turns of phrase, sentences as transparent and blue as the moon in order to smother the unseemly horror of the detailed account beneath their graceful telling.

The result was that people became crazy about this languishing folklore reinforced by the masters. But the masters did not have to work very hard to keep it going. All they had to do was adopt the local Creole, the secret-sharing language in which the intimate and formal words for "you" merged, and then root out even so much as the memory of how immobilized Louise and Longoué had been until Louise set out to teach Longoué the harsh, lilting words. Thus there were as many languages created for mouths as there were levels between the highlands and the sea. Not counting the fact that the language, rather than using its entire range, finally became distorted when it would jam up midstream in the throat of an old schoolteacher who was in love with her brand-new French and would naïvely complain in her flat voice, "I don't understand young people today, my dear, they just can't start a sentence in French *si yo pa finille an créole!*"

("Like that Eudorcie woman," said Mathieu. "You don't know her; she never leaves the Senglis house. She has a big, round face and laughs all the time; she walks tiptoe as if she's trying not to break her fat behind, and whenever Senglis wants a cup of tea to drink he shouts, 'Eudorcie, *fè an dité ba moin*,' and every time Eudorcie replies more crabbily than the governor's wife, 'Which would you like, sir, an infusion or a decoction?' and Senglis shouts back in exasperation, 'Infusion or decoction, what the hell, *man di' oü fè an dité ba moin!*'")

Oh! . . . Oh oh oh! . . . And does she make decoctions! Didn't she take lessons from Cydalise Nathalie who was an authority on the subject? Cydalise, who sold herbs behind the cabins like a true black woman, and who could get you pregnant no matter what unless some stronger will than hers was hiding in the crannies of an acacia root; Cydalise Éléonor would never go and spend so much money at Toron's for a bit of white sugar or magnesium powder. And even if she did Marie-Nathalie would never have gone back with a mule tail in her hand (like this fellow) to demand an explanation.

You can see him going into the pharmacy where he turns this way and that as if the jars were attacking him on all sides. Monsieur Toron, a fine mulatto, already knows what has happened. Full of fire he steps up exclaiming, "Well, how's that mule?" The old man stops, the sun stops spinning, he takes a deep breath and slowly raises his hand, he shakes the tuft of hair without saying a word. "What!" Toron says. "I can't believe it!"

"Yes, yes," the old man says. "You don't suppose Monsieur Anatole made it up wrong."

"What an idea! Anatole, come in here!"

The assistant came in, serious as stale bread and pure as the first morning, to take his turn in the dance. There they all were, the three of them shouting themselves hoarse inside the store behind the bamboo curtain covering the doorway. They turned round and round, each of them equally incapable of hearing what was being shouted in his face by the man in front of him, until finally Toron, as if abruptly blessed by inspiration, stopped all of a sudden, went to strike himself in the forehead but waved his hand grandly to call the other two over. He sat down in a chair and, looking the old man up and down, putting him through the strainer of his eyes, said crossly, "What color was your mule?"

The other man, transfixed by the question because by now he sensed the supernatural and conclusive cause of the remedy's failure, stammered, "But, but, the mule was gray."

"Now you tell us!" said Toron. "You should have been specific. We thought it was the usual color and Anatole weighed out the usual powder. Let's see now, Spanish bulls come in black and white and gray. What color are those bulls usually, Anatole?"

"White," said Anatole. "They are white, Monsieur Toron."

"So you see, if you had only told us your mule was gray! Anatole prepared the purest white-bull powder, you were the witness, there was not a single black powder in those packets, much less a gray one. The powder went bad in the mule's blood and it was unable to take effect."

"Yes," the old man said. "That's true. It was not able to take effect."

Cydalise would never have walked back into the store, firmly intending to get her four francs back, and then gotten taken in a second time by a pharmacist who cared as little about a person's life as he did about a mule's, and dragged this all out in the most lavish manner imaginable. For example, Toron, in order to get the old man to calm down for good, proposed to buy back the mule's tail for ten cents, because it would be interesting (he said) to observe what effect the finest gray-bull powder would have on the tail, and so forth. Cydalise would have pulled up three herbs behind some cabin and, pronto, it would be all downhill for Toron; he wouldn't even have time to say goodbye to his assistant.

Stéfanise even less. Though the tall woman who had taken refuge in Melchior's hut had consented to get along with Edmée, you should not think she was giving up anything at all. First she had adapted her voice to the situation: ever since Papa Longoué had been five, ever since the death of Apostrophe, she had to speak in a level tone, not loud and not wheedling because she was the one to provide information. But after that whom would she have shouted at? Had she not exhausted in one day all the shouting reserves she had? Whom would she have asked to tell her thank-you-very-much? Her voice was lost as a marker of the loss she suffered when Apostrophe departed: it was her way of mourning the deceased. And then, quite simply, she had given herself another task in life. When she found herself face-to-face with this mystery of sorts all made of skin and sweat that they called Edmée, and had understood first that this mystery was worth the trouble, and second that Papa Longoué was permanently attached to her—she had considered the mystery from all angles, cautiously, determined to mollify it. But she had failed every time she was confronted with that mouth locked with four locks, that bar across the triangular face. She had discovered to her amazement that stubbornness could take root far from shouts and noise. Consequently, her kindness toward Edmée resulted more from confrontation than from friendship. When René, the son of Papa Longoué and his wordless mystery (whom Stéfanise said pleasantly was "night gone hard as a *baramine* tree"), was there, she ignored the child (besides, she thought, being René you have no luck at anything) so she could keep on trying to seduce the mother exclusively. This was her last project, and no one knows whether or not she succeeded. Papa Longoué observed that the two women silently stuck together and bent over the same task more and more often with every day that passed. He never knew if Stéfanise had ended up conquering the "baramine" or if Edmée (that would have taken the cake!) in the end had deadened the will of the big woman and buried it within her silence. Stéfanise, it is true, did not live long enough to finish her job. One day when she went down to market she fought with a woman who was selling meat, something about some salt meat, an argument that degenerated into insults about "sorcerers, sons of Satan and his works" (the seller was shouting that) and about "scoundrels who take advantage of poverty" (the opinion of Stéfanise), and finally ended up in a riot. Stéfanise, after she had flattened the meat-seller like a cassava and managed to get away from the police, went back up into the hills waving a large chunk of unpaid-for salt meat as her spoils of war. But this meat was her last trophy. She died the evening of that very day after two or three hours of groaning. "Ou pa palé anpil," she said to Edmée. "You didn't say much." Those were her last words.

"She missed the turn in the road," said Papa Longoué, "and her heart didn't stand up to the shock." He himself felt like a cart falling into a ravine.

A year later the hurricane came and uprooted every mystery in the area. And two years later the official calendar left the eighteen hundreds and entered the nineteen hundreds. In the desert of La Touffaille, the mother was still keeping watch alone. That is, of all the Targins who had waited for who knows what miracle on the face of the earth, she alone remained anchored, inflexible, and refusing to surrender the land. Ever since they had celebrated the parody of a wake over the body of La Touffaille, the others (her man, her children) watched her closely; father, sons, daughters, without consulting each other and without venturing any hints or invitations either, all listened for the least hiccup in the mechanism of this stubbornness. She held on all alone, like an animal that is cornered by a silent clan but still scorns the circle around it. She did not grit her teeth any less at the announcement that the oldest son would perhaps go and look for a job in the city (seeking her permission first). Since she, of all of them, was the smallest, she seemed truly like a lit candle refusing to go out in the midst of a tall woods. Time went by, emptier and emptier, harder and harder, that is to say it was only swollen with debts, exhaustion, breadfruit and manioc, no respite, no joy. It was obvious that La Touffaille could not resist the will of the men bringing in cattle. Still she hung on, the primitive mother, simply silent on the edges of the noise or the exhaustion. In the days when the father was still going to see Senglis to argue over conditions, she had finally refused to listen to his reports. He would come back heavy with privilege (not the privilege of having known the conditions before the others, but of having looked a man whom none of them knew in the eyes, none of them having even caught sight of him in town on Sunday morning, a man who was playing with their fates nonetheless, and winning in advance) and overwhelmed by this privilege. It was not a conspicuous refusal to listen; she simply was not there whenever the father returned—that is all there was to it. Then the visits to Senglis stopped; the land, moreover, soon produced nothing but fruits and vegetables, which she along with her daughters would take to sell in the market. In front of the house the slope that used to descend so peacefully was now a mess—bleak, rusty earth with the old rows still marked by dried plants. The cocoa-bean trees out back were smothered in rot. Around the mango tree thistles were winning out as they were everywhere else in fact; at least there was plenty of rabbit grass. All along La Touffaille, in the stretch between the river and the coast where it was gradually silting in, there was thick grass growing, which probably meant that Senglis would come in. Yet she held on, erect beneath her basket, merging with the hubbub as women invaded the market (where her spot was reserved); friends called out to her familiarly and in their midst she suddenly regained her voice; brightening up, she would tell endless stories that she would pick up again Sunday after Sunday. She was serious and always reserved, but finally a smile would surface on her face, lifting her slightly pale cheeks out of her black skin. As if these market women, who stirred up such a commotion, such a hullabaloo of voices and movement around the trestles, were trying against all odds and using the fruits and vegetables they worked so hard to sell, to preserve the presence (if not the force) of the land up in the hills. As if Stéfanise, who departed after this battle, then Edmée, carried off by this hurricane, had entrusted the other women with the work of shouting out life, never stopping and never growing weaker.

But it was precisely after the hurricane came and went that there was nothing to hope for anymore. The father and children saw her, watched her attentively as she gradually shrank back into herself. At first there were repairs, the wide-open roof, the walls ripped open, the trees down. Then there was the burial of Edmée, this time with no wake, quickly disposed of in the general exhaustion: which meant that she did not immediately feel the emptiness that (inside her) made her seem to float along the surface of things. But in the end she could only go on in her low, monotonous voice about the hurricane's destruction, the heaping on of ruin, right down to the least yam plant—uprooted—that would become part of her list. Never mentioning her daughter who had gone up into the hills and been rolled back down like a ball, lifeless, by the wind as it descended. To forget her daughter, she relentlessly made an accounting of the material destruction, which, in fact, left her completely without hope or choices. The others kept an eye on her, they had understood that there was nothing left to do but wait. For her to make the decision herself. Consequently, as if out of remorse, they surrounded her with thoughtfulness and altogether unusual signs of attention.

She managed to drag out her confusion for a little while, forcing them to endure the wait, put up with it. Every Sunday she seemed to draw new strength from the market when she went there, reserves of patience for the following week. Ten times she would count the coins. Ten times she would measure gourdfuls of manioc, ladles of salt, spoonfuls of sugar. Until the day when, exhausted in turn from having to go like this and sell more and more shriveled piles of mangos and yams, breadfruit and sweet potatoes, oranges and plums gathered randomly here and there, she finally sat down and looked at them all around her, father, sons, daughters. Then she waved a vague sign of surrender, as if she meant to toss away all the vegetation to drift away with La Touffaille, far from her own exhaustion. . . .

Meanwhile the Béluses struggled along.

That is to say, in 1910 Zéphirin went off to join the dead, but neither by accident nor by fate. He too was simply worn away. Wear and tear with its pale, sticky hands gradually shaped for this Béluse the destiny shared by all, the local rule of death, and thus brought him back into the realm of the usual. This is how the Béluse family—who on their final day long had been reintegrated (being carried across the countryside, the woods and fields, down the colonial road and through roundabout alleys to the town cemetery) with the community of the dead, at least—managed, through Zéphirin, to merge with the masses. Because his death itself (that is, the way death came to him) no longer set him apart. Before he ended up living like everybody else, before abandoning the Longoués, their raging refusal, these Béluses learned therefore to die of common wear and tear. Zéphirin, who did not have business as his calling the way his father, Saint-Yves, did, worked relentlessly to keep up Roche Carrée at the same time that he worked for Larroche; he died at the age of thirty-eight. So these Béluses struggled hard (this was their work) to join the common destiny spread by sweat over the forest, the towns, the huts, the trembling hills and the steep plowed fields; anywhere that the smooth, undifferentiated earth without sheer drops or rises now opened expanses to the weight of the sun. Of course Mathieu Béluse, Mathieu's father, would still follow Ti-René Longoué to the Great War on the other side of the ocean! But he, the Béluse, would return.

4

Ah, I tell you.

Then silence, the dry season around them, beside the scorched ferns Papa Longoué without a voice (Mathieu, like a fire that has gone out, settled onto the knife-blades of earth, supported by the daylight that rushed through the opening, there where words, it seemed, had consumed the screen of foliage, the tangle of vines and bamboo, and had opened up in the surrounding curtain a clearing and more than that, the ravages of things turned to ash and things made clear, calcination, brightness), an old, furrowed body, a stubborn spirit all of a piece, the shrewd child who—ever since the day when Apostrophe's death had hurtled him toward Stéfanise's cry—plunged him into that silence and mystery in which he had met Edmée. Silence. But, for example, how could he have spoken about his father Apostrophe, he only knew him in the indescribable darkness where Melchior had raised up before him the masses of dead people—beyond that, Apostrophe was only a shadow projected upon the wonder of childhood. Papa Longoué could just barely see his round face again, that black moon in the sky, bent over the child he was and probably as an old man had never stopped being, while the absentminded voice spelled out, "This boy here is going to have matured before he is grown." And how would he have been able to show Saint-Yves Béluse, the one so keen on business, or his son Zéphirin who died at thirty-eight, or their women or their children, the ones that grew up in the cabin or were sprinkled around all over the place, and how would he say if they had thrashed out problems, asked questions, suffered or hated, he who had never had enough of all his time to try and remember the eyes in that black moon, or if those eyes said something different from what was said by the voice coming down from that moon like night rain?

The smell of loose stones, the taste of hard rock in the pond water, burned wood that fell from the fire and scattered in sparks onto the black earth around the pot of sweet potatoes, and perhaps yes the stench of dried mud on the hands and arms of the woman (upon whom Saint-Yves imposed the job of turning the carafes and cauldrons—who knows how she had learned to make them—that he himself fired after sawing up some wood and before sawing some more, and that she then took to sell at the edge of town), and Zéphirin the child who would pick up the bits of broken carafe, piling up a rough treasure of black bottoms, handles that had come off, cracked necks; then the wearing away: years, nights, and the kiln neglected and the ebony trees also, until the day when the victorious forest had reasserted its rights over that handful of earth with its clay hole—the run-together browns and glowing purples (gushing from the green madness) covering with its shadow the harsh red wound that had dug into the ground—and the hardened footprint of Saint-Yves, three prints to the right of the entrance to the hut that neither the scalding downpours nor the fine, warm rains of August had been able to erase—then, and at the same time, of course, but in another world, on the other side of this hill (neither more nor less than any other hill) that none of the inhabitants knew was singled out like this to bear both extremes of the same future, Apostrophe watching Stéfanise sweep the floor of the hut: the tamped down, smoothed out earth gleaming like varnish, so that the dust slid under the *corossol* branches of her broom like raw sugar on the patina at the bottom of a cauldron—and standing up with a sigh, pushing restlessness and impatience aside once and for all almost as if he were brooding in silence and beyond any thinking: "Ah! This country is not yet for us, no, it is not for us." And, probably to catch hold of the thing he could not define, taking the little barrel on his knees, he delicately and meticulously drew the loose staves back together with a string made of vines.

And how would Papa Longoué, after he had named the mystery, have been able to analyze it or demonstrate it or even simply evoke it, he who found he was completely dazed standing there before the unfathomable nature of this triangular face; there was nothing he could do about being drawn and enthralled by this absolute, final silence, and he had never been able to do anything other than notice the bones rising to the surface beneath her skin as Edmée gradually became thinner and thinner, not like a *baramine* but more like the branch of an *épini*. The mystery—what other word was there for this person who was wasting away without drying up: the bones rising to the surface more every day but still covered with a bit of solid flesh, gleaming skin that was neither flabby nor creased? All he had been able to do all those years was mutter as he sat every evening in front of the hut, tormented by this silence, and the piece of bark across his knees like a bit of wood weighing nothing: "Today she is even thinner and soon a big wind is going to carry her all the way down the hill"—not daring to believe that saying this he was seeing into the future, but using this daily joke in an attempt to fend off the lowering threat that would press down on his eyelids at night and suddenly wake him up, smothered and blinded, like a man drowning in the liquid mud of mangrove swamps.

This nightmare that was not a nightmare (because in fact he was not dreaming about anything and was only in touch with this horror when he was startled awake in the darkness rocking to the song of chirping insects) had increased in intensity and made him as edgy as an animal at the smell of storm or death. Until the time when the mystery and the silence were covered up for good by the preposterous roar of that wind (a wind that seemed red because it burned your eyes so badly) that blew for two days while still sparing everything on its foundation, but merely readying it all for the real hurricane: an eruption of thunderclaps and streaks of lightning into the madness that seconds before still had seemed to be the air you breathe and move through, a raging battle among slabs of wood and sheets of iron and steel—it was five in the morning but night fell for the second time—and the river of air roaring between the planks of the cabin and carrying everything outside, tearing the door off (the cabin itself reared back against the ground like a stubborn mule), the moaning that groaned constantly inside your ears, the burnt smell that tickled your nose at first and then blocked it all the way inside your brains, finally the rain, torn from the sky and swept along with the trees, the crates, the sparks of straw like firebrands on your body, barrels that were ripped apart, and the two of them (she weighed less than a bag, and he was burdened with the child who was not yet terrified but almost having fun) braced against the back wall of the cabin and then carried off into the clearing and gradually propelled toward the path downhill—but the triangular face still unruffled, eyes closed, the line of her lips like a thread, while he was shouting to her to hang on, and it was funny to be opening one's mouth in this thunderhole—and he had been plastered against the mango tree and held there by the weight of the wind, painlessly nailed to the trunk with the child against him and feeling the sky fall in deadly ruins into the surrounding hill, and he had seen her slipping gradually toward the slope, becoming more and more contorted as the hurricane's force increased, and he had tried, yes tried to get to her, to go down with her (despite his concern with saving the child whom he had managed to wedge between himself and the tree by twisting all the way around) but those hands of air that were plastering him against the mango tree did not allow him to die; and he had seen her disappear down the path, probably already dead, her body carted from rock to rock, her dress torn off long before, her arms and legs in knots around her head—and he had stayed there in the flood and the glimpses of uprooted things, in the pewter filings of the abraded night, in the fire of air and whirlwinds, knowing that there was no use in fidgeting, or moving, or trying to get away, or searching for that body that had practically flown off down the hillside, and he had closed his eyes; he detached himself from life, from the rage for life churning lethally around him, and he gradually shrunk down against the base of the mango tree as the slowly weakening hurricane had relaxed its stranglehold and when finally a sunbeam had struck him between the eyes (René now clutched tightly in his arms and crying but unable to make him turn loose), he had realized that silence and mystery had returned to earth: because he had seen the water all around him where it had stuffed itself into every crack and cranny and trembled on every last smooth surface, cascading softly down the slope between the uprooted rocks and the carpet of tree trunks and lianas, between boards stuck in the mud and sawed-off trees, into the sparkling mess where the bamboos were glowing like green embers; he had finally heard the murmuring of this mud-flow become solider and thicker than silence and more mysterious than the sea's horizon: it was the voice of the forces from the first day hovering over primordial waters that had no past and no memory.

René, hanging on around his neck, finally roused him. A lack of understanding and distance grew up between the two that began with this hurricane, and the father never managed to cut through it. The child was eight and sensitive enough to feel such a day of terror forever; it seems that for the rest of his life, in spite of the care his father had surrounded him with during the event, he confused Papa Longoué, the hurricane, and fear. This was how the wordless quarrel between them began; it was never to end. Papa Longoué unwittingly complicated it all even further; because when he went off to look for Edmée he did not want to take the child—the roads were gone and the dangers were great; and clumsily, ignorant of how things were done, he tried to dry René's clothes and his body (but how could he, in this world that suddenly was made of water and mud?) and afterward he put him in a back corner of the hut, probably to protect him in case the wind came back, and he left him there, suffering from the damp, the loneliness, and even the cold, when it would have been more normal to put him out in the sunshine. René suffered even more from the little bit of time he spent like this in the cabin (he very quickly escaped outdoors) than from the hours of delirium he had endured in the hurricane.

Papa Longoué found Edmée in a water hole. Only her back emerged from the mud that was already warm. He picked her body up without looking at it and in doing so released a yellow, almost sulfurous waterfall; he wrapped her as best he could in his old shirt of coarse, torn wool; then he carried her away. Not toward the cabin but in the direction of the sea, toward La Touffaille. As if the hurricane had actually razed the cabin, or as if he thought it was the decent thing to give Edmée back to her family for this final day. Life trembled all around. In a daze people were vaguely clearing away the ruins before them, looking for the wounded and extravagantly mourning the dead. No one paid any attention to this thin, almost naked man, who was carrying an even more naked woman in his arms. He found the family gathered in front of the devastated house at La Touffaille. They could see him coming from a great distance and Aurélie began to moan. He laid his burden at the mother's feet and then stood there motionless and silent as if this were not something that concerned him. In fact, no one spoke to him, no one looked at him meanly. Burial took place that very day, a collective burial blessed at the cemetery by the parish priest, and surrounded by vague health measures. Graves and tombs were not where they belonged; ravaged by the storm, they had no crosses or sand or artificial flowers; they were like plugged-up crab holes in a field of mud. The priest was unaware that in one of those boxes that he was sprinkling with holy water one after the other there lay the wife of a *quimboiseur*. Everyone was worn out, exhausted. The heir to the Longoués followed the crowd, not knowing how he had come to the town like this and gone into the cemetery, half naked and anonymous. He was not to see the Targins ever again. When he returned to the cabin Ti-René was gone.

What else have I ever done other than try and not lose the chain back to the first day? Everything in my body was born in order not to forget the ones who left too quickly, the things done-well-done, the land you turn over so you can dig out knowledge; but truth goes by like lightning, you stand there transfixed with your hand outstretched and the wind rolls through your fingers like a river. You listen to the mystery, the silence until something as big as a hurricane uproots you, then the waters cover your body, then the sun penetrates you like a remedy. Ah! Mister Mathieu, you claim that I know nothing about today, that I never go down to the tarred road, but today is the son of yesterday, and you are Mathieu the son of Mathieu who came to tell me about the hole in the ground where my son Ti-René, who had been gone you might say ever since the day of the hurricane, had finally fallen at the end of his journey. Ah! You have eyes, there is light in your eyes, but you are a long way from knowing what goes on inside one's head when one sees Melchior, a tall unhurried black man, scorned by those gentlemen, and ignored in his ignorance, but he is the one who dominates. And the tall woman hanging over her voice like a pot over the fire. There are bulls that go up into the hills and no one is ever able to find them again. At night I go down to the spring and while I fill my jug with the gourd I hear them calling to each other through the darkness. There are two-story houses along the main road in town, and as for me I am someone who is curious. I would like to get into one of those second-floor rooms and look out through the window to see if the road is still there. What else have I ever done other than every day bring into that day a bit of the sunlight from the day before, in order to throw light even today on where the cattle went, on how Melchior came down, and even to breathe the smell of that great ship throughout the forest you see here. You pay no attention to an old body raving on, but why do you claim that I know nothing about today? I tell them all the time: "Go give the doctor a shout, he has some very strong medicine," but the doctor costs five hundred francs. I tell them, "Me, I'm just an old black man with no connections," and they answer, "Alfonsine is going to die, her neck swole up overnight." I tell them, "Can't you smell that boat?" and they answer, "That's enough foolish talk, Papa Longoué, you're going to end up crazy." And I tell them, "Misery is not like a day going by, misery has no morning, no midday, and no night," and they answer, "You see the things you see clearly, even if you never budge from this cabin." But what do I do, even if I pick up my hoe to go dig out a few plants, other than gather up into today all the nights I have spent seeing my dead again, plus all the days I waited for Ti-René Longoué. But he never really came back, even if his body turned up around here from time to time. Because they have an animal inside their skin that carries them off far away, they all look beyond the sea; and that is why I saw, long before it happened, that René Longoué was going to leave this cabin and go away way beyond these woods.

Because the first character trait the quimboiseur saw in René was his wildness. When his father found him again on the night of the hurricane, the child did not even once ask for his mother, which was already a sign. It seemed the day he had spent wandering alone in the incomprehensible pile of crushed vegetation, yellow water, and mud (with the wind's siren still whistling through his head) had left him impervious. Not stunned, not stupid, but satisfied within himself. Papa Longoué talked to him, but he never really listened and was always straining toward something out of sight or out of hearing. He was skeptical and aggressive, sneering openly when Papa Longoué talked about Stéfanise (whom he had known) or Melchior or Apostrophe. Even his mother seemed to leave him cold. "Your mother was your mother," said Papa Longoué, but the boy kept fiercely silent.

At the age of thirteen he was hired in a tannery, where he learned to work leather. His father saw him less and less often and every time they had an argument. People said the young man was *foubin*: thoughtless, caring little for the disasters he was capable of triggering. He was, however, a serious worker and moreover a most obliging friend. But he was extremely thin-skinned and could not bear anyone's alluding to what might be described as his father's occupation. He liked to fight, not so much because he was a troublemaker as to convince himself that he was part of the community. For him a fight represented an extreme means of making each other agree. His friends did not understand these tendencies at all and complained that that tanner, Ti-René, was a devil wearing clothes. What's more he was shy (especially with the brazen women who hung around the tannery) but did not try to use this shyness and not play by the rules. Still he could not keep people from thinking of it as a supreme tactic.

Only with his father did he give vent to his wild nature. But Papa Longoué believed he had grasped the real reason for this attitude, what really lay hidden behind it. He patiently accepted his son's outbursts, his sneering, his bitter remarks. He learned how to mollify without flattering him, how to trouble without reproaching him. And gradually Ti-René changed. He began to ask his father questions, wanting explanations about Edmée—how he had come to know her, why she never spoke—and about Stéfanise who had always ignored him. Though he never consented to study the *quimbois* (he quite simply did not believe in it), he listened to the monotonous story materializing from the past without acrimony, and perhaps sometimes rather affectionately. The place where it all went sour was when Papa Longoué would vehemently insist that René leave the town and settle in the highlands again. In those moments the boy would really let out a yell and then just leave and let the quarrel drop. His father did not yet know that, in fact, he had no place to live but wandered wherever he felt like going, just about everywhere. He especially liked the unsettled outskirts of towns where the inextricable tangle of sheet-metal huts all crammed together and lit by candles created a sort of intimate refuge: it was good to go there and drink rum and hold up his end of interminable discussions in the darkness, or to dance there freely around a drum in front of one of those small public bars that, as it happened, people called "private." There he found plenty of occasions for arguments between two impassioned points of view. The city was the center of words and gestures and fighting.

Papa Longoué knew perfectly well that all of this was simply to cover up the single, intense desire to go away, to get out, to leave the land around him like a too-full gourd, to swim through space beyond the horizon. Even if he never said so clearly, had not Apostrophe thought that this land was not for them, not yet for them? Deep inside themselves they were incubating the fervent hope to know someplace else where they would no longer be objects, where they could have their turn to see and touch: they left the hill, but— thought the lonely *quimboiseur*—it was not the city they were looking for, it was the cloud packed down behind the line of the sea, the cloud that never came to fill the clear sky on this side.

The declaration of war, that is to say the call of a great unknown battle for an incalculable reward, one that really no one could have known how to estimate (because it was not desired as the usual, easily exchanged, concrete goods, but because it hovered diffusely in one's hopes like a fine dust filed from good fortune, a promise of the other place full of adventure), filled the country—and particularly Ti-René—with enthusiasm to the same extent that Papa Longoué greeted it with quite the reverse—every manner of doubt and annoyance. "Stay here," he said. "No authority is going to come and look for you. What came over you down there? Going to war? First do you even have any idea what a German is like? They don't understand any of the languages we speak. When you see one you will not even be able to give him a good insulting before shooting those damn guns." But there was nothing to be done, René Longoué would not even discuss it. From the moment he put on the uniform and right up until the boat left, his father wished neither to see nor hear him. René tried several times to get some admiration, at least, in his new outfit, but Papa Longoué withdrew under the trees behind the cabin, and the soldier remained alone in the clearing aimlessly shouting, "You are a savage! There's nobody more a savage than you!" Then he went back down with heavy feet.

He boarded ship on the first troop transport without having embraced his father. The whole country was stirred up over this departure; there was great gaiety and no one could ignore the event. From the highest hill, Papa Longoué watched the steamship going out. Upright, alone, more abandoned that day than he would ever be in his life and motionless among the palm trees lining the ridge, he saw way out before him and below him the boat, smoking like a fire made with green sticks rocked by the wind, on the green of the sea (for them the first departing boat, after all the ones that did nothing but come), and between the boat and himself the checkerboard of silent, deserted fields in the sun. "Go," he thought. "Go son, my son and not the son of Melchior, the one as savage as Longoué but unbelieving as Apostrophe. If you do not come back to the land there will no longer be a land for me. Go, son. Because no one answers when I cry out with my arms." And he opened his arms wide before the space stretched out before him; then he laughed and said, "You are going to end up crazy, ho Longoué!"

(René Longoué who, with the boat still in the middle of the harbor, and after conceding a brief glance—as if ashamed—toward the dark green hills, was already organizing a crap game in the hold that had been fitted out for them. Suddenly violent, with the rash ways that would be his until the end. He would only recognize the authority of white officers, and even then only starting with lieutenants. For example, he thought it was degrading for someone in command to be under something, and consequently flatly refused the authority of sublieutenants, considering it wrong that he was supposed to call them simply "lieutenant." Those were the things that preoccupied him, those were his problems. Otherwise, challenging was his law. He spent the greater part of the crossing in shackles, fiercely laughing it off. "What are you?" he shouted. "A sergeant. Do you think a sergeant can set me on my feet?" Soon he was criticized for being harmful to his compatriots as a whole because of his conduct and his bad reputation. When he was free he would manage to get into the kitchens and carry off great piles of grub. The others were no pussyfooters when it came to sharing those bits of luck with him; satisfied and scornful he would just laugh up his sleeve at them. He was unruly and untamed, but then all his exuberance fell away when the boat entered the port of Le Havre. They had been long in the grip of cold weather, which he laughed off, claiming to feel nothing and making a show of removing his shirt from time to time. But the land where the mist went on forever, the melted snow underfoot, the dazzling flocks of white roofs, the feverish beehive activity, the congestion, all that jeering familiarity of a war that had not yet proven to be endless, cooled him down for a long time. As a result he was even more arrogant with his comrades, mocking them for how clumsily they moved in this new environment—he who, at the beginning, would jump whenever one of the automobiles that fascinated him so much would suddenly appear, honking its horn, in the roads blocked by frozen mud. It is true that his undeniable powers of seduction made the locals, particularly the children, take an immediate liking to him. They called him Blanchette, and he was able to boast of a certain number of dinner invitations, which made him quite the celebrity. His ability to speak French improved because he hung around with white soldiers, whom he had discovered were just as powerless as he when faced with the officers' authority. He easily incorporated any number of English or Canadian words into his French, and even some proverbs from Normandy.

But all these tendencies did not save him from becoming the laughingstock in an incident that took place behind the lines in northeastern France. Invited to dinner with a family across from the barracks where his regiment had taken up quarters before moving on to the war zone, one evening he found himself seated in front of a strange vegetable (that the lady of the house had presented him with saying, "I hope you like artichokes, we still have some left"). So there he was, sitting there, absolutely without a clue as to what he should do with the thing, and everybody else around the table, pretending to be polite, staring at him, waiting to see how this young savage would use his hands, his napkin, his plate. "Yes," he said with a laugh. "Is that so," said the father. "Yes, yes," he said again, then suddenly, "Excuse me, I have to leave, I'll be right back!" Then leaving his flabbergasted hosts at the table, he dashed across the square, shoved the guards on duty aside, burst into the barrack room, shouting out of breath, "Quick, quick, how do you eat artichokes?" And the others, or at least the few whites among them exploded with hilarity and gave him the most preposterous advice: "Take a handkerchief, wrap the artichoke up in it and hang it around your neck; then you hop around the table on one foot," until, when the entertainment was over, one of them finally provided him with some instructions. And he, in a temper, raced back across the square, breathlessly sat back down at the table from which no one had budged, and then with a broad smile exquisitely proceeded to dissect the artichoke, which then made him sick to his stomach.

This incident was the end of his prestige, which vexed him no end. And this anger made him take excessive risks at the front, breaking the rules to do so, moreover, and then boasting about it. But he suffered long periods of prostration that were not caused by the war. On the contrary, it seemed that this man would never have any idea of the intensity of the throes of death all around him, nor of the danger constantly threatening him. His sergeant, a solid professional in charge of training the colonial troops, told him, "You are nothing but a braggart," to which he replied, having quickly learned his way around the language, "This braggart pisses on your ass."

The officers did not give him good evaluations but thought well of him; they did not apply the same rules to this regiment that usually pertained to relations between the troops and their superiors.

One of them, for example, who had noticed him in combat, would ask him before every attack, "So then, this is the day, Blanchette?" a remark that would definitely not have been acceptable in another unit. It was amazing how this tanner from the tropics was ignorant of fear. In the end people no longer gave him any credit for this bravery but attributed it to his "special" nature; consequently, even after the three sorties where his actions made a great impression, he was never proposed for either a promotion or a medal. He couldn't care less. One day, once again out ahead of his comrades and his officers during a line assault he leaped, for the pure gymnastic pleasure of it, into a hole full of stagnant water at the exact moment that a shell landed there. "I knew I'd get him," flashed through the sergeant's mind. They found his dog tag. That was all there was left, the disembodied identity or reality of that tooth-and-nail fighter, the man who had been René Longoué.)

And for a long time I knew it, I had gotten a piece of paper maybe five years before his return, and I buried this piece of paper in the woods near the cabin, more or less at the spot where Louise, Longoué, Melchior, and the others were supposed to be. I knew it, but I wanted to hear it from his mouth because he had been present when it happened. And he stood there before me, Mathieu Béluse who was not yet the father of Mathieu Béluse, the man who had remained over there for two years after the end of the Great War, he was beating round the bush and I told him, "He can't, under any circumstances, come back to life. So sit down here on this crate and tell me about the day, the time, and the place." He sat down, a very dignified man, he could not believe that I was crying deep inside, he drew me a picture of the field hospital, ever since that day I have been able to see the tents rolled up in front, the straw and the men wearing armbands, really I know everything about field hospitals, he explained how you get to the front line, how you get back, all the names of the companies and the regiments, the numbers, the uniforms, I said to him, "But were you there with Ti-René?" He said, "For ten years, Papa Longoué, we were inseparable," and I said, "Ah! Because you are a Béluse, the son of Zéphirin who was the nephew of my mother Stéfanise," and he said, "Yes, Papa Longoué." But already he was a man of complete dignity who soon would go off to be a supervisor at Fonds-Caïmite and for ten years was Ti-René's friend. One of them made mischief and the other came along behind to fix things up. Yes, and his dignity made him tell me about the entire war, for example, about a man standing guard who had become overcome by fear and had killed his captain when the latter came back from inspection, and all I really wanted was to know what the hole was like, at the end of ends, he told me, and even to console me, to divert me, he told the story of another man in another hole and a shell falls between his legs but the shell doesn't explode, this man stays there without moving, he screams and screams, and when they moved him he went mad; yes, I think about all of that. And Mathieu finally went away around six in the evening, I saw him going down; who would have said that the son of Béluse would come up onto the hills to ask me What and Why? Today there is another war. What has there been in it for us, except a big hole that time has leaped over with a single jump? And today, when you get right down to it, how many holes are open in the earth at the very moment I am speaking, and who knows how many men have gone mad before dying?

"The French have taken Bir Hakeim," said Mathieu.

Then silence; the old man and the young one sitting on the dryness as if they were glued to things that were immediate; but in their thoughts they were crossing the world's density, spaces packed in one on top the other, not to go to some precise, chosen place, but because they were full of a reddish glow, a crackle inside them and around them (the world: a fierce, unreal racket, swarming and still distant), and because they were letting themselves be guided by this force. Because they had not exhausted the depth of the dry woods, the skeletal vines, the brown dust on the ground that was reddened with fire itself; because they were burned by the blast, like a raucous breath, exhaled by the crackling branches; because they were spending their forces on these furrows dug into the trails by rainy-season downpours and carved into burning ovens by the height of the dry season. The two of them were taking off on the feeble clouds escaping into the sky, they were thrusting with all their blood, beyond the bristle of shucked-off, stripped-away earth, to a height where the water and the plain, the hurricanes and brush fires, the law of the drum and the written law reached them all at once. United by the same sort of rising flood pounding inside their bodies, the old man without a cause and the young man who was all scholarly and naïve, hurtled down to the world (its pitiful diversity), seeking perhaps to make out, among the clouds and mists, the long infinite country for which they had no words, and that they could only feel, indeed, as an absence; they only needed it so they could better grasp the immediate land remaining so elusive all around them.

"But you can see it," Mathieu said softly. "Now I know that you can see it."

Who can do that? It is so large. I see lions bigger than the Morne des Esses, they jump over mountains with a single leap; and I see rivers wider than the sea, you can throw the whole earth into them; I see the grass big as life swaying over your head, and when it catches fire mountain lions lie down on the flames to put it out! I see roads lined with magnolias, the straw thatch on roofs aflower with intense fragrances; the road goes up a tree, farther than noon. I see noontime, I smell the first morning wind that brings them together for work, and I hear music in the night when the stars come down among the branches and rest on a leaf. It is the infinite country: when you climb a mahogany tree, you are a brave young man, but you are an old body when you reach its topmost branch up there. Ah Godsalmighty! Daylight is weak, the eye can only see here and there. If your eye, only your eye, is very sharp the eye's field becomes empty before your very eyes. The country is too big, it moves from north to south — can you make out a country that breathes while you are sleeping, that is visible where your eyes are unable to see, can you, if you do not go down to the place where all the water comes together underneath, if you do not flow beneath your skin to find the light at the end of the canal, then the open sea in the light?

"But you can see the place," Mathieu said softly. "The houses, the forest, the river."

I see, I see the fool haggling with the men destined to be his masters, he thinks he is omnipotent; however the man giving him a machete, two little barrels of rum, and a dirty shirt is already thinking, "When we're all finished here we'll put him on board too." But this madman is blind and cannot read what is in the traffickers' eyes; so he opens up the path before them; he shows them the way to go through the forest darker than the soot of three thousand fires, and he takes them right to the middle of the gathering place after first slitting the dogs' throats himself.

"Ah! Full of the bitterness of revenge!" said Mathieu.

It was his passion to be the one chosen, the one in command. They had argued in front of the gathered people, each of them had spoken, but when night fell the choice had been made. Then he had fled into the woods with everyone after him because he had insulted the old men and invoked the dead in his favor. Then he lived a solitary life up until he began hovering around the line of slaves; and when the traffickers took him prisoner he had proposed a swap. He then counted on his fingers how many of the people who lived there could be brought in; so the white men had spread out before him a procession of objects from which he could choose. It was first of all his passion to be in command. It can be said that he was deserving; but the rotten root had taken hold in his belly and made it bloom with rot. And maybe the law was even in his favor. Maybe custom demanded that he be the one chosen. Maybe his father had performed the greatest services and he was thought of as the heir or continuation.

"Perhaps," said Mathieu. "Yes, perhaps, perhaps."

But there's no way you can deny that the other man had the power. The old men recognized his strength: he walked through the darkness and he knew where the horizon was, trees let him in on their secrets, animals obeyed, the child with scabies smiled, the pregnant woman left her bed. And so the choice between them came from the land all around them, and this is what led to the swap. A dirty shirt was the price of solitude. Because, in the frenzy of hatred, at the moment your ancestor picked up the machete and the two little barrels from among the stock laid out before him, he knew that his life from that point on would be eternal solitude. Lucky for him he was thrown into the pen then into the cell at the center and then into that boat where, though he did not see her, there was a woman leaning beside him; she was from a different part of the country and knew nothing of the whole affair: otherwise she would never have gone to live with him. And lucky for him that the other, I don't know what was in his mind, decided in fact to let him live all the way to the new land, and then on this new land until he died of slavery.

But who here remembers the boat? The space beyond is dense, it has all closed over like a well-cooked sea urchin. Then they felt something itching slightly inside them, feet picking themselves up to walk, wings sprouting to fly. For them somewhere else is the magnet. There is nothing against that. Which means that right now you sit there speechless, Mathieu Béluse, and you have been sitting there so long listening to me that you are turning into dust in front of my hut. . . .

And he did not say—but he knows it better than I do, thought Mathieu—that adding to this fascination with someplace else, this call of the horizon, this abdication of all flesh in the blissful dream of "faraway places" there was the comedy of destitution playing itself out to the point where it would be ridiculous to try to say which act came first, which second, or point out its setting. And, for example (thought Papa Longoué), Ti-René had been working for two years in that tannery — so that was three years after the volcano erupted and destroyed the big city and tossed its ashes all the way to the salt marshes of the south — when the mother sat down one day at La Touffaille with a few leaves on her knees and with her hand had pushed aside all that midday heat.

The siren at the Central Factory was blaring, and the noise made the flies spin in panic above the table. The three boys and three girls stood up and looked at their father, waiting for him to say something. "OK," he said firmly (he had always thought the decision would be his in the end, he calmly kept right on thinking this), "I'll go see Senglis next Saturday and I'll accept his conditions." Then silence struck like a cudgel after the siren's final blast, and the flies descended at once onto the vinegar burning into the wood of the table. The words had been said: the father would see Senglis. Senglis: a name more than a man, a presence with no presence, almost a bead in a rosary. Not one of them could have said whether or not this Senglis loved his wife, drank his coffee with a spoon, or sometimes turned over the ground in his garden to watch it turn yellow. He was a number in a line that was endless, maybe not even the first one who wanted to take La Touffaille. Not one of them (not even the father) had gone any farther than the entrance to the "château." He was a just colorless number, not even a figure, in an infinite series. They understood that he had been in no hurry to grab La Touffaille; he had plenty of time. Time does not count for those who have people preceding and following them. For ten years he could have grabbed them by the neck, but no, he preferred roundabout ways; he preferred to smother them slowly. Now finally it was said: the father would go see Senglis. The sons immediately began taking inventory for the move. It soon turned out that each of them had gone up into the mountain secretly to check on the land. The girls asked if the spring was far from where the future house would stand and if there weren't snakes there. Mostly there were *campeche* trees. The father calculated that with the payment proposed they would buy a small stock of hens and rabbits; it would be better to raise animals than plants up in the hills. . . . Outside the hard mud sparkled. A soft crackling of heat lulled the earth and the trees. But the land was already not theirs; they could neither sell it or turn it over officially because they had no title to the property. They merely signed a certificate of abandonment. Perhaps that was why Senglis had not rushed them.

The mother stood up and went to the door; she squinted into the dazzling dry-season light. Perhaps she was thinking about the people who did not have even a certificate of abandonment to sign. When you thought about it, if they were so destitute at La Touffaille, how much more true must that be of the people packed into the huts near the factory, the factory's outbuildings? For the last time the mother looked at the slope bathing in the glare that streamed down it. But even the dazzling light itself was no longer theirs. The sound the heat made was no longer theirs. And the mother raised her hands to her eyes and leaned against the door. Behind her the others bowed their heads. —Having a bit of earth amounts to nothing when the earth as a whole does not belong to everyone.

Croix-Mission

Chapter 12

1

MATHIEU REFUSED to go up to the *quimboiseur's*. He shouted at his mother, Madame Marie-Rose, that doctors should be able to cure him—they earned enough money! "Good Lord in Heaven," said Madame Marie-Rose, "a child barely nine years old and he's arguing with his mother!" And she, a woman who so often took the switch down from behind the door, this time stood there and showed no reaction to her son's stubbornness.

From farther back than he could remember, Mathieu had never argued. First his Aunt Felicia was in charge of his upbringing, then his mother herself and his eldest sister and he had grown up in the shadow of these women who, like all women in that country, took responsibility for educating the children. Although he bore the name Béluse because his father had recognized him, Mathieu depended on his mother alone for everything. Madame Marie-Rose had four children, two girls and two boys; the eldest daughter married in 1934 and her husband worked in the city, only returning home for weekends. Which meant that this sister who was fifteen years older had been a third mother (after Madame Marie-Rose and Aunt Felicia). She still would jokingly ask Mathieu, just to remind him of those early years, "Ti-Mathieu nèg', sa ki rivé' oü?" and he would answer in a singsong voice, the way he did when he was four: "My aunt beat me." But neither the aunt nor the sister would have been able to contain the child's turbulent nature; only his mother was successful. Though she could scarcely read and write, she would hold the book wide open on her hands as if it were breakable and make him recite his lessons. Mathieu had never been able to fool her and recite one lesson instead of another or improvise when he was at a loss. She would guess by his tone of voice that the child did not know what was in it and out came the switch.

They were bound together in silent complicity because Madame Marie-Rose was proud of her son and his school successes; but some strange sense of propriety had steered them both away from showing their affection the way a boy and his mother usually did. It must be said that Mathieu lived in dread of Madame Marie-Rose's strict ways. So he was amazed that she was so considerate about asking him to go up to the *quimboiseur's*. The eldest sister's child was almost dying, and Mathieu was refusing to obey his mother.

"Aren't you ashamed?" she said. "Your sister's child. Ah Virgin Mary, defend us. There are no buts or whys about it. The doctors have said he is going to die, you have to go up there to get Papa Longoué."

Mathieu was panicked: having to ruin an afternoon climbing up there in the sun and finding himself all alone face to face with the *quimboiseur*, four miles from where anyone could hear him, lost in the forest of acacias. As if the child had guessed that by going up into this forest he would leave forever the reassuring emptiness, the droning absence, the calm death that made them survive in the shadow of the Croix-Mission, where every evening he would sit on the cement stairs to have the best view of the two neighborhood tough guys strutting around. To walk for four miles first on melted tar then in extremely hot gravel and then between lines of bamboo on hard dirt that cut your feet; and to find yourself alone facing the *quimboiseur* while silence descended onto the hill or the wind hissed through the foliage.

Mathieu was well acquainted with the man. A few weeks earlier he had been at the barbershop belonging to Sainte-Rose, and the *quimboiseur* had come in and sat down on a stool; and while one of the regulars strummed a banjo and Sainte-Rose bustled about with his scissors, repeating his eternal refrain ("Les fers sont maniables et tangibles, en décadence comme les noix dans les pieds!")—his child's gaze met the man's gaze in the mirror. They stared calmly, vacantly at each other for one long moment, until the child lowered his eyes; when he had jumped out of the chair (a big one made of wood and woven straw) hurrying off to play, the man said to him: "Young man, you have the eyes, you can believe me." The memory was still vivid, at least as sharp as his memory of the day his uncle's skiff had sunk in the bay at Le Diamant; and if he closed his eyes he saw again simultaneously the gaze of the *quimboiseur* and the long bluish light that had swallowed him and slowly rose up into him and around him when he plunged into the sea and before his uncle dove in to save him.

So in those days he was afraid of the *quimboiseur*'s power—although he asked himself that particular day (racing out of the shop and unpleasantly surprised to feel the hot breeze on his temples) why that man came to have his hair cut. Wasn't he able to stop hairs from growing? . . . And when Madame Marie-Rose ordered him to climb up into the acacia woods, he had seen before him a big dark mirror from which burst two eyes with no eyebrows.

Madame Marie-Rose had held her ground, and there he was on the road that Saturday afternoon. His mind strained toward the moment when he would stop in front of the cabin ("all the way at the top of path, you can't mistake it") and shout to give himself courage, "Anybody there?" And he was so preoccupied with that moment that he did not notice how far he had gone, did not see the two lemon trees at the end of the mud road, or the big flat rocks piled one on top of the other in its final curves; suddenly he found himself seated inside the dark cabin, perched awkwardly on a crudely carved stool, after hearing Papa Longoué say to him, "Let's sit down and follow the path." Then he awoke from his hypnosis and almost enjoyed himself, watching the bony old man with his eyes shut who really seemed to move along inside himself, while his voice that seemed full of sleep murmured on, "I go down, I go down, I take the tar road to the left, I pass in front of the sawmill, I go over the bridge, I go up the main road, I turn at the corner by Bonaro's store, I go past the garden, the Lord's house, I turn again at city hall, and there it is, it's the road behind, one cabin, two, three, a little path, that's where it is, I go into the yard, there is a paved walkway." (Ah là là! thought the child, as if he didn't already know the place all these hundred and ten years he's been alive!)—but then he jumped, because there in front of him this mummy was almost shouting into the cabin's darkness, "I can't go in, I can't go into the house, the tablecloth is on the table upside down and the statue of the Virgin on the shelf has to be turned around!" Then the old man stood up, perfectly normal, and said, "You go on back down, I can't go in." He added, "I know you, I saw your eyes at the barber's."

Then the preposterous story that followed: Mathieu exasperated by all those miles, his bursting into tears when he got home, his mother's entreaties, his sister quietly weeping, lamenting her husband's absence, the nephew burning with fever in a tray filled with sheets and covered with a sheepskin, then going back up Sunday morning (while his friends played war in the Canteen garden), the whole scene all over again, the *quimboiseur* "in a state," going down into his mind, the parody of a consultation, finally Papa Longoué normal once again and smiling at him mischievously. And the worst thing was—everything tallied: the tablecloth was upside down, the statue of the Virgin was on the shelf; then, by some miracle Mathieu never understood, the *quimboiseur* decided on a remedy that cured the child.

However, even after these two visits had been forgotten, that is for the five years during which he did not once remember the *quimboiseur*, inside his mind and perhaps in the very equilibrium of his body Mathieu retained the deep shadowy shape of the cabin and the airy quality of how the road reached to stream narrowly down from this shadow to the flat heat of the colonial road. And there was inside him still, all this time, the sensation of its gradually becoming brighter and of a weight growing heavier, that had borne him down along the three roads—mud, stones, tar. But it was not the road that called him back to the old man, nor was it the desire to know the future nor even fascination with a power that he no longer believed in during this period when, at fourteen now at lycée, his mind was associating with even more seductive powers. Rather, what he went back to look for in the cabin was the abyss of shadow and lightness, the patient immobility so distant from his own nature.

He remembered how, at the time he had gone to consult the *quimboiseur*, the country was all stirred up and madly celebrating.

Something called the Tricentennial, now proverbial among the schoolboys because it had been drummed into them day after day, a litany: "1635, the jurisdiction of France established; 1935, Tricentennial of French jurisdiction." An eruption of banquets, speeches, receptions. And four times now (probably the two round-trips of some parade) he had found himself on the side of the road waving a flag, surrounded by cheers that really fed upon themselves because the object of the wave of sound (a shiny, black automobile) moved quickly between the two rows of people. Because the passion for anything coming from somewhere else beyond the horizon had long since been born and had now grown strong, along with a bedazzled confidence in anything that, legitimately or not, proclaimed that it emanated from and represented that somewhere else — coming every time like a miraculous bit of the world, like a meteor passing through the enclosed space here.

Mathieu remembered how, from his earliest school years, he had been carried away, made light and impalpable, vast and exuberant by reading a sentence like, for instance, "The northern seas are populated by whales"; or, for example, by a photograph of limestone plateaus in the Causse region of France in his geography book. It was more widespread, therefore, more tyrannical even than attachment or jurisdiction; it was already the secret desire to leave, to participate, to exhaust the incurable diversity (though this diversity endlessly tempted one to reduce it to a single truth) of the world. Mathieu, nonetheless, brooded over the little green book, about sixteen pages long, that reported its version of the history of the country: The Discovery, The Pioneers, The French Jurisdiction, The War with the English, The Natural Goodness of the Natives, The Mother — or Great — Country. He never got any satisfaction or peace from it. Though he was certainly not conscious of it, he was always anxious and restless, and he and his friends found their only recourse was to identify with the movie heroes when they would go, twice a week, to be carried off into another world. Soon the frenzied showings full of disaster, seen from the seats of El Paraiso and interminably discussed on the steps of Croix-Mission, were not enough. Nor were the great jumble of books he devoured (even including the copies of Complete Films that he discovered at a friend's aunt's house; she was sophisticated and had an incredible stack of them from which he helped himself on the sly). When war was declared in 1939 and came to kindle another fire or enthusiasm and the soldiers boarded ship, flowers on their guns, while the crowd sang:

Roulé! Roulé, roulé, roulé
Hitlè, nou kaï roulé' où anba monn'la!

This hill, this monn'la to the bottom of which they were going to roll Hitler, did not take Mathieu back to another hill, the one he twice went back down four years before. He was openmouthed with admiration for the men who were leaving. In the huge crush of people, he ran all the way to the Transat, then the whole length of the pier, with the same crowd going crazy, following the slow progress of the boat toward the line of the horizon where it vanished. (For them it was the second boat that really left, after all the others that did nothing but arrive.)

But then the war quickly drove them back into their salt marsh. From 1940 on there was no longer any question of thrilling departures; on the contrary, a significant armed force was dispatched to convince them to stay put. The vast world was once again closed. Mathieu found himself (one Saturday when he had returned home from the market town nine miles away, taking shortcuts through the countryside) seated again in the same chair in Sainte-Rose's barber shop; and, although there was no one else there other than the barber and the banjo player, he saw the eyes in the big mirror.

"What has happened to Papa Longoué?"

"Ah my friend," said Sainte-Rose (now that Mathieu was fourteen and at lycée the barber made no bones about treating him as an equal), "he is still up in the hills."

"Does he get his hair cut?"

"Never ever. The day you saw him here, my dear, he only stayed ten seconds after you left. He never comes to the city." (Sainte-Rose would have died rather than say "town.")

And this is how Mathieu met up with his old fear again. He closed his eyes; he felt himself dissolving into the blue of the sea, going down and down like a kite into the limpid light of transparent seaweed and sunlight through mist; once again he saw the eyes, not in the mirror, but at the bottom of the blue water that hung there inside him. The old fear and present agony merged. And the next day, a Sunday morning, he was on that road for the third time, though he did not know why, drawn by the shadow from up above, the lightness, the immobility.

Papa Longoué immediately said to him, "Ah! Boy, it will be hard for you to be content with your life," as if he were picking up a conversation that had been interrupted the day before. The boy stayed all day, saying nothing, or almost nothing. The silence between them was as full of vibration as the breeze on the canefields at the foot of the hills. They watched each other and took each other's measure. And gradually they reached the point where they would evoke the great-grandparents and past generations. That is to say that Mathieu, once he knew which way to go, made the old man tell the story while the rising wind slowly covered them with its flood.

Papa Longoué, who had done his best to approach Béluse's son, now wondered why this young man was coming like this, not talking, seating himself on the ground in front of the cabin. A boy already more educated than the clerk at city hall. It was the shadow, the immobility, the depth of bygone truths that he was seeking, as if they were a poultice to cover the anxious restlessness bubbling up inside him.

Sometimes someone would come down the trail, a cane cutter or charcoal vendor; Papa Longoué would receive this person who had come to consult him and Mathieu would wait. The past. As far as the past was concerned he had only his experience as a schoolboy (he was the last child in the family, the one who had no concern other than school). And all he could remember of the past from school—whenever the *quimboiseur* left him to give a "séance"—were scattered, unexpected bits like green mangos falling one by one.

The schoolyard, sprinkled with tall grasses that the pupils tied together, three by three, with a big knot at the top, repeating the phrase ("three dogs, three cats, if she comes it's not for me") meant to keep them from being called on in the next class. The line of students in front of the door to the classroom (under the sign with its ornate letters: "Sleep nine hours—That's the secret—Of vigorous old age!"), all of them taking care to keep their fingers crossed, the big finger of their left hands wrapped over the index finger, this too intended to ward off the teacher's attention so they would not be called on. The children caught speaking Creole, the shameful and forbidden language, lined up, hands thrust forward, fingers together and curled upward so that each child could get five blows from the ruler. The principle, a fine, stout, implacable man, regarded as strange by the students, who would keep them after school (or at least the ones preparing exams for the next level) and would walk between the desks with his ruler under his arm calling: "Let's go, let's go kiddos, in 1515, in 1515?..." And the ruler would sweep onto the top of a skull every time some terrified pupil was slow to honor the victory over the Swiss at Marignano on his slate, while the others raised slates with the correct answer way up over their heads in relief. The thin little girl (she laughed all the time, he was enthralled by her grace) whose dresses, always freshly ironed, he admired and who had such a wide mouth that, if not for her ears to stop it the split would have never ended—so that naturally she was known as "Thankyou-ears." Another little girl whose toes turned out at right angles when she walked and hence was given the name "Ten-past-ten." Small wars declared in class—how the news would go around the room; then when school was out, inside a circle formed by the others and from which there was no escaping, the line drawn between the adversaries that the aggressor had to cross; and the two who were fighting would set to fiercely, sometimes their quartermaster issue pens would break off in a hand or an arm and then the points would have to be pulled out, leaving two red holes purplish with ink in the skin. The loud shouts of the procession accompanying a boy who refused to fight ("Hi *cayé, hi cayé, hi cayé—é—hi cayé!*" He ran away!) all the way to his mother's house, where invariably she would take the switch to him. But the same thrashing awaited proud victors as well.

The examination that qualified you for a scholarship, and that comma probably or that correctly placed accent to make a past tense that had earned him the chance to go down to the city lycée that would also provide his midday meals. His Aunt Mimi who provided his lodging and evening meal for a small fee. His old school friends, his old rival, gone back to the canefields and henceforth more distant from him than a Syrian salesman from a watch that works . . . But really, he did not like this lycée. His affections and his busy memory kept returning to the schoolyard that was as overgrown as a real savanna, and to the principal's garden (the holy of holies), where the best students were appointed to ring the bell.

Before school, but also steeping in this life zone where the boy readily saw himself: church. And first, five o'clock mass which meant being obliged to get out of bed in the dark and rush (like the wild, panicky wind) into the back road and finally collapsing breathlessly into the half-light of the sacristy where one of the sisters was already bustling about. The underhanded battle, between the nine or ten brats that they were, to climb the hierarchy and as a result obtain the right to carry the cross at 25 centimes a ceremony rather than the censer (15 centimes) or the cruets (10 centimes). The secret scorn (aggravated by the grudge of a decent worker) directed at the one (the only one) who did not get paid because his parents were well-to-do and would not allow him to take money for a religious service. Also the vertiginous singing in the church, the incense that conjured up primeval forests, the sugared almonds at baptisms, the sweet smell of wine at mass. Abbé Samuel, a Canadian who would yell at the acolytes whenever he lost his temper, "Get out! Go home!" The book of responses where the Latin words stood out in black capitals against the instructions printed in light italics. The office where the vicar, seated in his rocker behind a table with a glass top, would hand over whatever they had earned (recorded in a notebook), and sometimes—as a charitable bonus—a pair of canvas shoes sent by who knows what religious organization. Finally those twenty or twenty-five centimes (depending on the number of births and deaths) that every month he would scrupulously take home to his mother, who earned a hundred and twenty francs working for Dr. Toinet.

Associated with this morning mass there were the five buckets of water he would go and get from the yo-yo fountain on the street (called a yo-yo because of the handle that was lots of fun to turn) to fill the big barrel set up in front of his house before going to school. The days when he was late or when his friends, already on their way, saw him waiting his turn at the fountain, behind an old lady who shook too much to move very fast. And associated with that, the rabbit grass he had to find every evening in the middle of the town, when the hilly fields dense with nettles where people dumped their garbage had died back. The sweet creepers (the best possible rabbit grass); he had located areas where it grew and watched the waning supply apprehensively.

In sharp contrast to all this, the nightmare day he had endured in one of the wooden wings of the hospital; taken there one morning by his mother, left in a bed with flies for company, bewildered by the sight of the skeletal old men all carrying little flyswatters (the principal attribute of the place), disoriented by the sweet yet distant nuns, one of whom—to his astonishment was as black as he was and seemed the most surly—who came at midday and again at three o'clock to make the whole room recite an impressive series of Our Fathers and Hail Marys—so that the rhythmic drone of the sick people counterbalanced the buzzing of the flies. In the middle of the day, the ghastly, insipid herbal tea that was brought in buckets with a few hunks of stale bread already soaking in it. That room—unreal. One side of it reserved for children his age who were crippled, weak, or wounded (one of them, green and emaciated, had been eating dirt for months and months. He was going to die). At four o'clock in the afternoon Mathieu had climbed out of bed; he had followed the grass path lined on either side with cement gutters; he had gone out through the big door left open just this once, and still wearing the pajamas of coarse gray cloth, paying no mind to the people in the street who called out to him, he went back home to his mother, to the two small rooms she rented from Monsieur Bedonné, right next to ten others all in a line beneath the same tin roof, all part of one building. "I'm not going back there," he had calmly declared when she discovered him there in the bed. Madame Marie-Rose, after hesitating a moment (and the only time in history —but probably because for her the hospital represented something like an introduction to death), gave in.

But what was this past, what were these memories if not the still warm thread of his existence, the sequence of images and sparks where each day he would find the impetus for the next? Could he a child—reflect upon his childhood? And supposing he did so, could he put enough distance between this principal's garden or this lattice pavilion in the hospital with no cures, or this sacristy hallway hung with red robes and capes, at least enough for these places to shine like suns? He longed for the place so distant that its light would reach him like an arrow of flame in the region where eyes can no longer see. There was another past, there were other nights to get through before, breathless, he would reach a morning's half-light. He sensed this with all of his body. And of course, for as long as he did not come out there he would be afraid of the dark. And though he was skeptical and no longer believed in the power of the *quimboiseur*, behind that wrinkled forehead and beneath the words spinning faster and faster, he also was watching for a country whose quaking, whose extinguished or forbidden truths now freely rekindled, troubled him even more seriously.

And so it was that between the ages of fourteen and seventeen he lived (wild, shaggy, gaunt from hardships and outbursts) at this peak, this extreme. Swinging back and forth between the vertigo of that darkness swallowing up the real past (the remote line of filiation) and the clearly throbbing pain of the present, or rather of the emptiness that was present. This feverish state did gradually diminish however. From one Saturday to the next—though sometimes he wouldn't go up for a whole month—he made some progress toward the deep tranquillity of the cabin, and meanwhile in a life of secondary importance he did the things lycée students usually do, making no attempt to hide the detachment and distance that made him hard to like. And gradually he made friends with some of the boys without knowing that they were just as distraught, just as arrogant, and just as anxious as he was. Until this day at the height of the dry season when he had traveled with the old seer into a place that was both a dream country and, at the same time, the trembling past of a real country; he understood then that the road down the hill led to everyday life, that taking that road one went from the acacias to the fields, from the fields to the town; but what was there, nevertheless, was only a semblance of life. Because as more light was gradually let in it met up with nothing: real life remained without an object; the tar's flat heat never raised itself to any level that was worthy of life—as long as that shadow from the hills had not come uncoupled from the cabin where it slept for so long in order to rush, gentle and unstoppable, into the surrounding land. The past. Mathieu spoke softly to the *quimboiseur*: "Now, Papa, you can tell me what was in that little barrel."

"Now," said Papa Longoué.

And the old man rummaged around under the belt to his pants and pulled out a purse made of heavy yellow cloth tied with a hemp cord; he opened it and spread it out on his hand, holding the thing out toward Mathieu. The boy bent down. He saw nothing in the bottom of the purse except maybe a minuscule amount of grayish dust that could just as well have come from wear on the cloth. He looked at the *quimboiseur*. But already the old man's voice was rising clearly into the dry air as if it were torn from the trembling depths of the past, a voice now clear and distinct, a reflection of the bamboos, the ferns, the lianas dried up all around them by the dry season into skeletons, a voice with no depth.

"So," said Longoué, "La Roche was standing there in front of the cliff covered with acacias, right where when you come down you see those two lemon trees. He was quite a distance from the others, a man whose actions are unpredictable: he might have been laughing or he might have been crying, who can say? And when they went back home he put the little barrel down in front of the kitchen door. None of the slaves (none of the ones he called "his people") would have reminded him about the thing, the barrel; they knew what was there. Louise would not have mentioned it either. La Roche had shown her the little barrel before he went off on the hunt, saying: 'We'll see if he really intends to put his sign on me when I have caught him.' Ah! Those are words I know by heart! So Louise said nothing about the thing sitting there outside. What's more, the next day Louise was on that contraption, and as for him, he drank more *tafia* than a person can take all at once. OK. Longoué comes in the kitchen door and almost trips over the barrel; he leaves taking Louise. Then the next day, when the terrified people come to tell La Roche that there was nobody on that cross contraption anymore, he comes out all sunk in rum, using the back door as a result, and the first thing he sees is not the useless contraption but his little barrel. Then he really laughs and instead of ordering his race horse to be brought so he can pursue them, he picks up the barrel and carries it inside, leaving his people to wait for him. Then, for one whole day perhaps, he remains in the big living room sitting in front of the barrel as if he meant to hypnotize it. And at night he put it in the storage room where Louise used to sleep, and forbade anyone to move it. Yes, that's what happened. But Longoué also knew what that little barrel concealed. Louise had told him. And when La Roche throws the thing at his feet ten years later he instantly thinks that the creature has come back to him because of his own weakness; because he had gone to break up and scatter the head made of mud underneath the root in the woods. So, ever since that time, no one would open the little barrel in the hut. Longoué himself told La Roche, 'Too bad if the creature turns against me.' Because (the *quimboiseur* said, stretching his open hand out to where the purse revealed its specks of dust), this is what was in it. A snake."

The wind shuddered against his leg and Mathieu instinctively rubbed himself as if warding off some threat; keeping an eye out for the still possible snake at his feet. Then they both sat motionless and dreaming with the dust before them.

"You see that thing," said Mathieu. "Nothing but a little barrel.

So it sat there in front of the door that whole night spent celebrating, and Louise went to bed right next to it. And the creature was alive inside it. Then La Roche carried it into the storeroom; he may even have put it on Louise's pallet. How many years before the crazy beast falls to pieces? Maybe it was beating its head against the wood. Or perhaps it coiled up at the bottom and went to sleep there. Then it dried up, the skin unraveled, and finally the entire body was nothing more than loose dust. And Stéfanise picked it up and put it on her head."

"And notice how fearless La Roche was. In any case he tried to turn the sign around on him. He would have crammed the creature into Longoué's mouth. Or maybe, right in front of the stunned hunters, he quite simply would have handed him the little barrel. An unpredictable man."

"And," said Mathieu, "that is how he could bear to sleep with the creature wide awake beside him, behind a wooden partition and inside a house where doors were only there for show. And any of the men you call his people could slip in at night and just open the little barrel. But he was shielded by his madness. He lived a hundred years when Senglis would have died ten times over."

"He had the mark on him," said Longoué. "Because it is easier to kill suddenly than to force the means of death in the future."

"Because you think that . . ."

"Yes," said the *quimboiseur*. "That is why the little barrel remained shut. Neither Longoué nor Melchior nor Apostrophe nor Stéfanise. Keep the creature good and warm. So it won't stick its tongue outside. It had been turned back against Longoué then. But when Ti-René died there was no longer any reason not to. I made the purse, and the same day that I buried the certificate of his death I opened the little barrel. There was dust in it and a bit of parchment still. Since then it has all gotten lost inside this purse. But it is here on my skin."

"Ah!" said Mathieu stunned. "You are a worse rascal than I thought."

The old magic man laughed silently.

During this period, therefore, the boy did not suffer at all from a sense of wasted energy. On the contrary, life was more and more a great cavalcade for himself and his friends, he felt a crackling enthusiasm, an intoxication with the world from which the endless world was absent. But every now and then he would be annoyed that he was unable to grasp the all-quivering shades and tones of the chaotic, passionate words around him, because he had a growing inner awareness of this language. He was more receptive, more trusting and perhaps more naïve than any of those close to him, and so, already opening up before him, was a long and patient vigil, one that was neither excessive nor exciting, where he would watch for a light coming from down there. He experienced how it was possible for people (he did not even go so far as to say: a people) to leave, to run dry, leaving no real descendants, no fruitfulness in the future, enclosed within their death which was truly the end of them, for the simple reason that their speech was dead too, stolen. Yes. Because the world, for which they listened either passionately or passively, had no ears to hear a lack of voice. Mathieu wanted to shout, to raise his voice, to call from the depths of the little land toward the world, toward forbidden countries and faraway places. But the voice itself was unnatural and Mathieu could sense that: he himself, strangely sent off to the frontiers, split there between the straightforward universe of cane and clay and straw (where speech was no help in *watching* or *digging* for anything) and the other zone, the one of people who speak but where he sensed that what they said was nothing, just smoke already bluish against the abyss of the great sky.

What Papa Longoué was calling "the Béluses" was no longer the monotonous clan that, following the example of the Longoués, repeated themselves one after the other in the cabin at Roche Carrée. Mathieu Béluse, the father, had seen the world; absolutely nothing would have kept him in that cabin. He had worked at a number of different jobs before entering the very select group of plantation supervisors. He had not taken a wife, at least not legally, and people claimed he had had an affair with a Frenchwoman. A good many children around there were acknowledged to be his. He liked to say of himself: "It's been used a lot but not worn out." At some exam or other in his youth he had forgotten a comma or an acute accent and he never let you forget it. He would grant himself brief intervals of meditation between two periods of full employment and people would suppose he "was counting tamarind leaves from down on the ground." But he was a man of intelligence and, as the *quimboiseur* said, dignity. In that vague zone restlessly astir with those who had escaped alive from the canefields, he gradually watched himself be outstripped by a generation that had had more advantages. He was rather scornful of them and his reaction was to apply himself with a clear conscience to his job as overseer where his authority was undeniable. In the end he became supervisor of an estate. Because of his sense of honor and justice, anchored (as if part of his structure) in his imposing stature, in a different world and with different means he would have been a patriarch by vocation: one of those poor but radiant men who spread their light around them. But the generations were jostling for position and Mathieu the father was no follower; he read the illustrated weeklies from France and endlessly commented on Daladier's politics as something the country had to deal with.

Mathieu the son had little to do with this father. He did not feel entitled to anything from the Béluses, but on the contrary he enjoyed the company of his uncles, his mother's brothers. One of them in particular (of course this was before the war and the great haste it brought about) would stop his horse whenever he came to town and go inside to play with the child. The Béluses, multiplied, dispersed, and young, were beginning a different story. Mathieu had never known his grandfather Zéphirin. What little he knew of him had been told him by the *quimboiseur*: Zéphirin too was a shadow. The scattering of the Béluses started with him. As for Zéphirin's wife, Mathieu's paternal grandmother, the boy had only associated with her every other Sunday when they came out of mass; she was a strong believer and never missed a service.

Occasionally he would get irritated. Not yet knowing how uncomfortable life is when you can never say "long ago" and know what it means. Not understanding at all why he seethed with this passion for distant countries. Not finding any of the places in the land where the land had shed its skin. These three things he lacked were enmeshed with emptiness and vertigo in his mind. But someone who cares about the horizon and can expand inside his shack is already a privileged person. He used to go up to the cabin, dig in the past, and take the earth's measure.

Sailors loyal to Pétain occupied the country, their ships on patrol keeping it closed off. Mathieu had seen sailors getting out of trucks on land belonging to people who had very little where they helped themselves to everything they could carry (breadfruit, yams, bananas). Flagrantly brandishing their power, they came down hard on the blacks. The sterile sea impassable. And yet, young men cramped up inside the country did cross the sea to enlist in the Allied armies. When people worried about some man who had suddenly vanished, there was a ritual response: "*Sille pa neyé, i Ouachigtone.*" If he hasn't drowned he's in Washington.

Life subsided. It got bogged down. It was getting ready (with the war over, its anemic calm, the explosion marking its conclusion, the air stirring over the area, the dizzy spell) for the flat rhythm to come. And soon it would feebly mark its time with rum and barley water in special structures erected for the town fête, blood pudding and hot pies at Christmas, the Princes' *quinquina* on New Year's, crab *matatou* and *riz-debout* for Pentecost, Noilly-Prat on Easter Sunday (holy water on Palm Sunday), bread with butter and milk chocolate for first communions, a drink at city hall on armistice day, and during the intervals between all these sacred treasures (for which anyone of them would have gone bankrupt), the same monotonous abstinence.

But on the fringe of this demoralized existence, where the towns and cities lay sleeping, shone a high plateau, a great rich detour, a chaos of wisdom gleaming from the land, calls buried away, innocent listening, fertility as dark and dispersed as the Lézarde River, a burst of the thickest waters, cries that are too forthright, child-hoods, milk sand, and in this region of unstable and fertile things, Mathieu Béluse met Marie Celat. No one seeing this young woman could keep from exclaiming, "Ah! Mi Celat!" Look at Celat! There she is! So that soon she was usually and poignantly called Mycéa. Beauty that balks and then surrenders like a *corde-mahaut*. But Mathieu dismissed the girl with the dark eyes, he was sure he would have improbable loves; he was out of his mind. Uneasy when confronted with this girl who, the first one of her family, introduced herself saying "I am Marie Celat." Sensing perhaps that inside her the stubbornness, the powers, the clairvoyance of the Longoués was preserved. But Mathieu did not know, or rather he had forgotten that the Celats were the *Longoués from down there*.

"Ah Mister Mathieu!" said Papa Longoué who was amused, "you are afraid of that girl. You have not yet come to terms with the fight on board the *Rose-Marie*."

"Just what does that have to do with it?" exclaimed Mathieu.

"Go look at the registers," muttered the old man. "The registers will tell you."

Those were moments when Mathieu preferred to direct the force of his exasperation somewhere else. "When you think," he said (a few raindrops crystallized suddenly in the dust in front of the cabin; and Papa Longoué went along with what he was saying, yes yes yes), "when you think about it! This fat lump's great-grandfather was on that boat, no mistaking the fact, but if she sees what she calls a black peasant come into the corridor she makes a dash for the living room and closes the door. Ah! Who she is and what she's like are not worth telling you about. And suppose she hears me talking about the acacias or about Liberté, whom I like so much, he was so able wasn't he?—suppose—first she understands none of it, and then she exclaims: Here's this Monsieur Béluse, a young man with an education, and all he can find to talk about is the stories of black maroons! Ah! Papa, no that is not poverty, no. Poverty goes along with it but first it is because of having half a brain, an arm cut off, a leg long gone. And all that is buried so far away in the earth, Papa."

The old man said, "Yes yes yes."

Mathieu railed against those obtuse people who came back home wearing an announcement of their travels like a star on their foreheads; they emerged from their trips just as unburdened as before—not even a speck of dust in their hair—nothing to them. He heaped words of abuse on the half-wits (all of them provided with some little job where they would be strung up in their self-inflation to dry there like ears of corn) who insinuated—with great to-do—that they were descended from the Caribs. Did you hear that! Descended from Caribs! Because they simply wanted to erase forever the furrow through the sea. These contemptible runts really knew nothing whatsoever about the Galibis: a people whose men were so proud that when Christopher Columbus landed with his weapons in 1502 he was struck by their daring and their dignity. Christopher Columbus, who considered himself chosen by and answerable to his god, found himself face to face with men who claimed that their mountain peaks, the Pitons du Carbet, were the cradle of the human race. Those same men had driven the Ygneris out of this land before they in turn were exterminated, every last one of them, and replaced by the hundred loads of cargo landed from ships. They would all rise up from the Baie des Trépassés, the dead-men's bay, to protest that they had no descendants and that, at least, they were not about to go and rot a second time in the breath of people who were so unnatural as to deny their own ancestors!

The old man said, "Yes yes. Yes, Mister Mathieu."

And Mathieu did not notice that that was the precise moment when, carried away with his angry speech, he had begun the chronology and set up the first milestone from which the centuries could be measured. Not the gap of a hundred years unfolding one after the other, but the space traversed and the boundaries in the space. Because every day, whenever they wanted to express irritation or admiration for someone, they would say, "That black man, he's a century!" But none of them had yet shaded their eyes with their hands and said, "The sea we cross is a century." Yes, a century. And the coast where you debark, blinded and with no soul or voice, is a century. And the forest—kept in its prime until the day you became a maroon, simply to open up before you and close back around you, the forest that later would gradually waste away, felling almost on its own the huge tree trunk with its roots where the head of mud gripped by the creature made of vines had been placed—is a century. And the land, gradually flattened out and stripped bare, where the man coming down from the hills and the man waiting in the valleys came together to hoe the same weeds, is a century. Not centuries all decked out in ribbons in the clever artifice of the Tricentennial, but centuries knotted together by unknown blood, voiceless suffering, death without echo. Spread out between the infinite land and the land here that had to be named, discovered, and borne; buried in those four times a hundred years that were themselves lost in wordless time, or—it comes down to the same thing—in that little barrel where the age-old beast turned gradually to dust and then to nothing.

"People draw pictures of countries," said Mathieu. "They tell you that the Ubangi-Shari is like this and Montevideo is like that. You go away with the picture in your eyes; they get you stuck. But what is a faraway place? A somewhere else? It is when you have dug so much in the land close by that in the end you feel the trembling that comes into your eyes, that sings you. The long-ago extinguished speech that suddenly emerges all at once from everywhere!"

"Yes," said the old man. "But it's no use complaining, Mister Mathieu. You are destined for that girl! And who is to say that you will not go away like René Longoué and fall into a waterhole just two steps away from the Ubangi?"

Immersed in the damp before rain, neither of the two friends was conscious that the younger of them, though repeating or almost repeating the words of his elder, seemed to be teaching him some eternal truths all the same. Light leads on ahead and now Papa Longoué was coming to the end of his road. He was there, unmoving, until the moment when he would go down, never to return. He would certainly not follow Mathieu in his journey. On the contrary, as the young man shivered and curled in on himself like a dried-up plant (a great darkness had struck both earth and sky at high noon, the timid bamboo sang, their dark-green foliage had turned pale green and was now the only patch showing in this daytime night; all the bursting smells—acrid from allspice, thick from the ferns, delicate from the fruits of creeping lianas—had rolled over the two men with the violence of a huge ocean wave; finally, large drops crashed into the dust where they were instantly absorbed, and from the earth a moist warmth rose that stuck in their throats and was sweetly soothing—then a storm of intermittent showers, warm and bright, merged with the smells, the shadows, and the warmth of the earth)—"come on," said Papa Longoué. "There you are burning hot as a cooking-pot! Let's finally go into the cabin."

Chapter 13

*Ever since my wait for you began I mud nettle I uprooted smoke close beside the
dawning dream*

*The land smolders and with the machete takes–purest idea–its earth blood,
more fiery for the past two times a hundred years.*

(Now acacias everywhere burn me, I dreamed of three ebony trees!)

*He sings not time but the hard unmoving idea that never goes dry: sun, sun,
and whose splendor has not turned yellow*

In any autumn.

(A bird rose up among wings that are entwined.)

*Not the summer–when the cloud will have rolled into its sap and its heat is
fragrant*

With frozen yesteryears–

*But the motionless explosion the sap boiled out of, ah! When the rock beneath
our feet . . .* — then Mycéa would come in, intent on her cures, exclaiming, "Ah là là! You are about to wear yourself out, I don't know
what's got into your body, a person would think you are racing
against this fever to find out which of you is maddest."

When, in fact, what was maddest was the surge of heat where the
dense history torn from the mud of oblivion was hanging up; and
the resounding craziness, taught, inculcated (*"you would not know how
to know or act; you are unaware of the advantage of seasons, the rhythm that
provides measure and is the introduction to method, the fortifying cold and brac-
ing dawn: all that smoldering sun overwhelms and stupefies you"*) vanished
into shouts that did not last or into constant clumsy words teaching nothing. Because the land, real, perched on the cliffs, gently
uphill from the beaches, now leveled out everywhere and uniformly squared and striped with fields, was no longer that fearful,
unknown place where the boat dumped you; there was no marked
boundary any more (not even one marked by sea-grapes or manchineels) between the cultivated land here and the foam driving

before it the dust of the world. The island, abolished as it was, no longer recognized the sea as the road from somewhere else into which Louise had wanted to fling herself. Since they could not run way out beyond the horizon, then was not their lack, yes, caused by their failure to dig into the red dirt and unearth at its center the source of the sea?

But Mycéa who had taken no time to get past the poetic bits of childishness born of dizzying ignorance, Mycéa who by now was no longer the young girl with dark eyes but already the woman worrying over her husband's welfare, went out of her way to point out how unpleasant the days were, the daily battle, the prosaic necessity of drinking and eating. She had the sense that she had to battle not only Mathieu's fever and the illness consuming him during this period—possibly the aftereffects of a deprived diet during the war—but also his tendency to fly off the handle, his uncontrolled outbursts. She knew for sure the real causes of this imbalance in Mathieu, the "baggage at the bottom of it," as Papa Longoué would have said; but she pretended not to understand much of what he was saying, perhaps out of a sort of modesty, and perhaps because her therapy for him involved being diplomatic. Or sometimes she would answer him bluntly, "But what do you think, that's all over and done with. Once your clothes are washed you have to starch them." Those were times when she turned back into the ordinary young woman bringing her mischievousness to bear on the surface of existence. Consequently she spared him the need to confess the worries, the dreams, the impulses that worked according to some law he could not firmly enunciate and had some meaning he could not extract. And, unconsciously, in doing so, she showed that—without having climbed up to the cabin in the acacias and without ever having met with Papa Longoué face to face—she had heard the long story and endured the long dizzying revelation. Perhaps she knew in one of those intuitions that suddenly bear you off into the indescribable night, why, beyond the everyday density of existence, Marie Celat and Mathieu Béluse were predisposed to each other. Why, together, a Béluse and a Celat, secretly watched over throughout this story and called to knowledge, would go beyond knowledge and finally begin to act: not with evanescent gestures or fiery passion with no tomorrow but the act, yes the fundamental act that would become permanently established and find its *state of being*.

So Mycéa shared in Mathieu's fits of anger; but, because she also knew that ahead of them, there in the future, other more concrete and harder tasks awaited, she broke the thread and pushed the dazzling light of the past far behind her, and with ironic jabs or deliberately prosaic remarks she fought off the kind of vertigo that Mathieu had inside him. She sensed that it was both fatal to ignore this vertigo (failing to understand where it came from) and fatal to wallow endlessly in it.

Though she had known nothing about Papa Longoué's life, the death of the healer on the other hand disturbed her—the moment, that is, when finally relieved of his burden (because in the final days of his life he had succeeded in communicating to a chosen descendent—Mathieu Béluse—the bodiless, faceless worry that was his lot), he had lain down inside the cabin beside the old women who had come running to watch over him, had put his hand in front of his face as if to cut himself off from the present more effectively and better see the forest of the infinite country, as if to follow Melchior and Stéfanise better or better smell the odor of the boat they came in—and he did not move again until the moment of his final breath.

Papa Longoué, his old gray sweater clinging to his skin, his bony limbs, his eyes drilling a sun into the cabin shadows. He heard the wind outside, the slow rise of the wind that only he could hear, "It's all that wind," he said; the old women raised their heads, they tried to overhear the secret of that wind that the *quimboiseur* was communing with. They had dug a grave behind the cabin because, once dead, Papa Longoué would truly have refused to go down to the cemetery; he would have stared down the men who might take the risk of carrying him down to the town; and he would have turned into a *soucougnan* just to come back and torment them. The grave had been ready for three days; from time to time a neighbor would come to see whether or not the old man had "passed," so they could bury him right away. No one could have borne sitting through a wake in that cabin with the *quimboiseur's* body lying there in the shadows for a whole night. Moreover, the cabin would be closed immediately after they buried the dead man.

Mycéa paid attention to those things; she had picked up Mathieu's trail along the path climbing into the bamboo; she took over for Papa Longoué but she refused to cover her eyes with her hand; she stayed close behind that vertigo in order to know it better—in order to fight it. Mathieu himself was waiting to get well before going back up, possibly for the last time, so that he and Papa Longoué could provide the indefinable chronicle with something like a conclusion, and at least decide if "logical sequence" in the end had won out over "magic."

But a few days after he began to get better he found out (from an old woman who came, carrying a large bundle and moaning in the sunshine) that Papa Longoué was dead and that the old man had asked that the bundle be given to Mathieu. And when the old woman had gone—she had hung around in the hopes that Mathieu would open the package in her presence—he split open the big guano sack (already knowing what was inside it) and pulled out the piece of bark with the maroon carved in *effigy* upon it, the little barrel patched back together with the cloth purse among the leaves.

"Well that," Mycéa murmured, "is the end of the world," as she studied the old remains being unwrapped.

The little barrel was fascinating; and as for the piece of carved bark it was astounding how much it reminded one of the profile of big Lomé, a farmer in the uplands who was believed to have *quimbois* powers. Mycéa, who was well acquainted with Lomé, wanted to know; Mathieu was preoccupied and answered her, "Oh, just old stories . . ."

He was familiar with death. First his Aunt Felicia; they had stuck bits of cotton wadding into her nostrils, her ears, and her mouth.

Petrified (barely seven years old), he had watched over the delicate bits of white standing out sharply against her black skin and made sure that a last breath did not make the cotton move. Then there was his cousin, brought in from the country, bleached out and rachitic, already worse than dead from anemia. That was during the war. The cousin and he slept in the same bed. And he knew one night that his cousin was dead. And he lay there without moving on the straw mattress beside the body and it seemed like he could feel it getting heavier and heavier. Until six o'clock in the morning when his mother, Madame Marie-Rose, had gotten up to boil the water for coffee.

He was familiar with death; he could see Papa Longoué's. The panic-stricken old women who ran to tell the man, and evening shadows were already flooding over the peaks. Then the man in a sort of breathless race against the approaching night, who came hurtling through the leaves and took Papa Longoué in his arms like a stuffed doll and carried him to the grave, covered him with sackcloth and immediately began to fill in the hole so that soon it was almost invisible beneath the grasses as they lay back down. And, in the presence of those three or four motionless women, with darkness already upon them, the man closed the door to the cabin and wedged it shut from outside using the wooden case that Papa Longoué usually sat on. And they went away without dispersing as if they were afraid that one of them might be called back and forced to stand vigil over the empty cabin.

And even better than this hurried burial, Mathieu saw the true departure of the *quimboiseur*, the real descent described so often to him by Papa Longoué. The solitary old man made no attempt to resist the force pulling him down; he called his ancestor Longoué, he called Melchior, he went down the hill. He lit his pipe, he looked at Mathieu standing near the two lemon trees and said, "Ah! It's you Mister Mathieu." Then, standing calm and upright before continuing toward the ravine he said, "What did I do all my life other than wait? You have come. But your path goes off in this direction and mine goes straight down the other side. It was decreed that I would never walk on the tar road! So our bodies must separate. You cannot sing everything in one singing or grasp the whole hill in one hand." Then he pulled on his pipe and, turning away, slowly vanished beneath the shadows. Mathieu saw him leave.

What was maddest therefore was this land heat surrounded by water; but it was also the vertigo of people who had forgotten the sea and the boat they came in and who could not even take a skiff to cross the waters. Papa Longoué was gone; and perhaps there were some people in the country who were thinking, "Ah! The old madman has finally moved on." But in fact how much madness fueled by rum and hopelessness was whirling through the circus all around them? If they had to rank it, the madness would certainly be sturdier and bolder than malaria or the yaws; accepted, normal.

The flute player without a flute, for example, who relentlessly sang the same phrase on the same note: "I wept so much for you— MY BELOVED!" The man who would run from one passerby to the next with his hand outstretched and shouting, "Cordial phalanges! My blood and my family." Alcide who for twenty years had been working on a plan to redistribute the land and who wrote to the pope and the president of the United States. Alexandre who made vehement, scholarly speeches, beyond the grasp of ordinary people and rich in Latin quotations (he had a degree in literature) to heap scorn upon his audience. The man who suddenly refused to budge. Garcin who started a religion and was an authentic visionary. All were witnesses who went unheard. Actors with no act. Sunken suns.

All of them drunk because they had never felt the long filiation that Mathieu had sensed was there and, thanks to Papa Longoué, had some contact with, and which made him drunk in another way. Exhilarated by this revelation of bygone days like light, like a bolt from the blue.

So—in his vision—he kept talking to the old *quimboiseur* as long as he could still see him under the branches of the forest. And, "It makes you dizzy," he said, "the speed of falling without breathing without shielding yourself instantly into a light so solid that you crash into it . . ."

Because he would have preferred to proceed peacefully following the long, methodical procession of causes followed by effects, logical chronology, history unfurled like well-carded cloth; to see the entire length of the land initially untouched, in that primordial solitude where no echo from elsewhere sounded (where no lost soul was discussing whether to suffocate in the enclosed heat or to take off for the parade), then, in a way that was coherent with details and things that happen over time—the forest turning brown and rock becoming plowed land—to record the slow settling of the land, the calamitous embrace that earned these "people" and this country their inseparability; then also, still using logic and being patiently methodical, to examine how a La Roche and a Senglis became isolated, listen closely to this moment, ponder why the ground that provided them with wealth had stopped speaking to them (if it was because they had always thought of it as raw property, an asset that no delusions of hatred or love would compel one to risk) and then—but there, examining its nuances—study that other moment when the "people," having left the canefields and washed off their sweat, began to turn into what was referred as "nice," the time when just any old imbecile of a governor—his flamboyant suit, the trace of scorn playing along the surface of his gaze while he listens to a flowery address—believed he was authorized, after six months of practice, to explain the country (and why should he not do this too since so many others had done so?), lapsing into the astounding profusion of das and doudous, nounous and nanas that constituted the acknowledged resources of the tradition. And also, perhaps, yes also to seek out the deep regions where this whole circus would fall apart, that is to say the place, the time, the wretched underside where, however, safely preserved, there were a black knife and a few ropes, an old sack tied to a boutou, the chain of life and bleached bones.

Yes, all of that depending on order and the gradual rising of the wind through the gorge of acacias, all of it reasonable and conclusive—rather than the way he, Mathieu was suddenly adrift in this country that seemed new to his eyes, suddenly seeing (for the first time in how many centuries) those houses, built you would think in a different universe, where the Larroches and the Senglis hid themselves away more securely than behind any sheer drop-off of cliffs; suddenly seeing Longoué (who had come into La Roche's house in the middle of the night) and Louise (who as a child had run around under the branches of the two *acajous*) and hearing them cry that they had no descendants, none at least who had re-discovered the trail that led past the acacias.

Because he would have preferred Oh present old present Oh faded Oh day and ashore I patience ("suddenly, motionless against the blue, white façades far back behind shady gardens, that was all you could make out of the Larroches or the Senglis, about their souls or their houses. Dreary dramas stagnated there perhaps: a de-generate son—the results of the happy system of marriages were not always good—who was locked up, or a violent love going ran-cid in the half-light of a bedroom and no longer daring to race outside or to swoop down and wreak havoc on the hedges and branches, or perhaps there is an illegitimate child whose mother is black and whose education one must think about paying for") you the lookout old lookout foam in your mouth and deep you mummy and to remain to take root to sink to bury Oh past ("Nei-ther Families of course nor Dynasties, the old ground-in rough-ness, the proud unnatural dream, neither this budding of cruel forces that had established its power in La Roche or Senglis or Cyda-lise Éléonor, but something faint, indistinct, the bead of a rosary, the cousin with a place at the Bank, the son-in-law a storekeeper at the seashore, all bogged down in the dreary, bloodless, and greedy power from which the land had been withdrawn—but distant, evasive, definitely incapable of understanding that a little barrel can contain the salt of a curse—and dreaded and implacable, wrote their name in the register of those who because of their nature, be-cause of their birth, have the right to argue") Oh acacia I earthed day fallen horizon Oh past you infinite country the country you rock, and "Damnation!" cried Mycéa. "Here comes that fever gal-loping back! It's going to your head." Mathieu smiled and answered (meanwhile she stuck out her lips to let him know he was really headed for trouble), "No, no. Those are all the leaves of life and death that have to be left now to rot."

And because, in fact, other roads were opening up, because the cabin's shadow no longer drew him upland anymore but on the contrary (by bringing the past back into the feverish present) would from now on, perhaps, lead and help everybody on the surrounding farmlands, Mathieu learned all over again what Mycéa said was "civility." He knew the characteristic wildness that had so long distanced him from ordinary people took its strength from restlessness and confusion: it was already ceding, not, of course, to the brilliance of clear knowledge, but at least to the drunken euphoria of what he himself had called "light that is so solid," the revelation. Mycéa encouraged him to begin learning about real life again.

Sometimes, still shivering from his fever's heat, he would go back at nightfall to sit on the steps of the Croix-Mission. The two braggarts had not changed; every evening they confronted each other in dizzying contests of oratory, and Mathieu was never able to report the best of it to Mycéa. Enemies and accomplices, Charlequint and Bozambo (the first was really named that—Charles-the-Fifth, and the second owed his name to his resemblance to a movie hero) would set Mathieu up as judge of their contests because he was the one with education. Both of them were toothless, and they found that this peculiarity was the perfect starting point for their debates. That evening Charlequint, his face theatrically turned up to the sky, thought a bit, then:

"Ho Bozambo," he said. "Your mouth, honestly, it's a park with no benches!"

"Ah!" said Bozambo, "you speak and what I see is that you have a mouth but it's naked as a jaybird!"

Mathieu applauded and shouted, "Bozambo!"

"You're always showing preference," said Charlequint.

"He's not showing preference. Whoever stuck two ears on the back of his head didn't forget to unplug the canals!"

The Croix-Mission plunged into shadows caressed by the light shining down from an old wooden post. The dilapidated shacks, vague ghosts, showed half-hidden behind plum and mango trees; on the corner Madame Fernande's store let a very slow trickle of smoke slip out through the half-open door—the result of her gas lamp that had never wanted to work. That was it. Mathieu steeped in the symmetry of the days; merged with everyday life and the merriness of hard times, he saw none of the hills around them. The gray, hairless dogs ran to the top steps of the Croix and raced back down full tilt until their own speed sent them tumbling to the foot of the staircase. Charlequint, who spent five months of the year working at the factory, and Bozambo, who sold crabs or polished automobiles (depending on how he felt), confronted each other. The town, calm and decrepit, spread out around them; sometimes the impregnable crenellation of a bleak zone of vegetation thrust itself between the sides of two shacks.

This was the country, so tiny, all loops and turns; possessed (ah, not yet, but grasped) after the long, monotonous journey. The country: reality torn from the past, but also, a past dug up from things that were real. And Mathieu saw Time henceforth bound up with the earth. But how many of those around him could sense or assess the hidden work that lay behind appearances? How many could know it? (Could knowledge thrive if it was not shared this way? Would this understanding, instead, not go on endlessly creating the anxious exhilaration that was perhaps nothing but a cruel mark of solitude? Is it not above all when it is shared that knowledge bears fruit? No one in that country was wondering, for example, if Pointe des Nègres had not been the scene of as many deliveries as Pointe des Sables; if its name had not come from the slave market that was held there once upon a time, or perhaps from the pen they had built there to fatten the Negroes up. The past. What is the past if not the knowledge that braces you in the earth and thrusts you in huge numbers into tomorrow? Two weeks earlier women from the countryside had come down to the city; the police had arrested a cane cutter who was in charge of a "rebellious movement"; it was established that this union leader "had broken his arm" by falling down in the room where he was being questioned; the police had fired on the crowd; the dead and wounded had soured in the sun before anyone had been able to pick them up. But that, that was not the past; instead it was the mechanism inherited from the past that, by dint of monotonous repetition, was turning the present into a dying limb. Ah! The present can never be gotten back, you run, eyes blinded in the heat, you fall—punitive raid yesterday or the gunning down of strikers today—then suddenly you emerge into the future, your head exploded against that light that is more solid than mahogany.

The long descent begun with the calm mystery of the cabin under the acacias ended up therefore in this everyday market town. But what was this town? It certainly did not mark some limit at the end of the road. Because if one had to keep on tracking down this vertigo, to define it, could one not say that it was born of ignorance (or fear) of the future, as much as from the too brutal revelation of a past? Yet to come, and Mathieu did not know it, was the time they would wear blinders. The monstrous, crawling, strutting, ridiculous stupidity where people who had escaped the canefields and now had a little money wallowed as they pulled in their lips to savor the Declaration of the Rights of Man and to bless the Mother Country. All those people who would despise in themselves the flesh of their flesh, and who would only go back to the infinite country in order to offer evidence of the good La Roche had done; only to assist La Roche and thus prove that as far as they were concerned they had renounced not simply their past but even so much as the idea that they might have had one. And time, the vast, hopeless, desert of time it would take just to open their minds onto the past Time bound up with the earth and to bring them back to the top of the hills!

"But it is not time that is required," said Mycéa, "it is action."

Then the *Companies* in which the men in control of the country would quietly hold stock but which had their offices in Bordeaux or Paris. Men who specialized in profit who couldn't care less about the old stories or the fights with black maroons. The Lapointes who would no longer be slave traders on adventurous ships but affluent businessmen with housing allowances . . . — That is another story.

"Between me the earthworm and Papa Longoué," said Bozambo, "it's night and day. That man hid himself away under the acacias; you'd go there and shout: 'Anybody home?' And you'd see a big snake standing on its tail who would answer you, 'No, my son.'"

"Ah!" said Charlequint, "my sister Marie-Thérèse who is said to be married to fat Loulou, and my sister Marie-Stuart who has lost her hair, they both saw a snake the same day at the same spot; it was a vision. Because my sister Marie-Thérèse works at the bar No Bread No Water, and my sister Marie-Stuart lives in Terres-Sainville."

Yes, the snake, the creature, thought Mathieu. And however hard we tried to fill the country with mongooses until the creature was as good as gone, organizing fights where we knew the mongoose would win—the creature, repudiated and aroused, comes after us. If one considers that it was not just La Roche carrying this snake dust into the woods shut up tight inside a little barrel in which vast amounts of time had settled, to give it as a challenge to Longoué, whom they called La-Pointe, and thus return the sign with which he, La Roche, had been permanently marked: if one considers that the colons brought those creatures by the hundreds teaming in boxes made fast to the bottom of the hold and ready to seek revenge, and then turned them loose in the woods, because it was the best way they had found of fighting the maroons. And the man who, even surrounded by an armed regiment and a pack of trained dogs, would not have gone into the upland forest; he had to have the boxes opened on the edge of the woods and, wearing heavy boots, he had them chase the dozens of creatures into the roots where he counted on them to exterminate the maroons. An idea so comprehensive and so magnificently appropriate, that maybe the creature itself had suggested it, shooting it into the head of this colon (an idea certainly worthy of Senglis), who was the first to get up one morning shouting: "Snakes! We're going to chuck snakes at their legs!" And when the maroons all came down from the hills after abolition, so there was only a single body of men left to blister under the sun, mongooses, in turn, were brought into the country to destroy the creature. But the creature was there, it was lying in wait. Because, though mongooses chased it and dug it out from under all the roots, it slept nonetheless in the little barrel; and in every minute, invisible grain of that dust it had become, there was an eye lying in wait for us. And we have never stopped fearing it; even after that old man with no descendants or hope had broken open the little barrel and beneath the sun directly overhead held out in his hand, the dust of a curse that had done its work. And if the curse fades away and vanishes, ah! Is it not quite simply because the cloud of memory is finally rising into the full daylight of this sky? And because we are perhaps already no longer on the branch where one wind after another set us quivering for no reason? And every day the effort increases as if it came from someone who was constantly being born of the vision of his own birth. Bozambo, ho Charlequint! Because I now know that beneath your unlikely words the land's great goumin has grown, its great battle silently yells at the top of its lungs; the land, scarcely sure of itself, finally is caught and actually rolls over, pregnant and profound, and its belly opens up to let its children out. I who speak to you this way without speaking I already understand the words you are shouting at me under your breath while you magnificently light up this complete silence with your words. And even if you erect before us (you and me) the screen of things that are too dazzling, fascination, the toy's sparkle, intoxication, automobiles, machinery, all the things they throw into our hands to make us forget the time going by and if you gape like children in the dust of the car recklessly flying down the tar road and even if your shouts are about us (you and me) in the first place and not about the inaccessible other and even if they cast the fine powder of mockery and the dust of the low road ah! without speaking or rather beneath roundabout words to make you laugh you are shouting you Bozambo myself Mathieu Charlequint ourselves the dawn of the beast that, reunited with itself (its dust back together again stretched out under the root and in the barrel's hole where time recreated as a body is settling) finally

288 *Croix-Mission*

looks at us and do you know pardons and perhaps appeased there under the root coils back up not to lie in wait but finally to fall asleep while the wind the wind oh the wind...

"Ah, what I was saying is," said Bozambo, "you stand there in front of him and you say, 'No, Mister snake. I'm going right straight back down, Mister snake. And well, have a good day, Mister snake.'"

"But none of that is going to keep the cars from coming, they say, like minnows in a dipper. Redder than lobsters."

"They say blue like the King of Prussia."

"And they say the freeway is going to run from north to south for the cars."

"They say straight as a broom through Charlequint's hair!"

"That's true. And they say, look children, do you know how to make a tar road as straight as that? You don't even know what you are. You are sons of the mother."

"They say, Monsieur Béril who knows how to talk, he has admitted this everywhere, he is the true son of the mother."

"They say that all that is madness, don't listen to faithless, lawless men. Nothing changes."

"And you shout: 'I didn't mean to, Mister Snake. Beg your pardon, Mister Snake. At your service, Mister Snake!'"

And what was maddest was in fact that it took so much giddiness and so much madness to perform a job that had looked so simple: knowing the quivering moss beneath a root, a footprint in earth hard as marble, the cry of frigate birds over a harbor where the smell of a ship has settled in for centuries. As if—above the earth's flight where no one could examine the point of rupture any more, that chosen place where the forest and the plowed fields had enacted their bloody contest—in fact the long forgetting (rooted in the body) clouded one's sight, and, and dangled the deceptive powder on the eternal leaves before one's eyes, the unmoving Perlimpinpin urging you to close your eyes and rock like a *filaos*.

"But everything changes when you want it to," said Mycéa. "We must run with our feet on the ground and not weaken, unite and not retreat."

"I wonder," murmured Mathieu, "if you've got more Louise or more Stéfanise in you?" And, while she clicked her mouth in reply with one of those *tchips* women use to rid themselves of pesky questions that are obscure or ridiculous as far as they are concerned, he thought once again about their friend, Raphaël Targin (whom they had called Thaël for so long; until the night he had sat vigil over Valérie's body, alone with his dead wife in the house up in the hills), who had simply abandoned the house, with no cries or lamentations, and who after killing the two dogs who had murdered Valérie (dead as it were before she had ever lived) had come back to tell Mycéa, "This is it, I'm going away for a while. Goodbye."

Because Raphaël Targin was not like himself, Mathieu Béluse. Instead of trembling with impatience in the face of what had to be done, he would calmly set to work and not look up until the work was done. He had quite simply left the house where he had hoped, as the last of the Targins, to set down roots. He too had left. Because the land, though it was the same now everywhere and in balance (after having escaped from that duality—hills and valley—that had brought it into conflict with itself for so long), sometimes still brooded over corners where two dogs were able to kill, where an old *quimboiseur*, the final branch from an enormous root, would die almost stealthily; where despair and solitude settled in. Because, since it had never truly belonged either to those who worked it or to those who possessed, the land had something unreal about it, as if it were suspended in the air, and wretchedness and suffering themselves could not make it any heavier; and on the contrary, it anxiously humored those places that were so dazzling in the sunlight but where, however, things that were uncomfortable and unsettled could suddenly degenerate into fruitless tragedy. And Raphaël Targin, whose great-grandfather had moved into this house in the uplands (hoping thus to prosper as an outsider), had to begin all over again in turn: the search, the choice, the house to be built, the life to put in order.

"But Thaël will be back," said Mycéa. "He is stubborn. He sticks tight as arnica."

Maybe she was conscious, moreover, of the parallels between a Targin man and a Celat woman: the stubbornness to carry on through the dimness of time, and a thickness, a tough density of body and mind. From Aurélie to Raphaël, these Targins had cleared the logwood trees, built their cabins, laid out vegetable gardens, planted huge trees, fed the animals, found the time (and the grace) to weed two flower borders along the path by the flamboyant tree—until the time when the only one left in this worn-out house was the young man who had entrusted his dogs to a neighbor's care and shut the door, drawn to the town, aroused by some force. Separated one by one from the stock: the father, the mother, the three sons and the three daughters (not counting Edmée who never had time to know the new cabin stuck onto what was referred to as the mountain), the third son's wife, his children and the children of his children—down to Raphaël who was definitely not a man to say: "I'll put this off to some other time," and who had merged with the brightness of the vast world all at once (just as, without any fuss, the Celats had earlier combined with the mass of people), probably just waiting for the moment, the hour, the spot where he could step forward and say: "Here I am. I am Raphaël Targin." Because there were no "other times" for the Celats or the Targins. There was only the same solid, earthy patience.

"The way to put it," said Mycéa, "just supposing I get drawn in to your madness, the fact is, in short, we have to learn what we have forgotten, but that, learning it, we have to forget it again. As for myself, what I like in all that tale you're telling me is when Louise says to Longoué: 'I know my mother; La Roche doesn't know I do, but I know her.'"

Wanting to make Mathieu admit that on that day something else had been started that replaced everything before. Because memory had set its seedling in the new land—about a lineage begun there (and not in some marvelous faraway place); that Louise, perhaps, had spent her life thinking about the known and unknown mother who had suffered far from her—and so close by. Affectionately wanting to make him understand that she, Mycéa, far on the other side of the ocean, had also searched for that bodily other half, without which no happiness could last. But that, now that this was said, they needed to get hold of some more reliable tools. Because Papa Longoué was dead. Because more precipitate ways of understanding and acting were required. Because the sea had intermingled the men who had come from so far away, and the land to which they were delivered had strengthened them with different sap. And the red lands had mixed with the black lands, the rock and lava with the sand, the clay with the flash of flint, the backwaters with the sea and the sea with the sky, giving birth in the battered calabash floating on the waters to a new human cry and a new echo.

And she, Mycéa, was suddenly thoughtful, adrift. She stopped at the top of the ridge where you could look out at the sea (the burning salt swelled in your eyes the instant you pushed aside the last branch—unbearable white patches of sky broke through the explosion of static heat—you staggered, almost weightless as if inflated by the salt air—far away you saw the foam, the gamboling fringe of the sea, and then where the foam left off came the slow thrust of savannas, the burned fields, dried mud, low grasses, thickets, the swell of sweeping branches, the jumbled ridges, the wind rippling across the uplands—when you breathed it was the mingled air of evaporating sea, souring sugarcane, the overpowering fragrance of the thick leaf), and she said pleasantly to Mathieu: "So then, here we are, it's 1946; it's been a long time since they crossed the sea." Then she moved away to be alone or better enjoy the silence, and absentmindedly poking the nettles or amaranth with the tip of her foot, she called out to Mathieu: "We'll see Thaël soon. This is where he turned over the soil and he'll be back to check if it has turned yellow."

And her certainty contained the world that was finally open and bright and, perhaps, so close by. The countries that rushed toward you from all directions and spoke to you with their sands, their red clays, their endless rivers, the din of their people. The real lands and the knowledge from far away that was beneficial to your knowledge. A boat, a boat that was open and transparent as well, one that would finally make delivery be followed by departure, departure be followed by arrival. The black hole of time and forgetting, from which you are emerging. The land around you that is not like a rat trap where you feel yourself going rancid: there is the sea (the sea is there!) and that line strengthening along the bottom of the deep waters to moor one speck of earth to another speck of earth, the coast that is here to the visible coast one faces.

And what difference would it make what spot in the country Raphaël Targin would choose to set himself up and begin again? It would be just as difficult anywhere. And then, there were no longer any chosen places; as for the places that were marked, if not cursed, gradually they became surrounded by luminous knowledge. The Longoués, lords of the upland hills, had run dry. The Béluses, who had pursued them so long (to recapture them or perhaps defeat them), were spread around and did not know one another. The city, the town, the level road in the sun was not the boundary marker, the extremity, what La Roche would have called "absolutely, the end." Had not René Longoué sought there in the gravel of huts inextricably packed together the maternal warmth stolen from him when Edmée, his mother, had been sent hurtling down the hill by the wind? There would never be another volcano—let us hope— needing to spew forth its ton of ash onto the conglomeration of unconsciousness and brazenness. A volcano was no longer needed because now humanity itself, relentless even if uncertain, had watched that light come from far away dawning from the depths of the earth beneath its feet, and had scratched the layer of nettles (watched the depths of the seas) to strip away the light.

The Longoués had run dry. And indeed the infinite country back there beyond the ocean was no longer that marvelous place those who were deported had dreamed of, but the irrefutable evidence of the old days, the source of a revived past, the repudiated portion that would in turn repudiate the new land, its population and its work. The Longoués who had run dry were buried in everyone. In a Béluse whose exhilaration and impatience took knowledge right to the edge of the road where soon it was shared with everyone. In a Targin, an impassive body created for action, that is for the moment when the giddiness and madness *subside*, around the root that has taken root again. Life is what never subsides. It seems to get bogged down. It waits patiently, imitating the grasses and vines in the dry season, it gathers strength in the fiery blaze, it curls up on the burning earth. It distracts the impatience of its flow (with flamboyant or ironic words—like Bozambo's or Charlequint's on the steps of the Croix-Mission). "It comes from so far away," thought Mathieu, "and it is put in irons, thrown to the dogs, it becomes so blurred, perverted, it's not surprising that it stumbles and curls up in a ball, it waits; but you, don't lose faith in it." And in the calm, monotonous benevolence rising from the night, and far away over all the islands and the mown fields and the echoing forests, he saw the tall transparent ship that sailed through the lands. He heard the sound of chains being manipulated, the rhythmic beat of *yesyesyes*, the canes snapping off under the propeller, in the sun, yes, in the height of the hot season—this is fever this is a world the world and the word sinks in the voice gets louder the voice burns in the motionless fire and inside his head he is spinning bearing off sweeping away ripening—and it has no end ho and no beginning.

Timelines

LONGOUÉ

1788   The first one lands
      Sold to Acajou Plantation
      Becomes a maroon
      Kidnaps a slavewoman
1791   Has a son: Melchior
1792   Has a son: Liberté

BÉLUSE

1788   The first one lands
      Sold to the Senglis estate
      Becomes part of the house staff
      Coupled with a slavewoman

1794   Has a son: Anne

1820   *The first "Targins" move in at La Touffaille*

LONGOUÉ	BÉLUSE
1830 Melchior the *quimboiseur* in the forest	1830 Anne takes a woman whom Liberté wants
1831 Liberté killed by Anne	1831 Anne kills Liberté
1833 Melchior has a daughter: Liberté (grandmother to the Célats)	1834 Anne has a daughter: Stéfanise
1835 He has a son: Apostrophe	1835 He has a son: Saint-Yves
1848 The maroons come down	1848 The slaves are freed

1858   Apostrophe lives with Stéfanise

1872   Papa Longoué is born   1872   Saint-Yves's son Zéphirin is born

1873   *Birth of Edmée Targin*

1890   *Edmée leaves La Touffaille to live with Papa Longué*

1890   Papa Longoué has a son: Ti-René

                                        1891   Zéphirin has a son: Mathieu

1898   *Death of Edmée*

1905   *The Targins abandon La Touffaille*

1915   Ti-René dies in the war

                                        1920   Mathieu returns from the Great War

                                        1926   Birth of Mathieu the son

1935   First meeting of Papa Longoué and Mathieu for a "séance"
1940   First of a regular series of visits by Mathieu the son with Papa Longoué
1945   Death of Papa Longoué

                                        1946   Mathieu Béluse and Marie Célat (Mycéa) are married

CPSIA information can be obtained at www.ICGtesting.com
Printed in the USA
LVOW01s0858160715

446233LV00021B/183/P